BIZARRE BEHAVIOR

As if the heat wasn't already unbearable, the temperatures continued to soar. The first of countless bizarre-behavior incidents occurred and later made the newspapers and TV broadcasts.

It was over a hundred degrees at the time. While the ice-truck driver was inside the building, a young woman spotted his cargo and began taking her clothes off. The driver returned just in time to view the rather buxom female climbing onto the truck bed, clad only in her skimpy underwear.

Ignoring his pleas to desist, she lay herself down on the nearest block of ice. As the gathering crowd watched, she assumed a supine, spread-eagled position, a wide smile on her flushed face.

But as the temperatures rose, this incident was considered mild—compared to the outlandishness that was to follow. . . .

READ THESE HORRIFYING BEST SELLERS!

DROUGHT!

BY RALPH HAYES

ZEBRA BOOKS

KENSINGTON PUBLISHING CORP.

ZEBRA BOOKS

are published by

KENSINGTON PUBLISHING CORP.
475 Park Avenue South
New York, N.Y. 10016

Printed in the United States of America

ONE

It was not surprising to Jodie Jameson that the Century Salon was crowded to overflowing with patrons on that warm May day. The temperature outside on the street was unseasonably high, and the Century not only offered a plush, coolly air-conditioned interior with Victorian elegance and refined taste, but also such premature summer weather specialties as garnished cold plates and tall, frosted drinks. Also, Jodie thought as she sat at a white-linen-clothed table and listened to the murmured conversations of people around her, Lou Falco's choice of this restaurant for their midday rendezvous was not unpredictable. Falco, ever since they had begun seeing each other, had always wanted a special setting when he had something important to tell her, and he had made it clear on the telephone earlier that he had something very exciting to discuss with her, on this spring day.

Jodie presumed it had to do with them.

"Good day, madam. Are you going to be dining alone?"

Jodie looked up and saw the stiffly-erect, green-jacketed waiter beside her table. The formality of the management at the Century had always put Jodie off a little, with its haughty manner and aura of proud diffidence, but Falco liked it and Jodie had never tried to dissuade him from coming there.

"No, I'm waiting for a companion," Jodie told the waiter. "He'll be here any moment, you can leave the menus."

"Would you like to order a drink?" The fellow was poker-faced, with a slight English accent that seemed out of place in Wichita.

"No, thanks, not now," Jodie told him.

The waiter left the large, folded menus and disappeared, and Jodie found that she was smiling to herself. It was difficult to understand how the mere serving of food could take on such stuffiness. She looked around the wide room, with its tables of guests, talking animatedly. The Century was a renovated turn-of-the-century restaurant that had been modeled after many in Gay Nineties Europe. There were high ceilings with skylights, fluted columns, potted palms. Thick carpeting lay underfoot and Persian tapestries hung on the walls. Food was served on silver trays, and water in cut glass goblets. But the ambience there had always seemed somber to Jodie, with protocol too rigidly ordered, and behavior too harshly disciplined by managerial restraint. It was a place where people of Wichita liked to be seen, and Jodie thought that was why Lou Falco liked to come there.

Jodie had no sooner mulled that thought briefly in her mind, when Falco came striding across the room, making his way between crowded tables to where she sat waiting for him.

"Jodie! You beat me here, you must have arrived early!"

Jodie smiled a little tiredly. "I wanted to get away from that mad-house at the Health Department for a while."

6

He leaned down and touched her lips with his, and Jodie got a flash of memory of two nights previously with Falco, at her place, when there had been a lot of hot flesh and shallow breathing and Falco full inside her. "I'm up to my ears in slide preparations, blood analysis, and bacteria counts, and now I've had to take on most of the boss' work because he's out with some stomach disorder," she added.

Falco had sat down. He was a rather tall, slim fellow with very dark hair and eyes and an aquiline nose, giving him an Italian-Irish look that was very appealing to women. "You should have gotten out of that place long ago," he said airily. "It's thankless, unprofitable work."

Jodie narrowed her cobalt eyes on Falco slightly. With mounds of reddish-auburn hair piled high on her head and a light eye-liner on her eyes, she bore an Egyptian, Nefertiti look. "Unprofitable, Lou? Whoever said that public health work was supposed to be profitable?" She raised a water glass to her lips with an easy, fluid movement and sipped from it. She was a beautifully molded girl, with dramatically sculpted cheekbones and a strong chin. Falco had once described her mouth as sultry, but Jodie did not understand why. The daughter of a widowed national guard officer stationed in Topeka, whom she visited every Christmas and Labor Day, Jodie also had a brother who was a drop-out from the same local college where she received her degree in bacteriology, Wichita State.

"If a thing is worth doing, Jodie," Falco grinned, "it's worth showing a profit at. That's Falco's First Law, remember?"

Jodie was interrupted by the waiter, though, before she could reply. They gave him their orders, and Jodie noticed again the way Falco loved parrying and thrusting with the waiter, out-cooling and out-haughtying him, playing the suave business executive. Falco ordered steak, and when Jodie settled for a chef's salad and a drink, Falco reproached her before the waiter, telling her the restaurant would go bankrupt if all its clients followed her cue. Jodie had always resented these little masculine displays. The owner of his own contracting and land development company, Falco was an ambitious, dynamic young man. But he was also at times thoughtless toward her, and occasionally overbearing. As he gave some last-minute instructions to the stiff-backed waiter about how he wanted his filet mignon, Jodie sat there and wondered if Falco were going to offer her a more permanent liaison on this sunny day in May, maybe even marriage. If so, she had reason for fear and doubt, because she was not at all sure, at this point in their relationship, that Lou Falco was the kind of man she wanted to spend the rest of her life with.

"You didn't order your usual dessert," Jodie told him after the waiter had left. "You like the crepes here."

He reached over and put his hand on hers. The hand was a tanned, strong one. "I was kind of hoping dessert might be served later, at your place."

Jodie glanced around her, but nobody had heard the remark. "Oh, no, Lou. Not at noontime. I have work to do back at the lab."

"That's not the way you talked the other night in bed." He was grinning his most provocative, Robert Redford grin at her.

She pulled the hand away, gently. "Lou, don't talk like that in here. People might hear us."

He arched his dark eyebrows. "Hey, you're not a

college girl anymore. You've been out in the big world for several years. You can pick any game show topic that pops into your beautiful head and discuss it out in the middle of Kellogg Street if you wish."

Jodie was straight-faced. "You said you wanted to discuss something, when you called. Is this it, Lou?"

The grin disappeared off his face gradually, almost unnoticeably, like a minute hand on a clock, falling off the hour. He looked down at his water glass for a moment, then back up to Jodie.

"I've just made a very big move, Jodie. A business move. Remember how I told you that I wanted to expand, open up another office?"

Jodie frowned slightly. "Why, yes, I remember. You thought there were great opportunities in Kansas City, in urban commercial real estate."

He nodded emphatically. "I've been dealing for weeks, Jodie. I didn't say anything to you because I wanted it to be all set. I've opened up an office in Kansas City."

A small tension that had built inside her diminished slightly. "Oh. Well, that's great, Lou! Congratulations. You'll have your hands full now, I'll bet, flying back and forth."

He was shaking his head. "No, you don't understand, Jodie. I'm leaving Wichita. My main office will be in Kansas City. I'm going to live there, I've already rented a penthouse condo and signed a year's lease on it. I'll build later, of course."

The tension mounted again, inside Jodie. He was going to ask her to go there with him, give up her job and friends, tear up her roots. *Don't do it*, she pleaded silently with him, inside herself. *Don't ask me to go. I won't know how to handle it. I'm not prepared emotionally for this kind of life decision.*

He was holding her fearful gaze now. "I don't want it to end between us, Jodie."

She looked away. *Oh, God.*

"I want you to come see me on weekends. Just as often as you can. And, of course, I'll be here from time to time."

Jodie's face changed, and she turned slowly back to him. "What?" she said deliberately.

Falco's face was serious, somber. "I said, there's no reason we have to think this is it for us, just because we're going to be separated by geography. Kansas City isn't that far away." He reached and touched her hand again. "I'll pick up the tab any time you want to fly east, I mean it, air fare and all. I'll be going first class from now on, Jodie, and I can afford it."

Jodie's mouth had dropped slightly open, as he explained his idea of future long-distance love between them. She could not believe for a moment that she had been so deluded about the truth of what they had between them. She had thought that Falco took her seriously, that he would at least have insisted she go to Kansas City to live with him out of wedlock. The tension inside her released itself quite suddenly, and issued forth in a short, giggling burst of laughter.

Falco frowned toward her. "Did I say something comic?" he said in a curious tone.

Jodie looked down, shook her head slowly, and burst forth in another subdued laugh.

"What the hell, Jodie. I'm trying to tell you something big here, and all you can do is sit there and tell yourself jokes."

Jodie caught his gaze finally, straight-faced. "I'm

10

sorry, Lou. It must be this restaurant, it does strange things to me. I'll give your idea some thought. Of commuting to Kansas City to play house."

He gave her a look. "I didn't mean it that way, and you know it. I just want to preserve what we have. For future growth, for God's sake. Who knows what might come of it?"

For the first time, a mild anger crowded into Jodie's chest, like acid spilling from a closed container. She tried to keep the emotion out of her face. "Yes, who knows?" she said. "I might successfully compete with your Kansas City playmates and win the big prize some day. To have Lou Falco all to myself."

"Jodie—"

A woman at a nearby table turned to glance at them, but Jodie did not notice. "There will be others, won't there, Lou? There are others now, I suppose, on those trips to Kansas City? Do you have a—regular like me there, Lou?"

He was scowling heavily now. "You're being a kind of brat, Jodie. You know we made no promises to each other. I've never told you to quit dating, and I don't expect to be told I can't. But you've been special to me, I mean that sincerely. You'll continue to be special, wherever I'm living."

Jodie told herself it was foolish to be angry. She would have had to say no to him, if he had asked her to accompany him across the state to see him embark on his bigger career. She had never been convinced that Falco liked her nearly as much as himself, and that was a bad situation on which to build permanence. But his offer to her was so niggardly, so devoid of real affection, that it humiliated her in a way that had been unforeseen by her.

11

Quite suddenly, she decided that she did not want to continue to sit there in that stuffed-shirt eatery with patronizing Lou Falco and wait for a haughty waiter to serve her a luncheon salad. She rose from her chair, calmly and coolly.

"That's nice, Lou, I'm duly grateful. And I wish you all the luck in the world, in Kansas City. But I don't want you to look for me at your new condo there, short-hop flying bores me. Now, I think I'll get back to the lab, I feel like my time can be put to much more profitable use there. Falco's First Law, remember?"

He rose, too. "Jodie, don't do this."

"Goodbye, Lou," she said.

A moment later, she was gone.

Jodie tried to forget Lou Falco that afternoon, as she got back to work at the Health Department. She put on a lab coat and supervised the scrutiny of some microscopic slides—despite her youth she was the senior bacteriologist at the local office of the department—and then ordered a couple of bacteria counts on area farm wells. When she returned to her small, white-painted office in mid-afternoon, with its Paris watercolors on the walls and Jodie's antique oak desk cluttered with files, someone had left her desk radio on, and a local disc jockey was reading off a weather report.

"... and after five straight days of ninety-degree temperatures, the prediction for tomorrow is about the same. This summer just might be a hot one, folks. As for rain, our farmers are still watching the sky hopefully. There has been only point seven inches of precipitation in the past thirty days, and that comes in a period when wheat and corn growers depend on plenty of moisture for crop growth. The

12

local Weather Service people say that we may see more of the same, at least over the next week or two."

Jodie snapped the radio off, and sat down at her work-jammed desk. The weather would be no problem for the Health Department unless the city reservoir got quite low, and that was not likely. Jodie thought of her friend Leah Purcell, who worked at the National Weather Service for a meteorologist named Keefer, and wondered whether Leah were being beseiged with calls from farmers, trying to get a better feeling about what was coming for them.

The phone on Jodie's desk rang, and she picked up the receiver a little tiredly. The day had worn on her more than she thought, with Lou Falco in the middle of it. She identified herself, and Tom Purcell's voice was on the other end. He was mayor of Wichita, an old-line politician who had been in the state legislature for a while, and Leah was his daughter. He knew Jodie's military father well, from the few years when Jodie and Colonel Sherwood Jameson had lived in Wichita together, Jameson stationed there.

"Jodie, I have some good news for you," Purcell's voice came to her. It was a deep, well-modulated voice, a voice that knew how to cajole and persuade when it was necessary. *"I've just come from Ben Webster's place, where I met with Ben, one of our commissioners, and both hospital administrators. Ben just got word from Topeka, Jodie, approving his request that you be made acting director here during his sick leave."*

Webster was Jodie's boss who had been out sick with a stomach problem for a couple of weeks, and whom she thought was about to return to his duties. "But he won't be gone all that long, will he?" she finally replied to

13

Purcell. "He said he was feeling better, the last time I saw him, just a few days ago."

"His doctor says he needs some time off, Jodie. Ben is worried about the work getting done there, and he knows you're the only one he can really trust to get it done the way he'd want it. It's a real opportunity for you, Jodie, and I'm proud of you. Congratulations."

Jodie was dumbfounded. She was already doing her boss' work, and expected to. But she had never suspected any development like this. Webster was trusting her with a lot of responsibility. She was excited, and scared.

"Thanks, Tom. I don't know what to say. Except that I hope Ben gets back here quickly, to run this department right." She looked up, and a young girl clerk was showing Leah Purcell into the office with a smile. Leah said hello silently, with just her lips, and Jodie gestured for her to take a chair, as the clerk left. "Guess who just walked in, Tom? Your wandering daughter is here to visit me."

"Tell her that her mother expects her home for dinner," Purcell said lightly. *"We're having Leah's favorite kind of roast, despite the heat. And ask her to let you get your work done, Ms. Acting Director. We don't want the health of the community to go to pot on the first afternoon of your promotion."*

Jodie smiled. "I'll tell her, Tom. And thanks for calling for Ben. I'm very honored."

"You deserve it, honey. We'll talk later."

When Jodie had hung up, she relayed Purcell's messages to Leah, and Leah made a face. "That's the trouble with living at home, Jodie. Big Brother is always watching you. I'm looking at apartments now, some place where Will and I can have some privacy."

Leah, who was several years Jodie's junior, showed not

the least submission to the heat outside. In a wispy summer dress, she looked as cool as a refrigerated drink. Slightly shorter than Jodie and not as pretty, Leah was one of those girls who is not quite blonde, whose eyes are not quite green or blue, whose facial structure is not quite remarkable. But she gave the appearance of being pretty, because of her jaunty figure, her vivacity and her raw energy. She wore her hair short and feathery, stood and walked in arrogant poses, and knew how to show herself off attractively in the clothing she wore. She manned a realtime communications terminal at the Weather Service station, had been Jodie's friend for a number of years, and was currently dating Jodie's younger brother Will.

Jodie was smiling. "It's beginning to sound serious between you and Will."

Leah shrugged, sitting on a leather chair beside Jodie's desk. "Your brother is quite a hunk, Jodie. I'm not the only one to notice. When he was on campus he had to beat the coeds off with a club. But why is he always so darned serious? Talking about politics and political reform and causes all the time. You're not like that, thank God."

Jodie sighed. "Will has always been one to worry over other people's problems," she said. "To get involved. If he'd go back to school and get his degree, he could be a moving force in state affairs some day, I suspect."

Leah shook her head. "He's more like Dad than either of them would care to admit, I think," she offered. "By the way, why did Mr. Mayor call you? Just to find me?"

Jodie smiled and rose from her chair, walking to a wall and studying one of the French watercolors. Just after college she had gone on a summer tour of Europe, and had loved it. Those were days without responsibility, or emotional ties. She turned and scanned the perimeters of the room, as if it had suddenly constricted in size. "He called for Ben, Leah. I'm going to be running this place for a while."

Leah beamed happily. "Gosh, that's just great, Jodie! I'm really impressed!"

"I'm scared to death," Jodie said. She came and sat on the corner of the desk, near Leah. "Maybe I'm still emotional from my noontime meeting with Lou."

"Oh, the land baron. How are things with you two, Jodie?"

Jodie gave her a look. "He's going off to Wichita, Leah. Permanently. He didn't even tell me he was planning to. He thinks it would be nice if we saw each other occasionally at long distance."

"Oh, God, Jodie."

"It's all right, Leah. If he'd begged me to go with him, I would probably have said no. It's just the way he went about it all. I'd like to have been treated as if I'd meant something to him, I guess."

"I'm so sorry. Do you think it's finished, then?"

Jodie regarded her soberly. "I suppose it was finished a while ago, when I realized that Lou would always care more about making money than he ever would about one woman. I suspect he's been seeing other girls right here in Wichita, bushy-tailed little sex kittens who like Lou's money. I should have ended it this spring, Leah, but it was comfortable with Lou. It was like belonging to someone."

There was a momentarily heavy silence in the room, crypt-like in its sudden intensity.

"God," Leah said.

16

Jodie decided to change the subject. "How are things at the Weather Service? Is Ed Keefer getting any crank calls?"

Leah tried not to look dejected for Jodie. "Oh, not many. He helped organize some cloud seeding operations north of the city, because there were some big farmers there who thought that would bring on a deluge, of rain. But it didn't work. There aren't enough clouds for proper seeding. Dr. Sprague at the university says there's a researcher out in California named Latham who thinks this dry spell might last a lot longer than we think. I hope he's wrong. One of my favorite summer activities is swimming, and I don't want the pools closed down."

Jodie was smiling again. "Well, I doubt it will come to that. Get the bikini and suntan lotion out, and hope for the best."

Leah returned the smile. "I will, Jodie. And maybe we can see more of each other this summer. There are some drama group productions coming up, and Will won't go to them. Maybe you and I could take them in together."

Jodie touched Leah's bare shoulder lightly. "That's a nice idea," she said.

When Leah left the Health Department that afternoon, she felt very badly about Jodie's sudden separation from Lou Falco. This was the second rather serious affair of Jodie's that had gone sour, and nobody deserved it less, in Leah's opinion, than Jodie. Two years ago, Jodie had gone so far as to become engaged to a biology professor at Wichita State, where he was working on a research grant. The professor had not really been Jodie's type, he lived in a world of electronic microscopes and formaldehyde and withdrew further and further into it.

17

Jodie cancelled wedding plans at the last moment, and the professor was shocked. Shortly thereafter he joined a research team at Columbia, and Jodie never saw him again.

Leah hoped that her relationship with Jodie's brother Will would fare better, but sometimes Will reminded Leah, in some respects, of both the professor and Lou Falco. He withdrew completely into himself at times, when things were bothering him, like the professor Jodie had thought she loved, and he harbored a grudge against institutions and the establishment that gave him an air of callous cynicism, often, reminiscent of Falco. But whereas they both professed disrespect for the society that was their milieu, Falco had no compunction about using it to line his pockets. Will Jameson thought that was hypocritical, and they had had a couple of arguments about it.

Leah had a date with Will that evening, out at the Phillips farm where he worked on salary. In early evening she had dinner with her parents, as Purcell had asked her to do, then on the way out to the Phillips place, just five miles south of town, she stopped at a small wheat farm to check on the report from there that the farmer's well was running dry. She made the stop, and got her data for Ed Keefer, and was surprised to learn that several wells in the area were low on water. Keefer was keeping track of the water table in the area, and this new information seemed to lend support to the assertion of some farmers that the high plains were dryer than even the surface soil showed.

Leah arrived at the Phillips place in mid-evening. She knew that she and Will would be alone, because the Phillipses had gone away for a couple of days. She and

Will popped some popcorn and opened up two cans of Coors beer, and watched a variety program on TV for a while. They huddled together on a long, tweed sofa in semi-darkness, alone in the print-wallpaper, bay-window living room of the big farm house. Leah was close against him, her legs up under her, leaning on his shoulder. Above them, a ceiling fan moved the warm air. About halfway through the variety program, Leah happened to turn to Will and she saw that he was not watching the television. He was staring off beyond it.

"Hey. What are you thinking about?" she asked him.

Will shrugged. "About Falco doing that to Jodie." He shook his head slowly. He was a tall, good-looking young man in his early twenties who bore a strong family resemblance to Jodie. His hair was darker than hers, with only a hint of red in it, and his eyes were a darker blue. But they were obviously brother and sister, he and Jodie. Will was one of those young people who had decided to get back to the land, in order to get in touch with himself and the world. He hoped to grow his own crops some day, plow his own fields and reap his own harvest. But that ambition had been pushed into the background in the past year. He had joined some campus protesting about the new registration for the draft, and then recently had gotten involved with a local group who wanted restitution for war veterans who had been injured by agent orange and other chemicals.

"She lets people take advantage of her," he went on. "She has this rose-colored view of the world."

Leah leaned forward and punched a button to turn the television off. The background noise was gone. "Is there anything wrong with that?" she said.

Will regarded her curiously. "Come on, Leah. The

people in charge drop napalm on babies, sell us poison in our food to make a quick buck, and store nuclear waste under our houses. Do you think all is right with the world?"

Leah thought a moment. "No, of course not. Maybe it won't ever be perfect, Will. But it's not such a bad place, either. There are conscientious, brave people all around us who work hard every day of their lives to make it all better. People still read Shakespeare, pledge their love, plant rose gardens."

"Is that what you want me to do? Plant a rose garden?"

"It would be a start," she said slowly.

"Toward what?"

"Toward joining up with those who are working within the system to make it better," Leah suggested.

"Like your father?" he said.

Leah frowned. "What the hell does that mean, Will Jameson?"

He looked away from her. "Nothing," he said. "I didn't mean that."

"My father cares, Will," she said darkly. "It may not seem like it to you, but he cares. He fought almost single-handedly for better health facilities in this town, and for new schools."

"Look, you're right," he said. "I'm sorry." He did not mean it. He lumped all local politicians together as pro-crastinators and self-seekers who did only what they absolutely had to for the public. But Leah was all he had. Her and Jodie. "Let's forget all of that tonight."

Leah's face softened slightly.

"Let's just enjoy each other," he added. He pulled Leah to him, and kissed her gently.

Leah resisted him for a brief moment, then participated. She had never been able to thwart Will's advances. He made her hot all through her whenever he touched her. When the kiss was finished, she was breathless. She had been sure, in March, that he was going to ask her to marry him, despite his low wages at the farm. But now things seemed different. Will was slowly changing. His hand was on her sheer blouse now, fondling her curves there.

"Maybe we ought to go up to my room," he said quietly. He had a bedroom upstairs in the house, with his own private entrance outside.

Leah was full of her own heat. A few weeks ago she had considered aborting their physical intimacies for a while, until she understood Will's head better. But now that his touch was on her, and she had the taste of his mouth on hers, she could not deny him.

"It will be stuffy up there," she protested weakly.

"Who cares?" he said.

They climbed an outside stairway together, and on the way up Leah looked up at the sky and it was dark and clear, with no clouds. Will's room was a small, almost-airless place with two flung-open windows and the smell of old wood. There was an iron bed, and three chairs, and a chipped-up desk. At the far end of it, through a low doorway, was a tiny bathroom. Mrs. Phillips' white curtains hung at the windows, but were pulled aside for air, and her chenille bedspread was rolled down to the foot of the bed. Over the head of it, on fading wallpaper, Will had hung a framed manifesto of some kind, declaring war on the White House.

There was a dim-watt bulb glowing in the bathroom, but no light turned on in the bedroom. They left it that way. They disrobed together, facing away from each

21

other. When Leah finished, she turned to him and he was standing there watching her, only a few feet away. He was slim and muscular, like a long-distance runner. She closed the distance between them, and felt his hands on her full breasts, and then her hips.

"What do you want, Will?" she whispered into his ear. "What do you really want?"

There was a short silence, and then his reply: "I don't know."

Leah remembered, standing there in his warm embrace, the way Jodie's face had looked when she was telling Leah about her meeting with Lou Falco earlier that day, and yet how special that relationship had seemed to Jodie, at one time. Will turned and led her to the big bed, and she climbed onto it. A fully developed girl, she was athletic-looking with her clothes off. Will knelt over that athletic body now, touching and caressing it, and soft sounds issued from her throat. Will was breathing shallowly already, and a fine dew of dampness made his skin glow in the dim light. Leah took hold of him, and was surprised at his quick readiness.

"Oh, God, Leah."

He came down beside her, and his hand was suddenly hot between her thighs. More sounds came from inside her, more urgent ones. When the full union came, she made a low outcry of pleasure, and then came the sweet excitation, and the fiery crescendo of passion, and the climactic release that made Leah's cries fill the room and Will's fists knot the sheet beside her head.

Lying there beside him afterwards, Leah realized that the love-making had been a bit more frenzied than on previous occasions, and with a sense of recklessness on Will's part, and maybe even of repressed anger.

Finally she looked over at him. He was staring fixedly at the ceiling. Intently, as if trying to read some meaning into the dark wallpaper pattern there above him. Ordinarily he was very relaxed after they had finished, but not this time. He looked just as he had before they began, except that there was a heavy dampness now on his inflamed flesh.

"You didn't like it," she said, after a long while.

He turned to her, blankly. "Huh? Sure I did."

"You didn't enjoy yourself," she said.

He regarded her somberly. "Oh, Christ, Leah." He looked back up at the ceiling, fiercely.

"Jodie thinks you should go back to school. Take some courses that interest you, like ecology. Quit hiding out here behind a tractor and get out where you can make a difference, Will. I think so, too."

When he turned to her again, there was something harsh in his blue eyes, something she had never seen there before. "I'd like for you to do me a big favor, you and Jodie. Get to hell out of my head. I mean it, Leah. I love you, but I need some space to do my own thing in. Are you listening?"

Leah turned away quickly. He had never spoken to her like that before. He had gotten angrier, even used obscenities in frustration. But he had never erected such a solid wall between them with a few words.

"I hear you, Will," she said in a low, hollow voice. "I hear you very clearly."

She stared at a black window, a few feet away, where the curtains now were moving slightly in a dry, hot breeze that was rising almost unnoticeably off the high plains.

TWO

When Hollis Sprague had been named to head up the Department of Meteorology a few years back, at local Wichita State University, he had already won the respect of other men in his field for his work in upper atmospheric air currents. Unlike Ed Keefer, Leah Purcell's boss at the National Weather Service at Rawdon Field, Sprague was a theorist and researcher in the weather, a man who taught aspiring students the differences between cumulus and cirrus, circumpolar vortex and magnetic field, storm metastasis and atmospheric air flow. He was a close friend of Tom Purcell, a friendly adversary of Ed Keefer, and a popular lecturer at College Hill.

At mid-June now, Sprague was one of several scientists across the county who were becoming privately concerned about the lack of rainfall over the Great Plains and Southwest. In Kansas, no measurable precipitation had occurred since early May. Only heavily irrigated wheat and corn were growing at all in Kansas and Nebraska, and much of that was turning brown in the fields.

Early in the third week of June, Sprague was obliged to fly to the University of California at Berkeley on an errand unrelated to his professional specialty, to speak with administration officials about a federal grant problem that concerned schools within a specified category. That business was finished in his first morning there, so he tried to locate a colleague there whom he had already mentioned to Ed Keefer in Wichita, an atmospheric physicist named Mark Latham who in May had made a public statement that there were serious upper atmosphere disturbances across western United States that were causing the severe dry spell. Latham, a young man only in his early thirties, had studied under Irving Krick, had already done avant-garde work in forecasting, and was regarded as one of the very top men in the field. He had visited Wichita State on two occasions at Sprague's invitation, as a guest lecturer, and Sprague considered him a friend.

Latham was not available to Sprague that afternoon or evening, because he had gone out on a field trip to make some station observations. Sprague had called Latham from Wichita, but then had arrived in California ahead of his plan, and Latham was not expecting him. When Sprague called Latham the next morning, a Saturday, he was told that he could find Latham at a nearby abandoned air strip, with a couple of his lab assistants. Sprague made plans to drive out there immediately.

It was only mid-morning when he drove up to the small, decrepit building that sat at the end of a narrow asphalt runway, and stopped his rental car there. The old air strip, not far from Berkeley and the campus, had fallen into disuse until recently, when balloonists had begun using it. The runway was cracked and weed-grown in the middle of a wide, brown field. The building was a weathered frame one with siding falling off it and dust

25

caked on its two broken-glass windows. A busted-hinge door hung open like a dark invitation.

There were two young men standing on the sun-bright concrete apron before the building, and they turned and stared toward Sprague as he got out of the blue Toyota sedan and walked over to them, squinting in the mid-morning sun.

"Good morning, gentlemen," he said to them. He was a man in late middle age, with silver hair and horn-rimmed glasses. He had a puffy, fleshy face with bags under his eyes, and a lecture-room voice and manner. He was in his shirtsleeves now, looking rather thick-set as he stood there with the breeze moving his silvered hair.

The two returned the greeting, informally. One wore street clothes, the other a blue jump suit. They had been staring into the sky when he came up.

"Not a bad morning," Sprague said to them.

"It's getting hot," the taller of them replied, the one in the jump suit.

"You ought to be in Wichita," Sprague grinned.

The shorter one, wearing a short-sleeved shirt and dungarees, frowned slightly at Sprague. "You're from Kansas?"

Sprague nodded, extended his soft hand to the fellow. "Hollis Sprague. I'm a meteorologist at Wichita State."

They both pumped his hand, taking more of an interest in him. "I hear it hit a hundred back there a couple of days ago," the tall fellow said.

"That's right. It's gone over a hundred three times now. And the crops are burning in the fields. We're hoping it's temporary, of course."

"So are we," the shorter man said. "There have been some brush fires already around Los Angeles. It could get worse maybe, too, before it gets better."

"Did Dr. Latham tell you that?" Sprague said.

The tall fellow's eyes revealed mild surprise.

"That's right," the shorter one admitted.

Sprague smiled. "I was told I could find him out here. Where is he?"

The shorter man turned and pointed toward the horizon of trees not far away. "He's just coming into sight now. Over there."

Sprague looked and for the first time saw the multi-colored balloon moving slowly toward them in the warm breeze.

"He's just arriving from the airfield," the tall fellow said. "He'll be down in a couple of minutes."

The two young men went out into the tall-grass field and waited there. One of them waved to the balloon. As Sprague watched, up closer now, the balloon made its descent, moving languorously and beautifully to ground, like a softly gliding bird. Latham was strapped to a kind of seat that was suspended from the balloon. In a short moment his feet were scrambling on the ground, and the balloon was falling over onto its side, but being dragged along through the field by the light wind. Latham was dragged with it, and could not keep his footing. But in a couple of minutes, the two men from the concrete apron had grabbed the shrouds and were hauling the lighter-than-air craft to a stop. Controls were adjusted by Latham, now on his feet again, and the balloon bag began to deflate. Latham unbuckled his gear, looking like a test pilot out there, and one of the other men spoke to him, and he looked toward Sprague. In another moment he was on his way over to him.

"Well, well," he grinned. "Hollis Sprague." He came

onto the concrete and approached Sprague in an orange jump suit, looking bigger and more physical than Sprague remembered him. He shook Sprague's hand, and gave him an easy smile. "I'm sorry you had to come clear out here, Hollis. I didn't expect you this soon. I always try to get up in the air on Saturdays."

Sprague returned the smile. "I got here early, Mark. A last-minute change of plans. But I wanted to see you before I go back."

Latham put a hand on Sprague's shoulder. "Come on, why don't we get in out of the glare? Our little shed doesn't look like much, but it's more comfortable inside."

Latham's voice was rather deep, and held the edge of authority. He was taller than Sprague, and youthful-looking. Dark brown hair blew into his serious brown eyes as they walked, and a heavy jaw jutted forward from a square, handsome face. He looked more like a young college football coach than a research scientist.

They walked into the old building together, and it seemed very dark and cool inside for a moment. It was just one medium-sized room, with layers of dirt and dust on the floor and the remains of a desk and chairs at the unfinished, barn-like walls. Latham went and sat on a corner of the scarred desk and unzipped the jump suit down to the waist. He wore only a T shirt under it.

"Are you going to stay tonight?" Latham asked Sprague genially. "I know a nice little Italian restaurant in town, and I know how you like tagliatella bolognese. You could sleep at my place."

Sprague smiled, shaking his head sidewise. "You make it sound very attractive, Mark, but I'm due back tonight. If I had more time, though, I'd like to hear about your

28

hobby. I didn't know you flew sport balloons."

Latham shrugged square shoulders. "I've been at it for about three years now. But it's more than a hobby with me, Hollis. I use these sport balloons to hone my skills with the big fellows."

"Big fellows?"

"Yes, the constant-altitude balloons we use to get a good look at the upper currents. The kind you and I sent up when I was visiting at Wichita State, only there are even bigger ones now."

"Oh, the Skyhooks," Sprague said, using the nickname for the big weather balloons. "But those things aren't manned, Mark."

"Ordinarily, no. But some of us are going up with them, now. I go up every once in a while. As you can imagine, we're learning things up in the higher altitudes. There are some things that instruments can't tell us, without putting up enormously complex and heavy equipment. The National Weather Service people like your Ed Keefer call us balloonatics." He grinned. "But we have some names for them, too."

Sprague laughed. "I'll bet. I've called them a couple, myself." He recalled in his head the ongoing dispute between the government weather people and experimentalists like Latham, and even himself. The government taking the position that the weather cannot be predicted beyond a day or two and believing that weather control is impossible, and the Krick-Latham people trying to predict weather a month, six months, or even a year in advance, and making cautious statements that the weather can be controlled, with further experimentation and data available to the scientific community.

Latham had glanced through a dusty window, toward

where his two assistants were now folding the deflated balloon in preparation to loading it aboard a small van parked on the far side of the building. He turned back now to Sprague. "Well, if you won't stay for a real visit, Hollis, what brought you out here this morning over rutted roads and dusty tracks? Are you going to ask to borrow our computer at the lab for some of those fancy calculations of yours?"

Sprague's face slowly went sober, after a responsive smile. "No, nothing like that, Mark. I just wanted to get your feelings on this growing dryness out our way. I mean, what the hell is the explanation? Your long-range predictions didn't foresee this, nor did ours at Wichita State. We've talked about sunspot activity, upper atmospheric disturbances, pollutant indices, possible changes in the magnetic field. But nothing seems to explain what's developing here in the Midwest and West. I don't think anybody is really concerned yet, but a few of us in the field. My friend Mayor Tom Purcell keeps assuring me it will rain at any moment. But I don't see it happening. Do you?"

Latham shook his head. "I sure don't, Hollis. Everything points to its getting drier, before it turns around. Our evidence shows a definite alteration of position of the jet stream."

"I was afraid you'd say that," Sprague said heavily.

"The development is completely contrary to our predictions for this summer," Latham went on. "It's almost—unnatural, on the surface."

Sprague eyed him sidewise. "Unnatural?"

Latham nodded. "Yes, if I didn't know better, I'd think the phenomenon was man-made."

The statement hung between them, in the close air of

30

the shed, like a black fog. Sprague regarded Latham silently, turning over wild possibilities in his head. But men of science did not like to engage in unfounded conjecture, so he did not voice his thoughts.

"That's an incredible idea," he finally said.

"Maybe not," Latham told him. "There are those who think the vortex can be influenced in a number of artificial ways. As a matter of fact, I'm one of them. But at this stage of our knowledge, meddling with basic systems would be little short of madness."

"I'll second that," Sprague muttered.

"I don't know what there is to be done at this point, Hollis," Latham said. "Panic is surely premature. I think we should all watch developments for a few weeks. Maybe it will all change back as quickly as it came. Maybe you'll be up to your ears in rain by August."

"Maybe the moon is made of green cheese," Sprague said sourly.

Latham smiled. "In the meantime, I'll make a few calls to colleagues at M.I.T., and elsewhere. Maybe Washington, too. I have a couple of far-out theories I want to eliminate from consideration. If you need anything back there for your own calculations, give me a call. A piece of equipment, a helpful idea. I'll be glad to help, Hollis. Let's keep in touch until the crisis is behind us."

"I appreciate that, Mark. That's what I came to hear."

"Hey, listen. We're all in this together, aren't we?"

Sprague nodded a little wearily. "Probably more so than in any other area of human endeavor," he said.

Latham drove Sprague to the airport, later, but they both avoided talking further about the weather, there or in Kansas. Sprague learned that Latham had been

31

separated from his wife for over six months, and offered his condolences. Latham did not talk about that, either. Sprague's jet took off at 4:43 p.m., and Latham watched it fly away toward the Great Plains. On the way back into town, he found himself glancing upward to the sky, where several snowy vapor trails lingered up there from jet planes, man-made, snaky clouds in the low heavens. He found himself wishing very much that they were rain clouds, building up and moving eastward over the Great Divide.

Latham also thought of his separation, on his way back to the Berkeley campus. Christine had left him in early December of the previous year, but it was just like yesterday to him, her walking out of the house with her luggage and their future. She had flown off to San Francisco to help out in an art gallery there, owned by a friend of hers from school days. There had been no children, so that was no problem. Latham had often thought, since their split, that maybe there should have been. Maybe Christine would have given more thought to running off to the bay area at every falling out, if there had been something more to bind them together.

The trouble was, Christine had had too much, materially, in early life. She came from a rather wealthy family, with her father a San Francisco banker, and had had everything she wanted, until marrying Latham. When the honeymoon was over, she had quickly become interested in their standard of living, and felt that meteorological research was a grossly underpaid profession. At first she asked him to move around, take better job offers at other universities. When he would not do that, she located a job for him at a private weather service, where Latham could have had a junior partnership and the chance of making big money. But Latham liked the research at Berkeley, and said no to the company and to Christine. That was when she had thrown a screaming tantrum and left, stiff-backed, for San Francisco.

But it was more than just money between him and Christine, too, Latham reflected as he approached the campus that afternoon, in rather heavy traffic. It was a matter of Christine's trying to run his affairs, take decisions out of his hands. She used to make jokes about having to "take care" of her absent-minded professor, to her friends. But in recent months, the situation had lost its humor. She had opposed his balloon flights, had contempt for his professional friends, and had insisted on his attendance at parties and social affairs that he had no interest in. The fact was, he and Christine were very different kinds of people. Latham supposed that they always would be. She had already gone to a lawyer in San Francisco, and had threatened divorce, but had not filed any papers yet. Latham figured she had not really given up on him yet, that she thought the separation would make him come to his senses and be more amenable to rehabilitation. This was a mere sanction at this juncture, a punishment meted out to break his will. Latham wondered what he would do if she came back, with her new ultimatums. He tried to keep it out of his head most of the time, so that he could get his work done without distraction.

The Berkeley campus was a big one. Latham was on it for ten minutes before he finally drove onto the small parking area behind the ivy-walled Department of Physics. A few minutes later he walked into the third-story laboratory and office complex used by Latham's

33

sub-department of atmospheric physics. There were rows of work benches, with a number of white-frocked researchers standing or seated at them. On one wall was a large, floor-to-ceiling computer, its colored lights winking mysteriously, its digital readouts appearing on TV-type screens. There were banks of communication consoles, and another wall filled with big anemometers that measured wind currents, and barometers, and a see-through ground map of weather fronts and a smaller prognosis map. One assistant of Latham sat at a weather radar console that monitored readings for wide radii of distance out from Berkeley.

Latham was about to move through one end of the lab into his small office at its end, from which he oversaw the activities of the department, when an assistant came up to him with a realtime communications print-out.

"Dr. Latham. Do you have a minute?"

Latham nodded. "Yes, of course, Bill. I thought only a couple of you were working this Saturday. Didn't anybody have anything planned for the weekend?"

The thin young man smiled. "I called a few of them, I hope you don't mind. We're getting some interesting stuff from our Skyhook we put up a few days ago, and so are some other research stations. The stream has shifted even further out of its usual routes."

Latham's dark eyes squinted down slightly. He had changed from the jump suit into a sport shirt and slacks, and his thick hair was neatly combed. "Are you sure?"

"All our calculations say so," Bill told him. Because of a white lab coat that was too big for him, he looked even thinner than he was. Rimless spectacles decorated a long nose, and serious eyes watched Latham studiedly as Latham digested the significance of the announcement.

34

"Damn," Latham said, as he read briefly through the printed paper his assistant had handed him. "This isn't good."

"That's what I thought, Dr. Latham. But the new air flow pattern is pretty definite. The stream is taking a more northerly route than it ever has before, and velocity has been reduced. It's God-awful abnormal. We're going to get a definite greenhouse effect, and it will probably be worse across the Great Plains. This high system we've been under will be almost unbreakable."

"Do we have any recent TIROS pictures?" Latham said.

"Not today," Bill told him soberly.

Latham took in a deep breath. "Well. There's no doubt that we have a meteorological event on our hands of the first magnitude. I wish I'd known of this worsening when Dr. Sprague was here. I'll have to give him a call when he gets back to Wichita. Are we still getting data in?"

"Yes, we are."

"Keep everybody here for a while, will you, Bill? I'll see that you all see it in your paychecks. I'd like to follow this for a few hours."

The assistant nodded. "We'd be here if we were working for nothing," he said solemnly.

In the next few days in Wichita, the high temperatures slowly rose from one hundred to one hundred five degrees. Air-conditioners ran at top power day and night, in homes, businesses, and manufacturing plants. Just eight days after Hollis Sprague's return from California, on a hot June mid-afternoon, the first of a number of bizarre-behavior incidents occurred and later made the newspapers and TV broadcasts. A Kansas Ice Company

35

truck pulled up in front of a place of business to make a delivery. It was over a hundred degrees at the time. While the driver was inside the building, a forty-year-old woman pedestrian spotted the truck, stood staring at the big blocks of cold ice for a long moment of sweaty indecision, then began taking her clothes off. The driver returned just in time to view the rather buxom female climbing onto the truck bed, clad only in her skimpy underwear. There was some yelling at the woman, but she ignored the pleas to desist, laying herself down on the nearest blocks of ice, in a supine, spread-eagled position, a wide smile on her flushed face.

As the temperature rose, there would be other such misbehavior.

Upon Hollis Sprague's return, Mark Latham had gotten in immediate touch with him about the new findings. But Sprague had not yet shared that technical and rather ominous information with local or state authorities. There were many calculations to be made, and pondered.

At the Health Department, Jodie Jameson received reports of a couple of more cases of hepatitis, caused by the lowering water pressure in some parts of the city, and the two hospitals together took in three cases of heat stroke. Tom Purcell was considering recommending the banning of lawn watering and car washing until further notice. Skies were clear and blue and cloudless.

Lou Falco had tried to call Jodie from Kansas City, one afternoon when she was gone from the office and lab, but Jodie would not return his call. She could not think of anything to say to him. The longer she went without seeing Falco, the easier it became, and the more certain she was that they had had nothing of substance between them. It was like withdrawing from a harmful drug, she supposed. If you could make it through the first few weeks, you could probably go for a long time.

It was on a Friday morning when Jodie knew that Leah Purcell had a day off from the Weather Service station that Jodie called Leah and asked her to join Jodie for lunch. Leah, who had moved into a tiny apartment of her own now and was already missing the luxury of her parents' home, accepted quickly. Her air-conditioner was a faulty one, and she was bored, sitting in the hot little flat. They met at a small cafe just off South Topeka and ordered such hot-weather items as iced salads, frosty pudding desserts, chilled wine. Afterwards, when Jodie mentioned she was driving out to a nearby farm to confirm the recovery of a hepatitis patient, Leah said she would like to ride along.

"We can take the rest of this bottle of wine, and get drunk!" Leah said enthusiastically. "They tell me you don't feel the heat, when you're already boiled!"

Jodie laughed at that. Leah made her laugh a lot, and that was what she liked about her most. "Tell you what. There was nothing very substantial about this lunch. We'll stop at the deli down the street, get us a big chunk of gouda cheese and a loaf of sourdough bread, and make a picnic of it, on the way back from the farm. I know a little stream where there's a nice shady waterhole to sit beside, and get as soused as you want."

Leah was very excited. "God, I can hardly wait!"

The drive out there was hot, though, and Leah's enthusiasm wilted. She started thinking about Will Jameson again, and how he was changing before her very eyes. They had seen each other only three times since that intimate night at the Phillips farm, and they had not made love at all. Will's mind always seemed to be on something else nowadays.

"That brother of yours is something else," Leah said as they drove over a narrow dirt road toward the farm. Around them were fields of dying corn, turned brown by the heat, and lack of water. Already farmers were talking about a bad crop year, even if rain came. "He's even blaming the government for the dry spell, now. Says the state should be financing the digging of wells in areas where farmers don't have them, to keep these crops from burning up. Says the bankers are against it. I don't know, Jodie."

Jodie glanced over at her. Leah was slouched on the seat beside her, staring ahead through the windshield. Her feathery hair was slightly breeze-blown, and her face was a little flushed. She was wearing a sheer blouse, like Jodie, only Leah's was low-cut, showing a full, eye-arresting cleavage.

"How are the two of you getting along, Leah?"

Leah shrugged. "Indifferently, I guess. When you don't talk much, you can't get into much trouble with each other. Will doesn't argue with me nowadays, Jodie. He just gives me meaningful looks."

"He used to do that when we were kids," Jodie said. "But I was bigger than him then, and I'd just knock him down."

Leah caught Jodie's eye, and Jodie was smiling.

"Hell, I'm sorry to bore you with this," Leah told her. "I promised myself I wouldn't."

The car bumped over a rut, and Jodie fought the wheel for a moment. Dust kicked up on the road around them, and the sun was caught hotly in it.

"You know I don't mind," Jodie said. "I want it to

38

work out between you almost as much as you do." She braked at an approaching driveway. "Here's the farm."

They drove up into the gravel driveway. The Grell farm was an old, falling-down place surrounded by fields of sun-singed corn, with three skinny, pecking chickens in a fenced yard adjacent to a weathered barn. The house squatted in the middle of all of that like a Reformation church that had been closed by edict. There was already an aura of defeat about it, an ambience of finality so rigidly entrenched that there seemed to be no possible release from its demon grip. Jodie and Leah debarked from the department's 1978 Ford with its sun-powdered finish and went up onto the front porch. Old boards squeaked under their feet. At a torn screen door, Mrs. Grell was waiting for them.

"Mrs. Grell?" Jodie said.

"Yes, ma'am. You the lady from the Health Department?"

"That's right, Mrs. Grell. I'm Jodie Jameson, and this is my friend, Leah Purcell."

Mrs. Grell turned her gaze on Leah, as she opened the screen. "The mayor's daughter, would that be?"

"That's right, Mrs. Grell," Leah said.

"Hmmph," Mrs. Grell grunted. "All right, come on in."

Jodie had had warmer welcomes, but she did not mind. Small farmers rarely trusted city people around there, and especially not City Hall-type people. She and Leah went into the living room of the old place. It was littered with newspapers and discarded clothing, and harbored a musty smell, as of museum basements.

"You want to see the faucet run water here?" Mrs. Grell said in a hard voice. She was a small, bony woman with gray hair and washed-out eyes of questionable hue. She led Jodie and Leah into a small kitchen with unwashed dishes in the sink and flies spot-marking the ceiling. She turned on a faucet in the sink and a dribble of rusty-looking water came out.

"You call that water?" she said to Jodie. "Why don't somebody do something about that?"

"There isn't much we can do, Mrs. Grell," Jodie said soberly. "Without some rain. Do you have a well?"

"A well? What do you think we are, rich out here? We can't afford no well!"

Jodie sighed. "Where is your husband, Mrs. Grell? I wanted to ask him how he's feeling. He didn't check back with the doctor, as he was supposed to."

"That doctor didn't do nothing for Hank," Mrs. Grell said testily. "Hank took right down again as soon as he got home. He's in the bedroom there, right through the parlor. Go on, you can talk to him, he's decent."

Jodie preceded Mrs. Grell into the bedroom, while Leah hung back in the living room. Mrs. Grell gave Leah a suspicious look as she passed her, and Leah ignored it. "Nice place you have here," she said lamely.

Hard sunlight was kept out of the bedroom by drawn yellow shades. Jodie squinted toward a low brass bed and saw Grell lying on it, a sheet covering him to his mid-torso. He looked as if he might have been sleeping. He focused on Jodie as she approached the bed. He was a blocky, tanned fellow with wrinkles in his coarse skin, and his arms were heavy-looking and muscular. The tan stopped halfway up his upper arm and partway down his torso. His face was square and heavily lined, and haloed by almost-white hair. He breathed shallowly, and there was no perspiration on his face, despite the heat in the room. He looked sick.

"You the lady doctor?" he said to Jodie in a gravelly voice dredged up from a dry creek bottom.

"I'm not a doctor," Jodie told him. "I'm a health care officer, Mr. Grell, a bacteriologist. Why are you back in bed?"

He shrugged eloquently. "I'm sick."

"You were supposed to go back to the doctor, Mr. Grell. Did you take the medicine he gave you?"

"Sure I took it," he said.

From the doorway, his wife corrected him: "He quit before the bottle was gone. I've got the last pills in the bathroom yet."

"You keep out of this, Ermina," he grumbled.

Jodie got him to let her put a thermometer in his mouth, and take his temperature. When she took it out, she looked over at him. "Your temperature is up, Mr. Grell, and you don't look so good."

"He won't go back to the doctor," his wife put in from the doorway. She turned toward Leah. "You can have a seat in there, if you want."

Jodie heard Leah mumble a negative reply. "Mr. Grell, you're going to have to return to the doctor."

He grumbled something unintelligible, and turned his head away.

"Hepatitis can kill you, Mr. Grell," she said solemnly.

He looked back at her.

"I'll send someone around to take you, if you want me to. But I want you to go tomorrow, do you understand? His office is open on Saturday."

Grell sighed heavily. He looked across the room, away from her again. "Hell. Okay," he said.

With a few last-minute instructions to his wife, Jodie

and Leah left the place, Jodie somber now. Leah looked back at the old house, through the back window of the car, and shook her head. "Jesus. How many are there like them out here in the back country?"

They were driving off, bumping along the rutted road. "More than I like to think about," Jodie said. "God knows how many unreported cases like this there might be, and diarrhea and other illnesses because of the water. And this kind of thing is just what I feared. That some of them are not accepting medical help after it's offered, and are relapsing into sickness that's completely unnecessary. If this goes on a while, I could have a problem on my hands."

They drove along the hot road, with its dust and ruts. When they came to a small crossroads corner, Jodie took a right turn and drove onto a slightly better road for almost two miles. They came to a small bridge that ran over a stream, and there was a pull-off parking area at the bridge, and a lot of shade trees. Jodie pulled over and stopped the car in the deep shade of a tall elm tree. The car radio was going, and soft music issued from it, and they both tried to put the Grells out of their minds for a while.

"This is it," Jodie told Leah. "This is my favorite picnic spot. I started coming here while I was still in college, and Lou and I came several times." She paused, staring through the windshield, thinking of one fall afternoon when they had laughed at their reflections in the placid, green water and joked with each other and, later, made love there among golden falling leaves. "Remember, I asked you to come out here once, and you were busy with something else?"

Leah was already reaching for the wine and cheese in

the back seat. "God, if I'd known it was like this, I'd have come anyway!"

Jodie had gotten out beside the car, but had not turned the radio off. She looked toward the stream, but could not see it because of the high bank on this side. Leah came out on her side with her arms full. "I think I'm going to like this. Do you think I could get Will out here? It might drain some of the tension out of him."

"It wouldn't hurt to ask," Jodie said. "I can tell you from personal experience, it's a place conducive to— well, shall we say, amour?"

Leah smiled widely. "I'll ask him," she said.

The music had stopped, on the car radio, and a spot news broadcast was starting.

"The current temperature in Kansas City is just at a hundred degrees, and in Wichita it's a hundred-two, down two degrees from the afternoon high. Humidity is five percent, and will remain low over the upcoming three-day period. Temperatures tomorrow are expected to be about the same, with no chance of rain in the forecast. No low front is seen on the weather maps, so no precipitation is predicted in the foreseeable future."

"I see my boss has been working this afternoon," Leah smiled. "Let's turn that stuff off, it's making me even more thirsty than I already was."

"Wait a moment," Jodie said, putting a finger to her lips.

". . . and we have it from good sources that just a half-hour ago, the main power plant of Wichita failed in several of its units, due to the terrific strain put on the system by cooling apparatuses, and that the city is now suffering a brown-out that could last an indeterminate period. Mayor Tom Purcell has issued a statement to the press saying that

43

strict measures will have to be undertaken until the plant is back to normal production, including the turning off of all air-conditioning units in the city, except in hospitals and other medical facilities. We'll have an update for you on this at six-thirty."

Leah frowned sharply. "Oh, God, Daddy! We'll all suffocate!"

Jodie reached in and turned the radio off, sober-faced. Now there would be more health problems in the city, with the temperatures going up with almost every day that passed.

"Come on," she said solemnly to Leah. "We have our stream, and our cheese, and our wine. We have this afternoon."

They walked over to the bank together. "You're right," Leah was saying. "We have hours and hours before we have to get the deodorant blues. We'll open up our bottle of wine, and lie down in the shade, and just—"

They both stopped at the top of the stream's bank, and stared down. Jodie could not believe it for a moment. Where there had been a full, green swimming hole under the bridge before, a place with bushes and greenery and shade and the smell of water, now it was very different. There was a shallow, acrid-smelling mudhole down there, the water only a foot deep and very brown. Water barely trickled into it from upstream, and was barely noticeable in leaving it. Most of the stream bed up and down river from the wide place was bare and dry; white stones, cracked earth, bleached wood debris. The greenery along the banks had turned a dull gray.

"Oh, God," Jodie said.

"Are you sure this is the place?" Leah asked.

Jodie nodded numbly. "This is it, all right. I didn't

44

realize, Leah. Living in town. This must be happening all across the state."

Leah clutched the food and wine to her breasts. "I know this is crazy. But I'm a little scared, Jodie."

Jodie put a hand on Leah's arm. "Come on, Leah. Let's get out of here. I'd rather drink our wine back at my place."

Leah made no reply. They turned and walked slowly back to the sun-faded Ford with its silent radio.

It would be a long drive back into town.

THREE

The mood of the city slowly changed, with the new ban on the use of cooling units. Locals had been patient about the weather up to that point, and hopeful. Now they were neither. A somber aura settled over the area like a solar eclipse. Tempers flared without reasonable cause, and depression hung heavily in the air.

Jodie had been right in her assessment that a fouled-up power system could cause her trouble. Emergency rooms at the hospitals filled up quickly and then heat-stroke victims began coming to the Health Department for help. A clinic had to be set up there to supplement hospital facilities, and department doctors who ordinarily were involved in research and administrative matters suddenly found themselves tending patients. With the lowering of the water supply, locals started coming in also with hepatitis, dehydration, and severe stomach ailments.

Reactions of citizens to the ban on air-conditioning was an amazing thing to behold. People had become so accustomed to the luxury of temperature control that they were like junkies being taken off a hard drug when their cool air was turned off. Tom Purcell, because he had had to make the announcement of the ban, was badly maligned by the man on the street, and even by the news media. People were certain that there must be some logical alternative to cutting off their air. But there was none. In fact, the local power company was asking locals to use only absolutely necessary power for cooking and lighting their homes. A repair crew was working feverishly to repair the generators that had broken down, but it was expected to take weeks to get the units in operation again. And even then, residents were told, there could not be unrestricted use of power, or they would have a repetition of the present crisis.

People became surly. The approval of use of portable fans run on 110 current was not enough for them. Many did not have fans, anyway, and stores quickly ran out of them and were having trouble ordering replacements. Many citizens disobeyed the ban and ran their air-conditioners. Policemen patrolled suburban neighborhoods and issued summonses to guilty lawbreakers. There was a five hundred dollar fine for violation, and the same for unauthorized use of water, such as lawn and garden watering, and car washing.

On two different occasions, locals shouted obscenities and accusations at Tom Purcell as he arrived at City Hall, comparing him verbally with Adolf Hitler and, remarkably, Josef Stalin. One local attorney warned he was filing a suit to test the constitutionality of the municipal ordinances restricting private use of power.

Jodie suddenly found herself working twelve hours a day instead of the usual eight or nine. In addition to doing Ben Webster's work, she was obliged to help out personally in the temporary clinic at the department. She could not treat patients, but she could do the lab tests on them, accomplish certain nursing duties, and supervise their handling. Jodie's superiors in Topeka had been in touch with the federal Department of Health, Education & Welfare in Washington, for possible financial assistance and technical supervision, and there was a rumor that HEW might send a task force team to Wichita to study the worsening conditions there and make recommendations for aid. Finally, just at the end of June, Jodie got word from Topeka about the subject and met with Purcell to advise him of developments. When Purcell's friend Hollis Sprague heard of the meeting, he asked to be included, and he was. The three of them met at Jodie's office on a very hot summer morning.

"The HEW official coming here is a woman," Jodie told them as the three sat around her office with a portable fan humming from the top of a file cabinet. "Her name is Betancourt, and she's only been with the department for less than a year. I checked on her, and found that she's a political appointee who knew nothing about public health when she took her job as assistant to the Secretary."

"I'm sorry to hear that," Sprague offered. He and Purcell were dressed in shirtsleeves, with open collars, no ties, and Jodie wore a wispy summer dress. Everybody was dressing for the weather, now. "Do you think she'll be able to help?"

"I don't know," Jodie said from behind her desk. "If she comes here with her ears and eyes open, willing to listen to what we have to say, and see what's going on, maybe so."

"Sometimes the uninitiated can see things more clearly than the more experienced but often jaded eye," Tom Purcell put in. He was about Sprague's age, but not as soft-looking. He was fairly trim, with a fading athletic look, and he had serious brown eyes and a touch of light gray in his sideburns that dramatized slightly his otherwise rather colorless hair.

"That's very true," Sprague agreed. "When will Ms. Betancourt arrive, Jodie?"

"Some time in the next few days, we think," Jodie said. "She'll have a Water Resources Council official with her, and a couple of her own aides. I asked our people in Topeka if HEW suggested they had any specific plans for assistance, and they said none were mentioned."

"Well, I can tell you one thing," Purcell said. "If the feds do get involved, there'll be more delay and red tape than you've ever imagined was possible."

"Hear, hear," Hollis Sprague said, smiling slightly. He looked a bit puffier in the face than he had in his meeting with Latham in California, and more tired. His silvery hair was combed neatly back now, and he peered at Jodie over the horn-rimmed glasses on the bridge of his nose. "And, frankly, delay is something we will probably be ill able to afford, in the coming weeks."

Tom Purcell turned to Jodie. He had always treated her like a second daughter, and there was much affection between them, especially since she and Leah had become so close. "Jodie, Dr. Sprague talked to this fellow Latham while he was in California. You may recall him, he's a weather researcher that's visited the Wichita State campus on a couple of occasions."

"I remember the name," Jodie said. "But I never met him."

"He's just a young man," Purcell went on. "But considered as quite brilliant in his field, Dr. Sprague tells us. He's been studying these new weather patterns this summer, and has some interesting data, according to Dr.

49

Sprague here. Dr. Sprague thought it would be nice if you were present when he relayed those findings to me, and that was the primary reason for his coming along this morning."

Sprague shifted in his chair, and cast a serious look toward Jodie. "I've already spoken with other colleagues around the state here, and with the governor's office. This sudden drought we're experiencing may turn out to be much more dramatic than any of us have suspected. There are jet stream alterations that are pronounced and extremely dangerous, and this sort of change doesn't undo itself overnight."

"You think this could get worse?" Jodie asked worriedly.

"That's exactly what I think, and what Dr. Latham thinks," Sprague said. "I wanted you and Tom here to know the truth as we see it, and I think Betancourt should know it when she gets here. The water problem could get worse, and the farm crops problem."

"How much worse?" Purcell asked.

Sprague blew his cheeks out into fleshy globules. "God only knows. I don't want to predict a high plains disaster. But I think we have to consider the possibility that we could be in real trouble here in a few weeks."

"God," Jodie muttered. She recalled that muddy creek bed where she and Leah had been going to have a picnic, and something tightened inside her, grabbing at her like a clammy hand.

She looked up at Purcell. "Dad called yesterday, from Topeka. The governor has alerted Dad's National Guard units, in case they're needed anywhere to help harvest crops early, or dig wells, or that sort of thing. He was quite concerned about how we're faring here. I tried to

50

be optimistic."

"I hope you told him that our health situation is in competent hands," Purcell grinned.

Jodie returned it. "He gave you his best, Tom. He said that with you running the city, we would probably outlast all this weather with a maximum of sanity."

Purcell's face went straight-lined. "I hope to God his confidence is not misplaced," he said almost inaudibly.

It was that same afternoon that Will Jameson picked Leah up from work at Rawdon Field, in his broken-down old Chevy. Leah had invited him to her new apartment for a light dinner, and she was in a rather gala mood when she hopped into the car, despite the oppressive heat. But Will was not.

"God, it was airless in that office this afternoon!" Leah said lightly as Will drove away from the parking lot and out toward the street in the hot sun. "Hey, wait till you see what I bought for us. A beautiful ham, glazed to perfection, and I made some egg-and-potato salad. Your favorite."

Will looked ahead, wheeling the car out onto a small street into light traffic. He wore dungarees and a work shirt, and his dark hair was slightly ruffled over his forehead. "That's nice, Leah. Are you sure this isn't too much trouble for you, though?"

She noticed his sober face. "Of course not, Will. I'm very excited about it." She felt her cheeks flushing with the heat in the interior of the car. Air-conditioning in cars was not banned from use, but Will's car did not have a unit. "Is everything okay?"

Will glanced over at her. Despite the heat, Leah looked unwilted. Her make-up had held up through the day, and she was bra-less under a sheer blouse, showing herself off seductively to him, and she looked very nice, considering. But Will did not notice. "Why not?" he said. "Why wouldn't everything be okay? Except for the fact that we don't have water to drink that tastes like water, and people are dropping like flies from the heat, and our wheat and corn are roasting in the fields like they were in a bakery oven, everything is just great."

Leah frowned. "We're all in the same boat, Will."

He drove along toward Leah's apartment, gripping the wheel tightly. "Are we?" he said. "I hear they drink bottled water at City Hall, and that they get all of it they want."

Leah's frown deepened. "There has always been bottled water at City Hall, as an alternative to installing a lot of water fountains. And they don't get all they want. I know, I've been down there."

"Phillips' wheat is burning right down to the ground," Will said in a low voice. "He tried to get a bank loan for a well and center-pivot sprayer, and they turned him down. Said he would have to go through the federal government for help. It's that way all around here, and nobody is doing anything about it. Nobody gives a damn. Not at City Hall, not at Topeka. And sure as hell not in Washington."

The apartment building where Leah lived loomed ahead, and Will pulled over to the curb as he reached it, under the sparse shade of a turning-brown maple tree. He cut the engine, and when he turned to Leah, she was scowling toward him.

"Will, every time you talk like this, you get me all upset. My father happens to be one of those that you're unreasonably criticizing, damn it! What do you expect him or the governor to do—make it rain, for God's sake? They're not medicine men, withholding their magic from you. And nobody is getting any favored treatment in this water shortage, except the sick. Ask Jodie, if you don't believe me."

He leaned on the steering wheel, staring out over the hot asphalt of the street. There were damp places under his arms, and across his chest, where he had perspired onto the thin cloth. "Jodie is just like you," he said darkly. "She believes all that crap they taught us in school, about how our Great White Fathers take care of us and protect us from evil, and how we must place our trust in them. Well, there are some of us, Leah, who no longer accept all that bullshit. Since Vietnam, things are different. Some of us are going to demand more of the people we put into office, and if we don't get it, we're going to do something about it."

Leah regarded him quizzically. "We, Will? Who is this 'we'? Why are you using the plural pronoun so often nowadays?"

"I'm talking about a group," he said, facing her again. "An action group, Leah. People who refuse to sit on their duffs and see the common man poisoned, cheated, lied to and made a fool of by the establishment clique. People who intend to fight back, to rebel if they have to."

Leah stared at him. "Rebel? I've never heard you use that word before. What is this group you're talking about? Who are they?"

He started to tell her, then turned away. "What's the difference what we call it? The important thing is that we believe in something, in taking action against the evil we find around us."

"Evil!" she exclaimed. "Oh, God, Will!"

He looked back at her quickly. "Your naivete is un-limited, Leah," he growled. Then his face changed, and became harder. "Unless maybe you see the whole thing all too clearly, but have been brain-washed to believe that rank and position deserve their privileges, here in Wichita and elsewhere."

Leah felt the anger boil into her head. "Brain-washed! By whom, my father? Is that what you mean, Will?"

"If the hat fits, put it on him," he said tautly.

Leah turned toward her open window, red-faced. "Damn you!" she said in a low, uneven voice.

Will knew he had gone too far, made unfounded accusations because of his own anger. But he was in no mood to apologize, he could not force himself to do it.

"Maybe this is the wrong night to have that meal together," he said quietly.

"Maybe it is," Leah said quickly, parrying the thrust with a vengeance. She reached to open the car door, and felt his hand on her bare arm.

"Leah, I didn't mean to—"

"Go to hell, Will!" she said harshly to him, her breath coming shallowly. Then she climbed from the car, slammed the door behind her, and quickly disappeared into the building.

That argument, though, was not the only one of its kind across the city during those hot days. People all over town were accusing the local and state government of inaction, with others defending those governmental entities. Some arguments were heated but controlled, and others got completely out of control in the high temperatures, with shouted words and occasionally flying fists.

Emotions were high, and they were rising with

the heat.

It was just before the July 4th weekend that Paula Betancourt arrived in Wichita with her small entourage. Besides her two aides and the Water Resources Council man, there was also a lesser civil servant from the Department of Agriculture who, for the purposes of this task force, was subordinated to and coordinated with Betancourt.

Betancourt was not what Jodie had expected. A rather large woman physically, she was serious, attentive to the many complaints that she was inundated with, and acutely aware of her shortcomings for the job given her. She understood immediately that she needed much guidance from those she was sent to help. Jodie and Tom Purcell quickly arranged a gathering of Farm Bureau people, area farmers, hospital administrators, wholesale distributors for the grocery chains, water company executives. With Jodie, Purcell, Sprague, and Ed Keefer in attendance, Betancourt and the Agriculture man addressed the group, telling them what they were there for, and asking about drought problems. The Water Resources official also took a short turn. The meeting was a loud one, and when it was over, Jodie, Betancourt, Purcell, Sprague and Keefer retired to Betancourt's hastily-furnished office at the Health Department for a more relaxed conference. Betancourt sat behind a long metal desk, looking as if she might be the next heat-stroke victim, and the other four sat around the room on metal chairs, in a loose semi-circle. Two fans fought to lower the room temperature, but with little success.

"It wasn't as bad as you think," Jodie told Betancourt, after a negative appraisal of the big meeting by Betancourt. "I think they might have liked you, under all those scowls."

"The hell they did," Betancourt said. She was a big-boned, rather masculine-looking woman with solid facial features and a businesslike look about her. She wore almost no make-up, and there was a hint of gray in her thick brown hair. "They want to tear my heart out."

"That was just the farmers," Purcell grinned. The grin slowly evaporated. "They're becoming desperate about their crops, Paula. They think more of their farms than they do of their lives."

"Maybe your presence here will take some of them off my back," Ed Keefer said lightly. "They drive Leah and me crazy with calls about the weather. They blame us for it, you know. They think there must be something we can do about it." He grimaced sourly. He was a thin, lanky fellow with a long, lean face and a dark mustache. His hair was thinning out on top, and his dark eyes were generally moody and defensive, lately. "I tell them to call the university and talk to Dr. Sprague here, that he's the guy that claims miracles with the weather."

Sprague gave Keefer a sour look. "We don't claim to create it, Ed. Only to be able to predict its behavior, something some people think the Weather Service has given up on."

Keefer turned to Betancourt, ignoring the familiar jibe. "Dr. Sprague is scaring everybody here in Wichita with talk of this weather going all summer or longer. Based on some far-fetched calculations by some fellow named Latham, in California."

"Do you think it will go that long?" Betancourt asked Keefer.

But Sprague replied for him. "Mr. Keefer's methods of prediction don't allow him to forecast the weather more than a day or two in advance, Paula."

"And you and this Latham can do better?" Betancourt said.

"We think so," Sprague replied. "We take more factors into account than the Weather Service has ever admitted are relevant. We have more to work with than Ed."

Keefer grunted out his low opinion of that position.

"And you believe that this dry period could last right through the growing season?" Betancourt went on.

"I think it's likely that we've already seen what there will be of a growing season," Sprague said solemnly. The pronouncement hung in the hot room like the shadow of a plains vulture over a parched landscape. "That's why we must concentrate our attention on people now, primarily."

Betancourt sighed heavily. "You make it all sound rather grim, Dr. Sprague."

Sprague shrugged. "Droughts can be deadly, of course. The Greek city-state of Mycenae was wiped out permanently by drought. Before the end, the population went crazy. Temples, palaces and granaries were burned and looted by wild mobs, dying from thirst, hunger, disease. In the Great Famine of Bengal, in 1769, which was caused by drought, over ten million people died. The one in North China in the 1800's killed over nine million."

A heavy silence filled the room, and there was only the sound of the humming fan, moving the hot air around them.

It was Ed Keefer who spoke up first. "There you go again, professor. This isn't Mycenae, and the Great Plains aren't the Peloponnese."

"Isn't there something we can do to influence what's happening, then, as opposed to the helplessness of the Greeks?" Jodie wondered. "With all of our modern technology?"

"The only thing we know about is seeding," Keefer remarked. "And you at least have to have clouds, for proper seeding. We don't."

"What Ed here doesn't like to admit," Sprague said, "is that we know little more about the weather than they did in ancient Greece. There are some people who claim the weather can be influenced and controlled by man, but not enough is known yet to put theory into practice. Work is being done on the effects of radio signals on the upper currents by certain researchers, including Dr. Latham. They're not at the stage yet, though, at which they can responsibly attempt to make their own weather."

"Then for the present, at least, we're stuck with responding to the effects of our hot spell," Purcell said. "And that's what we have to get on with."

"Well," Betancourt said, "I've already requisitioned financing for some well-digging on the smaller farms, and we'll try to get all of this sick livestock butchered at temporary sites and buy the meat at parity prices."

Jodie leaned forward on her chair, pushing a curl of thick auburn hair away from her face. "I don't mean to sound unsympathetic toward the farm situation, Paula," she said. "But as Dr. Sprague mentioned, it's already beyond irrigation and livestock problems at this point. We're running out of water here in Wichita. If we manage to find water by digging ordinary wells, I don't see how we could use it to irrigate crops. We'd have to save it for drinking. Isn't that right, Tom?"

"I think Jodie is right, Paula. Our water reserve has never been so low. If this thing continues for another couple of weeks, the health problems could be very serious."

Betancourt stared at him, and then at Jodie. "I didn't realize it was that bad here."

"Some people's faucets have almost dried up," Jodie said. "Bottled water, beer, soft drinks are all gone from the stores around town. Supermarkets are quickly running out of their stocks of canned goods. Distributors are not bringing new stuff in because it's needed in a lot of other places, too."

Betancourt looked around at their sober faces. "They showed me films from the thirties, at the Department. Tumbleweeds piled up against fences, dust-filled ditches alongside the roads. Bare, baked land. The savannah blowing away, with nothing left for greenery to grow in. But that all happened gradually. Not like this."

"If this trend continues," Sprague put in deliberately, "comparing this to the thirties will be like comparing a tornado to a slowly-rising summer wind."

Betancourt held his somber gaze, and a fan hummed in a corner.

"I don't want to sound like I'm pushing any panic button," Jodie said. "But we have to plan to get some water in here. If that reservoir goes dry, dehydration will set in very quickly. A camel can lose up to twenty-five percent of its body water and survive, but people can lose only twelve percent. Get us water, and medicine. We're already running low on drugs to treat hepatitis and dysentery."

"Medicine should be easier than water," Betancourt admitted. "Other areas of the country are beginning to feel the drought, too. They won't want to give up their water to send it here."

"What about de-sal plants?" Keefer suggested. "There are several of them around the country, in ports. They get water from the sea. Why can't we just gear up to meet our needs here?"

"I checked that out, Ed," Purcell told him. "The plants in operation are strained to capacity for the needs of their own communities. And building one would take months, maybe a year or more."

Betancourt looked very tired, and she had been there only just over twenty-four hours. "I'll make some calls," she said. "Our Water Resources man may have some ideas, too. I'm sure we can get you some relief from some source."

"I hope it's soon, Paula," Jodie told her. "I hope it's very soon."

No comments were added to that remark.

There was little left to say by the others, before they broke up their meeting solemnly.

Now it was time for action.

In the next few days, the high temperatures went up again, over a hundred ten toward a hundred fifteen. No cloud marred the perfect blue of the torrid sky. Residents of Wichita were gasping for air. Summer school closed down, and many small businesses. People had begun boiling their faucet water, at Jodie's request. More and more of them ran air-conditioners illegally, and some were arrested. Police began pulling the outlet cords out of the sides of the machines, when they found a violation. A sizeable crew worked day and night to get the power plant operating at full capacity, but as soon as they would get a unit working, another one would go out.

The Weather Service was so assailed with phone calls that Leah Purcell was given a full-time job of answering them, and it was wearing her out. A couple of crank calls came in, warning that the Weather Service station would be bombed, and Ed Keefer asked for Tom Purcell to send a policeman over to watch over them, and Purcell persuaded the police chief to do so.

Leah and Will had stopped seeing each other, after the argument in his car on that hot afternoon. Will was changing fast, and Leah was not sure she understood the person he was becoming. Will did not contact her, and Leah did not seek him out. Things were different, now. Leah did not feel that she had the time or energy to worry over Will. He would have to look out for himself.

Jodie had never been busier in her life. The clinic set up at the Health Department was jammed with sick residents, and Jodie not only was helping out more and more there, but now she was assisting Paula Betancourt make decisions about federal assistance to the area. She had no more calls from Lou Falco, and was glad of it. Falco was quickly merging into the past now. It was as if Jodie were moving away from him on a train, with Falco standing on the station platform, smiling his Robert Redford smile—an insincere smile, Jodie now deduced—but fading from view with every moment that passed, and from importance in her memory.

Had it not been for the emergency that now faced her in her work, Jodie would have been depressed by this juncture in her life. She had opened herself to two different men so far, given of herself freely to them, and then found out that there was no future in the relationships for her. An affectionate girl, Jodie needed to give love and to receive it. But the world did not appear kindly disposed toward the satisfaction of that need, and that cast a shadow over Jodie's outlook for her future life despite her success with her job.

Jodie, though, had little time to think of herself, during those early July days. She was in conference with Betancourt, or Purcell, or hospital administrators most of the day. As for Purcell, he was harried by new problems he had never confronted before. Water pressure was higher in some parts of town than in others, and that created inequities in water usage that Purcell was called on to make right. At night, local youth gangs had begun breaking into grocery stores and looting them of anything drinkable—beer, frozen juices, canned vegetables. The police were having a difficult time keeping up with it.

Jodie had not seen her brother Will for a while, and wondered how he was doing out on the Phillips farm. She knew that he and Leah had had a fight and were not speaking, and she tried to keep out of it. But then one morning when she stopped past a small supermarket to get a few things for her evening meal, she ran into Will quite by accident. She rounded a corner into an aisle where she hoped to find some canned asparagus, and Will was standing there staring at a can of fruit that he held in his hand.

"Hey, Will! What are you doing here?"

Will turned quickly, a scowl on his lean face. He looked different to her, more severe in his appearance and manner. "Oh, Jodie." He did not smile. "Good to see you."

Jodie came up and touched his arm. "I thought you did your shopping out on the edge of town."

"We do, ordinarily. But you can't get this stuff out there." He was wearing a back-pack on his shoulders, over his work clothes, and Jodie noticed that it was bulging with something. She peeked up over the top of it, where a cover hid its contents, and saw the edge of a can of cherries in there.

"Have you seen Leah lately?" she said to him. She had her thick hair up again, but there were little ringlets of it that lay damp against her arched neck, behind her head. Her face was slightly flushed, too, from the heat.

"You know I haven't," he finally replied, replacing the can to a shelf, and picking up another one.

"I think she misses you, Will," Jodie told him. "Why don't you call her?"

He made a sound in his throat. "Did you see the prices on this stuff? They've tripled prices, Jodie, just because they know we'll pay it. They're taking advantage of our desperation, for God's sake." There was an anger in his voice that was disturbing to her. "Well, I won't pay it, by God!"

Jodie looked at the back-pack again, and saw the hidden edges of cans bulging in it. "Will, are those cans of food in your pack?"

He did not look toward her. "It's goddam thievery, is what it is!"

Jodie knew that Will had never stolen anything in his life. But times were different, now. He was different. "Do you intend to pay for that stuff, Will?" she asked him deliberately.

He finally looked at her, with a hard, hostile look. "Mind your own business, Jodie."

"Oh, God, Will!"

"I'm not your little brother any longer, I'm all grown

up now. I play the game my way, Jodie. If these bastards can make up their new rules to gouge me, I can make up some of my own. It isn't just me. We're all doing it this way now. It's called beating them at their own game."

Jodie was suddenly very scared for him. "Don't do it, Will. The Phillipses can afford the new prices. This isn't the way to make things right."

He turned away from her. "Excuse me."

But Jodie followed after him down the aisle. "Will, listen to me! If you won't pay for that stuff, I will! Here, you can have some of my money! Will forty dollars help you?" She stopped him, and held out two twenties to him.

Will stared darkly at her for a moment, as if he were dealing with an insane person. Then he suddenly reached and jerked the back-pack off his shoulders, glaring at her all the while. He tok it in both hands, and savagely threw it onto the floor between them.

"There, damn it! Are you happy now?"

Jodie jumped, startled, and stepped back away from him. Down at the end of the aisle, a woman shopper turned and stared at them. Will glowered at his sister now, breathing shallowly.

"Will! Take it easy, it's me, Jodie!"

"I'm telling you, by God! Keep out of my life! You and Leah both! Neither of you understand any of this, and you never will! You can be put upon and cheated and kicked in the head all you want to, but don't count me in on it! I'm doing something about it!"

Before Jodie could respond to him, he turned and stormed out of the place, with several people looking after him wide-eyed. Jodie stared at the sack of food cans on the floor for a long while, shaken inside her. Then she replaced the cans to the shelves, and left the store without buying anything.

She tried to call Will at the farm that evening, but Mrs. Phillips told her apologetically that he was not answering the phone to anybody. Jodie felt very badly about it all, wondering if she had handled the situation correctly.

She also found herself wondering, though, if Will and his new friends in town were some of those who were breaking into stores at night and looting them. It was an ugly thought. She wished her father were there to talk to Will, to reason with him. But Will was alienated from Colonel Jameson, too, and had been for several years. Will did not like the idea that Jameson had made a career of the military, had participated in the Vietnam fiasco, was still training young men to kill. Jameson and his son had had arguments about it for a while, and then they had stopped arguing. That was about the time that Will had dropped out of college at Wichita State. Now, when Jodie visited Jameson in Topeka, she went alone, because Will would not go see his father.

The morning after her confrontation with her brother, Jodie left the health lab before noon for an early lunch, and to stop by Tom Purcell's office at City Hall. She wanted to find out what the city was accomplishing to stabilize water pressure evenly throughout the city. Paula Betancourt almost went with her, but was obliged to meet with a hospital administrator at the last moment. Jodie had her meeting with Purcell, catching him just before he left for a luncheon with a visiting mayor who was having similar problems to those of Wichita, in Iowa, but not so severe. The other mayor went on to lunch with an assistant of Purcell, and Purcell stayed on for a few minutes to confer with Jodie. Their business did not take

65

long, but just as Jodie was preparing to leave, declining Purcell's invitation to join him and the others at a small restaurant nearby, Hollis Sprague came by, flushed in the face and sweating heavily.

"Has it been on the TV here yet?" he asked Purcell after Purcell and Jodie had greeted him curiously. They had never seen Sprague unsettled before, in an emotional state. He was always calm, controlled, thoughtful. But not at that moment. "Have you heard the latest on our worsening weather?"

Purcell shook his head sidewise. He and Jodie were standing beside his long walnut desk in his private office, and Sprague faced them from the center of the thick-carpeted room.

"No, we haven't heard anything," Purcell said, glancing at Jodie for her confirmation. "What is it, Hollis?" He ordinarily addressed Sprague informally in private, between them, or if only someone close to him or Sprague were present.

Sprague was shaking his head sidewise. "It was Mark Latham that figured it out. He talked to somebody at M.I.T., and that person spoke to someone at the White House. After about five calls to Moscow, it's been confirmed. The damned Russians did this to us!"

Jodie and Purcell were staring at Sprague curiously. "Now wait a minute, Hollis," Purcell grinned a little weakly. "I know it's popular to blame the Soviets for everything nowadays, make them the engineers of all our ills. But isn't this going a little too far?"

Sprague forced himself to slow down. "No, listen to me, Tom. Both we and the Russians have been toying with the notion that the jet stream and upper atmospheric patterns can be influenced by super-powerful radio

66

signals. But the Russians are far ahead of us in this area. Latham had heard that they might actually be experimenting with the theory, by trying to alter weather patterns on the Asian continent. Well, he was right. After a very dry year in the Steppes last year, a study group of atmospheric physicists, like Latham, convinced the Kremlin to allow them to orbit a satellite for the specific purpose of creating rain across the Steppes and Siberia. In March of this year they secretly orbited their satellite, which they called Dozhtbog, or Raingod. It was a great success, from their point of view. They got their rain in Siberia, and privately hailed the experiment as a landmark of science. But they delayed announcing it to the world community until they had watched the 'downstream' weather for a while."

Jodie's face had lengthened through the brief report. "You're saying that their rain in Siberia caused our drought in Kansas?"

"That's exactly right," Sprague answered. "They interfered with basic weather patterns, Jodie. They actually forced the jet stream slightly out of its usual path, with powerful radio emissions. Without knowing or caring what happened here, downstream."

"My God," Purcell muttered.

"I didn't know things like this were possible," Jodie said in a low, subdued voice.

"We weren't sure they were, until now," Sprague said. "Of course, this represents the grossest kind of irresponsibility on the part of the Russians—irresponsibility as great as any military adventure."

"Maybe it was a calculated injury to us," Purcell theorized. "The Russians haven't exactly been our bosom buddies in past years."

"Nobody at the highest levels thinks so, Tom," Sprague said. "Even the Russians would not profit by turning our Midwest into a dust bowl. They buy too much grain from us. No, I suspect they're genuinely embarrassed by all the criticism they're getting from around the world. They gambled that the stream would move back quickly to its original route across the Pacific, but it didn't. People like Latham feared just this kind of result, with meddling, and that's why we've never conducted such experiments here."

"I just can't believe this," Purcell said, anger boiling in his voice. "I can't believe it."

"Our State people are already in Moscow, making unprecedented demands for reparations that could bankrupt the Russians if they honored them. The Russians disclaim legal liability, but have offered to send a study team over here to help us take action to correct the situation."

"How would they correct it?" Jodie wondered, a small hope in her voice.

Sprague was shaking his head again. "They think the stream can be altered back into its old route with further bombardment of radio signals, from this end. They've got Washington interested, and the Weather Service and NASA are sending a whole scientific team here, to Kansas, to look closely at the situation. Ed Keefer thinks they're coming right here to Wichita, and that when they get here, the Russians will be with them."

Jodie was stunned by all of that. "Damn them," she said. "Damn them for playing with our lives." She thought of Will, and his rebellious cynicism, and for a moment she was on his side.

"Well, at least maybe something will be done now,"

Purcell said. "If they all get here in time."

Sprague cast a weary look at him. "Latham is dead set against our inviting the Russians here to further meddle with things they know so little about. He says that it's one thing to move the stream out of kilter, and quite another to knock it back in. I agree with him. Even if you accept the moral responsibility for what *we* could do to downstream communities—Europe, Africa—you're still stuck with the probability that it won't work. Or if it does, it will take longer than we have."

Jodie was frowning. "Well, I'll tell you, Dr. Sprague. With all due respect to this Latham, I think we have to do *something*. We send a lot of wheat to Europe and Africa, too. If the Great Plains are hurt beyond short-term recovery by this suddenly ferocious weather, our 'downstream' grain customers will suffer, too. But more importantly, if this continues into August, people will be dying here. And I mean in large numbers. Some will move out, but not enough of them. As for the probability of success, maybe the Russians and NASA will fail. But maybe they'll succeed, too. And that would be pretty wonderful."

Sprague nodded. "Yes, it would. But don't get your hopes too high, Jodie, that the Russians will save us. In my opinion, in the end we'll probably have to save ourselves."

Tom Purcell grunted his understanding. "That's the way it often seems to work out," he said quietly.

FOUR

Jodie lay sprawled hotly on her bed, a sheet twisted partially off her, a full right breast and a long left thigh exposed to the stuffy air of the room. A slender hand lay on the exposed breast, and moved over its nipple gently, caressingly.

Jodie had had little sleep in the heat that barely dipped below a hundred that night, and she had wakened with a dream-memory of Lou Falco floating in her head, and in her aroused body.

The dream had begun during sleep, one of the few periods of real sleep all through the long, hot night. Then she had begun waking up in the middle of it, not wanting to, wanting it to go on.

Falco had been slowly undressing her, in the dream, his tanned hands on her everywhere, touching, inflaming. Skirt had come off, then blouse, and then the tanned hands were forcing themselves beneath the flimsy cloth of a bra, crawling over the contours of her breasts, exciting her. For some reason, in the dream, she was reluctant to let it happen, and she was squirming and moving under his grasp, trying to avoid what he was doing to her, yet wanting it very much, on a deep, primordial level. That made the whole thing more breathtaking, more passionate. The bra came off with protests mumbled by her, and then the last piece of cloth slid down over her hips and thighs, with her kicking it off, helping him now, not being able to help herself. Then it was her taking hold of him, and finding that she needed both hands to guide him to her, and being emotionally grateful for it. It was at that hard, pulsing union that Jodie awoke and knew it was not real, and a flooding of disappointment came bursting through her, and she forced herself back into a half-sleep to let her conscious mind direct the climactic stages of the love-making, with Falco working and working on her, making her reach for him, and clutch him to her hot flesh, and cry out with the pleasure of him inside her.

She lay there now with her hand on her naked breast, cooling down slowly inside.

"You bastard, Lou," she murmured aloud.

She threw the sheet the rest of the way off her, and stretched. Her thick auburn hair was fanned out on the pillow, and her flesh was rosy-colored with the heat of the room, and from inside her. She was a finely made girl, all soft curves and arches and satin skin. She lay there motionless for a long moment, then sat up and swung her legs off the bed, in graceful, flowing movements. Just the motion of getting out of bed caused a fine dampness on her flesh, and she felt breathless for a moment in the stuffiness of the room. She picked up a small clock from the adjacent nightstand and it said the time was 7:33.

"God, I overslept, after all that restlessness," she chided herself.

She could not take a shower. Tom Purcell had asked residents not to bathe for a while, except to sponge off with cloths. She got up, walked into a tiled bathroom, and washed herself down with tepid cloths, and was slightly refreshed. That was the worst part of what they were all going through, there was no way to rejuvenate oneself from day to day. You could not sleep in this heat, nor even rest in it, and you never felt really crisp and clean. Jodie always felt a little wilted, even when she started off the day. That could wear on you, after a while.

Dressing slowly in the bedroom again, Jodie thought of Will. Taking a few cans of food from a store was not the depth of his new misbehavior, she was sure. She was also sure Will was letting himself get involved with people who were doing much worse than that. The petty stealing was merely an isolated act of defiance on his part, a crazy whim induced, possibly, by the mind-frying heat. But she sensed that it was all more serious than that. If Will had convinced himself that acts of defiance were needed, that civil disobedience were called for, he would not be satisfied with minor acts of theft. Will never did things in a small way.

When she was dressed, Jodie decided to call their father and discuss Will with him. She got on the phone at her bedside and dialed the long-distance number for Jameson's office, and after several rings, a female voice came on the line.

"I'd like to speak with Colonel Jameson," Jodie told the woman.

"*May I ask who's calling?*"

"Yes, this is his daughter, in Wichita."

"*Ah, I see. Well, Colonel Jameson has not come in yet, Miss Jameson. He was stopping on his way in for a meeting with a supply distributor.*"

"Oh," Jodie said.

"*I'd be happy to give him a message.*"

"No, it's all right," Jodie assured her. "It was just something personal that can wait. I'll try again, when I get a chance. Just tell him I said hello, and to try to keep cool."

A small laugh. *"I'll do that, Miss Jameson."*

When Jodie had hung up, she just sat there on the edge of the bed staring at the phone for a long moment. She wished her father were here in Wichita, so he could see Will himself, and understand what was happening to him. Now, more than ever before, it seemed like Topeka was a long way off.

When she left for work, not long after the phone call, she was feeling rather low.

Across the breadth of the city that morning in mid-July, Wichita was boiling with ever-rising heat. In a normal summer the city was one of the warmest places in the country. The explorer Garveth Wells had once remarked that at its August worst, it could compare to Cairo, Egypt in dry heat, where oven-brick cobblestones baked in the African sun and camels groaned under its onslaught. But nobody, not even Wells, had ever seen anything quite like this in a center of human population.

Gone now was the dappled green of that parks-and-university town that had paraded its cool shade and its blossom-grown vistas. The prairie community lay brown and scorched like some Saharan outpost, under an unrelenting, blast-furnace sun. The tall elms along South Topeka wore withered, dust-choked leaves like winter coats out of season, adding to the feeling of heat, and at Linwood Park the grass had gone dry-yellow as ripe wheat. On College Hill, where Hollis Sprague wrestled in his mind with the worsening weather disaster, ivy-grown halls had taken on a sere, arid look of stony desperation.

73

Wilted pedestrians out on sun-blinded Kellogg Street sported damp-stuck summer clothing that could not protect them, dabbed at flushed faces, and worried about heart attacks. Steaming automobiles hissed out their agony on the interstate, stalling in travel lanes. The entire city now crouched, sweltering, under an undulation of thermal waves from baking concrete and asphalt, with City Hall and other central edifices striking cowed silhouettes against a violent sky. Blistering-hot, humming-quiet, yet percolating inside with the unflung curses and unshouted obscenities of officials and employees, they were airless shelters of ill-hidden panic and potential, shimmering madness. Fear and discomfort were producing frustration, anger, hysteria.

In the midst of all that, on that torrid afternoon, Ed Keefer's National Weather Service boss arrived from Washington. He was an assistant director and his name was Stanley Kravitz. With him were three NASA technicians, several Weather Service meteorologists, and a big computer on loan from NASA. The computer arrived by truck and was installed in Kravitz' new command post, a quonset-type building at McConnell Air Force Base on the southeast outskirts of town. Two other trucks also arrived with electronic equipment, later in the afternoon. This headquarters was to be the center of all anti-drought activity in the state, and Ed Keefer's Rawdon Field station was, of course, subordinate in function to it. In early evening, two Corps of Engineers officers also arrived at McConnell, but were not a part of the Kravitz team. They had been sent to confer with Paula Betancourt and the Water Resources Council official, to figure a way to make more water available to the area.

There were also command posts being set up at

Oklahoma City, Omaha and Des Moines, but the one at Wichita was the important one, because it was where conditions were the very worst, and it was where NASA and the Russians were gathering. The Russians were to arrive the next week, flying in from San Francisco.

When Tom Purcell prepared to leave work at City Hall that early evening, after a hectic day with reporters, Kravitz, and irate citizens, Hollis Sprague arrived in time to delay him. He had been studying Mark Latham's calculations on the disturbance of the jet stream, and had gotten in reports from across the country as to worsening weather conditions. He heaved himself onto a leather chair in Purcell's private office, where he and Purcell and Jodie had conferred a few days previously, and his face was very flushed, as if he had just run a mile.

"The whole Midwest is slowly burning up, Tom," he said. "And Oklahoma and Texas. There has never been anything quite like it, in the history of our country. Nothing so widespread, that came on so quickly. California is brown, with fires starting in the southern areas regularly. Water is being rationed in New York and New Jersey. Only the few ports with de-sal plants have sufficient water, and they're running short because of excessive use."

"If this goes into August," Purcell said, seated on the corner of his desk, "we're going to have a real disaster on our hands, Hollis. Did you hear what happened in Iowa City? A mob attacked City Hall, demanding water and food. Several people were injured, in a clash with the police. We're getting more and more looting here, tied to break-ins. Chief Kelly has his hands full nowadays, believe me. There's some campus group behind a lot of it, call themselves the People's Brigade. They think we're holding back water from them that they have coming, or some such nonsense."

Sprague nodded. "Our president is looking into the group, Tom. But it's difficult to stop such activities, in times like these. I understand the White House has put National Guard units on full alert."

"Yes, including our Topeka guard, commanded in part by my old friend, Jodie's father."

Sprague rose from his chair, and went and stood directly in front of a rotating fan that sat on a file cabinet. He stared around the paneled room, at the American flag in a corner, the state flag in another one, the watercolor paintings on the end walls. There was a feeling of restraint in the plush office, an aura of rather rigid order. Sprague wondered if that order would dissolve, in the next couple of weeks.

"I don't like what's happening out at McConnell, Tom," he finally said, standing there perusing a nearby watercolor. "There's a gearing up to do something, anything. The Russians will be here pretty soon, and my feeling is, they're going to run the show. Our government people will give them full reign on this satellite project, plunging all the way from a no-control posture in regard to weather, to an anything-goes attitude, without knowing much more than they did thirty days ago, or for that matter, thirty years."

Purcell shrugged. "Well, if they fail, we're no worse off than we are right now. I think Jodie was right when she said we have to do something, Hollis."

"Yes, we should be trying to come up with some solution to this rather unprecedented problem," Sprague said. "But we will be worse off with a Kravitz failure, if we should have been seeking alternate solutions but

76

weren't, because we were depending on NASA and the Russians to save us."

Purcell regarded Sprague soberly. "Might there be alternate solutions, Hollis?"

Sprague had turned back to him. His face was a little less flushed, and his shirt did not look quite so damp. "It's possible. I'd like to see a second study team here in Wichita, Tom, a conference of weather scientists from the universities that would confer with and cooperate with Kravitz' team, but would have funding to take their own, independent action if it seemed required. Maybe they would agree with the Russians, that a second alteration of the jet stream by radio emissions is the only course open. But if they did, we'd all feel a lot better about proceeding with such a plan, I think."

"Theoretically such an idea is sound," Purcell said. "But you can be sure the federal government won't invite your experts to argue with NASA and the Russians. And I doubt I could convince the governor, at this stage, to fund such a program. Even if I could, it would take longer than we have now to get it going, at this juncture."

Sprague came and seated himself on the chair again. "You're probably right, Tom."

Purcell eyed him pensively. "What about this Latham you're so high on? He's already up on this thing, and he's been here on your campus before. Maybe I could get a telephone commitment from the governor to bring just him here, Hollis. To confer with you and your people in your department. That would be better than nothing, wouldn't it?"

Sprague let a thin smile creep onto his fleshy face. "A hell of a lot better, Tom. It's a good idea."

"The university would have to bear some of the responsibility, of course," Purcell said. "You'd have to set up a second command center in your department there, and furnish the use of university equipment. Can you get authority for that?"

"There ought to be no problem at all," Sprague told him. "I'll get in touch with Latham and put the proposition to him."

"If he says yes," Purcell added, "make a list of equipment you might need that you don't have available, and I'll ask the governor to write us a check from some state grant fund or something. We could be set up to go within just a few days."

Sprague's smile had widened. "I'll get right on it, Tom."

Now that Kravitz' task force was established at McConnell (although equipment was still being moved in from several sources), a White House aide was sent to make certain there was nothing else Kravitz needed, and to urge full speed ahead, before he flew on out to California to assist Betancourt in getting a shipment of water from San Diego. The President was very worried now, but he did not really know what to do other than what was being done.

The White House aide, a man named Stevens, arrived at Rawdon Field the morning after Purcell and Sprague's private meeting. Because he was the President's personal emissary, there was a great deal of unwarranted furor about his coming, both favorable and antagonistic, so Tom Purcell ordered security measures at the airport.

The plane was met there by Purcell, Stanley Kravitz, Ed Keefer, Paula Betancourt, and the two highest-ranking NASA men. The group drove from Rawdon to McConnell in three limousines, windows up and air-conditioners on in the hundred fifteen degrees heat. There was a rather surly-looking crowd on the waiting ramp at the airport, but no incident occurred there.

Unfortunately, at McConnell it was a different story. The People's Brigade had gotten wind of the aide's arrival days in advance. It was the group which Will Jameson had joined a couple of weeks ago, and which had now become quite active. They had started off by breaking into three different food stores and stealing any liquids they could find, including canned goods. Will had been with them on the last two occasions, and during the most recent one he had almost been caught by the police. They had consumed much of the stolen goods themselves, and had distributed the rest, God-like, in the poorer neighborhoods of the city. Taking from the powerful and rich and giving to the weak. Like modern-day Robin Hoods, one member had said.

On this hot morning, they were waiting for the limousine convoy from Rawdon Field, and Will Jameson was with them. The Brigade was even more adamantly opposed to the NASA-Weather Service cooperative effort than either Hollis Sprague or Mark Latham. Most members, including Will, believed that it was immoral to even consider giving the licentious Soviets even further license to wreak havoc with the upper atmosphere by inviting them to Wichita, even if there was a chance they could help, and that the money so spent could have been used to ship water in, drill wells, and render free aid to victims of the drought. They did not know that the aide Stevens intended to assist in obtaining water, nor that ordinary well-digging was out of the question as a means of drought relief. Just as above-ground streams and rivers were going bone dry, so were the usual underground water supplies, the ones found within striking distance of farm well diggers. The Brigade did not possess sufficient technical knowledge to know that it was already too late for such procedures to make any substantial difference.

When the motorcade came into view of the main gate at McConnell Air Force Base, the lead car contained Stevens, Tom Purcell, Stanley Kravitz and Paula Betancourt. The extra security at Rawdon was gone, with only a couple of motorcycle cops leading the convoy at this point. It was they who first spotted the Brigade members as they converged on the gate area with their placards. The signs read, *Water Not Russians*, and *Save Wichita Now*, and *People Power*.

The cars had to slow for the gate, where two military guards stood waiting to pass them through, so the demonstrators were able to converge freely on the motorcade for brief moments. Will was at the forefront, dressed in farm clothes and a straw hat to keep the sun off, and he was waving a placard and shouting at the passengers of the automobiles.

Inside the car at the front of the procession, Purcell and Kravitz were not really surprised by the demonstration, and took no alarm, but Paula Betancourt was afraid, and the aide Stevens caught her mood. Purcell was apologizing to Stevens for the placards, and the trouble, as their car pulled up to the gate. Shouting faces crowded in on them from all sides, as the nervous guards at the gate examined the driver's pass and motioned the cars through. But just at that moment, a rock came crashing against the door glass beside Purcell. Then, a second one spidered the windshield, loudly.

Kravitz, a heavy-set, beet-faced fellow sitting in the rear with the White House aide and Betancourt, leaned forward and yelled at the driver. *"Get to hell inside with this thing! Now!"*

Outside the car, Will had come up close and was hitting on the hood of the limousine with the edge of a thick placard as it moved away. *"Dirty bastards!"* he was yelling. *"In your goddam air-conditioned limos! Turn on our water, do you hear us?"*

Tom Purcell thought he recognized the voice, and turned and stared into Will's enraged face just as the car lurched ahead and through the gate.

"Jesus," Purcell muttered.

Will had probably not even seen him, he guessed. As the other cars came through the gate, Purcell looked over his shoulder and saw a couple of Brigade people heaving small missiles at the guards, and then a guard fired off a pistol over their heads. The noise stopped with that report, as if it had been turned off with a radio button.

The convoy proceeded on across the base, with those inside the cars sober-faced. The aide Stevens made a small joke about it, but Paula Betancourt had to take a tranquilizer when they arrived at Kravitz' headquarters.

That same afternoon out at Berkeley, Mark Latham got word of the setting up of Kravitz' headquarters at McConnell. His assistant Bill brought the news to him, then the two of them just sat quietly in Latham's small office at the end of the lab, and digested the significance of the development.

"They say there will be some brief preliminary studies of the area, and its upper atmosphere," Bill concluded his report. "Then, when their buddies the Russians arrive,

81

they'll go ahead and make calculations for the orbiting of a satellite, unless there are so-called contra-indications, at Cape Kennedy. They'll construct the guts of the satellite right in Wichita, at McConnell, then fly it to Florida for installation in the payload of the rocket."

Latham, dressed like his assistant in a white lab coat, shook his head slowly. "I called Russ Atkins at M.I.T., and he talked to the President himself. To try to de-rail this Moscow Express. It didn't work. Everybody's in a panic now, Bill. Nobody's ever seen anything quite like this. Also, they don't perceive the Soviets as the villains they really are in this scenario. Congress is more concerned that we were not notified of the Siberia experiments than that they were performed at all. There's a feeling, encouraged by a couple of our own scientists, that the Russians are brilliant pioneers in weather-making who will push a few buttons and make all of this go away, then give us an era of absolute weather control."

"Do you think it's possible they can do just that?" Bill wondered.

Latham, sitting at his desk with its piles of papers and files, leaned back on his chair. "I wish to God I could answer that in the affirmative. Of course, almost anything is possible, particularly in this field. But if our own calculations have any validity, their chances of correcting what they've done through more playing with the circumpolar vortex are probably slim to none. They could create more havoc with the basic systems. We don't really know what happens with a forced massive pressure system shift. You're fighting ocean temperature, solar activity, magnetic field. Playing with the jet stream is too complex an interference, Bill. It's not like cloud-seeding. We just don't know enough, yet, to be meddling in this God-like way."

"Well," Bill said. "We are, whether or not we should. I just wish the Weather Service or NASA had invited some American physicists to join them in their study."

Latham shook his head. "They don't want too many cooks stirring the stew," he said. "They particularly don't want any opinions that might delay this panic-motivated project. I suspect that—"

The phone on his desk rang, and Latham excused himself to answer it. There was a long-distance operator, and then Hollis Sprague's voice was on the other end.

"Well, Hollis," Latham said after their greetings. "I didn't expect a call from you today. Are you getting along all right with the bureaucrats back there?"

Sprague's voice sounded weary. *"I haven't even been introduced to the big brass, Mark. Ed Keefer and this fellow Kravitz are keeping well away from College Hill."*

"How are things there, Hollis?" Latham asked.

There was a short pause. *"Mark, they're getting worse than we ever thought. Kansas farmers have lost their crops. Period. And now they're losing their livestock. Dehydration, disease. The stink of death lies heavy across the plains, Mark. And now it's infesting the city here. People are succumbing to this heat. A small percentage has moved out temporarily, to the north and east, to try to get out of this blast-furnace. But most just hang on and suffer. It's pretty bad when you can't get out of it, Mark. I damn near fainted yesterday myself, when I walked into a closed room. I've never seen anything like it."*

"It sounds pretty terrible, Hollis."

"Mark, Tom Purcell and I got our heads together and decided that we ought to be putting an effort forth separate

from and independent of the Russian-NASA project, in case that one fails somehow. Tom says he'll beef up our technical facilities here, if I can get you to join us in our department here for a short time. I told him if there was anybody who could come up with some alternative plan to that of the Russians, it would be you."

Latham hesitated before replying. "That's very flattering, Hollis. But I have to tell you, I don't know if there is any way to short-cut the effects of the Dozhtbog orbiting. I've given it a lot of thought here. We all have."

"I know, Mark. But maybe you could learn something from on-the-spot observations that would give you some ideas. I've wangled a couple of Skyhooks, and I think we can get hold of a better computer. All expenses would be on us, Mark. Of course, I know I'm asking you to walk into an inferno here. But there isn't much I can do about that."

Latham hesitated again. "When would you want me there?" he asked Sprague.

Sprague laughed throatily. *"Yesterday,"* he said.

Latham glanced across his office at his assistant Bill, who was listening intently to this end of the conversation. Latham sighed slightly. "Well, I'll have to clear it with some people here. But barring any unforeseen problems, Hollis, I'll be on a plane tomorrow morning."

Sprague's voice changed, and was softer. *"Thanks, Mark. We really need you."*

When Latham had hung up, he sat there staring across the room, reflecting on the anxiety he had heard in Hollis Sprague's voice.

"You're going to Kansas?" Bill asked him, after a moment.

Latham nodded. "It looks like it, Bill. You'll have to run things here for a while. And I may be on the phone to you from Wichita, to give you a problem or two for our computer."

"So Sprague doesn't trust the Russians to save the country either?" Bill grinned.

"I think he has his doubts," Latham said, returning the grin. "I just hope he doesn't place too much hope in a competitive effort by us. There just may be no answer to all of this."

Bill grunted in his throat. "I wouldn't express that view in Wichita when you get there."

Latham did not make many preparations for leaving, beyond getting approval from the university authorities. With Christine gone, he had nobody to answer to, at home. It was just a matter of packing a small bag and getting on a plane. In addition to some toiletries and light clothing, he packed a few notes he had made based on observations along the West Coast, and flew off the next morning early for the Midwest.

As Latham's Boeing 707 jet approached Wichita a few hours later, in early afternoon, Latham stared out through his window at the parched plains below and was surprised at the arid look of it all. It was dry and hot in California, but nothing like this. A few more weeks of this, he thought, and the high plains would be largely uninhabitable.

The jet floated down at Wichita like a condor, skimming the oven-hot runway gracefully, touching down effortlessly among the heat waves off the concrete. When Latham debarked, Sprague, Purcell and Jodie Jameson were there at the airport to greet him. Leah Purcell had been going to come with her father, but Ed Keefer had kept her busy helping his boss Kravitz settle in at McConnell.

Upon debarkation, Latham was met with a wall of heat in the direct sun such as he had never experienced before. It was almost a tangible buffer that he felt he must push through, to gain the shade of the terminal building. Inside, after he had passed through the baggage pick-up, the three welcomers met him at the end of the concourse, Sprague extending a pumping hand, and then Purcell. What almost stopped Latham short of them, when he got a glimpse of her, was Jodie, standing beside Purcell. Her auburn hair was caught up behind her head, and ringlets of it stood at the sides of her face. She wore light make-up that accentuated her cheekbones and big eyes, and she was wearing a wispy, lemon-hued dress and high heels, both of which dramatized her quite remarkable figure.

Latham was mildly stunned.

He thought he had never seen quite so beautiful a girl.

"We're very glad to see you here in Wichita, Dr. Latham," Purcell grinned from behind a sweaty, reddish face. "We know that you're taking time from important work."

Latham shook his hand. "Hollis Sprague here convinced me that nothing I was doing in Berkley could have quite this importance," he said, "and I agree with him. I'm glad to be here."

Sprague turned to Jodie. "Jodie, I'm pleased to have you meet Dr. Mark Latham. One of the very top atmospheric physicists in the country, in my humble opinion."

Latham mumbled a protest, and Jodie offered him her hand and he took it. Their eyes locked in a sudden, tight embrace, and Jodie felt a ripple of excitement flow through her so unexpectedly that she was certain it showed in her face. "My pleasure, Dr. Latham," she heard herself saying.

Latham was embarrassed by his staring at her. He grinned, and caused a repetition of the excitation effect in her. "On the contrary," he said.

"Jodie is our acting director at our Health Department," Tom Purcell was telling Latham. "Her last name is Jameson, and she's a good friend of the family. Jodie has her hands full at the moment, trying to keep up with our new health problems from the heat wave."

"We're getting federal help now," Jodie said, "but it all takes time." Latham released her hand, and she wondered if she were blushing. "Do you think you can make it rain for us, Dr. Latham?"

Latham gave her an easy smile, and brushed thick brown hair off his forehead. Jodie did not know what she had expected, but no scientist she had ever met looked anything like Latham.

"I don't know, Miss Jameson. I'm not nearly as certain about that kind of thing as our Russian friends."

"Well," Jodie said, "at least we can take some of our eggs out of the Russian basket, now. That gives us all a lot more hope."

Sprague had a car on the parking lot, where the heat was forbidding. He wore cotton gloves to unlock the car door, because its metal was hot to the touch, and he warned Latham about it. The air-conditioner in the Ford Fairlane was turned on immediately, but they all still sweated inside the vehicle. Jodie sat up with Sprague, who drove, and Latham and Tom Purcell sat in the rear, where Purcell advised Latham of the many political problems that had arisen with the drought. As they drove into town, Latham saw the withered trees and brown grass, the boarded-up grocery stores, the dust and baked earth everywhere.

"We've sent one Skyhook up already," Sprague was telling Latham as they drove along in light traffic, "independent of the Weather Service here. We can't worry about offending this fellow Kravitz at a time like this. We're getting small dust storms now, Mark, and the pollutant dust is making things even worse, we think."

"Is the index pretty high now?" Latham asked.

"Higher than we've ever seen it," Sprague said.

Latham looked toward Jodie. "That caused some health problems in the thirties that were pretty bad," he said.

Jodie turned to him, and nodded. "Yes, and we're getting a repetition now. Farmers are coming into the clinic with so much dust in their lungs that they can hardly breathe. One wheat farmer from near here insisted on plowing a field through a brief dust blow a couple of days ago, and it killed him. He choked to death in his own bedroom, before we could get him any help."

"The heat is making people act crazy, too," Purcell said heavily. "There's a minority who are convinced there's something we can do to stop all this, that we're delaying for various political reasons. Or they complain that only the rich and powerful are getting water. That sort of thing." He thought briefly of Will Jameson's psychotic-looking face, at the McConnell demonstration. He had not told Jodie about seeing Will there. She had enough on her mind.

They were moving along a relatively quiet street, toward the center of town. Sprague gripped the wheel with his gloves still on, looking worried and tired. "Even some municipal facilities have had to close down because of employee absences," he told Latham. "Tom is having a real problem keeping anybody on the job. If we could just—"

Sprague stopped his summary and braked the car slightly. A hundred yards ahead of them, something was happening in the street. A beer truck had parked at the curb up there, to make a now-rare delivery to a store, and it was being mobbed by a group of young men. Two of them lay on the pavement beside the truck, injured, blood covering the face of one. A third figure, in a coverall uniform and obviously the driver, was also on the ground. The side of his head had been staved in, with a bottle or some other heavy object. He looked dead.

"Oh, God!" Jodie gasped out.

Sprague had driven up close now, in an effort to get past the trouble. But as they came up almost even, with the young men yelling and busting the tops off beer bottles near them and drinking with foam on their faces, Tom Purcell suddenly got red-faced and spoke angrily to Sprague.

"Stop here a moment!" he said loudly.

Sprague gave him a doubtful look, but slowed the car to a stop near the truck. Then, before anybody could stop him, Purcell had thrown open the car door at the rear and stepped out into the street.

"*You there! Get off that truck immediately! You're in violation of the law!*"

Several of the looters turned to stare blankly at him, beer running from their chins onto their clothing. "*Hey!*" one of them shouted, a swarthy chicano. "*That's our do-nothing mayor, dudes! The big white fuzz!*"

"Tom, you'd better get back in here," Jodie said fearfully to Purcell, rolling her window down.

"Look, the ee-stablishment has arrived!"

"I'm telling you!" Purcell yelled. *"Get away from that truck! I can have the police here in two minutes!"*

Latham crawled across the rear seat and climbed out beside Purcell. He was about to ask him to get back into the Ford, when Purcell started toward the downed driver.

"Hey, you want a beer, Mr. Mayor?"

An unopened bottle came hurtling at Purcell. He ducked, and it hit the car behind him, smashing its glass on the metal of the Ford just above Jodie's open window. She felt a shard of glass rake her bare arm, and spattered beer splashed onto her face and clothing. She let out a small yell, and rolled the window back up.

Outside on the hot pavement, Latham grabbed at Purcell's arm and pulled him back toward the car. Another bottle came, and hit Purcell in the side of the head, grazing him. He fell against Latham heavily, and then Latham was pulling him back into the car. Purcell hit the rear seat weak and dazed, crimson worming down the side of his face from his hair. Latham jumped in beside him, slamming the door shut hard.

"Drive on, Hollis!" he said quickly to Sprague.

Sprague jerked the car into gear and hit the accelerator. Two of the assailants had come out in front of the Ford, to bar its way, but jumped aside as the vehicle skidded past them, burning rubber. There were some last shouts from behind them, and then the riot scene was fading from view quickly.

Purcell leaned against the back seat, holding his bloody head. Sprague was gripping the wheel as if he might never let go of it. Jodie turned and saw Latham bending over Purcell, examining a shallow wound. It appeared that the mayor would be all right.

"Drive right to the hospital," she told Sprague.

Sprague nodded tightly. "Right."

In the rear seat, Purcell put a hand to his head, and it came away with blood on it. He had been lucky, though. He turned and regarded Latham numbly.

"Thanks," he said in a low, frightened voice. "And welcome to Wichita."

FIVE

Paula Betancourt and Jodie took a tour of area farms that next day, while Latham was getting organized in Hollis Sprague's College Hill lab. Sprague had been right, the crops were lost for the year in Kansas. It was pretty much the same story in Iowa and Nebraska, too. Thousands of chickens and other poultry had died in the heat, and cattle were now dying. They saw dead cattle along the roadside, fly-buzzing corpses that were yet unburied, or butchered. They passed a chicken farm where a great stink came from the grounds, and Jodie knew without being told that the low buildings were filled with dead birds.

It was all very unpleasant.

Temperatures at midday were inching above one hundred fifteen now, and still the power plant operation would not support air-conditioning. Block leaders were deputized for the purpose of disabling air-conditioners and other appliances that took power needlessly, and there was a great uproar against this kind of outrage against privacy and individual freedom.

On Latham's third day in town, Jodie, Betancourt and Purcell stopped past the university lab to see how Latham's settling in had gone, and found him and

Sprague very hard at work deciphering some recent observation data from universities around the Midwest. A computer expert from another department at Wichita State had figured a way to make use of a big computer of a local private company, through the smaller one in Sprague's lab, and the governor was guaranteeing the bill. Latham was busy reading a print-out from that computer when the visitors arrived, but he interrupted his work to show them what the Latham-Sprague team was doing. After a brief meeting among the five of them, Purcell excused himself to go off to another meeting, and Jodie and Betancourt invited Sprague and Latham to lunch at the barely-operating school cafeteria nearby. At the cafeteria, which was serving only sandwiches and stale baked goods with a half-cup water allowance per person, the foursome sat at a trestle table with their spartan sandwiches, and somehow Jodie ended up sitting beside Latham, with Betancourt and Sprague seated across the table from them. Sprague did most of the talking while they were eating, and then Betancourt was asked a number of questions by Latham, about commitments around the country to send water and food to Wichita. She had obtained several, and the first shipment of bottled water was due to arrive in the city in the near future.

"It's hard to understand what you're up against here, until you get here and see it," Latham said. "I understand people are coming in to the Health Department just for water, Jodie." They were all on a first-name basis now, except that Jodie could not bring herself to address Hollis Sprague by his given name.

"Oh, yes, that's true," Jodie said. "People come in badly dehydrated, some haven't had a glass of water for days. The reservoir is so low now that some residences have no water pressure at all. They turn their faucets on and nothing happens."

"We're trying to find out who isn't getting water," Paula Betancourt told him, "so we can ration some out to them. We have it in quart containers at the Department. People have begun to line up in the mornings there, to get an allowance." It was hot in the big cafeteria room, and her face was flushed and dewy.

Sprague was finishing his sandwich after the others, and he now put a remainder of it down. "I can't eat in this heat," he said, his flabby face slightly pale. "I don't have any appetite."

"You've been overworking, Hollis," Latham said. He and Sprague both wore open-collar sport shirts that were damp on their backs. "You can slow down, now that we have a team organized."

"I'll slow down when it rains," Sprague said dismally.

Betancourt turned to Sprague. "How are our government friends doing over at McConnell? Do they know you've brought Mark here all the way from California?"

"Oh, Kravitz knows it, all right," Sprague said. "But we haven't heard from him. I think he's afraid to acknowledge our presence at College Hill, for fear that would amount to some kind of official recognition of our parallel project."

"What happened to the White House aide, Dr. Sprague?" Jodie asked. "Paula says he was pretty disturbed by the demonstration outside the air base."

"I think he left already. Didn't he, Paula?"

Betancourt nodded. "He's supposedly going to apply some pressure at San Diego to get us some water. Then he'll go spread a red carpet for the Russians, I understand, at San Francisco." She turned to Sprague, beside her. "You did some work in Moscow as a young man, didn't you, Hollis?"

Sprague started into a brief history of his early career for her then, information that both Jodie and Latham knew well. Latham turned to Jodie, and started a second dialogue underneath the Betancourt-Sprague one.

"I'm told you're a bacteriologist," Latham said to her.

Jodie smiled prettily. Just sitting beside him, despite the physical discomfort of the airless room, she felt little pricklings of pleasure undulate through her. It was embarrassing. She had never reacted this way before with a man, not even Lou Falco. There was no use trying to hide it from herself. She had met the man only twice, and she wanted him physically. It was ridiculous, and unnerving. It made her feel like some hot-pants high school cheerleader.

"Yes, my degree is from Wichita State," she said. She felt foolish, talking about "her degree" with a respected Ph.D. in a difficult science field. "I was going to go for a master's, but couldn't turn down this job at the Health Department."

"I'm sure you've learned more there than you would have in another year or two of college," Latham said. "I—gather you haven't married."

Jodie was wearing a low-cut, bare-shoulders little dress to keep cool through the day, and suddenly she felt almost naked, with his full attention on her. She put a hand to her cleavage. "No, Mark. It hasn't worked out like that for me."

Latham made a low sound in his throat. "Maybe you're lucky," he said.

She looked quickly toward him. "Do you mean—"

"Yes," he said. "I've been married for three years."

"Oh," she said. It was not until that moment that she knew she had been hoping he was single. A small disappointment crowded up into her chest, like the fog from dry ice.

"Christine doesn't think much of meteorology," he grinned.

"Well. My friends have never thought much of bacteriology, either," she offered. "I suppose we can't expect too much."

He liked her answer. "No. I suppose not."

When Jodie had returned across town to the Health Department with Betancourt later, and Latham was alone at the university lab, studying his notes in a modest office set up for him there not far from Hollis Sprague's, Latham found that he could not keep his mind off Jodie. She made him a little breathless just to be beside her. Every gesture she made, every turn of her head, made her more beautiful to him. He had never looked at other women since his marriage to Christine, never coveted any. He was not the kind of man to look around, he was too preoccupied with his work. But Jodie was different. She was intelligent, pleasant, and more desirable than he liked to think about. He could not believe she was unmarried.

In late afternoon, Sprague got a call from Kravitz. He wanted a conference with Sprague and Latham, at McConnell, at their convenience. Sprague conferred with Latham, and told Kravitz they would be over within the hour. Both Latham and Sprague thought there ought to be a dialogue between the two teams, and Sprague did not want to miss the opportunity to begin one.

Both Latham and Sprague were impressed by the facilities at McConnell. Inside the quonset building was a study lab similar to that of Latham at Berkeley, only there was more of everything. The NASA computer was still being installed on one long wall, but it was awesome, even without having come alive.

Kravitz had taken to himself the largest of several offices that lined one side of the building. Outside these offices was a wide, high, hangar-type room where all the equipment was. NASA and National Weather Service technicians busied themselves throughout that room, as Kravitz showed Latham and Sprague around and then took them into his office.

Sprague was surprised to find Ed Keefer and Leah Purcell there. They were there to help tie in some equipment of theirs at the local Weather Service with that in the quonset building, and Kravitz had invited them to stay for the meeting with Sprague and Latham.

"Well, Ed," Sprague said as Keefer and Leah rose from chairs to greet him and Latham. "It looks like your Marines have landed."

Ed Keefer nodded soberly. His thin, lanky frame looked particularly bony beside thick-set, red-faced Kravitz. He was very aware of Kravitz' high position with his organization, and that Kravitz had orders directly from the President, and acted very subdued in Kravitz' presence.

"We're getting things under control here," he told Sprague. "We want to be ready for the Russian scientists."

Sprague and Latham exchanged a small look, and Kravitz noticed it.

"Ed, this is Dr. Latham from the University of California," Sprague said. Latham had already been introduced to Kravitz, and Kravitz had been very cordial. "Dr. Latham, Ed Keefer and his assistant Leah Purcell."

Latham and Keefer shook hands, and Keefer's face showed that he was greatly pleased with meeting Latham. Leah then offered her hand, and Latham took it.

"Leah is Tom Purcell's daughter, and a good friend of both Jodie and her brother Will," Sprague told Latham.

Latham's face brightened, and a small grin crossed it. "I'm glad to meet you, Leah. I'm very impressed with your friends."

Leah understood that he meant Jodie, and found herself hoping that there was something happening between this handsome physicist and her best friend. She thought momentarily of Will, and how she had not heard from him since their argument. She had almost driven out to the Phillips farm a couple of evenings ago, to try to find him there, but had changed her mind at the last minute. After the way Will had talked to her, it seemed unfair to her that she should be the one to make overtures of peace, now.

Kravitz offered them all chairs, and they sat down around Kravitz' metallic desk, while he settled in behind it. Sprague watched his face, and saw that things were going to get more serious shortly.

"I've heard about your work in California," Kravitz said to Latham. All the men were in loose-fitting shirts, and Leah was wearing a thin dress that showed off her fine figure without her conscious effort. "There are some who say you're doing pioneer work in an important area."

Nobody in the room missed the qualification placed on Kravitz' compliment, and Sprague, particularly, was nettled by it.

98

"I suppose the importance is a moot question at this point," Latham replied easily.

"I'd guess," Sprague put in moodily, "that Dr. Latham knows as much about the circumpolar vortex as anyone in the country."

Kravitz grunted, and Ed Keefer squirmed uneasily on his chair. "Well, I hope all of that comes in handy some day, I really do. Although I'd guess that the Soviets are one up on us in that area, wouldn't you, Dr. Latham?"

A small tension crackled around them in the hot room with its corner fan and bare gray walls. A window behind Kravitz was closed tight against the late sun.

Latham shrugged, not taking offense. "I don't really know. I know their work in radio emissions is impressive. But it needs a lot more study before we can be sure it will be useful."

"I'd second that," Sprague said.

Kravitz pursed heavy lips. He owned a master's degree in meteorology, and had thought of going into research himself, at one time. "Maybe some of us feel that way because of wounded pride," he grinned tightly. "It's tough to be beaten out in our own field."

Sprague was angered. "Do you call this being beaten out, Mr. Kravitz?" He waved a hand in the hot air. "This thing the Soviets and their radio emissions have done to us?"

"They say they can correct this condition," Kravitz said. "They tell me it's a mere technicality. Maybe they're right."

Latham shook his head sidewise. "My calculations tell me they're not."

A humming silence filled the room. Ed Keefer gave a little nervous laugh. "Well, we'll know pretty soon, I guess. I just hope we don't have to speak Russian to find out. Isn't that right, Leah?"

Leah tried a smile. "I had a hard time with high school Spanish," she offered.

Latham turned to her and smiled, thanking her with his eyes for her effort.

"My people in Washington want to know what you're doing here, Dr. Latham," Kravitz said quite suddenly. "They're concerned that Dr. Sprague here is mounting a competitive effort on campus that could be counter-productive."

"Dr. Latham is here at the invitation of the governor," Sprague said stiffly, "and the board of regents at the university. Not to mention the local mayor's office."

"But the federal effort here has to be pre-emptive of any state or local program," Kravitz said somberly. "Surely you understand that, Dr. Sprague. This can't be allowed to be a free-for-all. There's too much at stake."

Sprague was tight-lined in his face. "What we would like, Mr. Kravitz, is for our lab and yours to work together in a cooperative effort. We just could learn something from each other through this. We don't think this should be a Russian-dominated and Russian-directed project, exclusive of our own efforts."

Kravitz' face was straight-lined, too. "This is not a Russian project, Dr. Sprague. It is a U.S. government project, sponsored jointly by the Weather Service and NASA. The Russians will be here as advisors only."

"Which means," Latham put in, "that they'll make the calculations, set your radio computer to issue the signals they tell us to issue, and tell you when and how to orbit our satellite."

Kravitz turned to Latham, and his face darkened even

more. Keefer and Leah Purcell sat quietly on their chairs, embarrassed and uncomfortable. "We're damned glad to have the Russians' help. Without it, we'd have only you and Dr. Sprague to try to get us through this," Kravitz said evenly. "And, unless you're keeping some grand plan a deep, dark secret, I'd guess that you have no idea how to end this killer drought."

Leah wished she had not been invited to this volatile meeting. She sat there with her head down, staring at the floor, hoping her presence would be forgotten.

"Dr. Sprague told me that his team is working on the problem every day, Stan," Ed Keefer said nervously.

Nobody paid any attention to him, or acknowledged his comment. Latham sat forward on his chair, his dark brown eyes narrowed slightly on Kravitz. Kravitz was just the kind of bureaucrat Latham had thought he would be. "I don't have an easy answer to this, Mr. Kravitz, nor does Dr. Sprague. I'm not sure there is a viable way to influence what's happening here in the high plains. But since we have very little hope that the Russians have the answer, either, we think it's imperative that there be continued effort through all available sources until this disaster is somehow behind us."

Kravitz leaned forward, too, onto the littered desk before him. "Well, now let me tell you the government's position on this, Dr. Latham," he said in a low voice. "We don't care how much calculation and computing you do over there at College Hill, and how many of those Skyhooks you send up. Just so long as you don't get in the way of this very important project here at McConnell. The word direct from the top is that you are not to take any positive steps on your own to put any of your theories into practice, in the area of weather control,

101

without clearing them through this headquarters first. Do you understand that quite clearly?"

Latham was beginning to dislike Kravitz very fast. "I understand you, Mr. Kravitz. But let me tell you something, too. There are a lot of people in Kansas, and elsewhere, who think it's a big mistake to even consider giving the Russians the opportunity to further meddle with the circumpolar vortex. This decision of Washington to invite them here was forced on the citizens of this state and the nation by the White House. There isn't a hell of a lot we can do about it, I know, and we're not going to waste time arguing the point. The thing is, we're stuck with the Russians' coming. It seems to me that the federal government can show just some of our tolerance toward it, with regard to our own efforts. If we should get lucky and think of a way to save this Great Plains area from burning up, I sure as hell would not want to have to go through fifty Washington bureaucrats to get an okay to go ahead with it. The people and government of this state have some rights, after all, to influence their own destiny."

Leah turned toward Latham and stared hard at him. She had never heard anyone speak like that, and with such authority. She found that she was in complete accord with everything Latham said, and she was very impressed with him.

Kravitz had risen ominously from his chair. "The people of this state are being taken care of as well as they can be, by their chosen representatives in Washington," he said in a hard, tough voice. "Any steps you might take independent from those representatives might jeopardize our effort here at McConnell—each project could be negating the good effects of the other. By its very nature, this problem requires one central authority to coordinate efforts to solve it. This headquarters represents that authority. We will not tolerate competitive activities, Dr. Latham, and any attempt to engage in them will be severely dealt with."

Now Sprague rose, too, and Latham. Sprague was furious, anger flushing through him hotly, like boiling oil. "This is an outrage, Kravitz! You're not speaking to hoodlums, by God! Our project just happens to have the support of much of the university community, in the Midwest and elsewhere! Of course we wouldn't endanger your program with meteorological activities. But we don't like being threatened, either, by Jesus!"

"Hollis, Stan here didn't mean to make it sound like a threat," Keefer put in soberly, rising to stand with them. "It's just that there has to be some control over all this. Isn't that what you meant, Stan?"

Kravitz' face was stony. "Just don't interfere with what's going on out here," he said. "That's all we insist on. But it's not a negotiable position."

Latham made a face. "We'll try not to get in the Russians' way, Mr. Kravitz," he said deliberately. "After all, we all want the same thing, don't we?"

Kravitz held Latham's gaze. "I'd like to think so," he said.

Sprague moved to the office door, then turned to Kravitz sourly. "If we should come up with anything that sounds as if it might help," he said to him, "do you want us to discuss it with you here?"

"Why not?" Kravitz said. "It just might be something that would help us in our own efforts."

Sprague's voice held a bitter edge. "That's always an outside possibility, Mr. Kravitz," he said.

*   *   *

In the next twenty-four hours a dust storm swept across the face of Kansas that tied up traffic, choked the lungs of farmers and city dwellers alike, and eroded the topsoil of the prairie. Farmers were abandoning their homes now in fairly large numbers, and some were coming into Wichita where there were few facilities to put them up.

In the same twenty-four hours with the storm, a fire broke out in the brittle-dry plains about ten miles east of Wichita, destroyed several farms including the Phillips spread where Will Jameson worked, and for a while threatened the city.

Will, already bitter about the effects of the drought, was infuriated by the loss of the Phillips farm. He helped them save some furniture and farm equipment, and then move it to some relatives of the Phillipses to the north about fifty miles. He then moved into town, onto the same campus where he had gone to school for just over two years, and not far from the Latham-Sprague project lab. The headquarters of the People's Brigade was located on campus, and Will wanted to be near it. The fire at the farm had sent him down to another lower plateau of emotion. He and the Brigade had warned county officials that there was a great danger of fires, and had asked for fire safety lanes to be cut through open prairie grass at regular intervals, and between farms. But there was no money for such activities, and officials doubted it would help much. Now Will, who had become one of the leaders of the Brigade, was further embittered toward authorities because, in his head, they had failed the people of the area once again.

Jodie did not even know Will had moved into town, as

she had not heard that the Phillips farm was one of those lost. She was so busy now at the Health Department clinic, and in making the rounds of the hospitals locally, that she hardly had time to eat, during the day. People just could not take the heat that now rose each day to somewhere between a hundred-fifteen and twenty degrees. But it was clear now that the city would never have enough power to begin cooling the interiors of homes and buildings again, until the drought was over. So people kept coming in with heat prostration and dehydration, and it became more and more difficult to find places for them, and water for them. Hepatitis was at epidemic level already, and stomach ailments were rampant. Jodie asked the hospitals to pay closer attention to these patients, and got into arguments with administrators about it.

A clinic had also been set up on the campus at Wichita State, and Jodie visited it almost every day. It was there, two days after the Phillips farm fire, that a graduate student who knew Jodie stopped her in a hallway and mentioned Will's return to campus. Jodie did some snooping around and got his new address, a dormitory house on the edge of campus where several Brigade members lived. She tried to find him there that late afternoon, but he was nowhere about. When she stopped back past the clinic, which was near the meteorology lab, she ran into Mark Latham coming out of the clinic building.

"Oh, hi, Jodie," he smiled at her.

She stopped under the shade of a withering box elder tree. "Hello, Mark. Business at the clinic?"

"That first shipment of water that was flown in today. Some of it was supposed to come here, and I was checking

105

to see if they got it. I had volunteered to go get the ration if it hadn't arrived. But it came, all right."

"It's too bad it was so little," Jodie said. "But Paula Betancourt assures me that other shipments are on their way. I hope so, because our reservoir is almost dry."

"God, I'll be glad when the sun goes down," Latham remarked. A fine dew of perspiration stood on his brow and upper lip, and his sport shirt was damp in places. "I don't think there's any way to get used to this."

Jodie, despite her bare-shoulders, bare-back dress, was not faring much better. "I guess it would be more tolerable if we could have all the liquid we want. My mouth is dry half the time."

"Say, that gives me an idea," he said. "There's still a small cafe open down on Douglas Avenue, and I hear they serve Italian. Why don't you let me treat you to some neapolitan spaghetti, or some fattening lasagna?"

Jodie hesitated, remembering that he had said he was married. "I have a better idea, Mark. Why don't you stop past my place, and I'll do the cooking? I can't spare the water to cook spaghetti in, but I still have two cans of prepared lasagna I can warm up, and a loaf of French bread, and some grated parmesan."

Latham grinned handsomely. "You're on!" he told her.

Later, at home, Jodie was all fluttery inside about his coming, despite the fact that she figured nothing could come of their knowing each other. It must have been the drought, she figured. Things took on a different perspective now, like in wartime. You lived more for the present, without thinking of consequences.

Latham arrived right on time, which impressed her, and they had an enjoyable, quiet meal together, sitting out on a tiny balcony off her living room, to get the air out there. Afterwards they stood together at the railing of the balcony, sipping wine, Jodie leaning on the railing with Latham facing her. He thought her face was especially beautiful in the peach-hued light of dusk.

"I understand you lost your mother, Jodie, but that your father is a military man in Topeka." He sipped the red wine, making it last. It was liquid.

"Yes, that's right," Jodie said. It was very quiet, outside the building. She used to hear birds in the nearby trees at this time of day, but their calls were absent lately. She wondered if they were all dead, or dying. "Dad is on standby alert now. A couple of units have already left Topeka, to help keep order on the streets of Kansas City and Salina. The street violence has been greater in those places, it seems, than it has here. Even though the water and heat problems are worse here."

"Tom Purcell has maintained a fine police force here," Latham said. "But things are escalating some, I hear. There was a rowdy demonstration on campus last night. Some kids that call themselves the Brigade."

"Yes, the People's Brigade," Jodie said acidly. "I think my brother may be involved with them, Mark."

"Oh. Will, is it?"

"Yes, Will. He and Leah Purcell had such a nice thing going between them. Then he started getting mixed up with all of this pseudo-political stuff. They had an argument about Leah's father, and now they're not speaking."

Latham smiled. "They'll probably both get their tempers under control when the temperatures drop."

"That's a distinct possibility," Jodie said, flashing a tired smile of her own.

Latham suddenly was quite close to her, without her having noticed how he got there. He was staring into her eyes, and it embarrassed her.

"Jodie, you may have figured this out yourself, I don't know. But I think you're pretty special."

Jodie met his gaze with an open one, then averted her eyes. "I appreciate that, Mark. I feel the same way about you. You've made a remarkable career already."

He smiled. "That's not what I'm talking about."

Jodie met his gaze, and little waves of skin-tingling sensation swept through her. "Mark, I don't think—"

She paused, and he set his wine glass down on the balustrade near them, and suddenly she felt his arms around her waist, drawing her to him. She turned her head, but then felt herself irresistibly drawn to face him again. Their mouths touched, and she found herself in the middle of a hot, sensuous kiss. After a long moment she broke away, breathlessly.

"Oh, damn!" she gasped out.

Latham frowned at her slightly. "What's the matter?" he asked her.

"I—didn't want to let you do that."

"Why?" he said.

"Because I knew I'd like it."

"Is that so bad?"

She looked into his dark eyes. "I just got past a bad experience with a man, Mark. At least I think I'm past it. And now here I am, inviting a married man to my apartment."

Latham nodded. He turned and leaned on the railing beside her. "I should have told you, Jodie. Christine and I—well, she moved out a while back. We're separated, and she says she's filing divorce papers."

"I'm sorry, Mark," she said.

He shrugged. "First marriages are often foolish ones, it seems. Some people have to learn how, like driving a car. I don't blame Christine, and I don't blame myself. I think we both tried hard."

"Then you think it's over between you," Jodie said.

"I think so."

"You don't sound so sure."

"Neither do you," he grinned.

Jodie returned it. "I guess you're right."

"I don't mean to scare you, Jodie. I know how you must feel. It's just that—well, I liked you from the first moment. In the concourse at the airport."

"I'm flattered, Mark. I really am. It's just that I'm a very cautious girl, now."

"I understand."

"Can I get you some more wine?" she asked him.

He shook his head. "I'd better get back to the lab. I have an hour's work to get finished. I'd—like to see more of you, Jodie, while I'm here. Do you mind?"

Jodie hesitated. She had never been involved with a married man in her life. And this one was not even sure his marriage was finished. She hesitated a long moment, then turned and looked into his eyes again. "No," she said. "It's all right."

Latham did not stay more than a few minutes longer.

When he was gone, Jodie felt really alone for the first time in weeks.

SIX

"Here. Right here east of Denver. Another dust storm, but it looks as if it will miss us."

Leah Purcell was pointing out a new dry storm movement to Ed Keefer, on their wall ground map. Keefer stood there shaking his head. "If we even mention the possibility of its coming, people will ring our phones off the hooks. Good God, why do they blame us? You'd think with the Russians coming, they'd finally have some patience with this."

"Not all of them are as sure the Russians can change things as Stan Kravitz is," Leah told him. She walked past a couple of young men sitting before monitor screens, and leaned over a third one. "Yes, here's a report from Pueblo. The blow is shifting to the north of us."

Keefer, in his shirtsleeves, came over to her, pink-checked in the fan-blown heat. "That's good news. We probably won't have to issue an advisory."

"The last time we had to, the wind blew away a lot of loam from area farms," she said. "And helped fan that prairie fire that did so much damage."

Keefer cast a sober look toward her. "Will Jameson was involved in that, wasn't he?"

Leah turned to him. She did not have the crisp look of a

couple of weeks ago. She finally was showing signs of submission to the ugly heat—in her flushed face, her wilted clothing, her tired manner. Nobody was immune from it, and Leah had held up longer than most, despite her trouble with Will.

"That's right, on the Phillips farm." She had gone to Will after the fire, after Jodie had located his whereabouts, and tried to talk with him. But he had been withdrawn, morose. She was sure now that she was losing him. "He helped save some things out there."

"I've been hearing things about Will, Leah." Keefer turned toward her, from the monitor, and lowered his voice so the other employees would not hear.

"What things?" Leah said defensively.

Keefer shrugged. "That he's a troublemaker. A cop friend of mine has seen him on the street with some unsavory people."

"Unsavory? What the hell does that mean?"

Keefer glanced around them. "Hey, I'm sorry I mentioned it. It's just that you're important to me here, and I'd rather you didn't run into trouble in your romantic involvements."

Leah regarded him acidly. "Look, I can handle my private life, Ed. And I'd just as soon you didn't spread any gossip about Will that might not be true, if you don't mind."

He put his hands up as if to ward off a blow. "Okay, okay. It's your life. But I get the distinct impression that Will is very different from his sister. That's just one man's opinion."

"Fine, now you've voiced it," Leah said. "I don't want to hear about it again, Ed."

"Like I said, it's your life."

Outside in the city at that moment, in the direct brilliance of the sun, it was already frying-pan hot. There was no pedestrian traffic now through the heat of the day, almost no vehicular traffic. Even the police kept off the streets. If a fire started in a local house or building, the fire department responded to the call, but mostly they could only stand around and watch the fire burn itself out. Sand and chemicals were used for containment, but there just was no water for fire-fighting.

That in itself was a dangerous situation.

Over at McConnell Air Force Base, Kravitz and the NASA technicians were all set up and ready for their foreign visitors, and a mood of tense waiting prevailed. At the Wichita State lab, Latham and Sprague were working on two ideas at once. One involved a direct attack on the weather system of a much less dramatic nature than the one the Russians intended. It involved setting up machines to send a chemical particulate up into the air, on the theory such an operation might reverse the strong greenhouse effect that prevailed over the high plains. There was a body of thought in scientific circles that this sort of thing could work on a limited basis. But now Latham's latest calculations showed that, with nature's own dust in the air now from recent storms, the chance of accomplishing anything was almost nil. Also, the machines needed for such ground-to-air chemical dusting were situated all over the country, and it would require weeks, if not months, to bring them to Kansas. It was a possibility for later, long-term help. But what Kansas and the Midwest needed was immediate relief, something Kravitz and his crew were promising.

The other project Latham and Sprague were considering was one that did not directly involve influencing the weather. Latham had conferred at length with Paula Betancourt and her Water Resources Council man, and had gathered a lot of information on the long-forgotten Ogallala Aquifer.

The Ogallala Aquifer was a known rock-bound reservoir of water deep in the bowels of the earth, running haphazardly across the Great Plains. Beneath the level reachable for ordinary farm wells, the aquifer could only be tapped by means of super-deep artesian wells drilled with special, expensive equipment. It had been done on occasion for important projects, and it was one source of water supply for city reservoirs across the Midwest. But one well tapped only a limited area of the aquifer, so that to get more water up, more wells would have to be drilled.

Such a project was now uppermost in the minds of Latham and Sprague, as a means of giving temporary relief. They had conferred with university geologists, and they and the Water Resources man all agreed that water could be obtained by artesian well drilling, with a little luck.

"The trouble is," Latham told Hollis Sprague that morning, as they talked in Sprague's tidy, ordered office, "that we don't have any way of knowing how much loss there has been in the aquifer, until we spend the time and money to drill some wells."

"I called a couple of friends in the oil industry, in Texas," Sprague said, sprawled on his desk chair and looking very tired and a little sick. "One of them said he might give us some free help. But he wants to hear our plan in detail."

Latham was standing beside the desk, sweating in his clothing. "Who is he?" he asked.

"His name is Emmet Douglas, and he owns several refineries near Dallas," Sprague said. "He has all the equipment we'd need to get, say, a half-dozen test wells drilled around here. I think what he needs is somebody to let him know how intense the need is."

"I'll fly there," Latham said. "I can leave later today and be there tonight. I'll tell him what it's like here."

"I don't know if we can spare you," Sprague said.

"Hollis, this is the only good idea we have at the moment. And Kravitz can't have any objection to it, since it doesn't involve any weather-meddling. At least we don't think the aquifer tables influence surface conditions."

"Well, I'm sure you could be as persuasive as anybody who would go," Sprague said.

"Say, wasn't Jodie trying to get some medical supplies from Dallas?" Latham said. "I could take her along, and she could pick them up herself. She indicated that quite important drugs were ordered, and that there has been quite a delay."

"I believe you're right, Mark. Take her with you, it would be a much-needed brief break for her, from the clinic routine."

"I'll ask her at lunch today," Latham said.

Latham was surprised, later, by Jodie's quick acceptance of his offer. She had been worried about getting the medicines from Texas, and was very receptive to the idea of bringing them back with her aboard a jet. She was also excited about Latham's proposed attempt to recruit the oilman Douglas to the well-drilling project.

The air-conditioned flight to Dallas was a welcome relief from the heat for both of them. By halfway through the flight, though, the temperature inside the aircraft

114

was too cold for them, at around eighty degrees, and they both had to bundle up. Because they had had to live in one-fifteen temperatures, their bodies had adjusted to heat, and ninety degrees now seemed quite cool.

Dallas was just as brown-looking as Wichita, but the heat was not climbing to much over a hundred. The newspapers there were full of items about dying range cattle, and cities all through Texas and Oklahoma were besieged with a new problem: snakes and other wild animals were beginning to come into town, to find water. It had become quite a problem.

Douglas' offices were in downtown Dallas, in a tall, glass-and-steel building with his name on it. He holed up in a penthouse suite, with long mahogany desks, paneled walls, and beautiful secretaries. Latham and Jodie arrived there in early evening, after making a taxi stop at the drug warehouse where Jodie got her order sent out to the airport, to go aboard their return flight with them, at almost midnight that same night.

"Well, well," Douglas greeted them, as they entered his spacious, plush office that dusky evening. "You folks must be desperate up there in Wichita, to make such a quick trip down here. Emmet Douglas here, folks. You must be Latham and Jameson."

Latham and Jodie introduced themselves, and Douglas seated them in richly upholstered chairs. His office was air-conditioned and comfortable, and they appreciated it.

"We have a serious health problem in Wichita and all through Kansas, Mr. Douglas," Latham began. "I know you've had some cases of heat stroke here, too, but up there it's out of control. Miss Jameson here can tell you better than me, she's our health officer there."

Jodie sighed slightly. She was feeling cold again,

115

because of the normal temperature in the office. "Mr. Douglas, our hospitals are full and overflowing with hepatitis cases, heat prostration, dehydration, and other diseases related to lack of water. So are the emergency clinics we've established, and infirmaries. The bad part is, there seems to be no end in sight, and every day the situation gets worse. You still have water here, we understand. But we've almost run out."

Latham took up where she left off. "Dr. Sprague spoke to you on the phone about aquifer wells. We think there just might be some reserves left in the Ogallala Aquifer, if we can tap into it. It would mean deep-well drilling, maybe as far down as a mile or two."

"That would be no problem," Douglas said, sitting at his desk. He was middle-aged, but trim-looking and rather handsome. He had serious gray eyes, and a look about him that showed he was a man who got things done. He had made millions in oil, and he had started out with nothing. "The knotty part would be in deciding where to drill. It would be a lot like looking for oil."

"That's what we figured," Latham smiled. "That's why we came here. We've put our heads together with a couple of fine geologists at Wichita State, and they think they've isolated a number of likely spots. They're busy looking for more right at this moment. Of course, you'd have the last word on where to drill. It's your equipment and manpower that would be involved."

Douglas sat there absorbing that. He was a man who did not mind silences in conversations. He liked to think before he spoke.

"I do have a couple of ideas of my own," he finally said. "I know the Wichita area pretty well. Dr. Sprague said something about eventual reimbursement from the state of Kansas."

Latham nodded. "He knows the governor in Topeka personally. The governor can't give you a written guarantee, but he says he'll put his career on the line to get you reimbursed out of state funds, if you agree to help out. If the well-drilling brings water to Wichita, we would try to convince Washington to foot the bill for similar projects all around the Midwest."

Douglas grunted. "It might come to that here, if this drought continues. Everybody is saying how those Russians are going to save our butts. Frankly, though, most of us Texans would rather dry up and blow away, rather than have a Russian save us."

He grinned, and Latham and Jodie exchanged smiles.

"Tell you what, Dr. Latham," Douglas went on after a moment. "I'll give you four test holes free. If they bring up water, we can talk about more. But in return for this generosity, I'll expect to be inured of the mineral rights at each rig site."

"You mean, if you strike oil, you want it to be yours," Latham said to him.

"That's right," Douglas replied.

Jodie looked over at Latham. "All he wants is oil? My God, that seems reasonable, Mark."

Latham smiled at her, then turned to Douglas. "I'm sure that won't be an obstacle. I'll call Sprague from here before we leave tonight, and ask him to call Topeka."

Douglas nodded. "Then you've got yourself a gang of roughnecks, Dr. Latham."

When they got back to Wichita in the small hours of the morning, that night, the deal had been sealed with Douglas and his Dallas Oil Company. Within forty-eight hours, Douglas would move equipment and men to Kansas. Coincidentally, it would be about the same time that the Russians were due to arrive in Wichita.

Latham wanted to kiss Jodie goodnight, when they parted at her place at almost three a.m. He did not say so, but she knew he did. She did not know why she avoided his attempt. She was still afraid, she supposed. Afraid of emotional ties, of commitment. She shortened their brief farewell by telling him how sleepy and tired she was, and then he was suddenly gone. Later, up in her apartment, she wished she had let it all develop more naturally.

The next day, Jodie's life became even more emotionally mixed up. She and Betancourt drove off to nearby Hutchinson for the day, to take some medicines there, and to study health problems to see if there was any way they could improve on what was being done there.

It was not a pleasant trip, despite the half-power air-conditioning in the sun-bleached department Ford. Devastation lay over the landscape like a withered claw. There was no wheat and corn now, there were only scorched fields and tinder-dry stubble. Farm houses were desolate in appearance or closed up entirely. Tractors sat in the middle of burned fields, dust-covered. In fact, dust was everywhere. On houses, trees, shrubs, fences, dead and rotting livestock. Some farms had been burned over, and there was only black char for as far as the eye could see, with ghostly, dark-ribbed barns and houses rising as grimly as Mayan ruins among the debris and litter.

The twosome spent late morning and early afternoon talking to doctors and hospital people, and then Jodie left Betancourt for a couple of hours while they split duties. It was just at the beginning of this period of separate work that Jodie received her big surprise of the day. She was just coming out of a clinic building, walking in the shallow shade of a line of poplar trees that were now almost bare, when Lou Falco came striding up the walk toward her.

She stopped short when she saw him, not believing her eyes for a moment. In that undulating heat, you saw desert-like mirages at times. But Falco was very real. He flashed a wide smile as soon as he spotted her.

"Jodie! For God's sake, what are you doing here in Hutchinson?"

"My gosh, Lou. I could ask you the same. I thought you were busy keeping out of the sun in Kansas City."

"I'm trying to get some financial backing for a really big development project, Jodie," he said. "There are a couple of doctors here who were interested, before all this weather trouble. You never know now, though, everybody is pulling in his horns until this thing is over."

Jodie shook her head. "Leave it to Lou Falco to think of making a buck at a time like this." She did not say it reproachfully, only in wonderment.

He grinned. "Well, I'll admit it's all slowed me down some."

Jodie was unconsciously comparing his looks with those of Mark Latham then. His smile was flashier, but more practiced; he was very dynamic-looking, but not as physical as Latham; and now Falco looked much more Mediterranean than he had to her before.

"Hey, Jodie, it's absolutely great to see you again," he was telling her. He watched her face, trying to read it. "I think you were avoiding my calls recently, weren't you?"

Jodie met his handsome look. "I didn't see much point in discussing us any further, Lou," she said.

"Look, Jodie. What I said there that day at the Century

119

came out all wrong. Do you have a little time? Let me tell you about it, over a drink."

Jodie told him she had to meet Paula Betancourt at a medical clinic several blocks away in just over an hour, but that she would go with him for a brief talk. He took her to a small hotel just a few blocks away, and then instead of showing her into the bar there, he asked her to come up to the room he had taken for the night. Jodie hesitated, then reluctantly accepted.

The room was rather modest by Falco's usual standards, Jodie thought. It was clean, but there was a tackiness about it that Falco would not have accepted if he had not been in a small town. There was a clear plastic cover over the lampshade at the night table, and stains on the carpeting, and a rather gross oil painting on velvet over the bed, of a half-clad woman reclining with a tiger. Jodie was still staring in awe at the painting when Falco came to her with the scotch and water he had mixed himself, from supplies he had with him. Jodie took the drink just to please him, and they stood there not far from the narrow bed, facing each other.

"The room is air-conditioned," she said. The clinics and hospital had been, but it surprised her that a hotel would be allowed the use of power for that purpose.

"Just barely," Falco said. "We have some in Kansas City, too, but not much. You don't look any worse for the heat, Jodie."

She smiled. "Looks are deceiving. Lou, you don't need to make any explanations, you know. I felt abandoned for a couple of days after you left, but I'm fine now. Our lives have taken us down separate paths, that's all. Nobody's to blame."

He sipped his drink. "You wouldn't believe how I've

missed you, honey. I'm not just saying that, either. I think about you all the time."

Jodie looked down.

"I've been going to fly back to Wichita and have another talk with you," he said. "In fact, I was thinking about going there from here. If I could raise you on the wire."

"Really, Lou, there's no need," she murmured. She looked around the room furtively, as if trying to find any place to fix her gaze except on Falco's face.

"I've been giving all this some heavy thought," he went on. "I'd like for you to come to Kansas City, Jodie."

She looked at him in surprise.

"I know you're not the type who'd like to move right in with me," he said carefully. "So I'd set you up in your own place, I can swing it now. In the same building with me, if you want it that way. I even checked into a job for you, at a private lab. There's an opening for an assistant manager. Your bacteriology degree would be perfect, I already asked."

Jodie was trying to assimilate all of that. "How can you be so sure I wouldn't want to live with you, Lou?" she said casually.

He raised his eyebrows. "Well, I was just guessing, of course." He touched her face softly. "Something tells me you missed old Lou just a little, too, huh? The long, snuggly nights at your place?"

She averted her gaze again.

"Well, I'd love to have you at my place, naturally," he said. "But I know you, little lady. You like to feel independent until you've judged a new situation, gotten a feeling for it. I'd want you to take your own place first. At least for a while. Then we could talk about sharing space later, when you have your feet on the ground there."

Jodie had been right in her guess. He wanted her there in the city to see regularly, but not with him in his own place. He wanted to retain his privacy. For obvious reasons.

It made no real difference to her, though. She would not have moved there under any circumstances: separate, live-in, or as his wife.

"Lou, I appreciate the offer. Really. I know what an expense such an arrangement might be for you, even if I paid the rent for a separate place. It's a generous offer. But I'm needed in Wichita, Lou. I'm running the department in Ben Webster's absence, and we have a big emergency on our hands at this moment. We have no idea when it might be over."

"Well, of course you could wait until the summer is over," he told her. "It's bound to cool off sooner or later—isn't it?"

"Nobody knows, Lou," she said. She caught his gaze for a long moment. "I wouldn't be going to Kansas City then, either, though."

He regarded her somberly.

"My life is in Wichita," she said. "I think I really ought to let it remain there, on a purely selfish basis."

Falco took their drinks and put them down on a nearby table. Then he pulled Jodie to him, and kissed her. She resisted him for a moment, then let it happen.

A moment later they were both breathless. There was no doubt about it, she thought, he still did things to her, physically. His hand was suddenly on her breast, caressing it through the flimsy cloth of her clothing. His lips were on her cheek, her throat.

"Please, Lou." Throatily.

"You remember, don't you? How good it always was? It can be that way again for us, honey. Just let me remind you. We both have a little time. Let me make it happen again, for old time's sake. Let me change your mind."

He forced her to the edge of the bed, and she was seated there, and then pushed back onto her back, her legs still off the bed, her feet on the floor. She pushed at him, but weakly. His hand moved the hem of her dress upward, over her thighs, and then found the hot place at the tops of them, and began working there. In just moments, it would be too late.

She moved him away, forcefully, and sat up. She stared down at her naked thighs darkly, as if to reprove her body for causing her trouble. His hand still lay on one of her legs.

"What's the matter, honey?" he said hoarsely.

She caught her breath. "I can't, Lou."

A frown took a slow grip on his aquiline face. "Can't? Why the hell not?"

"I don't know. It shouldn't make any difference. But it does." A fleeting thought crossed the back of her mind, like a sun shadow. Maybe she would have, if she had not met Mark Latham. Maybe.

She rose off the bed, and turned away from him, regaining her composure. "I shouldn't have come up here, Lou. I have another clinic to visit before I meet Paula." She pushed wrinkles out of her dress. "I hope you don't mind if I leave now."

Falco's frown had deepened. "Jesus Christ, Jodie. You drive a man nuts, do you know that?"

She turned back to him, pushing a ringlet of auburn hair away from her face. "I'm sorry, Lou. I should have known better. There can never be anything between us

123

again, it's all different now. I think you know that, too."

"Oh, hell, Jodie! Just because I've had to—"

"It's not that," Jodie said. "I've changed, Lou. You forced me to, I guess I should thank you for it. I want something more from a relationship, now. There's no going back, don't you see?"

"What I see is," he said, "that you're doing too much thinking about how things are and how they should be. A girl should let her body heat be her guide, baby. You think too much, you'll get worry lines across that lovely brow. That's Falco's Second Law."

Jodie did not like that response. She did not, in fact, like Lou Falco. She picked up a small purse from a table, and walked to the corridor door.

"Fortunately, Lou," she said soberly, "Falco's laws no longer apply to me. I don't come under their jurisdiction. Good luck on your development project, incidentally. I hope the drought doesn't spoil your plan to get rich quick."

All the friendliness was gone out of his voice, now. "Go to hell, Jodie," he said.

That same evening, about the time that Jodie and Paula Betancourt arrived back from Hutchinson, the People's Brigade was meeting at its campus headquarters in preparation for a nocturnal outing.

There were no haranguing speeches by the leaders this time, no shouting of slogans. That had all happened previously. Now there was a quiet earnestness as last-minute orders were given, and weapons were handed out. Will Jameson was one of those distributing the clubs, the wire cutters, the surplus Army water cans. They were headed for the city reservoir.

They were taking the water shortage problem into their own hands.

There were six car-loads of them. They left the campus headquarters at just before midnight and drove grimly across the night city to the reservoir on the northern perimeter of the city. When they arrived there, they got out of the cars quietly. A full moon stood bold overhead, like a spotlight on them. The temperature was breathlessly high.

The reservoir sat behind a high wire fence in an open, park-like area. Because of the drought, its locked gate was now guarded by four policemen, two of whom were on constant patrol around the perimeter of the grounds, outside the fence.

The Brigade's plan was to create a diversion at the gate—they were not aware that the police had begun to patrol the fence—while half of their group climbed the fence elsewhere and made off with a couple of car-loads of water.

The idea might have worked, except for the two cops on patrol. The Brigade split into two groups of about fifteen apiece, and at just after midnight, the first group made its presence known at the big wire gate, brandishing clubs and demanding water. The two cops there responded with threats and curses, but because the demonstrators made no physical move against them, they did not call for a back-up force from headquarters. There was a lot of shouting on both sides, and warnings with drawn guns by the police, but no real confrontation.

On the back side of the reservoir enclosure, though, things were different. Will Jameson's group there had sneaked up to the fence without being seen, and figured they had a clear path ahead for their plan. Will and another young man cut a big hole in the chain-link fence with special wire cutters, and the others got the water cans ready to take inside.

But then the two patrolling cops showed up unexpectedly out of the shadows.

"Hey, what's going on there!"

"You people! Get away from that fence!"

Will was startled by the sounds of their voices. He turned and saw the two policemen hurrying toward his group.

"Cops!" somebody growled.

"There were more than we thought!"

Will turned to the young men near him. There were also three girls there. They all wore dark clothing, and had smeared dirt on their faces. They looked like irregular commandos.

"Don't do anything," Will was telling them. "Wait till they get here. Act innocent as hell. Then take them when you can."

The cops had arrived. "What the hell you kids think you're doing?" the broadest one said harshly. "Did you cut that fence?"

"We wanted water," Will spoke up. "We just wanted water."

"We all want water, by God," the other cop said, an older, taller man. "You think you're going to steal what little we've got left here?"

"There are neighborhoods in the city where no water comes from the faucets now!" a young woman told them. "Two water trucks have come in, and those people are still without!"

"We're going to take water to them!" a young man, a student at the university, said heatedly. "And we're going to have some ourselves! Like the mayor and the police department have!"

"The mayor is working on a plan to distribute water fairly," the heavy cop said in a low voice.

"*He's been working on it for weeks!*" Will said loudly. "*People are dying in their homes, damn it! Or didn't you know that?*"

The cops noticed now that they had been surrounded by the Brigade people. The taller one pulled a walkie-talkie from his belt and pushed a button. He identified himself to the gate guards, and then told them what they had run into. "Better call for back-up, Mac, and send somebody around here."

But before he could replace the transceiver to his belt holster, Will gave a silent signal to the group. In the next instant they all converged on the two policemen at the same moment.

The broad, bulky cop aimed his .38 Smith & Wesson toward the first young man in, and fired in a small panic. The shot went slightly wild, though, and only grazed the fellow in the side. He was spun off his feet, doing a tight pirouette like a ballet dancer, and then hit the ground. But then the group was in on the cop. The other one did not even get his gun aimed. Two men and a girl were all over him, grabbing at his gun, throwing him to the ground. There was some wrestling around then, and some grunting, and both cops were disarmed. Will went to the downed Brigade member, and saw the blood on the follow's shirt. He was holding his rib cage and grimacing in shock and pain. "Jesus Christ!" Will muttered. "Is it bad?"

The fellow shook his head. "I don't think so."

Will turned to a couple of the group. "Get him back to

a car. The rest of you, through that fence! Let's get some water out here!"

The group began hurrying through the hole in the fence. Will went over to the downed cops, where they were being held down with their own guns by two Brigade men.

"You jerks!" he said loudly to them. He leaned over the broad-set one, the cop who had shot the Brigade man. "You'd shoot a man because he wants water? What kind of a bastard are you?"

Without even thinking of what he was doing, he hauled off and kicked the policeman in the thigh, hard. The fellow jumped, and gasped out in pain. *"You sonofabitch!"* Will yelled. He kicked him a second time.

There was a siren in the distance now, and heads turned in that direction in the blackness. Will turned darkly. He had thought that it would take a back-up unit much longer to arrive. "Christ!" he spat out. He turned toward the reservoir, where Brigade people were attempting to open a big spigot near a service building.

"Never mind, it's too late!" Will yelled. *"Come on back, let's get out of here!"*

A couple of them near the fence turned and came back through. But several of them were a hundred yards from the fence, inside it, and not all of them had heard him. He ducked through the fence hole and ran toward them. *"Come back! We have to leave now!"*

Now he had their attention, and they were all running back toward the fence. Will brought up their rear, making sure nobody had been left behind. They darted through the darkness swiftly, like bats released from a cage, fluttering breathlessly. When the first ones arrived back at the fence, the extra police arrived.

They came screaming up in their vehicles, lights flashing, tires raising dust on the gravel road that paralleled the fence. The two patrol cops were released, and Brigade people began scattering as riot police swarmed from a van and a patrol car, brandishing billy clubs and scowls, shouting obscenities.

What followed was a melee. In a frieze of swinging clubs and grappling arms, police and Brigade met. To their credit, the police did not use their guns. But they wielded the clubs with a viciousness born of frustration and the heat, and several Brigade members went down, bleeding from the faces and heads. One cop went down, and another was thrown violently against the fence.

Will was through the fence opening now, and saw that arrests were going to be made. *"Get out of here!"* he yelled to his comrades.

He started toward a hidden, parked car himself, but saw a member down right in front of him, a student he knew well. He stopped and grabbed at the fellow to get him up, and the injured student was dazed and numb. Will had just pulled the fellow to his knee, when he heard a policeman run up behind him. He turned just in time to see the club descend onto the side of his head, over his right ear. There was a blinding, bright-hued light in his head, and for a moment he saw himself as if in a slow-motion film, falling off the ledge of a building roof, floating down and down toward a darkness far below. A hoarse voice from somewhere in the void was shouting at him, *"Don't fall, Will! Don't fall!"* But it was too late, he was on his way.

Before he hit bottom, though, the scene dissolved and

changed, and he was surrounded by a black infinity of winking suns and clouds of nebulous gases, and he seemed to be traveling toward the very largest nebulous cloud, and he knew through some primordial instinct that ungainly demons hid in those dark gases, singing hymns of depraved evil and dancing their obscene dances to a malignant god named Dozhtbog.

SEVEN

Police headquarters was a hot, noisy madhouse during the small hours of that airless night. Newly installed ceiling fans whirred in offices, in corridors, in cellblocks. Red-faced rioters and delinquents shouted angrily at their captors, and surly-visaged looters and burglars waited, handcuffed, on chipped-paint benches to be booked. Harried officers took fingerprints, made mug shots, moved prisoners in and out of holding cells. They were doing a land-office business, and they did not have the personnel for the job.

Jodie, Leah and Mark Latham arrived in the midst of that three-ring circus of activity, to bail Will out of jail. Will had been unwilling to call anyone on his own, when he arrived conscious but groggy from the blow on the head. A department medic had given first aid to Will and a few others among the dozen or so Brigade people arrested, but then Will had refused to acknowledge the need for any more help, physical or otherwise. A policeman who knew that Will had been a friend of the mayor called Leah, and Leah called Jodie, whose head was still buzzing with memories of her afternoon episode with Lou Falco. Mark Latham had stopped past Jodie's place late to tell her that the oilman Douglas would arrive in

Wichita the next day, with a roughneck crew, so Jodie knew that Latham was probably still up. She was shook up about Will, and knew Leah would be, so asked Latham to drive them to police headquarters. Latham was glad Jodie had felt she could call on him for help, and picked up both Jodie and Leah and took them downtown.

Now, standing in that crowded corridor before the booking sergeant's desk, Jodie was overwrought about Will. They had heard that he was hurt, and she and Leah were very worried about him. Leah insisted on sharing the bail responsibility with Jodie, and they had signed some papers.

"Look, Sergeant," Jodie was telling the officer in charge at the desk. "We've been out here for a half-hour now. Where is my brother? Are you sure he's all right?"

"We demand to see him immediately!" Leah said loudly. She looked more mussed-up than Jodie, with her hair uncombed and her clothes thrown on hastily. "If we don't, by God, I'm calling my father!"

The sergeant made a face. "Ladies, ladies. I told you, we're bringing him up just as soon as we can. We've got a lot of people here tonight, and we're—"

A plainclothes officer came up to interrupt them. "Jameson is cleared for release."

"Ah, there," the sergeant said. "You see, ladies, I told you."

"We brought him to interrogation room C," the plainclothes man said. "You want him here at the desk?"

"Maybe you'd like a few minutes with him there," the desk sergeant suggested to the girls.

Jodie was trembling slightly inside her. "Yes," she said quickly. "That would be nice."

"I'll wait out here," Latham told her.

"No, come with us," Jodie said. "I want you to meet Will."

"All right," Latham said.

They walked down the corridor to room C. Jodie was thinking of how she would have to call their father in the morning and tell him what had happened, and it was not a pleasant thought. Colonel Sherwood Jameson had always warned Will that he was too rebellious.

"This is it, folks. He's inside. He's free to go any time you want to take him home."

Leah entered the room first, and saw Will standing facing away from them, at a table in the center of the white-painted room. He turned immediately, and his face became quite emotional when he saw Leah and Jodie. His head wore a bandage around it, and he looked weak.

"Oh, Will!" Leah gasped out. She went to him, and he embraced her. Her eyes moistened as she laid her head momentarily on his shoulder.

Jodie came over less emotionally, and then Will was embracing her, too. "Are you okay?" she asked him quietly.

He nodded. "Sure, Jodie. A crack on the head can't hurt me, I'm too thick-skulled."

"We were so worried, Will," Jodie told him.

"They told us you'd been hurt, but wouldn't give us any details," Leah said.

"That figures," he said sourly. "What did you do, bring a lawyer with you?" He was looking past them, to Latham.

"Oh, no," Jodie said. "This is a new friend, Will. Dr. Mark Latham. He came all the way from California to help us do something about this terrible drought."

Latham extended his hand. "Glad to meet you, Will."

133

Will hesitated, then took Latham's hand. "Can you make water out of sand?" he said.

Latham smiled. "I'm a weather man. But we're working on all aspects of relief, Will, at the university, under the coordinating efforts of Dr. Sprague. We're hoping to formulate some ideas about shortening the drought that would be less dramatic but maybe more effective than the Russian plan. And in the meantime, we're trying to get the area some water. We'll begin drilling artesian wells this week."

"Artesian wells?" Will said. "Why not just dig some irrigation wells around the state, to start off with? Why not spend some money on something practical?"

Latham narrowed his dark eyes slightly on Will. It was obvious that the young man had a lot of hostility in him. "We've discussed that with experts, Will. There isn't any water left at shallow levels. It's all evaporated off. We have to go deep, to have any chance. Down to the aquifer."

Will scowled toward him. "Is this the governor's idea of appeasing the people around here who are thirsting to death?" he said. "To go through the motions of drilling a couple of deep wells? What are the chances you'll hit the aquifer?"

"We really don't know," Latham told him. "But it's all we can think of to do right now, in addition to shipping water in."

Will laughed bitterly. "Ship it in!" he said. "We've had two small shipments, and where the hell did it go? To people who have the money or pull to get it, that's where!"

Jodie frowned deeply. "Will, that's not true! Paula Betancourt personally supervised the distribution of that

134

water, and it went to people who needed it! Is that why you were in that group at the reservoir tonight, because you think we don't care about the suffering here in the city?"

Will shook his head. "I can't argue with you, Jodie. You believe in the establishment, you always have. All I know is, there are people dying of thirst out there, and you and your crowd aren't doing anything about it. That means that my people will have to."

"Oh, God, Will!" Leah moaned.

Jodie was very dejected. "You know I'm going to have to call Dad, Will. He has the right to know that you've been hurt."

Will gave her a rather hard look. "Do what you think you have to, Jodie," he told her.

She sighed. "Will you come to my place for a while, Will? At least until you feel better?"

Will shook his head. "No, I have friends who'll take care of me. I appreciate your making bail for me, but I can't accept it if there are any strings attached to it. I have to be my own person."

"Nobody is asking you to capitulate to your imagined enemies," Leah told him. "Just let us give you our affection, Will."

Will looked into Leah's damp eyes. "I'm sorry about us, Leah. I really am." He turned to Jodie. "I presume I'm free to leave now?"

"Yes, that's what we were told," Jodie said.

"Then I'll be off," Will said.

"Let me give you a ride," Latham said. "I'll be returning to campus, after I let the girls off."

"No. I'd rather walk," Will replied, holding Latham's sober look. He went to the door and opened it, then

135

turned back to Jodie. "This isn't over, so don't expect it to be. We've had enough talk, and promises. If we don't get the food and water and medicine we need, we'll take it. If the power clique won't help us, we'll help ourselves. It's just that simple."

He turned, then, and left them all staring after him.

Jodie got almost no sleep that night, after leaving Latham and Leah. It was not just that Will had been arrested, and would have to face a trial, eventually, for his misdoing. It was not just that he had been clubbed over the head in a violent confrontation with police. It was the different look she had seen in his eyes, in that interrogation room at police headquarters, and the new way he spoke to her. There had been no affection in his voice for either Leah or herself, and no reaching out for a meeting of the minds. It hurt Jodie badly, because at one time she and Will had been very close.

That next morning, Jodie called Sherwood Jameson in Topeka. She called from her apartment, for privacy, and when she got through, it was a sergeant on the other end. He asked her to hold for a moment, and then suddenly Jameson's deep voice greeted her.

"*Jodie! How's my favorite daughter this morning? Is everything all right there in Wichita? Are you getting water there?*"

"Hi, Dad. We've gotten some water in, but it wasn't nearly enough. We have a health problem here now. A rather big one. But that isn't what I called about."

There was a short silence on the other end. "*Oh? What is it, Jodie, are you sick or something?*"

Jodie could imagine his square face on the other end, serious and sober, with its jutting jaw and steely eyes. Jameson had had to be both father and mother to Jodie

136

and Will for a number of years, and he had not shirked the job. He had been rather strict, but always fair with them. At the end, he and Will had not gotten along at all.

"No, I'm not sick, Dad," Jodie told him. She paused. "We're having a lot of civil disorder here, now. The police are having a difficult time handling it."

"*I know, honey,*" Jameson said. "*Tom Purcell called the governor yesterday, and the governor had a talk with the White House. I may be taking a detachment of troops to Wichita.*"

"Oh, my gosh," Jodie said. Even though her own father was a military man, she feared an escalation of violence, by bringing troops into the city. "Does Tom think that's necessary?"

"*He's worried about the safety of local citizens on your streets,*" Jameson said. "*And that looting will get out of hand.*"

"Well," Jodie said, "I'll be glad to see you, of course. But not under these circumstances."

"*If we get the go-ahead, we may leave as soon as later today,*" he told her. "*I intended to call you when I got a confirmation.*"

"I'll check with Tom to get the latest," she said. She paused again. "Dad, a group of militants is causing us quite a lot of trouble here. They call themselves the People's Brigade. Maybe Tom has mentioned them to you."

"*Yes, I believe he did,*" Jameson said.

"Well, they have a lot of complaints against local and state government, because of sickness and dehydration. They have the idea that a lot more could be done for relief. They attacked the city reservoir last night, and some were arrested. Will was one of those hauled in by the police."

"*Jesus Christ!*" Jameson said in sudden anger.

"He received a head injury, too, but not a bad one. He seemed all right when I saw him a few hours ago. I tried to get him to come here to my place for a while, but he wouldn't. You know how he can be. I'm a little worried about him, Dad. Maybe if you come here, you can find a chance to talk with him."

Jameson's voice was heavy, on the other end. "*Yes,*" he said. "*If he'll see me, Jodie.*"

"We'll go to him together," she said. "I think he's all right for the moment. But I'm afraid of what else he might get involved in. He's going through a bad time. He's lost faith in everything, Dad. He's been involved in too many lost causes in the past year or so, seen too many injustices. It's changed him."

"*Will was always bull-headed and uncompromising,*" Jameson said. "*I just couldn't talk to him. You were twice as easy to raise as he was. Your mother always used to say he had a lot of her maverick father in him. But maybe somehow it's all my fault, I don't know. Maybe I didn't try hard enough to understand.*"

"I suspect Will has only himself to look to for an explanation of his current behavior," Jodie said wearily. "Well, I just wanted you to know, Dad. I'm going to check today to find out exactly what the charges are against him. If you come to Wichita, I'll probably have all the details on your arrival."

"*Thanks for calling, Jodie. I'll be in touch.*"

But Jodie did not have to wait long to learn whether Jameson was coming. In mid-afternoon Tom Purcell confirmed the rumor, and in early evening the troops were there.

Jameson called Jodie from the airport, and told her he had arrived, and that he would get in contact with her after he had settled his troops in at the centrally-located armory.

Jameson had military trucks to haul his men into the city, but he used them only for part of the trip. He decided that it would make more of an impression on the law violators if the National Guard arrived in a very visible way, so he left the trucks at a public square about two miles from the armory, and marched his two hundred soldiers into Wichita.

The sun was almost down when they marched through the streets of the city, so the heat was not as torrid as it had been in the afternoon. They marched in four companies, in full battle regalia—helmets, canteens, ammo belts, automatic rifles on their shoulders. They came down the main streets and boulevards in close formation, their feet thudding in unison, their guns glinting in the dull light from the west. Nothing symbolized law and order more strongly than those marching troops, not the police force, not the visiting officials who had come, not the White House itself. When American troops were brought to an American town to keep order, a new, awesome mood was struck. Central authority was giving out a tough message: obey the law or suffer the consequences. It was a simple message, but a dynamic, dramatic one.

Part way along the march route, people began coming out onto the streets to watch the invasion of uniformed soldiers. Many faces were surly, a few were cheerful, sure the Guard could somehow make all their troubles go away. Down toward the center of town, a few at-large Brigade people crawled onto rooftops and hurled tin cans and other light missiles at the troops as they passed, as a protest against their presence. Sherwood Jameson, at their fore, ordered his troops to maintain ranks and not respond. At last, they arrived at the armory without incident.

The first stage of their temporary occupation had been accomplished without violence.

That evening later, Jameson deployed about half of his troops around the city, in accord with a plan pre-established with the police department and Tom Purcell's office. Purcell and Jameson met briefly at mid-evening, and had a fond reunion at the armory where Jameson had set up headquarters. Just as Purcell was about to leave, later, Jodie arrived to greet her father, and Jameson was happy to see her well. After Purcell left and Jameson issued some additional orders to a couple of subordinates about troop deployment, he and Jodie were finally alone in his hastily-put-together office.

"Well, we didn't get what you could consider a friendly welcome," Jameson said, when they were both seated in the fan-humming room. There were hints of Jodie and Will in his angular face, but all the lines in his were harder, more masculine than in hers, which featured her mother's big eyes and sensuous mouth. Jameson was healthy-looking, ramrod-erect in his green uniform and trim at the waist. He had just a hint of graying in his thick hair. "I think, though, that we made our impression on the town. We showed them we're here on serious business."

"I just hope it doesn't get too serious, Dad," Jodie said. "Remember, most of these trouble-makers are just trying to find water and food for their own consumption."

"Stealing is stealing, Jodie," he responded. "And violence is violence. A few policemen were hurt the other night. One is still at the hospital, did you know that?"

"I know, Dad," Jodie said. "I guess I just get scared of all those guns you came with."

"Unfortunately," Jameson said, "guns are all some people understand."

There was a knock on the door, and Jameson replied to it. An officer came in, saw Jodie, nodded to her. He had captain's bars on his shirt, carried a helmet under his arm, and wore a big, heavy-looking automatic pistol on his gunbelt. "Sorry to disturb you, Colonel. I just wanted to report that B company has been placed on rotating guard duty all around the perimeter of the grounds, in accord with your orders. Also, I just got a call-in from Captain Chulowski at City Hall, saying everything is quiet on the streets there."

Looking at the young captain, Jodie recognized an immediate difference between these men and the Wichita police that patrolled the streets. There was a more aggressive manner about them, a readiness to do battle that was almost palpable. Whereas the police obviously wished to avoid trouble, Jodie sensed that the Guard courted it, expected it, perhaps wanted it. If you happened to be a store owner whose property had been looted and vandalized, or a resident whose home had been broken into or who had been mugged by anarchistic youths, their presence was surely a calming factor. But Jodie worried that Wichita could become a battleground, if the drought lasted.

"All right, Captain," Jameson said briskly. The silver eagles on his shirt collar glowed impressively in the hard fluorescent light. "You're relieved for the rest of the night. Try to get some rest."

"Thanks, Colonel," the captain said. He nodded again to Jodie. "Miss Jameson." He turned on his heel and strode out, his gear clanking and squeaking out metallic and leathery sounds as he left.

"He seems like a determined fellow," Jodie said when he was gone.

"He's a good man," Jameson said. "My officers take all of this very seriously, just as if they were on a foreign battlefield. They know their lives are on the line, and the lives of their men."

Jodie did not like to hear that kind of talk. "Will this be dangerous for you?" she wondered.

Jameson grinned at her. "Not a bit, honey. Your old man just sticks other people's necks into nooses, remember?"

"I hear you were at the head of the column, when you marched into the city."

He shrugged. "Just a little show biz. There wasn't any real danger out there, on that first appearance."

Jodie looked at her hands for a moment, sitting there hot and tired. "I went to visit Will on campus," she said. "To set up a meeting for the three of us. I couldn't find him."

Jameson squinted down curiously. "Couldn't find him?"

"He's moved. The whole Brigade, as they call it, has moved. They and he are off-campus, now. Probably for extra security. The police have threatened to bring them all in."

"Damn," Jameson growled. "How could he get mixed up in something like this?"

"I'm afraid you and Will are going to be on the opposite sides of something for a while," Jodie said heavily.

"It won't be the first time," Jameson grunted.

"It will be the first time either of you carried a gun," Jodie reminded him somberly.

He cast a dour look toward his daughter. "You can be sure we won't be using guns unless we're forced to," he told her. "But if we're confronted with violence, Jodie, we'll be forced to respond in kind."

"God," Jodie said. "I wish all this were behind us."

Jameson gave her a grin. "Remember the Chinese emperor."

"What Chinese emperor?" Jodie said.

"I don't remember the name. The story is probably apocryphal, anyway. This Chinese emperor asked his three wisest advisors to put their heads together and try to formulate an eternal truth for him, a verity that would be as valid in a thousand years as it was at that moment in time. They thought and thought, conferred and huddled. Finally they came to him and announced one life rule that he could always count on to be the same, and that his descendants could count on."

He paused, and Jodie arched her pretty brows. "Well?"

"Their message to the emperor was," he told her, "'And this too shall pass.'"

Jodie smiled, nodding slowly.

"The only sameness in the universe is change," Jameson added. "Mostly, Jodie, that's not so bad. In a situation like this one, we can pretty much figure on things getting better, if we're patient."

Jodie made a small face. "There is a third possibility," she reminded him.

"We won't even consider that," Jameson replied soberly.

"All right," she smiled. "We won't consider that."

When Jodie returned home later, filled with mixed feelings about the presence of her father's National Guard garrison, Mark Latham was just coming out of her building, on his way to his car. He had stopped past to ask her out for a drink before they called it a day.

"There's a little quiet bar not far from here that still has some mixer for drinks," he told her as they stood on the dark parking lot. "It's too early to go to bed, isn't it?"

Jodie was glad to see him. He was so different from Falco. He was easy-going, low-geared, casual. He had interests other than himself. He cared for people, and about the way the world was. How ironic, she thought, that he was a married man, and that she had met him at a time when she needed someone more than she ever had.

She gave him a wide smile. "I have a better idea. I still have some chilled dry wine left. Come on up, and we'll share it."

"I haven't had that nice an offer in ages," he grinned.

Jodie turned on several fans as soon as they got inside the apartment, and opened the French doors onto a small balcony. The temperature had dropped more than usual that evening, and it was no longer a physical weight on their bodies. They sat on a sofa before the French doors, and sipped Jodie's wine, and

Jodie told him about the coming of her father. Latham said he thought the Guard was needed, if only to protect the reservoir and City Hall.

"I've got my fingers crossed that we may have some relief soon," Latham said, holding his glass of wine. "Douglas is here, and has okayed a couple of sites for drilling that our geologists suggested. He'll begin tomorrow."

"Aren't the Russians due tomorrow too?" Jodie said.

He nodded. "Talk about coincidence."

"Well, at least things are happening, Mark. Is there any expected change in the weather in the near future?"

He shook his head. "The equator-to-pole and ground-to-air temperature differences are unchanged, and the westerlies are stable. It can only get drier and hotter, for a while."

"We've been hearing that since May," Jodie said.

"I wish I could say we're onto something, Jodie. But we're not. All of our theories are more wild than those of the Russians, or impractical. I hope the well-drilling works to bring relief, because weather-wise it looks as if we have nothing better than the Russians, and I'm convinced now that radio fluxion is impractical."

"Well," she said, "drink and be merry, Mark. Tomorrow it may be a hundred twenty."

When they finished the wine, Jodie got up to open the French doors further, and looked out over the dark city for a moment, thinking of Will, and of her father. When she turned back, she was surprised to find Latham beside her.

"I was just wondering what's going on out there," she said.

He put his hands on her waist, and she felt the

familiar tingling through her. "Let's forget all of that for one evening," he said quietly. "Let's just think of each other."

Latham drew her to him, and kissed her. She did not resist him. There was a hot, passionate moment with his mouth exploring hers, and his hands on her ripe curves, and then he was looking into her lovely eyes.

"Jodie, I—want you," he said thickly.

"Oh, God," she breathed.

"Please, let's not think of what has been, for either of us, or how the present might be more perfect. Let's just take what we have, and enjoy it."

Jodie felt his strong hands on her, smelled the masculine odor of him in her nostrils. She had never been quite so physically moved by the touch, the proximity of a man. It was just that he made her aware of the closeness of their lips, or his hands to her breasts. Somehow his physical manner made her acutely aware of how proximate he was to the hot place where a throbbing union could occur at any moment, where his manhood could couple with and overwhelm her, take her wholly, ravage her.

"Give me just a moment," she whispered harshly to him.

She left him at the big doors, and went into her bedroom. Latham stood there, heat building inside him for her. Every curve of her, every soft touch under his hand, made the fever for her rise in him. He waited as long as he could, then went to the bedroom doorway and entered the darker room.

Jodie was standing beside her bed, facing away from him, having just laid a wispy piece of underclothing on a nightstand. She turned to him, nude, and he gasped inaudibly.

"Good Jesus," he breathed.

She came to him and they kissed again, with Jodie's bare flesh in his arms. His touch inflamed her breasts, her buttocks, her thighs. She began helping him undress, and in moments they were on the big bed together, side by side, in breathless expectancy.

"I don't care tonight," he heard her saying softly, more to herself than to him. "I don't care about anything tonight."

"Oh, God, Jodie!"

His touch was firmer, his exploration more complete than Falco's had been, and yet there was less rough carelessness and more affection in it. There was oral caressing, and gentle manipulation, and patience. There was an anxiety between them, too, that was like a gentle abrasion, but Jodie knew that that was because it was all for the first time. She could not remember when he mounted her, and when union came it was natural and effortless and smooth and breathtaking. Then followed a deep, gasp-accentuated probing, a fiery yet incredibly thorough plumbing of her deepest depths that was unknown to her before that beautiful moment, and she responded with a free abandon that came from some hidden and magical touchstone inside her. At the back-arching climax, she was engulfed by her own orgiastic release as he erupted emotionally on her, seeking and finding the forbidden secrets of her darkest, most private places.

EIGHT

That next morning, Jodie admitted it to herself.
She was in love.

In the middle of a furnace-like drought, at a time when
all her attention was needed on her work, and when
residents of Wichita were collapsing all around her from
the heat and disease, she had managed to fall in love with
a married man.

It was preposterous.

It was stupid, immoral, unforgiveable.

But it was real.

Latham had not left, after that first love-making on the
previous night. She had asked him to stay in her bed,
and there had been a long, sensual night of caressing, of
touching, of physical fulfillment.

There had never been anything like it in her life.

He had left not long before the first rays of a burning
sun lighted the eastern sky with a dull, crimson glow.

She had difficulty thinking of anything else, at the lab
and clinic that morning. At shortly after ten, Tom
Purcell came past and asked her if she wanted to join him
and Betancourt in welcoming the Russians at Wichita
Midcontinental Airport, where most of the big commercial jets came in. Jodie declined. She sensed that there

was going to be a squaring off between Latham and the Russians when they got there, and she did not want to be appearing to take sides.

At shortly after noon, an official entourage went out to the airport to meet the Russians, including Stanley Kravitz, a NASA man, Ed Keefer, Tom Purcell, and Paula Betancourt. Betancourt had come to believe Sprague and Latham, that the Russians never should have been invited to Kansas, so she had little interest in meeting them. But it would have been considered a slight to the Kremlin if a high-ranking U.S. administrator had failed to appear.

There were two scientists in the Russian task force, both of whom had been intimately connected with the orbiting of Dozhtbog, the Russian raingod, and with its design and development. There were also several officials with them of minor importance in the Russian government.

The older of the scientists was a Moscovite named Yuri Mazurov, an atmospheric physicist like Mark Latham who also had done a lot of work in radio signals and their effect on the weather. His assistant was a younger man, an Asian Russian named Ilyich Potamkin, a meteorologist involved in research like Hollis Sprague, but unlike Ed Keefer and Stanley Kravitz, who very cautiously applied the theory of science to practice, and with little imagination.

The group was welcomed cordially at the airport, but their own enthusiasm seemed restrained. They had now seen the effects of their weather-tampering on the Midwest of the United States, and were prepared to be defensive about it. There were no accusations, though, not even in jest. The Russians were too important

149

to offend.

In a limousine cavalcade even larger than the one that took the White House man Stevens to McConnell— Stevens had met the Russians at San Francisco, put them on the Wichita plane there, and then gone about other business in California—the Russians traveled in style to the military base, being careful along the way not to remark to each other about the arid dryness they saw on all sides, nor the boiling heat.

The Soviets were settled in nicely by the end of that day. It was August 3, and the temperature was expected to hit one-twenty in the middle of the afternoons over the next several days. The TV news was full of reports about locals being brought into hospitals and clinics and infirmaries, and the Wichita streets were jammed with military vehicles and armed men. The Russians were getting a close-up look at the havoc they had wrought from Siberia.

No incidents occurred at the airport, or at McConnell, either during the arrival of the Soviets or afterwards. But that did not mean the dissidents in the city had forgotten or forgiven. The Brigade was re-forming after the arrests, and Will was one of those who was helping reorganize. They were gathering strength again, and they already had another plan for protest.

Betancourt's efforts to get water to Wichita from other cities had not been eminently successful, but now a big supply was on its way from the nation's capital, by air. It had been gathered at Washington from all around the eastern seaboard, a little here, a little there, and this would amount to the biggeest relief the city had obtained since the inception of federal efforts.

Betancourt and Jodie had already made detailed plans

150

for an attempt to distribute the water equitably. It would go first to hospitals and health care centers, and then to the city's residents whose faucets were not giving them water in their homes. It would be free to those who received it, with the federal government paying the bill.

This was good news to most residents, but there were some, like Will Jameson, who did not believe the equitable distribution part. Their anger smoldered, as they waited.

Emmet Douglas was drilling in four different sites now, all outside the city but nearby, except for one well that was not far from the city reservoir. The going was slow and tough, and it was too soon to know results. Latham, Sprague, two geologists and Douglas had a big conference at Sprague's lab, and Douglas told them that the wells should be coming in within a few days, if they were over water. Latham and Sprague held their breaths, and waited.

Two days after the Russians' arrival, while the two scientists were already busy making calculations based on local upper-currents observations, Sprague called Stanley Kravitz and asked if he and Latham might meet the Russians and get a better picture from them as to what they intended. Kravitz did not want either of them around, but since he knew that the governor and Tom Purcell would back them up in such a request, he reluctantly invited them to his McConnell command base.

It was mid-morning when Latham and Sprague arrived at the quonset building squatting in the torrid sun. M.P.s stood at the entrance of the place, and had to check inside before allowing Latham and Sprague admittance. Inside, the air was cooled by air-conditioning against city ordinance, because of the Russians and because Kravitz thought top-notch work required it. Latham and Sprague were taken to the rear of the big, open room where all the humming equipment sat, and the Russians were back there with Kravitz, bending over a complex electronic component on a work bench. It was a part of a radio system that would go into the American satellite, when it was launched at Cape Kennedy, and Yuri Mazurov was explaining a feature of it to Kravitz. When a guard showed Latham and Sprague to them, the Russians turned to the newcomers with sober but acute interest.

"Ah, here are our university people," Kravitz said in a forced congeniality. "Dr. Sprague, Dr. Latham, these are our Russian friends. Yuri Mazurov." Mazurov violently shook Sprague's and Latham's hands. "And Ilyich Potamkin." Potamkin did the same, but with less zeal. "Both doctorates in their fields, and both internationally recognized for their contributions to weather control."

"I'm very pleased to meet you," Sprague was saying rather somberly to them.

Latham mumbled a formal cordiality, studying Mazurov's broad, meaty face. He was a man of about Latham's height, but he was older with more weight on him. His eyes were dark and piercing, and his grip firm. "I've heard a lot about you, Dr. Mazurov."

Mazurov grinned. "And I know your name also, Latham," he said in a deep voice.

Potamkin was a more retiring, quieter fellow, about Latham's age, with oriental eyes and the look of a young Genghis Khan, but a very pensive one. He was Mazurov's subordinate and acted it, defering to Mazurov in all matters.

152

"It looks like you've gotten us into a hell of a lot of trouble here in this country, Mazurov," Latham said lightly, dropping the formal title as Mazurov had done.

Kravitz gave Latham a hard look, and Mazurov's grin disappeared. He shrugged. "We suspect there are many factors involved in this jet stream incident," he said, "only one of which has been our radio waves broadcast. But in any case, Latham, our intentions have been good ones. We do not with calculation pollute the air, the sea, the soil on which we depend for our food. Can America say the same?"

Latham regarded the Russian studiedly. "Pollution is one thing, Mazurov. Wanton meddling with the basic weather systems is quite another, as you can see by looking around you here in Wichita."

"Wanton?" Mazurov said quizzically. He turned to Potamkin, and Potamkin whispered something into his ear. When Mazurov turned back, he wore a scowl.

"Your description of our scientific achievement is a harsh one, Latham. But, of course, to be expected from a spokesman for a school of thought so backward in comparison with our own."

"What the hell's the matter with you, Latham?" Kravitz said in a half-whisper to him.

"Not backward, Dr. Mazurov," Sprague put in, paying no attention to Kravitz. "Responsible. We've studied radio emission technique in this country, too. But we haven't been so reckless as to test it on our planet's basic life system without some assurance that a calamity can be avoided."

For the first time, Potamkin spoke up. He was much more reserved in his manner, and more courteous, than Mazurov. "With your permission, Dr. Sprague, I must dissent from the judgment that you have a calamity here in the Great Plains. I don't wish to sound callous, but the deaths of a few dozen persons does not amount to a national tragedy. In the great Russian famine in the early part of this century—"

But Sprague interrupted him. "We're not talking about the turn of the century, Dr. Potamkin. We're talking about now. In this country, at this time, the deaths we've had, and the sickness and debilitation of thousands more, with the destruction of a nation's crop, is a modern calamity. And it's not over."

"If your government had invited us here earlier," Mazurov said in his thicker accent than Potamkin's, "we might have saved lives and crops."

"If you had announced the proposal of your weather-tampering," Latham said coolly, "we might have dissuaded you from embarking on such an ill-advised experiment, and have had an ordinary summer here."

Mazurov regarded Latham darkly. "Is this why you came over here, Latham? To rebuke us for making the biggest breakthrough in weather science history? To offer us sour grapes from the primitive garden of your weather laboratory?"

"We came," Sprague replied for Latham, before the angry Kravitz could intervene, "to be briefed on your project here, and to urge you to confer with us at the university as you go along."

Mazurov turned to Kravitz with raised, bushy eyebrows. "Confer? Nobody said we must confer with scientists here," he said arrogantly to Kravitz. "Is this something the U.S. government wishes, Mr. Kravitz?"

Kravitz was livid. "No, it is not, Dr. Mazurov," he hissed out, glaring at Latham. "I invited these men here because I thought I could count on them to be cordial and cooperative. I'm sorry for you that it's turned out so different from those expectations. There is no need now, or in the future, to confer with the university about our plans here."

"Use your head, Kravitz," Latham said tersely. "The more ideas you have on this, the better off you'll be."

"That, by Jesus, is a matter of opinion!" Kravitz said loudly, his jowls shaking slightly. "I intended to have these gentlemen exhibit this electronic device for you today, to broaden your knowledge of what we're doing. But I think we've had quite enough of a dialogue here, if you can call it that. Our guard will show you both out now. And please check with me personally before coming over here again."

"You're a jerk, Kravitz," Latham growled.

"Guard!" Kravitz called out harshly.

"Don't worry, we're going," Sprague said. "But remember, this cooperation thing works both ways. If you won't talk with us, I see no reason why we should talk with you about what we're doing."

Kravitz pointed a finger into Sprague's face. "You get in our way, you two, and I'll close down that whole goddam campus! Don't think I can't do it, the Guard here will respond to presidential orders!"

"If you change your mind about sharing information, you know where to find us," Latham told him.

As they left, Mazurov called after them sourly. "Nice meeting you, gentlemen!"

It took the Russians only four days to put their radio together, and to set it for the work it was supposed to do. The newspapers reported that a Titan missile was ready at

Cape Kennedy in Florida, and that it was only days to launching. The tracking of the satellite, and the activation of the radio device, would be done at McConnell by NASA technicians, supervised by Mazurov and Potamkin.

The entire country—in fact, most of the entire world—was caught up with watching the drama unfold at Wichita, now. Every TV broadcast brought an update of developments at McConnell, not only across America, but Europe, Asia, Russia. Newspapers in every language carried feature stories about the big Russo-American effort to save the Midwest from burning to a crisp. Every magazine carried latest "body counts" of death across the Great Plains, mostly in the cities.

The stories were not exaggerated, for the most part, either. People were dying, and it was clear that more were going to die. It was impossible to keep up with the slaughter of livestock, and much of it rotted, stinking, in fields and barnyards. Even the stubble of wheat and corn was burned away now, and topsoil was being blown away from holding roots with every wind that came up. The winds were hot ones now, killing winds that blew dust everywhere, even into the cities. In Wichita it began piling up against the foundations of buildings, and sticking on tree trunks. It got into buildings through doorways, windows, air vents. It could not be kept out, when the wind came up. And it seemed as if the winds were more frequent, and fiercer.

Wild animals were not plentiful in the farmland around Wichita, but the day after the announcement by Kravitz that the Russian device was ready, two snakes were caught and killed in the southern suburbs, and one was a rattler. Over near McConnell, a coyote was reported scavenging for garbage at a commercial dump.

The creatures of the plains were beginning to converge on the cities, where there was food and water.

On the same day that the Russians made their announcement, telling the world that the radio device would now be flown to Florida for installation in the satellite capsule of the waiting missile, the oilman Douglas gave up on the first of his four wells, telling Latham and Sprague that further efforts would be fruitless. He had gone down over two miles into the bowels of the earth, and figured he was into the Ogallala Aquifer. But only a trickle of water was raised.

It was a bad sign.

Jodie was working long hours to keep up with the work at the overflowing clinic-infirmary at the Health Department, and Paula Betancourt was doing the same. There had been a brief delay in the delivery of water supplies from Washington, but now it was finally in the air.

Jodie and Latham were seeing each other almost every day now, and there was another long, hot night together at her place, and her relationship with Latham was a small island of pleasure in a world of growing misery and worry. She did not allow herself to think about what the future held for them, or what her moral responsibility was toward a faceless woman named Christine Latham. She let her love for Latham grow silently inside her, like a tuber in barren soil, not discussing it with him, not sharing the repressed anxiety it caused her.

Leah Purcell had moved back into her parents' house, because she had no water pressure in her apartment. She tried, too, to find Will Jameson, but without any luck. She and Jodie and Sherwood Jameson had a meal together and reminisced about Jameson's days in Wichita, and Jodie took Latham to the armory one day and introduced him to Jameson. Jameson was impressed with Latham, but when Jodie mentioned later that he was married, Jameson was shocked, and he asked her to quit seeing Latham. Jodie said Latham was her business, and would not discuss the matter.

Jameson's troops had their hands full. Despite the arrival of the Russians, which was lauded by the press as favorably as the coming of the U.S. Cavalry in the 1800s, the street people had not called a truce in their demonstrations and lawbreaking. There were several clashes between troops and demonstrators, and finally a gun was fired, and a demonstrator badly injured.

Restaurants were closed down now for the duration of the emergency. There just was not enough water available to them to cook meals for the public, and constant brown-outs cut their electricity at inappropriate times. Movie theaters had closed down, and almost all forms of entertainment.

Despite diminishing supplies of canned goods, there was still a problem with looting and stealing in stores that were still open. One afternoon late, when Jodie had taken Latham to a small supermarket with her in advance of cooking them an evening meal, they became caught up briefly in one of those incidents.

They had a shopping cart half-full of groceries when the disturbance occurred. A dozen young men came bouncing loudly into the store, not People's Brigade or some other organized activist group, just a loose bunch of toughs looking for trouble. They went up and down the aisles busily and loudly filling their carts with food from the shelves, and getting in the way of customers. One elderly man was knocked down, on the opposite side of the store from where Jodie and Latham were looking for a jar of oregano. Two of the group then left the store with full carts, without paying. An assistant manager tried to stop them, and a blond kid not more than eighteen knocked him down. Then the rest of the group proceeded to take over the store.

Jodie and Latham heard the disturbance, but by the time they understood what was happening, it was too late to avoid a confrontation. Two young men rounded a corner behind them, and a third came down from the opposite direction.

The first one to reach them from behind reached into their cart and picked up a head of lettuce Jodie had carefully picked out. He dumped it into his cart, grinned at them, and bent to see what else their cart contained.

"Hey!" Jodie said. "Go get your own stuff!"

Now the three of them were surrounding them, and a fourth was arriving. "Look what we got here, guys. A happy couple preparing for the end of the world."

Latham saw that they were in trouble. "Excuse us," he said darkly. "We want to move on down the aisle."

"Move on down, move on down, move on down the aisle!" a voice sang out to him, from behind him.

But when Latham tried to move the cart, a third fellow purposely blocked it with his own cart. "Hey, lady. Ain't I seen you on TV?"

The first one now joined in. "By God, this is that Health Department broad, the one that keeps telling us how this is all going to get better!"

"No kidding?" another one said. "Are you that chickee?"

Jodie was scared now. "Please excuse us," she said in a low voice.

"So you're the one that's been spouting all them lies,"

a hard voice said to her. She looked toward him, and he was a crazy-looking chicano with wild eyes. "All that bullshit."

Latham gave up on the cart. He started between two of their harassers now, and the blond kid shoved a cart in his way, thumping it against Latham's thighs. "You the boy friend?" he growled.

Latham felt anger crawl into his chest. "We don't want any trouble," he said carefully. "Just get to hell out of our way."

"Don't you know this is it, you two City Hall flunkies?" the one with the first cart said. "Don't you know this is the way it all ends?"

"They know," the fourth kid said. They had relinquished their carts, too, and now faced Jodie and Latham menacingly.

The chicano came up very close to Latham. "Do you read your Bible, man? 'Jehovah shall come with fire, and his chariots shall be like the whirlwind, to render his anger with fierceness, and his rebuke with flames of fire. For by fire will Jehovah execute judgment, and by his sword, upon all flesh. And the slain of Jehovah shall be many.'"

At the last words, a switch blade suddenly appeared in the chicano's fist, and he held it up for Latham and Jodie to see, a hard grin on his swarthy face. Two of the young men showed surprise in their faces, and concern, but the blond one broke into a grin, too.

"Oh, God!" Jodie gasped out.

"You lie to us about the end," the swarthy kid said to Jodie. "You don't want us to know. So we'll go peaceful-like. You're the spokesman of the Devil."

Latham saw that only two of them intended assault.

But there were still others in the store, he could hear them. He picked up a can of bean sprouts from his cart, and held it out in front of him and Jodie. "Don't try anything silly now," he warned the knife-wielder. "We're not your enemies, we're trying to do something about all of this. Now let us out of here."

In that exact moment, the chicano shoved the blade toward Latham's midsection, savagely.

Latham saw it coming, and stepped aside at the last second. The knife ripped through his shirt, tearing it audibly but barely missing his flesh. He slammed the can of food hard against the kid's head, and he grunted loudly and fell against the nearest shelf. Cans and boxes went everywhere, and the chicano then hit one of the carts loudly and took it over with him as he hit the floor.

Now the blond threw himself at Latham, and landed on Latham's back. Latham bent and hurled him off and over, and the blond hit a second cart and threw it into another nearby shelf. One of the remaining two youths backed way off, but the other one barred their way. Latham took Jodie's arm, gripping it hard.

"Oh, God!" she was muttering.

Latham dragged Jodie out through the ring of carts and past the last youth, who took a swing at Latham and missed. Others were now coming from down the aisle, running toward the scene.

"Stop them!" the last kid was yelling at his comrades for help.

But Latham was at the end of the aisle now, and heading for a door to a back room with Jodie. He yanked it open and shoved her through it, then saw that there was a latch on the inside. He slammed the latch shut just as somebody on the other side of the door threw himself bodily against it. The door held.

"Let's get to hell out of here," Latham said thickly to Jodie.

They ran out through the back of the place to a parking lot for employees, and then out onto a side street. One of the last working municipal buses was just pulling up to a stop nearby. They hailed the driver, and climbed aboard. The bus pulled away.

Just as it turned onto the main boulevard out front, Latham and Jodie looked through its windows and saw a couple of the youths come bursting from the front of the store, wild-eyed, searching the street with their eyes. They did not notice the bus.

It drove away with Latham and Jodie gasping-breathless inside.

That evening, Leah Purcell had part of an evening alone at her parents' house, and she got a surprise.

Will Jameson visited her.

He knew that the mayor and his wife were going out to a meeting that evening, and he waited outside in the hot night for them to leave. Then, like a shadow from the night prairie, he appeared at their door.

"Will!" Leah said wide-eyed when she let him in. "Where have you been, we've all been looking for you!"

He turned to her after he got inside, and he looked tired. "Somewhere where none of you can find me," he said deliberately. "Unless I want to be found."

"Jodie thinks you should see a lawyer, you'll have a preliminary hearing coming up one of these days."

"The courts are barely operating," Will told her. "Hardly anything is operating." He touched her cheek gently with his hand. "How have you been, Leah?"

162

Leah got a small lump in her throat. "Okay, Will."

"I waited till your parents had left," he said. "Especially Mr. Mayor. I had to see you."

"Oh, Will!"

He took her to him, and kissed her. Leah let it happen. The kiss was urgent, fierce. Will was breathing shallowly when it was over. "I need you, Leah. I need you tonight. Do you understand?"

"I—think so."

"Take me to your room, Leah. Or if you want, we can stay right here, on the carpet." He grabbed her roughly, desperately, and his hands were on her breasts, her hips. His mouth sought her throat, her ear, her lips. In a moment, she pulled away gasping.

"Will, this is so—unexpected," she whispered.

"I dreamed about you last night," he said. "I dreamed we were naked in the middle of McKinley Park, and we were making love. I was deep inside you, Leah, and we were doing it right out in the baking sun, getting parboiled there but not caring. Your skin was glistening damp, and you kept pleading for me to keep going, you wanted more and more. You were insatiable."

Leah averted her eyes from his gaze. "I've never thought of myself as a nymphomaniac," she admitted.

"But you do want me, don't you, Leah? You've missed our evenings together too, haven't you?"

"Of course, Will."

"Take your clothes off," he said levelly.

She looked at him. It was more like he was telling her, than asking her. "I'd rather not, Will. Not tonight."

He frowned. "Your parents will be gone for hours. I thought you'd be glad to see me."

"I am," she said. "But not for—this."

"You said you wanted to help me. You said you wanted to give me your affections," he said accusingly.

"I do," she protested. "But not this, not yet. Things have happened between us, Will. Things that have to be talked out and resolved."

"Oh, for Christ's sake," he said, turning away.

"Where are you living now, Will?"

"I can't tell you," he said, frustration heavy in his voice.

"You're keeping off the streets at night, aren't you?"

He looked at her, and grinned a very hard grin. "You mean, so my father's soldiers won't blow my head off?"

"The colonel wants to see you, Will, and talk with you. Why don't you go visit him at the armory?"

He scowled heavily at her. "Lay off it, Leah."

"Jodie is so unhappy because she can't locate you."

"Jodie is being well taken care of," he said. "Even if Latham is a married man."

"Oh, Will. You sound so damned bitter."

"I sound the way I am," he said.

"Will you at least promise me you won't get into any more trouble?" she asked him.

"I promise nothing," he said. "As long as the people of this city need water and food and medicine that's being withheld from them, we'll be trying to find a way to get it distributed."

"The reservoir is guarded by troops with automatic weapons," she said. "I hope your group doesn't have any more notions of taking it from there."

Will grinned again. "There are sources now besides the reservoir," he said laconically. The grin was suddenly gone, as if it had never been on his face. "Well, I won't keep you, Leah. There's nothing for me here, it seems."

The remark brought tears to her eyes for a moment. "If that's the way you feel, Will."

He stared hard at her for a very long moment, burning inside with hot desire for her, but very angry and frustrated. Then he turned and stormed moodily from the house.

The next day two things of importance happened, and one involved Will.

In the morning, Ilyich Potamkin flew off to Florida with the radio payload for the satellite, taking two NASA technicians with him. Newsmen were at the airport with cameras, asking questions, getting their hopes up. It was all very exciting.

In the early afternoon the flight arrived from Washington with hundreds of containers of water for distribution in Wichita and on farms in the outlying areas, and that caused even more excitement.

The plane was met at Wichita's Midcontinental Airport by the police, who had advised Sherwood Jameson they did not need his troops for help there. But Jameson sent a jeep-load of four guardsmen out there anyway, for extra security. That was a fortunate decision, because through some mix-up at police headquarters, only two squad cars were sent to meet the plane, with a total of four policemen. When the convoy of three trucks bearing the water drums left the airport for temporary storage at City Hall, one patrol car and the jeep preceded the trucks at their fore, and the other police car brought up the rear of the column.

If Jameson had been there, he would have delayed the transport until a more military procession could be arranged. But he was not there, so the convoy proceeded through the dust-clogged streets of town with just eight armed men to guard it.

It was a situation the People's Brigade and Will Jameson had been waiting for.

The column had gotten only a third of the way into the center of the city when the attack came, and this time it was not just with clubs and shouted invectives. There were a dozen of them in all, including Will, and each Brigade member was armed with some kind of gun. Most were handguns from private homes, but there were also two rifles and a shotgun. The shotgun was of small gauge, and one of the rifles was only a .22 calibre target gun.

The convoy was slow-moving and an easy target. The orders were to shoot only in self-defense, so the group swarmed down on the police car at the rear of the convoy almost silently, on foot. Suddenly they were all over the car, jerking the doors open, breaking glass, pointing guns. That vehicle and the last truck were stopped, and their intent was to hi-jack only that one truck of the three.

The cops inside the patrol car were taken by surprise by the rush at them, and suddenly they were being dragged out of the vehicle, disarmed, thrown to the ground. The truck driver was yanked out, and a Brigade member quickly took his place and began turning the truck around, to drive it away. Most of the members were to leave on that truck, while four of them, still on foot, stayed back to scare off pursuers. They were to fire a few shots into the air, to keep the police and troops up at the head of the column, then make a break for it on foot.

Naturally, things did not go exactly as planned.

The guards at the head of the convoy saw the incident as soon as it developed, and the whole convoy was stopped. As those two cops and four guardsmen debarked from their vehicles and started to fan out with guns drawn, the Brigade man in the confiscated truck had gotten the trailing truck turned partway around in the street, but now stalled the engine there, so that the truck was blocking the street in both lanes.

Will ran to the truck, holding a Smith & Wesson 61 Escort automatic pistol out in front of him and yelling so that veins stood out blue in his neck.

"Get it going, goddam it! Get it going!"

The Brigade driver ground the starter frantically, but the engine would not kick in. On the ground, a cop thought the group was sufficiently distracted to go for a revolver that was still in his holster. He drew the gun clumsily, and a hard-looking young man saw the movement. He raised a Webley .32 revolver of his own in a frantic, spastic motion and fired. The cop was struck in the thigh by the hot lead, and fell heavily onto his back, losing his gun as he grabbed, gasping, at his leg.

Several Brigade people turned to stare at the shot cop, realizing the thing had escalated into a higher stage now. A couple of pedestrians down the block retreated fearfully into doorways of businesses, and vehicular traffic had stopped a hundred yards back. Will Jameson turned and saw the bleeding cop, and his face went straight-lined. The driver of the truck was grinding the starter without success. The middle-position truck driver jumped from his vehicle and ran forward through the approaching cops and soldiers, who were now positioning themselves for firing.

"Hold it there!" a policeman yelled. *"You move that truck and we fire on you!"*

"Go to hell!" one of two female Brigade assailants yelled back. To punctuate her remark, she raised a pocket

revolver and fired it off over the heads of the defenders.

The cops and soldiers ducked down behind truck fenders and parked cars, and then an angry guardsman raised his automatic rifle and fired off several shots toward the Brigade. A young man not far behind Will grabbed at his chest and plummeted backwards to the street. He was the one with the .22 rifle, a gun he had never fired before, and he flung it away from him as he went down. It crashed loudly into the side of the police cruiser nearby.

Now there was more white-faced staring, as everybody cast dark glances toward the lifeless figure on the pavement. The Brigade fellow who had been in the truck jumped out with wild eyes.

"I'm getting to hell out of here!" he said loudly, and then he was running toward the rear.

"*You bastards!*" a young Brigade man was yelling now. "*You dirty bastards!*" He began firing off a World War II service automatic, and it banged out raucously in the hot air. The slugs caromed off the metal of the lead truck, but hit nothing.

Will ran toward the truck door. He was going to try to get the vehicle going. But a shot rang out from a policeman's revolver. "*Keep off that truck, we're warning you!*"

Three different crouched Brigade people replied, filling the air with cacophony. The last shot out hit the yelling policeman in the right eye, the hot slug traveling through his head like a lightning bolt and then blowing the back of his head away. Blood and bone sprayed onto the lead truck and a couple of soldiers. Will, not taking notice of what had happened, started up into the cab of the truck. One of the soldiers who had been spattered with the cop's blood rose red-faced and pulled off five

·shots toward Will.

The first shot hit the metal of the truck door beside Will, and the second grazed his left arm, drawing blood. The third thunked into a corner post at the back of the truck, the fourth shattered glass in the windshield above Will's head, and the fifth walloped him in the left shoulder.

Will was spun off his feet, his grip on the door of the vehicle torn loose, and he went hurtling to the ground. He hit there almost under the wheels of the truck, shock welling through his body as he gritted his teeth in raw, ugly pain.

Other soldiers were returning fire now, too, and another Brigade man went down, hit in the neck. Some were already running away, to get out of there before they were either killed or arrested. Will raised up onto an elbow, and saw the soldier who had shot him, standing up and preparing to fire on the Brigade people retreating. Will aimed the Escort automatic at the soldier and fired. The fellow was hit in center chest, jumping backwards as if pulled on a rope. Will knew, by the way he looked as he went down, that he had killed him.

Now a thick-set Brigade man was pulling Will to his feet, firing a gun as he did so. "Come on, Will! You stay here, you might as well have been killed!"

Will was on his feet, light-headed. But he found he could use his legs. A shot came, and narrowly missed his head. He and the other fellow moved behind the truck, and then used it for cover as they limped away from the battle scene, other Brigade people covering them as they went. In just moments they were around a corner and down an alley, piling into an old car with three other Brigade people there. Then the car squealed away in the heat, bumping over a curb as it left the alleyway. No pedestrians stared after it, no defenders were following.

Within an hour, they were holed up with the other survivors in a new secret headquarters on the outskirts of town, in an old abandoned barn.

Their water hi-jack had failed.

A policeman, one of Sherwood Jameson's guardsmen, and two Brigade members were dead.

Several people were wounded, and others had put their lives in danger, and it had all been for nothing.

Later that afternoon, the temperature rose to one hundred and twenty-five degrees.

NINE

The city was electrified by the news of the violent shoot-out between the defenders of the water shipment and the Brigade. Sherwood Jameson, outraged by the deaths of a guardsman and policeman, vowed publicly to find the "nest" of the Brigade "vipers" and roust them out. Jodie, who knew that Will was probably with them, worried at first that he might be one of the dead, then that he could be one of the escaped injured. But nobody knew for sure how many Brigade members had been injured, or who they might be, or cared much.

Jodie spent all the rest of the day of the attempted hi-jack trying to find out something about her brother, but failed. When she reminded Jameson that Will might have been with the attackers, he angrily said that if Will was, and he the colonel found out about it, he would disown Will as his flesh and blood.

A thorough police-and-Guard search occurred that night and the next day, almost house-to-house in the campus area, but they did not find the Brigade. Jodie and Latham had arranged to drive out to see Douglas at work on his fourth well, and Jodie decided to go, anyway, but it was difficult for her to keep her mind on what she was doing. She and Latham went out there—the rig was located about five miles north of town—in late morning, before the temperature got up so high.

Douglas had found water, finally, but not much. His third well had brought up water from the aquifer in dribbling amounts, hardly enough to bother purifying and distributing. Now Douglas was deep in the fourth well.

Latham and Jodie drove up to the rig in bright, hot sun, and a cloud of brown dust rose around them as they stopped the car. They got out wearily and walked over to the rig, where Douglas and a small crew of roughnecks were working. There was a tall derrick, and some heavy-looking equipment beside it, and an open-sided hut where they could get out of the sun. Jodie and Latham went up under the roof of the open hut and found Douglas there. He was dusty and tired-looking, and wore a grim look on his square face.

"How's it going?" Latham asked him. "Anything yet?"

Douglas shook his head. He was dressed in work clothes now, looking very different from the way he had in Dallas. He wore a yellow hard hat, and there was grease on his clothing. Latham had to admire the man. With his millions he had not had to come out there to oversee this operation personally.

"Not a drop," Douglas told them. "I think we're through the aquifer now, frankly. We'll be giving it up tomorrow."

"Oh, damn," Jodie groaned.

"Then what?" Latham asked him.

Douglas shrugged. Behind him, the big drill whirred and hummed as his sweating men tended it. "I don't think there's any point in further drilling in this area, Dr.

Latham. And I can't spend big money running all over the Midwest doing this, without some guarantee by the government. I'm not sure that even if I did, I could bring up much water."

Latham sighed heavily. "I understand, Mr. Douglas."

Jodie shook her auburn head, on which rested a cloth cap with a bill, to keep the sun off. "That water we got from Washington won't last long. It will just relieve the sick, not the healthy who are quickly getting sick."

"We're still getting a little water from well number three, on the edge of town," Douglas said. "That ought to help a little."

Latham grunted. "We need more than a little help. It has to be massive, and soon."

"Well," Douglas said. "I hear Potamkin arrived at Cape Kennedy, and is busy installing his electronic miracle into our satellite there. The launch is scheduled for day after tomorrow. It's just possible something might come of our own little Dozhtbog, isn't it? It's just possible that the Russians might make it rain?"

"I guess anything is possible," Latham said heavily.

Douglas looked at Jodie, and than at Latham. "Unless some miracle occurs here today," he said, "I'll be flying back to Dallas tomorrow."

"Of course," Jodie said. "You have a business to run."

"I see people leaving here now," Douglas went on. "Whole families in cars, vans, trucks. It is better in other places, you know. Maybe you ought to consider getting out while you're still on your feet. Even doctors are getting sick, I hear. Nobody is immune to all this. Businesses are closed all over the city, even most public offices are shut down. If it would ease your consciences, arrange to ship the sick out of here. Leave the city to the

173

sun, the vultures, and the coyotes. In three more weeks it will be a desert here, unless some relief comes."

Jodie regarded Douglas somberly. She knew that everything he said was true, about what was and what would be. It just sounded worse if someone voiced it orally.

"I can't speak for Dr. Latham," she said. "But I just can't leave here, Mr. Douglas. No matter how many people you try to move out, there will be many more that won't go. They'll need medical help, if this goes on. They'll need—comfort as they die." Her voice sounded hollow. She thought of Will, and wondered if he needed her.

Latham glanced over at Jodie. She had a lot of strength, more than Christine had ever shown. He looked back at Douglas with a small smile. "The same goes for me," he said. "My observations, whether they amount to anything or not, have to be made right here, in the center of the furnace."

Douglas made a face, and extended his hand to Latham. "Well. Good luck to you both then, in case I don't see you before I leave."

"Thanks," Latham said. "We just may need it."

When Jodie and Latham got back to town, with Latham going to Jodie's office with her to make a couple of calls there before heading back to the lab at the university, Leah Purcell was there waiting for them, and she was very excited.

"An old friend visited me this morning, at work," Leah said rather breathlessly. "She's one of them, the People's Brigade."

Jodie's mouth fell slightly open. "It's Will!" she said,

after a moment.

Leah nodded. "He's injured, Jodie." Jodie gasped. "But it isn't very bad, I guess. It's a shoulder wound, and no bone is involved. But he hasn't seen a doctor."

"Oh, damn!" Jodie said, her eyes moist.

"Where is he?" Latham said. The three of them were in Jodie's private office, and nobody else was around, at the moment.

"They're all in an old barn, out on the outskirts of town. My friend gave me directions to get there. She says Will doesn't know she called me, Jodie. But he needs sulfa, and blood. She thinks he'll accept it, if you bring it."

Jodie swallowed hard. "Well, I've got to go! I'll get it all together immediately!"

"I'm going, too," Leah said.

"So am I," Latham told them. "Those people have guns out there. I'm not letting you two do this alone."

Jodie hesitated. "All right, Mark. Let's get going."

It took only a half-hour to get ready to leave. Jodie crammed medicine and whole blood units and some paraphernalia into two black bags, and they all piled into his rented car, and he drove out to the area described by the calling Brigade member. It was an area that had at one time been farmland but was now encroached upon by the city. Latham drove to a place on a small side street where an abandoned house sat fifty yards from the road, falling down and overgrown by weeds. He pulled up to the curb there at Leah's direction.

"This is it. Back beyond those trees is the barn somewhere, out of sight of the road. That's where they are."

Jodie started to get out of the car, and Latham stopped her. "Wait!" he said sharply.

175

Jodie hesitated, and a police patrol car drove past them. One of the two cops looked toward them casually, but the car kept going. Latham waited until it turned a corner back toward a main boulevard. "Okay," he said then.

The three of them approached the house slowly, cautiously, because Latham knew there would be a sentry of some kind there. There was. Just as they reached the shade of a withered oak tree in the high-weeded, acrid-smelling front yard, a young man showed himself on the porch.

"Hold it!" he called out to them.

Latham stopped Jodie with his hand. Leah had already frozen, seeing the gun in the young man's waistband.

"You're on private property, you can't come up here!"

Jodie broke loose from Latham's hold, and stepped forward. "I'm Jodie Jameson," she said. "Will's sister."

The fellow scowled down at her. His gaze left her, traveled to Leah and then to Latham, hung on Latham a long moment. "What the hell are you doing here?"

"We know that Will is here," Jodie said. "We want to help him."

The Brigade man's eyes revealed anger. "Who told you he's here?"

Jodie glanced at Leah. "A friend," she said.

The fellow drew the dark automatic pistol from his waist, and let it hang loosely in his right hand, at his side. He came down the rickety, squeaky steps of the porch, and looked them over. "What do you expect to do for him?"

"Give him blood," Jodie said. "And medicate him."

"Is that medical stuff in those bags?" the fellow said. He pointed to the bags Latham and Jodie were carrying.

"That's right," Jodie said. She put the bag down and opened it up, and Latham did likewise. The fellow glanced into them. Jodie then showed him her I.D. "You see, I am his sister."

"That doesn't mean a hell of a lot," the fellow growled. "A soldier under his father's command just damn near killed him. I don't think Will thinks a whole lot of his family."

Jodie's face clouded over. "Do you want to let him die?" she said with a breaking voice. "That's what will happen, if he doesn't get some medical help shortly."

The fellow paused, then sighed. "Okay, I'll take you in. But you'd better be on the level."

They marched through two hundred yards of high weeds behind the house, past some dead trees, and the barn came into sight. It had some boards off, but it had a roof, and was in better shape than the house. Farmers almost always took better care of their barns than their own shelters, Jodie thought. As they came up close to the barn, a door opened and two young men came out. One carried a pistol, the other the shotgun that had been at the attempted hi-jacking.

"What the hell is this?" the broad fellow carrying the shotgun said in a very belligerent voice.

"It's Will's sister," the sentry said. "They want to give Will some blood."

"Jesus Christ!" the other fellow said, the one beside the man with the shotgun.

"A friend called me," Leah blurted out. "She just wanted to help Will."

"She?" the shotgun-carrier grated out.

Suddenly a girl emerged from the barn behind him, a brown-haired young woman dressed in fatigue clothing

177

and a gunbelt. She was slim, pale-faced. "It was me, Rick," she said quietly. "I called Leah."

Leah smiled at her. "Hi, Sherry."

The shotgun man glared toward Sherry for a moment. "Are you out of your mind?"

"Somebody had to do something!" she said. "He's still losing blood!"

The fellow turned back to the intruders. "Get inside," he ordered them. "Now."

Latham gave him a sober look as they filed past him and into the barn. Inside it was cooler and darker, and there was a smell of hay and rotting wood. There was a lot of debris on the dirt floor, and members had put down sleeping bags and litters to sleep on, in the main area of the building, and in the several stalls along one side. The three were taken to one of those stalls, as other members stood and stared at the newcomers, with surly faces.

"In there," the shotgun man said. "He's in there."

They looked into the stall, which had been cleaned up fairly well, and saw Will lying on a cot in there, his head propped up by pillows against a rear wall. When he saw them, his eyes widened slightly.

"Jodie!" he muttered. "Leah!"

The three of them went into the private enclosure, and a young man who had been sitting on a stool beside Will's cot excused himself with a dark mumbling. Jodie and Leah went and stood beside the cot, and Will glared up at them.

"How the hell did you get here?" he said harshly to Jodie.

"Somebody called Leah. We were told you needed help. We brought it to you, Will."

"I don't want your help," Will said. He had no shirt

on, and there was a bloody bandage over a wound up by his shoulder. It was just rags torn from clothing. "Now please get to hell out of here."

Jodie had sat down on the stool to open up the bags, and now Leah knelt beside Will, close to his face. "Listen to me, Will Jameson. We risked our lives to come in here. Now, damn it, we're going to fix you up whether you like it or not. We'll tie you down if we have to!"

Will looked at Leah, and his face softened slightly. He turned to Jodie, who was getting a pint of blood ready to inject into him. "Oh, hell," he said wearily. His handsome face was pale, and he wore a smaller bandage on his arm, where the shallow wound was located.

Jodie's eyes had moistened up again. "How did you get involved in something like this, Will? Using guns against the police—against the soldiers who came here to protect us?"

Will's eyes filled with a sudden hatred. "They fired on us!" he said bitterly. "We only defended ourselves!"

Jodie looked him in the eye. "They only defended our water," she said.

"Oh, Jesus," he said, looking away.

Jodie rigged the blood, put the needle in his arm and taped it there, fastened the hose up, hung the blood on a nail above Will's head. Then she and Leah began treating Will's wound. Sulfa was applied, and clean bandages. Jodie saw that with a little rest and the blood she brought, Will would heal quickly. He would not talk to them during the treatment. Leah kept up a monologue about Kravitz and the Russians, reporting to Will. The fellow with the shotgun looked in on them. Jodie finally unhooked the first bottle of blood and connected a second one.

"There. I think this will do it," she said. "But I'm not a doctor, Will. You ought to be in a hospital. Will you at least come to our clinic with me?"

"You know better than to ask that," he replied. He already looked better.

"Did you—shoot anyone, Will?" Leah asked him fearfully.

Will glanced at her. Latham noticed the pain flicker into his face as he replied. "Yes," Will said quietly. "The guardsman. I killed him."

Jodie felt a lurch inside her chest, as if a wild something were trying to get out of there. "Oh, no!" she whispered.

"Under what circumstances?" Latham asked him.

Will looked toward him hostilely. "We were just trying to get away. He was going to shoot more of us. I had to stop him."

Leah turned away, a hand at her mouth.

"If you turn yourself in," Latham said, "it could make a difference. We'll get you a good lawyer, Will. When this is all over, there will be a tendency to be lenient with lawbreakers during this ugliness."

Will cast a wild look at Latham. "When it's over? Don't you know yet, professor? This isn't going to get over! We're all going to die in this Russian-made furnace! Everybody that stays here!" He paused for a half-moment. "But some of us are going out with dignity. You can count on that."

"Oh, God, Will!" Jodie moaned.

There was a sound behind them, and the fellow with the shotgun was there. He was a beefy, pink-faced young man with very hard eyes and a bristle of beard on his square chin.

"We can't let them leave here," he said to Will.

Latham and Jodie turned to him. Leah had buried her head in her hands. "What?" Jodie said.

"You heard me, lady. You know where we are now. You think we're going to trust you to keep your mouths shut when you get back to that ivory tower of yours?"

Jodie rose from the stool. "We have no intention of telling the authorities where this place is." She turned to Latham, and Leah. They both acknowledged their agreement with the statement by shaking their heads.

"Hell," the beefy fellow said, "you *are* the authorities. This girl's father is the mayor, and yours is that bastard that brought those troops here!"

Will regarded the fellow with a stony look, unemotional, impassive.

"They're also the sister and close friend of Will," Latham told him. "You think they want soldiers busting in here with automatic weapons?"

"I don't know what they want," the pink-faced, brown-haired man said.

"You can't hold us here," Jodie said. "Dr. Latham here is working on ways to try to end this drought. I'm needed at the Health Department, and Leah helps keep track of what this hellish weather is doing from day to day."

"And none of you make a damned bit of difference," the fellow said bitterly. "What's going to happen is inevitable, now. We're all going to fry here, and there's nothing the Russians or you people can do about it. But we're sure as hell not going to fry in jail."

Will lowered himself to a lower position on the cot, and let out a long, ragged breath. "Let them go, Rick," he said very quietly.

The beefy fellow frowned deeply toward Will. "What?"

Will met his gaze with a hard one. "You heard me. They're not here to make us trouble. They won't turn us in."

There was a long moment of hard staring between the two. Finally, the one called Rick turned angrily away. "You're crazy as hell, Will. But we owe you. They can leave when they want to."

When the fellow was gone, Leah turned to Will. "Let me come back in a couple of days, Will. I can—"

"*No!*" Will said harshly, glaring at her with a look she had never seen before. He turned to Jodie. "Things are different now, they can never be like they were. Not for any of us. Please, get out and don't try to come back. I can't be responsible for your safety, if you do."

His face told Jodie that there was nothing more to say to him. Not at that time. With a mumbled farewell from her and Leah, the threesome left the stall and the barn.

They were allowed to return to their car without incident.

In ten minutes, they were gone from the neighborhood.

Both Jodie and Leah were sobered by that visit to Will, but the younger Leah did not quite know how to handle all the fears and frustrations that now gripped her. That evening she had dinner at Jodie's place with Jodie and Latham, and they noticed how very quiet she was. Jodie tried to think of something optimistic to tell her about Will's situation, but she could not truthfully do so. Will had killed a man in the commission of a felony. Even if he healed well from the bullet wound and survived the blast-furnace drought, he had that awful responsibility to face up to. Jodie had called her father in early evening to tell him that Will was all right, and when he deduced that Jodie knew where the Brigade headquarters were and would not tell him, he was furious. But Jodie said she had pledged her word. To help Will.

When Leah left Jodie's she drove to Rawdon Field to see how Ed Keefer had fared without her for most of the day. She knew he would be at the Weather Service station late, and wanted to give him some last-minute help if it was needed. She saw a few young men hanging around the outside of the terminal building as she entered, but thought nothing of it. Upstairs in the weather facility, Keefer was just about ready to go home. He had just taped a no-change weather forecast that sounded almost exactly like many previous ones, and the work had depressed him. Leah did not mention Will to him, but she could not get Will off her mind. She checked some ground maps while Keefer prepared to leave, and then they locked up, leaving only a night-shift technician on duty.

When they got down to the parking lot, which was dark and deserted, they walked to their cars together. But when they arrived at Leah's car, discussing the three-day forecast, suddenly a half-dozen men appeared from the shadows of other cars.

"Hey, weatherman! Where you think you're going?"

Leah and Keefer looked up to see themselves suddenly surrounded by hard, leering faces. But these were not youths, such as had molested Latham and Jodie at the supermarket. These were men in their twenties and thirties, a couple of them with farm work clothes on.

Leah squinted down at the faces, but did not recognize any of them. Neither did Keefer.

"What's for tomorrow, mister weatherman? Snow

183

and colder?"

Keefer put a hand on Leah's arm, his thin face full of concern. "What is it you want?" he said warily.

A brawny fellow moved closer to them, looking Leah over. "We hear some nasty things about you, Keefer. It's all over the county. How you knew about this drought in May, and didn't do nothing, you and your Washington friends. We hear you could have done the same as the Russians, and saved all this misery. Saved our farms. But didn't want to spend the money."

Keefer laughed hollowly. "That's absurd. The Weather Service has never experimented with radio-emission weather control. Not before this Russian-American effort. Your information is incorrect. Now, if you'll excuse us."

But nobody moved. Hard, angry faces crowded in on them.

"You sold us out, Keefer," the brawny fellow growled, standing his ground. "We know you knew what was coming. We also know you could have done something about it. Anything."

Keefer's voice hardened. "We predict the weather three days in advance," he said evenly. "And even then we're often wrong. Sometimes we cooperate in a cloud-seeding project. When there are clouds. That's the extent of our knowledge, boys. Believe me, you're giving us more credit than we have due."

"We ain't giving you no credit, mister!" a voice came.

"Now, please," Keefer said. "We're very tired, and want to get home."

Another fellow came up close, a tall, stringy-haired one with a scar on his chin. He was a farm laborer who had been laid off. "Look, guys. This here is the mayor's daughter with him."

Leah drew back a half-step, and now fear was crowding into her chest. "Please," she said.

"Well, I'll be damned," the brawny man said. "It looks like we caught two snakes in one bag."

He came up to Leah, and touched her lightly but ominously on the cheek. Keefer reached and shoved his arm away. "All right, boys. You've had your fun. Leave Miss Purcell alone. If you want to talk with me, I'll—"

The brawny fellow swung a ham of a fist into Keefer's face. Bone snapped in Keefer's nose, and he went stumbling against Leah's car, banging loudly against it there, before slumping to a sitting position on the pavement.

"Oh!" Leah gasped.

"We were just going to teach you a lesson to report to your Washington cronies," the brawny man said to Keefer. "But now it looks like we can let the girl into our little class, too."

"Yeah," the tall man grinned. "Let's start with her."

The tall man reached out and grabbed Leah by the arm, and she broke loose and fell against the car. *"No!"* she called out. *"Help! Help us, someone!"*

The tall man was joined by the brawny one and another, and one went and stood over Keefer, just in case. But Keefer was dazed, sitting there numbly with blood on his chin from a cut lip.

Leah tore loose from the brawny fellow now, and her sheer blouse tore down the front, and her ample cleavage was exposed to view in a tiny bra.

Suddenly the whole mood of the attack changed.

Every assailant was now staring at Leah's partially-naked body.

Leah tried to clutch the cloth to her. The tall fellow made a gutteral laugh in his throat, reached to her, and tore the blouse the rest of the way off. Leah jumped visibly, and a wail began in her throat. The brawny fellow grabbed at the bra, and yanked hard. It clung to her body in places, but then it came off, too. Leah's breasts bounced nicely for them as she tried to break away, crying in low sobs now. "Oh, God, please!"

"Leave her alone!" Keefer was saying thickly. "*Leave her alone!*"

The fellow standing over Keefer gave him a hard kick in the thigh, and Keefer yelled aloud.

Now all eyes, though, were on Leah. The brawny fellow exchanged looks with the tall one, and then the brawny one grabbed Leah's arm. She struggled, but he was strong. He dragged her to the end of the car, and threw her to the pavement between the end of that car and the next one. Keefer saw her skirt go up to expose her full thighs, and he heard the low, moaning protests from her as more cloth was ripped, and then a rather loud outcry from her, and then heavy, grating breathing by the brawny man. The others stood around and watched as best they could, grinning harshly. In a few long moments, the tall fellow began unfastening his trousers impatiently.

"Come on, give the rest of us a turn." Breathlessly.

The brawny man rose off her finally, and the tall one knelt over her with eagerness. Keefer tried to get up, and fell back against the pavement. He could see the tall man mounting her. Then the sound of a car, and headlights in his eyes. Behind the lights was a jeep.

"It's the goddam Guard!"

"They see us, let's get out of here!"

The tall fellow was up, staring. Then everybody was running across the lot and into shadows.

"Hey, you people! Halt!"

The last man kicked Keefer hard in the side, and Keefer yelled out in pain again. Then guardsmen were out of the jeep and running over, automatic rifles at ready, boots clattering on concrete. Two of them ran after the assailants, and a couple of others stopped to examine Keefer and Leah. When they saw Leah, they stared hard at her. She still lay between the cars, skirt up around her waist, bosom bare. There was blood running from her nose, and bruises were turning blue on her face, chest, thighs.

"Jesus," one of them said.

"Get an ambulance," Ed Keefer gritted out from where he lay. "Get an ambulance immediately. And see that she gets to the Health Department infirmary."

"I'll go call in," the nearest one said heavily.

TEN

"Leah," Jodie said softly. "It's me, Jodie."

Jodie sat at the side of the white hospital bed, where Leah lay staring toward the ceiling. At the foot of the bed stood Tom Purcell, his square face grief-stricken. Mrs. Purcell had gone out into the corridor, because she did not want her daughter to see her crying. Also in the corridor were Mark Latham and Colonel Sherwood Jameson, comforting Mrs. Purcell. Ed Keefer was in a long ward at the other end of the basement infirmary, with a broken nose and two cracked ribs. He had wanted to go on home, but his doctor had insisted that he stay the night.

Leah turned to stare at Jodie. She had not spoken a word since they had brought her in. Her face was washed off now, but the bloody nose was now swollen, and the bruises were more pronounced. She now opened her mouth and spoke for the first time. "Jodie."

Jodie's eyes watered up. "Yes, Leah. You're at the clinic now, and we're going to take good care of you."

Leah swallowed before she spoke. "They—they threw me down. Then they—"

"We know," Purcell interrupted her. "Don't talk about it, baby."

Leah focused on him. "I'm sorry, Daddy."

"Oh, Christ," he said unevenly, turning from her.

"You have nothing to be sorry for, Leah," Jodie said. "You're going to be all right, too, we've checked you out. It was a good thing Dad's men arrived when they did."

"Is Ed—?"

"He's all right," Jodie told her. "He's right here, too."

"It wasn't Will's people," Leah said throatily. "I know that."

"I'm glad to hear that, Leah," Jodie said.

"Those goddam animals!" Purcell mumbled under his breath.

"I don't want—Will to know," Leah added.

Jodie touched her arm. "Whatever you say."

A nurse came into the room, glanced at Leah. She turned to Tom Purcell. "Mr. Mayor, the colonel is going down to talk with Ed Keefer, and he wants to know if you want to be there."

Purcell nodded. "Yes, okay." He turned to Leah. "I'll stop back before we leave, baby."

Leah nodded, and the nurse and Purcell left together. Jodie caught Leah's dull gaze, and smiled for her. "Now, listen to me, woman to woman, Leah."

Leah held her gaze weakly.

"We're going to get past this. Aren't we?"

Leah stared at her.

"We're not going to let this hurt us. You're going to be strong, for you and for all of us."

Leah hesitated, then nodded. "All right, Jodie."

"It's like a car crash, or falling down a stair," Jodie said. "It's a crazy accident, Leah, that will never happen again. And you're no less for it, no more than if you'd broken an arm. Do you see what I'm saying?"

Another hesitation. "Yes."

"Now. Can I get you some juice? It will make you heal faster."

"All right, Jodie."

Later, when Jodie left the clinic for the night, Leah had fallen asleep, and was resting well.

Latham went home with Jodie that night, and they sat for a long time together there, saying very little. Then Latham left, only kissing her goodnight. Jodie seemed more reserved with him, more withdrawn.

It was the next morning that Latham got the surprise call from Christine.

Christine had heard that Latham had been called to Wichita to study the killer drought, and she was calling to find out if he was all right. She had never sounded friendlier, or more caring. Things were getting bad in San Francisco, too, but nothing like Kansas. She told him that she had put her lawyer off, and that she wanted them to get together again. Latham told her that he had to stay where he was, that he was needed there. Christine parried that he could work anywhere, and asked him to join her in San Francisco for a while, until it was clear what was going to happen. She felt alone, and afraid.

Latham rather liked the plea for a reunion, he had to admit. Christine was suddenly like her old self, before they were married, when she had been solicitous and warm toward him. It reminded him of old, good times with her. But he advised her that he could not leave Wichita with a clear conscience, not until some relief had come through one source or another. He told her that the radio satellite would be launched at Cape Kennedy the next day, and then it would be known very quickly whether the Russians had accomplished anything. He had to be there when that happened.

Christine hung up petulant, and Latham sat beside the telephone for a long time after her voice was gone from the other end. Just hearing from the world outside of Kansas was cheering to him. Sometimes it seemed as if that hellfire he had plunged himself in was all there was, that the whole Earth was afire.

Emmet Douglas left that day, with one well still bringing up a small amount of water, just enough to help relieve the sick. The temperature soared to over one twenty-five, and several deaths due to heat were reported. A high wind came up at noon, and blew brown dust into the city, clogging machinery, blowing into cracks and crevices. Several cars stalled on the streets in the dust storm, and dehydrated dogs that now roamed in packs slunk into dark corners and whined.

The following morning, Latham, Sprague, Jodie and Purcell all gathered at the university to watch the televised launching of the U.S. satellite, which had been dubbed some unpronounceable Aztec name for their god of water. Jodie went there directly from seeing Leah at the clinic, and Leah was up and moving around now.

In a private room in the same building with Sprague's lab, the four of them sat around the table model TV, two fans on them, and watched the countdown that the entire nation was focused on. The camera zeroed in on the steaming underside of the rocket, and then the warhead—the capsule that would orbit the electronic mechanism put together under the supervision of Mazurov. Potamkin was there himself somewhere, they all knew, worrying over last-minute details, probably getting in the way of the rocket experts. At McConnell, Mazurov and Kravitz were monitoring the whole thing on sophisticated NASA equipment, keeping their fingers crossed, since so many small things could go wrong at the last moment.

But none did. As the four watched in the small private office, the missile lifted off without a hitch or flaw, the camera following its soaring flight into the blue, hot sky of the Cape.

"Well," Sprague remarked, leaning back on his chair. "It looks like a perfect launch."

"I think that's at least one thing we know more about than the Russkies," Purcell said, from beside Sprague. He was slumped on his chair in a way Jodie had never seen him do before, looking extremely weary. Leah's assault and rape had been almost too much for him, in the midst of all his other current troubles. His wife was under sedation at home, and he worried about her, too.

"Wouldn't it be something," Jodie heard herself saying, "if the Russians pull it off?"

Latham looked over at her, and saw the hope in her lovely face. Even Jodie now was showing signs of wear under the ugly heat. She was getting fatigue lines in her face, and her skin was losing its healthy color. There were certain lights she found herself in, Latham mused, that actually made her look even more beautiful than before, with the pale skin and the auburn hair. But he knew that she was deeply fatigued and tense, and he worried about her.

"I hope to God they do make it," he said soberly, "without hurting the environment further. I'd give my career for it, if they could just show me I'm wrong, that it will really work."

Sprague went and snapped the TV off, and then heaved himself back into the armchair he had risen from. "Well, we won't have long to wait now. The radio signals will begin tomorrow, I understand, with Mazurov pushing the buttons from McConnell. They'll be sent out for several days, and then the rain is supposed to start." He gave an acid little laugh in his throat.

Purcell sighed. "If this does fail, Hollis, where the hell are we? Where does failure leave us?"

"It leaves us," Sprague said, "in a bad way." His silver hair was sticking out over his ears rather wildly, and his horn-rimmed glasses had slipped halfway down on his nose.

"This one well Douglas left us with just isn't sufficient to make much difference here," Latham said, "and I suspect it's going to go dry on us soon. Paula Betancourt has asked for further shipments from outside, but the prospects look slim. Nobody has enough water to be giving it away."

"I thought Paula was coming over with you?" Purcell said to Jodie.

"She was," Jodie said. "She isn't feeling well, Tom. She won't admit it, but I think she's getting sick. It's her stomach."

Purcell shook his head. "Several doctors have come down with various ailments. Businesses aren't functioning, and municipal government is grinding to a halt. Frankly, it's frightening. We need somebody around who can fight back."

Latham grunted. He, too, looked tired, slumped on his chair. He had not gotten much sleep, and there were dark places under his brown eyes, and he had lost over ten pounds since arriving in Wichita. "For all we've accomplished at the university here, I'm beginning to think you could have done just as well without us,

Mr. Mayor."

"You brought Emmet Douglas here, you and your College Hill team," Purcell said. "Number Three isn't bringing much water up, I know, but every little bit helps."

"How's your evacuation plan coming along, Tom?" Sprague asked. "Are you making any headway on it?"

"A little," Purcell said. "There are planes available to fly people out of here, if they'll go. Northern New England and eastern Canada are still relatively unaffected, and a number of communities have offered to take our people on a refugee basis. The sick should go first, of course. The trouble is, there's been a poor response here. People just don't want to leave. Most of them that would, have already. Of course, if the Russian project fails, there may be a sudden voluntary exodus. If that happens, we want to be able to implement it."

"I'm just afraid," Sprague said, "that locals won't have the impulse, now, to move from their homes. This terrible heat drains their energy, and their will. Stoicism sets in, the willingness to let the fates take control."

"I know what you mean," Jodie said. "We're seeing that in our patients. It can become infectious, too."

"Well," Purcell said, "I'm as afraid of anarchy as anything. Your father is having his hands full now, Jodie, I understand. Every night there's a new clash with troops or police by roving lawbreakers. It's not just here, either. In Omaha, mobs have taken control of the streets. There have been violent confrontations in Kansas City, Houston, Albuquerque. There are even riots in New York, now, and in L.A., as the drought worsens."

"Western Europe is drying up, too," Sprague commented heavily. "The Russian embassy was attacked in

Paris this morning."

Latham rose. "I guess sitting and talking about it won't help the situation much," he said. "I'm taking a small balloon up this evening, to make some personal low-atmosphere observations. I have a lot to do to get ready."

Purcell rose, too. "Keep at it, Mark. You and Hollis are our only ace in the hole."

Sprague made a wry face. "I would rather be anywhere, at the moment, than in such an unenviable position," he said quietly.

When the group split up, Jodie met Latham alone in a corridor outside the lab, and asked him about his balloon ascent. She wanted to just be near him for a few minutes, his proximity seemed to quiet her inside. Also, she knew that he was down emotionally, and she wanted to show some interest in his evening project.

"Why are you going up with the balloon?" she asked him.

"I've been up on the big Skyhooks on occasion," Latham said. "I find I can get more information if I'm with the balloon, than if we just send instruments up. I'm going to use the same technique on this low-level flight. I'll be in a sport balloon that I borrowed from a local club yesterday. Actually, I'm looking forward to it. It will be a welcome break from the lab. It might even be a few degrees cooler up there tonight."

"Where does this happen, and when?" she asked him.

"We'll get it ready at either Rawdon Field or out at Beech Landing Field, probably Beech because it's less trafficked. I expect to make the ascent at about dusk, say eight. The flight will take a couple of hours, and I hope to come down on a farm near Eldorado. There will be people there waiting to bring me and the balloon back."

Jodie's cobalt eyes gave a small twinkle for the first time in days. "I'd like to go with you."

Latham frowned slightly at her, through a curious smile. "Have you ever been up in a balloon?"

She shook her auburn head. "No, I haven't. But that doesn't disqualify me entirely, does it?"

Latham's frown dissolved away. "Of course not. I'll have to give you a few instructions about landing, but you should be all right. I had thought of taking an assistant along, to help read instruments. You can be of some help."

"Great," Jodie smiled. "When should I be here to leave?"

"Come about six and we'll have a short cafeteria meal together," he grinned at her. "If you can survive that, you can fly a balloon."

"It's a date," she said.

Jodie visited Leah twice that afternoon at the clinic, and Leah had been up and on her feet for most of the day. But Jodie learned that she had hardly eaten anything at all, and she seemed to have no interest at all in returning to her parents' house.

That disturbed Jodie, because physically there was not that much wrong with Leah. She would heal completely in a few more days, from the cuts and bruises. But deep inside her she was not really responding to that physical recovery, not yet. Jodie supposed it would all take time. Time to like the world again, and to be unafraid of it. In the circumstances of the drought, that would be more difficult than if the attack had come in some other period.

There was no way to know how Will was doing. But, Jodie knew that with a little luck he would be improving with every day that passed. She wondered if the Brigade had moved to another location, now that she and Leah and Latham had been there. If she had been in charge out there, she would have insisted on moving out of the barn, she imagined. Will's allowing them to leave the place had constituted a real danger to their security.

Jameson was very stiff-backed with Jodie now. He could not understand her reluctance to lead him to the Brigade's headquarters, since they represented the hard core of trouble-making, to the Guard. Even though Will was one of them, Jameson considered them the enemy, a force that continually placed the lives of his troops in danger. For his daughter to protect such a force, because a promise had been extorted from her, seemed to Jameson stupid and somewhat immoral. Suddenly it seemed that Jodie was in league with her recalcitrant brother, and that failure on Jodie's part was almost more unbearable to Jameson than his son's bearing arms against Jameson's own troops, because Jameson had given up on Will a long time ago, but his expectations in Jodie had always been very high.

That evening, Jodie and Latham had a rather tasteless meal at the almost-nonfunctioning cafeteria on campus, and then drove out to Beech Landing Field together, where assistants were just inflating a big orange-and-red balloon with hot air. By the time Jodie and Latham got some small pieces of equipment out of the car and walked over to the concrete apron where the balloon was moored, floating above their heads like a silent prayer against the heat, the assistants had the polyethylene aircraft ready to fly. Jodie preceded Latham up into the gondola, climbing into it over a light metal ladder. There was a head-high brazier within the gondola or fiberglass basket of the balloon, where a fire was burning and could be turned up or down with a simple control. There were stacked sandbags of ballast, a fuel tank, and meteorological equipment crammed into the basket with her and Latham. On the superstructure for the brazier were controls for valving off the heated air at the crown of the balloon's envelope or bag.

The sun had just set, thankfully, when Latham's assistants released the mooring lines and the balloon began floating upward into the evening sky.

Jodie was exhilarated by the ascent. It was nothing like flying in an airplane, with the noise and speed and vibration and claustrophobia. It was quite beautiful, she thought. Up and up the craft rose, with Latham firing the hot air occasionally, and adjusting controls. Jodie watched the ground and trees recede from them, as if converging on themselves in an adjustable wide-angle lens. The sky seemed to stay light longer as they rose upward, because their horizon kept widening. It was a barren scene that unfolded to them around the airfield and the city, but somehow it seemed less ominous with distance. Jodie was also surprised to learn that with every thousand feet of height the air cooled down a few degrees, until it became quite comfortably cool by the time Latham leveled the balloon off.

It was dark by then, and Latham turned on running lights on the sides of the gondola. He had chosen a route where no other aircraft were expected, so he figured it was reasonably safe for them. It would have been completely safe in daylight, but Latham wanted to find out what was happening at that level when the sun was gone.

They floated lazily on the breeze now, in a generally eastward direction. Latham set his instruments, and

Jodie helped, following his specific instructions.

"We're measuring sulfur dioxide, hydrocarbons, nitrogen oxides," he told her as he worked a control on an instrument attached to the interior wall of the gondola. "All these factors can be used in what we call Euler Equations," he continued. "Different atmospheric-level readings allow us to improve the accuracy of our predictions. It's all part of what we call the Caltech or analog method."

"Something tells me the behavior of bacteria is easier to predict than the antics of the circumpolar vortex," Jodie said, leaning over the waist-high gunwale of the gondola into the moonlit blackness below. "I think I'm glad I picked public health for my career, rather than meteorology."

"Everything is understandable if you have enough data at your disposal," Latham said. He came over and leaned on the gondola's bulkhead beside her. "The trouble is, this science was for too long in the hands of the numerical-prediction forecasters, like Kravitz and your Ed Keefer. By the end of the century, we'll be into a whole new era of weather understanding. That will probably mean control, and events like this one will no longer be possible. If we last that long, of course."

They drifted along. The night and the silence enveloped them. It was like being in a bat cave, hundreds of feet underground. Except that occasionally, far down below, a yellow light shone up at them, like a winking eye in the darkness. It was a farmhouse, or a crossroads service station, or maybe a lamp post. Jodie felt the tension drain from her slowly, replaced by a tranquility that was deep and pervading. The problems of those ground-dwellers far below were no longer hers, she was soaring above them and was untouched by them. She knew they were still there, intellectually, but she was not emotionally involved with them.

Also, if they looked up, they had a look at the stars that just was not possible from the ground. The heavens were sprinkled with twinkling lights from horizon to horizon; the moon with all its craters and mountains hung in the eastern sky brilliantly. All of that, too, contributed to a feeling of removal from the world's petty problems, a separation from them that was more than physical.

"I'll never forget this night as long as I live," Jodie finally said to him. The only sounds except for her voice were the low hissing of the pneumatic-torch fire and the wind rustling against the envelope of the balloon.

"I know what you mean," Latham said. "It's particularly beautiful in the middle of what we've been through. I'm glad you thought of coming, Jodie." He looked over at her. "It seems as if I've been through more with you in the past few weeks than I have with Christine in all the time I've known her."

Jodie met his gaze. She could barely make out his features in the moonlight because of the shadow from the bulbous bag that hung over them. She wondered whether Latham were really finished with his wife, emotionally, or whether he would soon be going back with her when she pulled the right strings. He had not said that it was final between them. He had only hinted at it. Jodie had no hold on him, she knew, despite their intimacy.

"You ought to call her and see if she's all right," Jodie said to him.

Latham looked over at her. "She called me, Jodie."

Jodie's face showed surprise.

"I don't know why I didn't tell you."

"It was none of my business," she said, turning away to look out over the edge of the gondola again.

"The hell it wasn't," he said. "I just didn't want you to—have it to think about."

"Christine is your wife, Mark," she said a little stiffly. "You don't have to explain any contact you may have with her, you know that. I have no claim on you."

"Oh, Jodie," he said softly. "I honest-to-God don't know my feelings toward Christine. But I know how I feel toward you, at this moment, on this special night."

Jodie turned and met his gaze, and wanted him more than she ever had. It was the caressing coolness in her face, and the stars, and the silent moonlight.

"I know what you mean, Mark," she whispered. It seemed almost a sacrilege to speak aloud. She looked out over the dark void.

"You do things to me inside that are almost unbearable," he said. "You tantalize me with every look, every tilt of your chin, each movement of your body. I want you every night, Jodie, I lie awake conscious of the great vacuum beside me, the void created by your absence. The frustration of deprivation."

"I feel the same thing," she said breathlessly. The cool wind touched her face, her body. The stars floated lazily past.

She felt his touch on her back, and it moved down onto the sweeping curve of her below her waist. She gasped lightly, and turned to face him. He pulled her to him forcefully and kissed her, his mouth hungry for hers.

It lasted a long, beautiful moment, and when it was done, Jodie was breathing audibly, like an underwater swimmer just breaking the surface.

"Tonight is forever," he said almost inaudibly.

"When we get back, let's go to your place and—"

Jodie put a slender finger to his lips. Then she reached and pulled the skirt of her thin dress up, drew the small piece of cloth at her hips down over her long thighs. It fell to the floor of the gondola, and she kicked it away. She had not had time to go home earlier, for a more practical pair of jeans, but now she was very content with that omission. She felt more feminine for him, and she was more physically available.

"It would be—different, down there," she whispered. "The mood would be gone."

Latham understood, and was grateful for her insight. He turned and adjusted a control to keep the craft on level flight, and then looked into her eyes that reflected the mystery of the night sky.

His hands moved gently over her soft contours. "Oh, Jesus, Jodie."

There was a moment of fumbling then, as she waited breathless, leaning back against the gunwale and shrouds. Then she felt the silky movement upward of her skirt again, and the new, hot presence, hard and questing against her, and before she really expected it, the full, insistent entry.

"Oh!" she cried out from her low diaphragm, in a hoarse voice. "Oh, Mark!"

Then there was the fiery caressing inside her, pregnant with heated promise, and the gossamer fingers of the wind on her skin, and the stars' wild flirtation with her in their cartwheel explosion across the black heavens, all symphonically orchestrated just for her. She gripped the shrouds beside her head, and she felt his strong arms pulling him deeply into her, and finally she gave herself absolutely to the raw, unbridled power of his passion.

ELEVEN

For the next several days Yuri Mazurov and NASA attempted to play God with the weather. The upper atmosphere was bombarded with complex, super-powerful radio emissions designed to influence the route of the most massive and powerful force on Earth, the ubiquitous, deity-like jet stream.

Wichita, meanwhile, suffered. Citizens were now succumbing in larger numbers to the intense heat, and to other causes aggravated by the heat. People began to fight for water. There was violence in the long clinic lines where water was being doled out selectively to those who could prove they had none. Fire hydrants had long ago been capped, to prevent their being opened by the lawless, and flow restrictors had now been installed on faucets in areas of the city where flow was inequitably high. Fire trucks and dairy tankers stood outside the hospitals and the Health Department, pumping emergency water supplies they had carried from the reservoir. The reservoir itself was down to a ten-days supply. When that was gone, people would begin dying of thirst in large numbers.

Even the massive water-cooled computers of NASA and the university were in danger of meltdown and malfunction, despite the high priority given to the one at McConnell. If that happened, even the Russian attempt to manipulate the jet stream would be aborted.

The President had been in touch with a number of foreign governments for help, and there had been quick response. Russia, feeling the responsibility for the disaster despite public denials, was getting several plane-loads of water together, and China was doing the same thing. Also pledging help were Brazil, Mexico, Canada, Great Britain, and a couple of Scandinavian countries. The problem was time, and no water had as yet arrived from any foreign source. At least one Russian plane-load was scheduled to come to Wichita, and one from Mexico City. But red tape was delaying supply.

On the second day of the Great Experiment at McConnell, with Wichita, Kansas and the entire country holding their collective breaths for hoped-for results, Christine Latham arrived quite unexpectedly at Midcontinental Airport. Latham, immersed in his meteorological calculations and caught up very deeply with Jodie, was stunned when he heard Christine's voice on the phone and realized she was in town.

"My God, Christine. What are you doing here in Kansas? Do you know what it's like here?"

"*I'm finding out fast, Mark,*" Christine told him. "*But I just had to see you. I've been—very lonesome in San Francisco.*"

Her tone was almost plaintive, and that was very unusual for Christine. Latham reluctantly told her he would come and get her at the airport, and tried to keep the reluctance out of his voice. She had picked the worst possible moment in time to renew old affections, reestablish old intimacies. But Christine was his wife,

204

they had strong bonds between them despite their differences and troubles. Latham could not just send her back to the coast without seeing her, hearing what she had to say to him.

They avoided talking about themselves on the ride into town from the airport. Christine was dismayed by the heat; it seemed to wilt her right before his eyes. Before it was even decided where she was staying, she announced her intention of leaving as soon as possible, probably within forty-eight hours. Christine had never held up well under any kind of physical discomfort, it made her angry and impatient.

Because Latham was staying in dormitory quarters at the university, and also because of the circumstances under which they were meeting, Latham short-circuited any suggestion of their sharing sleeping quarters by taking her to the local Davidson Hotel, not far from campus, and he got her a first-floor room there where the windows opened for outside air and fans were available from the management. Christine could not believe it when the bellboy told them that both the dining room and the bar were closed through the emergency, and she complained about the heat from the moment she got out of the air-conditioned car Latham drove her in. When Latham had tipped the bellboy and all the windows were thrown open and two big floor fans turned on, Latham and Christine sat down on facing chairs before the fans and rested there.

"I wish you hadn't come, Christine," he told her then. "This is no place for you. We could have talked again on the phone."

Christine eyed him sidewise. She was a tall, rather slim young woman with very dark hair and eyes, and the look of a Madison Avenue model. She wore her hair rather short, and it had natural curl in it. She was dressed in a sheer Lilly Pulitzer summer dress, an expensive hand-print creation, and stylish heels, and her neck and wrists were decorated with antique silver. Christine had impeccable taste in her attire and personal appearance, and it bothered her to show the slightest sign of wear, as she did at that moment.

"Our last phone call was very dissatisfying," she said with a wry look. "I sensed that I'm losing you, Mark. And I've decided I don't want to."

Latham was wearing a print sport shirt and light slacks, and he looked just a little haggard now, from the heat and the hard work and tension about the Russian project. "You weren't talking that way a few months ago," he said.

"I know." She smiled a coy smile. "But I've done some heavy thinking since then. Frankly, I was impressed that you've become so important lately. You are important, aren't you, Mark?"

"Hell, Christine, I haven't done a thing worth mentioning since I got here. It's the Russians who are the big heroes, don't you read the papers?"

"Your name was mentioned in a White House press release the other day," she said. "I just sat there and stared at the TV and said, 'My God, that's my Mark.'"

"I'm the same old Mark you left without looking back, not so long ago," he said drily. "No more, no less."

"Maybe," she said. "But I know now that I was too difficult, Mark. Your work does have its place in the scheme of things, whether you make any money at it or not. I was wrong to insist that you try for something better—that is, more financially stable. Ruthie at the gallery told me as much but I wouldn't listen to her. You have to learn things by yourself, it seems. What I've learned, Mark, is that I miss you when we're not together. I miss you a lot. When we both have gotten some rest, I want to talk about it. Okay?"

Latham nodded. "Okay, Christine." She had kissed him with a rash spontaneity at the airport, an act that was uncharacteristic of Christine, and she had made him wonder whether she might not in fact have changed since their separation. "But I have to tell you in advance. I can't spend much time with you here. I'm going day and night on this drought problem. And we're all waiting now to see what happens with this Russian experiment. I don't have a lot of time for personal problems."

Christine smiled a sexy smile at him. "I won't need much time," she said.

Latham made a date to meet Christine at the campus cafeteria that evening for dinner, and then he tried to put her out of his mind for a few hours. It was not easy, though, because he kept remembering that last hot intimacy with Jodie, and how content he had been in her sensuous embrace. He had thought that maybe something important was developing between him and Jodie, and now Christine was there to complicate things and confuse him. If Christine had indeed changed, if she did now put more importance on what they meant to each other, rather than focusing on re-creating his world to fit her specifications, that would give Latham something serious to think about.

The six o'clock news was full of last-minute developments from McConnell, both on the local level and the national. The Russians had made most of their high-power "broadcasts" and would finish them late the next day. Then the weather should start changing.

Sprague and Latham sent a Skyhook balloon up that evening, unmanned, just before Latham left the lab to meet Christine at the cafeteria. They wanted to make their own independent observations of the troposphere, to determine whether anything was happening up there. Latham personally supervised the launching of the craft by telephone, from lab to Beech Landing Field, and then he walked over to the cafeteria with Hollis Sprague.

Sprague was very cordial to Christine when they met outside the cafeteria, and Christine was charming to him. That, too, surprised Latham, since Christine had always been very aloof from his scholarly friends and associates. Sprague sat with them when they were through the cafeteria line—there were only a dozen or so other customers at the half-functioning service—and intended to leave them alone after he had finished a quick sandwich. He asked Christine a lot of questions about conditions in California, and the art gallery where she had been helping out, and generally avoided speaking of Latham and Christine's marriage. He finished the sandwich almost with magical swiftness through the conversation, and was about to excuse himself to give the other two some privacy, when he looked up and saw Jodie walking toward them. He had been holding a small paper cup in his hand that he had emptied of a tiny ration of water, and he set the cup down very carefully as Jodie approached them from behind Latham and Christine.

"My goodness," he said slowly, "look who's here."

Jodie came up to them breezily, trying to bear up under the heat. Her long auburn hair was piled high on her head, and the dampness of the flesh on her face gave her a very sensual look. She came up with a big smile, and placed her hand affectionately on Latham's shoulder just as he turned toward her.

"Hi, Mark. I thought I might find you here. Dr. Sprague."

"Good evening, Jodie," Sprague greeted her awkwardly.

Jodie was now looking into Christine's dark-eyed face, thinking she had never seen her at the lab.

"Jodie!" Latham said pleasantly. "What a nice surprise." He could feel Christine's eyes on him and Jodie, and tried to ignore it. "Sit down and join us."

Christine stared at Jodie's hand on Latham's shoulder, and Jodie saw the look. She removed her hand, and smiled at Christine. "I don't believe we've met. Are you one of Hollis Sprague's weather experts?"

Latham cleared his throat, and met Jodie's gaze. "Jodie, this is my wife, Christine."

A heavy silence fell over the table as Christine and Jodie regarded each other slowly for a long moment. Jodie was angry with herself for being so stupid as not to guess, and frustrated that she suddenly felt like a husband-stealer.

"Oh," she said clumsily. Another long silence. "I'm— very pleased to meet you, Christine."

"Christine," Latham said, "this is Jodie Jameson. She's our Health Department officer here, and we've all been working very closely together in the past weeks."

Christine had never been good at being nice to adversaries, and she had recognized Jodie at once as such. She had not smiled at Jodie, and did not now. "I'll bet you have," she said in a somber tone.

Latham gave Christine a look, then turned to Jodie.

"Christine arrived unexpectedly today. She wanted to see how we're doing with the drought." His voice sounded hollow to him, as if it were coming from a recorder rather than a real person.

"I hope I haven't spoiled any plans," Christine said smoothly. "I mean, in case you two intended to work together tonight."

Jodie narrowed her lovely eyes on Christine slightly. "Mark and Dr. Sprague get most of their work done in their lab," she said levelly, "and I don't get over there much."

"Where do you get most of your work done—Jodie, is it?" Christine said.

But Sprague broke in then, rather nervously. "Oh, Jodie is everywhere at once, Christine. The Health Department lab, the clinic we've set up there, the mayor's office. She has a big job on her hands now."

"I'll bet you and Mark have become close friends," Christine said to Jodie, ignoring Sprague.

Jodie held her veiled gaze. "As a matter of fact," she said rather defiantly now, "we have." She already disliked Christine, was glad that she had made love to her husband.

"We've all become rather close in these last weeks," Sprague put in with a weak smile.

The women continued to appraise each other coolly. Christine turned to Latham, finally. "I should be jealous, I suppose, Mark. She is a rather pretty little thing. But then I understand how a man has his physical needs. A little diversion in times of stress can serve its purpose, even if it is a bit tawdry."

Jodie's face flushed with anger and embarrassment, and Sprague averted his gaze tautly. A crackling of

210

winchwire tension filled the air around them.

"Christine has this nice way with words," Latham said to Jodie sourly.

Jodie looked at him. She had expected him to make some defense of their relationship, to tell his wife that it was not as she had described it. Now that he had not, Jodie was even angrier than before, and some of the anger was directed at Latham. She felt betrayed by him, and humiliated, and cheap.

"I think I'll have to decline your offer to join you, Mark," she said in a tight, low voice. "I have other things to attend to, if you'll excuse me."

Before Latham could respond, Jodie had turned and was hurrying away. Sprague rose to leave with her, but she was already gone by the time he was on his feet.

"Well, I think I'll get on back to the lab," he said, giving them an awkward smile. "If you need anything, Christine, let us know."

"I will, Dr. Sprague," Christine told him with an easy charm.

Christine and Latham did not once mention Jodie on the way back to her hotel. Latham was quiet and pensive, and Christine did not press him into conversation. They had already planned to have a couple of drinks together in her room, so Latham went on up there with her, and they turned on the fans. Latham declined a drink, and went and stood before a black window. Christine came up behind him, quietly.

"You have been intimate with her, haven't you?" she said.

Latham turned to her, and looked into her dark eyes. "Yes," he said.

"I was seeing an attorney in San Francisco for a while.

But there was nothing intimate. I kept hoping you'd call."

Latham held her gaze.

"I don't mind, Mark, not really. Not if it isn't serious."

Latham turned back to the window. "I don't know what's serious and what isn't nowadays, Christine," he said. "I thought it was probably over for us. You made me believe it was."

"I know, honey," she said. "That was my fault, I admit it. Let's forget all of that now, though. I want us to renew old bonds, Mark, get it all back. It can be different, now."

"I wish I could believe that," he said.

"You can, Mark."

She left him, disappeared into a bathroom. In a couple of moments she returned, and she had disrobed. She was wearing a loose-fitting robe that fell open at the front as she came toward him. She reached to turn off the lights, and it fell all the way open, revealing most of Christine's svelte shape beneath it. The room was plunged into a shadowy semi-darkness.

She came over to him, and began unbuttoning his shirt.

"Christine, I don't think we should—"

But she shushed him, and kept undressing him. He did not know what to do. It was all very confusing, in the midst of his bigger problems. He felt her hands on him, her slender fingers caressing him. A physical thing happened to him inside, and he relaxed and let it happen. She was, after all, his wife.

Somehow they moved to and onto the bed nearby, and then Christine's flesh was bared to him, and she was caressing and seducing in the way she had done so well in the old days of their early marriage. Latham could not stop it then if he had wanted to. Everything was familiar between them, every move practiced. It was like falling back into an old habit easily, without effort. There was an easy, fluid union, and then Christine's long white thighs were on him, embracing him to her, pulling him deep. Her mouth devoured his in an insatiable way, and her hands clawed across his inflamed flesh, and it was almost like their wedding night again.

When it was over, she would not let him separate from her. She held him locked physically to her, her thighs pressing him to her, possessively, proprietarily. Finally, after a long time, she released him, and a secession of union occurred that was reluctant and warm.

"God," she breathed in the darkness. "It was just like the honeymoon. Wasn't it, Mark?"

He had rolled onto his side and was facing her. "It was nice, Christine," he heard himself saying. Already he was sorry he had let it happen. He should have made Christine convince him that things could be different somehow, that she had really changed, before they were intimate.

"I knew we were still good for each other," she was saying now. "I want you to come back to San Francisco with me, Mark. Please think about it before you say no. We could wait this thing out together there, before you return to your job at Berkeley."

"I told you, Christine. I'm needed here."

"Oh, hell, honey. Leave it to NASA and the Russians. You admitted you can't come up with anything better than what they're doing. You don't need to play hero out here in the middle of nowhere. Who really appreciates the effort, that counts?"

Latham narrowed his eyes down slightly. "I'm not

213

looking for appreciation, Christine. But I just can't go at this time. Not unless the Russian project brings spectacular success in the next few days. And even if that happened, I'd return directly to Berkeley. There are things going undone there."

Christine smiled a smug smile. "I have all that worked out for you," she said. "Don't worry about it."

Latham frowned. "Worked out?"

"Yes, when Daddy talked to the dean of physics we arranged for a short leave for you, so we could have some time together in the bay area. Oh, now you've made me give away our secret."

Latham sat up on the bed. "What the hell are you talking about, Christine?"

She touched his chest with a slender finger. "It was my idea, but Daddy really gets the credit. He talked to the dean about you, Mark. Daddy knows a couple of men on the board, and the dean knows he does."

"Your father went to my boss?" Latham said incredulously. "About me?"

"Now just wait until you hear. Daddy told him that you're a big property now, Mark, because of all of this publicity, and that you're worth more to the university. He got you a raise, Mark, a substantial one. Your dean had little choice."

Latham stared at her as if she had suddenly gone psychotic. "I don't believe it," he said hollowly.

"Wonderful, isn't it? That's why I told you it was all right to keep on at the university, don't you see? It's okay for both of us now. You can keep playing with your balloons, and we can still have a decent standard of living. Of course, eventually you'll want to work into the dean's job. You could even be president some day, with a little push here and there by Daddy. What do you think, honey? Are you pleased?"

Latham's face had fallen into hard, straight lines. He rose off the bed and stared down at her, nude, his square frame hulking black against a window. "Have you gone around the goddam bend, Christine?" he said in a low growl. "You had your father go to my dean behind my back, and pressure him into giving me a goddam raise? Because your father knows people on the governing board?"

Christine frowned slightly. "Is something wrong, Mark? Don't you want to make more money?"

Latham just stared hard at her for a moment, then turned and faced a window, breathing shallowly, trying to hold his temper in check.

"Mark?" he heard her say to him.

He turned toward her hostilely. "Jesus Christ, Christine! I have a certain stature at Cal. Those people there are my friends, not my goddam adversaries! How dare you go to them and harass them with something like this, without even consulting me! It's goddam outrageous!"

Christine sat up, too. "Well, I'll be damned. It never occurred to me that you could actually get angry because I tried to help you. Help us."

"*I don't need your help!*" Latham fairly shouted at her. "I don't need your interference, Christine! I don't need someone to run my life for me! I told you that when you left, and nothing has changed!"

She turned away. "Christ!" she muttered.

"You haven't changed, either," he went on. "You wanted me to think you have, but nothing is different. You're generously allowing me to stay on at Cal, so long as I'll mount a campaign for president under your and your father's auspices. Do you think I'd accept a

215

promotion because of pressure from outside? Do you really still have the notion that I'd accept a salary increment because you've twisted my dean's arm up behind his back? On the contrary, I'm going to have to call him now and apologize for this unwarranted interference with the workings of his department."

"Apologize!" Christine said in astonishment.

Latham was pulling his clothing back on, roughly, angrily. "That's right, apologize," he said bitterly. "Let's face it, Christine, you don't have the slightest idea of what kind of person I am, after all this time, and you never will." He was tying shoelaces, bent over a straight chair.

Christine got off the bed, and stood facing him darkly, her slim figure defiant in the dim light from outside. "Oh, I'm beginning to, Mark," she said. "It's becoming clear that you want to go through life playing with Skyhooks and computers and anemometers, that you'll never have any real ambition."

Latham was buttoning his shirt now. "You shouldn't have come, Christine. I suggest you get on the first plane out of here tomorrow and fly back to San Francisco."

"You're telling me to leave?" she said.

"I'm asking you to," he replied to her.

"Then it would also be all right if I saw my lawyer again," she said. "He wanted me to file papers."

Latham was dressed. He gave her a hard, even look. "I think you ought to follow his advice," he said firmly. He turned and walked to the door, and yanked it open.

"You damned ingrate!" she said between her teeth.

He did not look at her. "Goodbye, Christine," he said with finality.

Then he closed the door behind him.

TWELVE

Latham tried to get in touch with Jodie the next morning by calling the Health Department, but was told she was not available. She was avoiding him, he knew, and he could not blame her.

In early afternoon, a geologist came to Latham and Sprague and reported that the last well of Douglas' drilling had gone dry, the only one that was bringing up water. The crew that Douglas had left there was capping the well and packing up for Dallas.

In late afternoon Mazurov terminated his bombardment of the atmosphere with radio waves, and the whole country focused on McConnell, where the results of the experiment were being monitored. It would be a day or maybe two before anything much was known, but the attention of the country was concentrated on Kansas now, where things would change first, if there were changes, according to Mazurov.

In early evening Christine flew away from Wichita, without further contact with Latham. Latham checked at the hotel and found that she had left, and breathed a sigh of relief. It was really over between them now, he was certain of it, and he did not want her around to give him any trouble.

Paula Betancourt had not worked in three days. She had gotten a stomach ailment from the bad water, and she was not getting well. Assistants were still getting her work done in part, but the assistance program was hurting because of her absence from it. No new probes were being made to find water from other cities, and the Russians and Chinese were not being pushed the way they might have been, to get their supplies in the air.

Neither Jodie nor Leah had heard from Will Jameson. A store was burglarized in the north section of the city, and the police said that they thought the People's Brigade was involved, but nobody had gotten a good enough look at the lawbreakers to identify individuals. Leah suggested to Jodie that she might return to the Brigade headquarters alone, just to see if Will was all right. But Jodie dissuaded her. Knowing how desperate the Brigade was now, Jodie figured they would probably keep Leah there, maybe even force her to participate in something illegal.

Sherwood Jameson was having his hands full, despite the imminent outcome of the Russian experiment. The dissidents and hooligans did not much believe in the Russian project nor care one way or the other about it. They continued to burglarize, loot, steal, and commit acts of violence around the city. The police could not begin to keep up with it, so Jameson was obliged to send his patrols out to quell disturbances almost every night, and shooting was taking place on both sides. Jameson had had no idea there were so many handguns around for illegal use. Two more of his guardsmen had been killed, and several wounded, in clashes with armed gangs.

That evening that Christine Latham flew back to San Francisco, giving up on her plan to rehabilitate Latham for a chapter two of their marriage, Jodie went to visit her father at the armory. She found him inspecting a squad about to go out into the night streets, and it was an impressive sight. The men were dressed in battle fatigues, and carried automatic rifles and submachine guns. They looked tough. Too tough, Jodie thought. When the inspection was over, Jameson took Jodie into his private office, and unbuckled a big gun from his hip as she seated herself on a straight chair near his desk. He looked very tired, and hot.

"You never stop past the department," she said. "I've only seen you once since I told you about Will."

Jameson was hanging the holstered gun on a wall hook. "I've been damned busy, Jodie. This drought isn't just sick people and dry faucets, you know. People are being killed in these night streets now. Some of them are my men."

"I know," she said quietly.

"There's a certain element in town who don't give a damn about when we get water. They've already stolen enough to last them for a long while, and now all they want is to be left alone to loot and pillage. They don't want it to be over. They don't want order restored. Did you know that two girls were raped last night, only a block from my troops at City Hall?"

"No, I didn't," Jodie said. She watched her father's face, and saw the extra tension in it, the anger.

"You can't be everywhere," he said defensively, as if he had been accused. "What we need is a couple more units in here."

"This will all quiet down if the Russians make it rain," she reminded him. "They say it could happen within forty-eight hours, Dad."

"Or not at all," he said sourly.

"Dad, I hope you're not still angry with me about the Brigade," Jodie said.

Jameson came and slumped onto his desk chair, then gave Jodie a look from under his brow. "You're a big girl now, Jodie. I can't make your decisions for you anymore. You have yourself to answer to these days."

"I don't suppose you've heard anything about Will?" she said.

"I haven't," he said flatly. "And I don't want to."

"You may not agree with this," she said slowly. "But I don't think most of those in the Brigade are really bad people. They're just people who would be sending letters to Congress, gathering petitions, and waving placards. If it weren't for the heat."

Jameson grunted in his throat. "Just a bunch of misunderstood malcontents, huh, Jodie? Somebody we ought to sit down and talk to?"

"Something like that," Jodie said.

He stuck his square jaw out. "We think it was one of the Brigade that one of my men was trying to talk to the other night. The fellow blew a hole in his head for the effort."

Jodie made a small sound behind her hand, and shook her head. "I know it's been bad," she said. "But they're not all alike, Dad. One of them called me to go help Will despite the danger I represented to them."

Jameson leaned forward onto the desk. "I can't afford the luxury of trying to distinguish the nice ones from the ones who are trying to kill me, Jodie. I'm getting tough with them—all of them. They only respect force, so force is what they'll get. We have more automatic weapons now, and we're getting more yet. We're getting grenades. We're going to clear the goddam streets if it takes tanks to do it. And if you happen to see any of them before I do, you can tell them that."

Jodie regarded him studiedly. It was obvious where Will got his stubbornness. He was more like Jameson than either of them knew.

"Dad, please exercise restraint when you're out there in the street," she pleaded with him. "This is not a war. At least hold your troops in check until we know whether or not the Russians have broken the drought. That shouldn't be very long to wait."

"You worried about these hooligans and outlaws that much?" he said in dark wonderment.

"About them, and about you," she said.

He grimaced, and rubbed his chin. "Jodie, I know you mean well. But you're not on top of things the way we are, not these kinds of things. You're not getting shot at every time you poke your nose out of doors. This uniform makes a nice target, you know. And it's a challenge to some of them. Something big is in the wind right now, and I'm certain it's a calculated showdown with the Guard, an attempt to humiliate us and break our will."

"Something big?" Jodie said. "How big?"

"There's a rumor," he said. "There's going to be an attack on some government or military facility. We think it's the Brigade that's planning it."

"Oh, hell," Jodie said dismally. He did not have to say what he was thinking. That she could help him abort any trouble brewing by the Brigade, by telling him where they could be located.

"I just hope that if there is a big confrontation," he said deliberately, "the killing is minimal."

Jodie rose, and turned away from him. "Maybe Leah

221

was right. Maybe one of us should go back there. Try to talk with them."

"The hell you will," Jameson said darkly. "I forbid it, Jodie, as military commander of this city! If anybody goes to them, it must be the Guard. With guns."

"Oh, God, Dad," she moaned. "I didn't want this responsibility. I just wanted to help my brother." She knew what would happen if she gave Jameson the location of Brigade headquarters. They would go in with guns firing, shouting battle cries and seeking targets. Will, and a lot of others, might be killed.

"Give it some thought, Jodie," Jameson said. "If we go to them, at least the injuries will be on the side they ought to be on. If they take us by surprise somewhere, there's no telling how many guardsmen will be shot or clubbed or beaten."

She turned to him. "Don't, Dad. Please don't." She walked to the open doorway. Outside it, men were moving about in their battle gear, and there was the odor of gun oil in the place. She turned back to him for a moment. "Incidentally, you don't have to concern yourself about Mark Latham anymore. His wife is here. Whatever we had between us is finished."

"Well, I'm glad to hear that," he told her.

As she turned away to leave, he saw just a slight moistness in her big blue eyes. Then she had disappeared through the doorway.

Across town that evening in a closed-down store building with boards over its windows and doors, the Brigade prepared for battle. The organization had finally moved its headquarters from the barn, fearing that Leah, Jodie or Latham would reveal its location either

222

purposely or inadvertently. Consequently, even if Jodie had advised Jameson of the barn's location, he would have come up empty-handed there.

Handguns were being checked, ammunition unpacked. When the Guard was involved in defense, they shot at you, and you had to be ready to shoot back. Or maybe even fire the first shot.

Will was up and moving about easily now. The shoulder still hurt as it healed, but it was not disabling him any longer. He kept a sling on that arm, but was able to use the arm for short periods without tiring it. It could be used to fire a gun.

Jameson's reported rumor was a story based in fact, because the Brigade did intend an assault against the establishment. But they, like everybody else, were waiting to see what happened now that the satellite had been activated. If there was rain, the issue would be moot as to whether the authorities were making fair use of available water. But at the first negative word from the news media, the Brigade would act.

They had decided to attack City Hall.

"It's defended by two platoons of guardsmen now, you know," the broad-shouldered Rick said to Will Jameson that evening as the two of them slumped by themselves in a corner of the big show-room of what had been a furniture store. There were a few pieces of old, used furniture in the place that had not been moved out, including the overstuffed chairs that Will and Rick now sat on, and some crates and boxes sitting about. Again here, there were sleeping bags and home-made pallets for sleeping on the floor of the place. Many members reclined on these, others milled about, rather zombie-like, trying to make the time pass.

Will was cleaning the S&W 61 Escort automatic he had wielded at the truck convoy skirmish. He rammed a cleaning rod through its barrel, moving it up and down, before he looked over at Rick. "Having second thoughts?" he asked the other young man.

Rick gave him a look. "I'm just saying there are other targets that are less well defended. Even the armory itself doesn't have that many armed men there, ordinarily. They're all out guarding other sites."

"We've been through all this," Will said a little impatiently. He looked harder now, perhaps more efficient than before. When he spoke, he spoke with authority. He had matured. But something else had happened to him, too. He had lost his empathy for anyone outside the organization. He had made the world his enemy. "Only City Hall has the importance that we need. It's a conglomerate of offices and bureaus and official authority. When we take the building, we stop all local government dead. Nothing functions from that moment on, except for the goddam police and fire departments, and they're about on their last legs, anyway. We'll make our demands from Tom Purcell's office, by God, and they'll have to listen to us."

"Maybe it would be more impressive to take police headquarters," Rick grinned.

Will looked at him. "Maybe impressive, yes. But not as devastating to the enemy. We want real disruption. We want a governmental vacuum. That means we have to attack the head of the goddam octopus."

Rick glanced at a newspaper on his lap, and saw a sub-headline about Jameson's troops and their deployment. "Are you sure you want this, Will? I mean, what if your father the colonel shows up there when we go in? What if he stands between you and the building and tells you to stop?"

Will glanced over at him again, pulling the rod from the gun. "He'll have to kill me to stop me," he said.

"What if you have to kill him?"

Will stared out across the big, low-ceilinged room, to where a couple of members were standing and talking in low tones. "I hope it doesn't come to that," he said at last.

Rick grunted. "Well. The way I figure it is, once we start our assault, we'll have the whole goddam Guard down on us, and the police in force. That means that we have to break through the initial defenders fast, and get inside the building, before all that back-up comes."

"There's only one platoon on guard at midday," Will said. "And through most of the afternoon, when the temperatures are highest. I think that's when we should hit."

Rick frowned at him. "I think we all thought it would be at night, Will. As usual. When they can't see faces. When we can have some chance of surprising them."

"Surprise is important," Will admitted. "But so is strength of the enemy. My dad taught me that." Bitterly. "In this case, I think the reduction of opposing forces at midday is more important to us than cover of darkness."

"You'll have to convince some of the others," Rick said.

"They'll understand," Will said. He was still thinking about his father, standing before City Hall with a submachine gun aimed at his, Will's chest, and wondering what he would do about it. "I'm sure they'll understand."

*   *   *

225

Jodie was hard at work the next morning when Latham showed up at the Health Department. She was in the clinic infirmary, involved in some nursing duties. Two patients had expired through the night, and four had been brought in between eight and nine a.m., both with bad cases of hepatitis. Jodie was moving between rows of temporary cots, assisting nurses and doctors, giving medication and taking temperatures. Then a nurse came and told Jodie that there was someone to see her in the corridor. Jodie removed a white mask she was wearing, and stepped out into a white hallway outside the infirmary, and Latham was there waiting for her.

"Hi, Jodie," he said quietly.

Jodie was somber, and tired-looking. "Oh, Mark. Is there something we can do for you here?" Her tone was formal.

"No, I just came past to see you for a few minutes," he said. "And to ask how you are."

"I'm feeling all right, except for the fatigue," she said. "How is your wife holding up under the heat?"

He sighed. "She's gone, Jodie."

"Oh?"

"I sent her back to San Francisco."

Jodie's face was impassive. "I suppose this is no place for a woman who doesn't have to be here," she said.

"It isn't that, Jodie," he told her. A nurse passed by, and he paused for a moment until she was gone. "It's really over with us now, Jodie. I told her to go ahead and file divorce papers. She's seeing her lawyer as soon as she gets back there."

Jodie averted her gaze, thinking about that. "I'm sorry for you, Mark. I really am. I got the idea that you were patching things up, when I met her at the cafeteria."

"That's the impression Christine was giving everybody. She had me fooled for a while, too. But then I found out that nothing had changed." He looked into Jodie's eyes. "I won't be going back to her. No matter what she does in San Francisco."

Jodie avoided his gaze. "Well."

"What I'm trying to tell you, Jodie," he said slowly, "is that I'm free to take up where we left off, and I hope you are. I—think I'm in love with you, Jodie."

Now she caught his gaze soberly. "You're in a very emotional period now, Mark. Losing Christine and all. So am I. I know that Lou Falco isn't for me, now. But I don't know who or what is. I—think we've gone too fast, Mark, and too recklessly."

"I don't want to put any undue pressures on you," he said to her. "Force you into any commitments you don't want to make. I just want us to go on finding out about each other, to continue enjoying each other's company. Don't turn away from me now, because of Christine. Christine no longer exists as a part of my future. Without you, there's nothing."

Jodie was very confused. All she wanted at that moment was to withdraw into herself and her work, and not have to decide on the wisdom of personal commitments.

"I'm sure that's an overstatement of reality, Mark," she said. "You have your work, just as I have mine. Maybe that's all either of us really need."

"It's not all I need," he said. "You will go on seeing me, won't you? I mean, privately?"

Jodie hesitated. She had decided against seeing Latham again socially, after the incident with Christine. Now she was not so sure that she should rescind that agreement

227

with herself.

"I—guess so, Mark."

He grinned a nice grin. "Good. I'm going to drive out to see Ed Keefer this morning, to try to find out if he can add anything to our observations on the Russian project. Would you like to ride along?"

Jodie was very tense about the developments on the McConnell experiment. "If I can get free here, all right. I'll give you a call in about an hour, will that be too late for you?"

"It will be fine," Latham said, feeling better.

Jodie and Latham did drive out to Rawdon Field together that morning, but Latham found her reticent and quiet all the way there. At the Weather Service office, Ed Keefer asked Jodie about Leah, and Jodie said she thought Leah would be returning to work in the next week. Keefer was working with taped ribs and a limp, and there was a policeman stationed outside the terminal building, to watch for any further possible trouble.

Keefer unfortunately confirmed what the skies overhead and Latham's own observations were already telling him. So far, the bombardment of the jet stream had not caused any significant change of weather, except that some dust storms were building up through the Midwest, and a few clouds had been spotted over the plains about a hundred miles north of Wichita. But there was no suggestion of rain clouds yet. Slowly but surely, tension in the city was turning to depression.

That afternoon, Yuri Mazurov admitted a growing doubt on his part to a local reporter. Ilyich Potamkin had flown back from Florida, and he too was worried that no immediate results were noticeable. In Siberia, when they had conducted similar experiments there, rainfall had occurred within twenty-four hours. Stanley Kravitz had already asked Mazurov if there might be value in repeating the complex conglomeration of radio assaults on the atmosphere, but Mazurov believed that there would be none, not at that moment in time.

In the late afternoon edition of the local newspaper, Mazurov was quoted as saying he thought the experiment had failed, which was an overstatement of the facts. But the announcement, also made on local TV, was received with explosive impact by the city.

People came out into the hot streets and chanted protests against the Russians, the local and state government, and the federal people. A rash of store burglaries occurred in broad daylight, and a police car was turned over and burned.

Latham called Jodie, and asked her to stay off the streets that evening, and she promised that she would. He told her that his calculations were not yet conclusive about the Russian experiment, and that he was going to tell the news media that. But he did not think that would make a great deal of difference in the way people were reacting.

The police and the Guard had their hands full that night, with disturbances all across the city. But the big trouble lay ahead for them. The next morning early, Will and other leaders of the People's Brigade began getting the Brigade ready to move out at just before noon, in the heat of the day.

Their objective: City Hall.

It was rather quiet that morning in the city, after the night of trouble. The police and Guard were licking their wounds, resting up from the night's activity. Three guardsmen and one cop had been rather badly injured in a downtown riot, and two demonstrators had been killed. Only a few maverick Brigade people participated. Will and the other leaders were keeping them in readiness for the important mission at City Hall.

At noon at City Hall, a part of the Guard troops had been removed by Sherwood Jameson, as usual. There were eight men on duty at the big concrete-and-glass building, guarding the entrances in a relaxed manner. They had the idea that they could relax until the evening, when the streets would become hectic again.

They were wrong.

At 12:17 exactly, two Brigade people showed themselves at the rear of the building, near a parking lot, and began shouting invectives at the three guardsmen situated there. A shot was fired over the heads of the guardsmen, and nearby pedestrians scurried for cover. The Brigade was hoping to create a diversion that would pull the sentries off the other entrances, so that they could swarm into the building with no opposition.

It did not, however, work that way.

The guardsmen on duty, under Jameson's orders, shouted into a walkie-talkie that was in touch with the other sentries, saying that they were under attack. But the order was to stay at all entrances no matter what happened, and to call for back-up. They did just that. By the time Will and his people began swarming into the square the building faced, shouting and waving their guns, Sherwood Jameson had already gotten the message that there was trouble at City Hall, and he alerted an entire company to move off to the trouble area, with automatic weaponry.

It was hot out in that sun-baked square, with its wilted trees and burned-brown bushes and sand drifts. Brigade people sweated heavily, as they came charging at the front entrance of the building, and the guardsmen waiting for them with their submachine guns and automatic rifles were flushed hot in the face, and there was an unreal feeling to it all, a feeling of loss of control. It was all slightly different from at night. Brains boiled in the flat-iron sun, and blood raced hotly through veins, and anger crowded into chests in a maniacal way.

"It's the goddam Brigade!" one of three waiting guardsmen said tightly, seeing the thirty or so young people running wildly toward them. "And they look like they mean business!"

"Throw the special interests out!"

"Stop corruption!"

"Out in the street with Purcell!"

Will, in the thick of them, carried his pistol out in front of him, at ready, waving them on. *"Let's go! They can't stop us now! Throw the bastards out!"*

The most nervous of the three guardsmen stepped back a step, fearfully, and then squeezed the trigger on his submachine gun. The hot air exploded with sound, like a jackhammer on concrete. Out on the open expanse of the area before the building, two Brigade members tumbled onto their faces.

Most of the others slowed to a halt, staring wide-eyed at the downed comrades. One had three holes stitched across his chest and abdomen and was lying face down on the hot concrete, lifeless. The other was holding his groin and yelling loudly. There was a lot of blood.

"Spread out!" the fellow named Rick yelled out, from somewhere behind Will. *"Find cover!"*

"No, keep on going!" Will yelled. *"Return fire and go in on them! We have to get inside the building!"*

But most of them followed Rick's suggestion and found cover of some kind before advancing further. Behind a couple of parked cars, small trees, burned bushes. Will kept on going, as did several others. A couple of them returned fire, but did not hit anything. A second guardsman fired off a rattling round of hot slugs toward them, from a crouched position in the big doorway, and one of those advancing with Will went down, hit in the leg and side.

Will glanced toward the fallen man, and swallowed hard. He fired off two quick shots toward the doorway, and then threw himself onto his stomach on the pavement. The other fellow who had been advancing with him did the same.

"Return fire!" Will shouted at the top of his lungs. *"We have to get past them, goddam it!"*

Now many of the Brigade people were returning fire, from cover or half-cover. The air was filled with raucous gunfire and made heavy with the acrid odor of gunsmoke. One of the three guardsmen grabbed at his face and toppled onto his side.

"I got one!" a voice shouted. *"By God, I got one!"*

Will turned toward where several of them were hiding behind the parked cars. *"We have to rush them! Now! It's our only chance!"* He still wore the sling on his arm, and it and his shoulder hurt badly since he had hit the pavement. He rose up onto one knee. *"Are you with me? This is what we came for!"*

Just at that moment, though, two guardsmen appeared at the left corner of the building, grim-faced. They had been relieved of duty on a side entrance, by radio, to assist at the main entrance. They saw the situation at a

232

glance, and both began firing automatic rifles toward Will and the others. One girl Brigade member had gotten up just as Will urged them forward, and now she was hit several times by the new firing from the left. She hit the pavement in a lumpy heap, her mouth open and working, her eyes staring into the savage sky.

"Oh, God!" Will muttered.

Now another guardsman appeared at the right-hand corner of the building, beside a dark brown bush there. He raked a hail of lead over the square, and a Brigade man behind a tree yelled and fell, hit in the thigh.

"*We're flanked, Will!*" a high voice came. "*What do we do?*"

But Will did not know what to do. He knew little about military tactics or guerrilla methods. He crouched there on one knee, his head whirling. If they only had grenades. If they had just one automatic weapon.

If they had picked a target with fewer guns.

Will thought of napalmed villages in Asia, and agent orange, and the Russian revolution. If the rebels had given up so easily at Red Square, there would still be czars ruling the Soviet Union.

But maybe that was not so bad.

He heard a sound at the far side of the square, behind him. He turned quickly, and saw the Army vehicles arriving. Jeeps and trucks, disgorging soldiers. Jameson's guardsmen.

Will had vacillated for too long.

They were surrounded by guns now.

He rose to his feet, frantically. "*Get out! Every man for himself!*" he yelled hoarsely. "*Disperse!*"

Some of the Brigade began firing toward the newcomers as they debarked from the vehicles, and a guardsman went down. Soldiers knelt and began returning fire with rifles. Brigade people now started running from the square, between the Guard forces. One went down hard, and then another. Some were getting out of the square, a few were not. Suddenly three were down.

Will knew he could not stop to help any of them. There was no time, no opportunity. He began running toward a side street, yelling as he went, and just at that moment, Sherwood Jameson climbed from a jeep and saw Will as he headed across the open space between them.

"Let's get out of here!" Will was yelling. *"Let's go!"*

"Will, stop!" Jameson called out in his deep voice, his service pistol hanging loosely at his side.

Will heard his father's voice, and stopped and turned toward him. In that split-second, a guardsman fired from the front of the building and hit Will in the back, just beside his spine. His head whiplashed violently, and his gun went flying, and he plunged headlong to the pavement.

Jameson swallowed hard. "Will!" he muttered.

Now most of the Brigade was gone from the square. A couple had thrown their weapons down and surrendered. Jameson turned and yelled to his troops. *"Cease fire!"* he called out. *"Cease fire!"*

The square before the City Hall fell silent. Jameson turned and dog-trotted toward the fallen Will, holstering his gun as he went, his heart sinking inside his chest. When he got there, Will was lying on his side, motionless, his eyes open. His limbs were unnaturally placed, and there was still a look of mild surprise on his face.

Jameson bent over him, and turned him over onto his back, cradling his head in his arms. A crimson pool had formed under Will's side, on the pavement.

"Oh, for Christ's sake, Will." Throatily. "For Christ's sake."

"I—heard you call," Will said.

"Damn," Sherwood Jameson hissed out. He turned and yelled over his shoulder. *"Get some ambulances here! Fast!"*

He looked back down at Will, and saw the odd color in Will's face. Will grinned weakly. "You finally—got my attention, Dad."

"Please, Will. Just lie quietly, for God's sake." A couple of guardsmen ran past, clattering their boots on the pavement. Others were bending over fallen Brigade people, disarming them.

"I'd have—gotten it, anyway," Will croaked out in a voice that was no longer his. A worm of crimson inched from the corner of his mouth. "Don't—blame yourself."

"Will, I'm so goddam—sorry," Jameson said almost inaudibly. His throat was all choked up tight, and he felt a moisture at the corners of his eyes.

"We both did what—we had to."

Jameson ran his hand over Will's thick brown hair. "Your mother always said you were a stubborn kid," he said.

Will tried another grin, but something inside him grabbed at him and jerked it quickly off his face. "Tell Jodie—"

Jameson bent closer. "Yes, Will?"

"Tell Jodie that I—"

But he never finished. There was a low, gurgling sound

235

in his throat, and his eyes widened slightly, and then life passed from him like a small flame blowing out.

Jameson was suddenly shaking all over. He could not seem to stop, it was as if he had been chilled to the marrow. In the bright, hundred-twenty degrees sun.

He finally reached and closed Will's eyes.

His lifelong battle with his only son was over.

THIRTEEN

It was 2:26 p.m.

Jodie had just gotten back from a quick lunch in the basement of the department building, and was trying to sort out some files on clinic patients. When she heard the sound at her office doorway, she looked up and Jameson was standing there.

He hulked large in the doorway in the green fatigues and helmet and battle gear. With the white walls all around him, stark and brilliant, he looked like an actor dressed for a John Wayne film, who had stepped onto a Fellini set by mistake.

Jodie saw the look in his face immediately, and a cold chill passed through her. "Dad! What are you doing—? Oh, God. It's Will!"

He just stood there, not being able to speak for a moment.

"What happened?" she asked in a dry voice, as she rose from the desk and came around it. "What happened to him?" But she already knew.

Something jerked at the corner of Jameson's mouth. "He's—one of my people shot him, Jodie."

She gasped, turned away from him.

"He—didn't make it."

Jodie's ears began ringing fiercely, and suddenly she could not get her breath. Big, choking sobs started in her throat, and then burst out of her in welling gushes. She felt her father's hands on her shoulders, and she turned and buried her head against him.

"It was my fault," he was saying to her. "He would have made it out of the square, probably. I stopped him by calling to him."

She looked up at him, teary-eyed.

"Why didn't I let him go, Jodie? Why didn't I for just once in his life let him go?"

"Oh, Dad." Sobbing, shoulders shaking.

"I killed my own son, Jodie." His eyes were wet, too.

Jodie got herself under control. She used a facial tissue on her desk, and turned back to him. "You—can't accept the blame for this, Dad. Will was—different in past weeks. He carried a gun. He had killed a man."

He went and heaved himself onto a straight chair, removed his helmet, set it on his lap. "It was at City Hall. They had guns, Jodie. It was no telling what they'd have done, if they'd gotten inside. As it was, four of my men were shot, and one is dead. Maybe I overreacted, maybe I could have handled it differently. If I had, Will might be alive."

Jodie went and sat on the edge of her desk. Nothing seemed real to her. Not the white walls around her, not the department, not Jameson, sitting slumped on the chair a few feet away. It all had a dream-like quality. It was a stage scenario, and they were acting out what could be, not what was. It would all be over in a few minutes, and they would get a big laugh out of their performances, and everything would be the same again.

Like hell, a voice inside her shouted.

Will was dead.

He was no longer a present tense, but a past tense. She had no brother, now. There was a crumpled, bloody corpse somewhere at the morgue, but Will was gone. Erased from existence wholly, as if he had never been. Vanished was the crooked smile, the stubborn manner— the brotherly kiss on the cheek. It was all so relentlessly irrevocable. She recalled that last time she had seen him, at the old barn, and tried to remember his last words to her. She could not.

"If you hadn't stopped them," she finally said, "the incident could have escalated into something terrible. You had a job to do for this community, and you did it."

Jameson sat there shaking his head. But Jodie's words had helped him. More than he knew, at that moment.

"Oh, Jesus. Leah," Jodie suddenly said, brushing at her eyes. "I don't think we can tell Leah just yet."

Jameson looked up at her. "Tom Purcell knows. I think he said he was going to tell her."

"Oh, God," Jodie said.

"Don't you think she can handle it?"

"She hasn't really put this assault behind her," Jodie told him. "I'm worried about her. I don't know how she'll react to something like this."

"Tom said they had been talking about marriage, not so long ago." His voice was heavy, tired-sounding. Quite suddenly he got up, rubbing a hand across his square face. He looked terrible. "I have to get over to the armory. Maybe you ought to take the rest of the day off, Jodie."

She shook her head sidewise. "No, here is better. I'll call you, Dad."

He nodded, and he looked ten years older to her.

239

"Okay, Jodie."

The next day there was a bad dust storm, and everybody across the city huddled indoors. The few clouds that had gathered across the plains had dispersed, and no more were in sight. Mazurov fretted and steamed at McConnell, and nobody could speak to him, not even Potamkin or Kravitz. Latham stopped past to offer his condolences to Jodie, and she appreciated it more than she ever would have thought. Latham had known Will at the last, had helped care for him at Brigade headquarters. That made him an inner-circle figure at the moment despite Jodie's reluctance to revive their intimacy.

Leah reacted very much like Jodie had expected. There were no tears, no talking about it. She went into a kind of trance from the moment Tom Purcell gave the bad news to her, and could not be dragged out of it.

On the following day after the storm, on a quiet, hot morning, Will's funeral took place. There were only a few cars at the graveside service, with a dozen people huddled around the open grave. Jodie and her father, the Purcells, Ed Keefer and Hollis Sprague, a couple of students from the university, Latham. A minister stood at the head of the yawning hole and spoke a few words over the casket.

"'However, now Christ has been raised up from the dead, and the first fruits have been harvested from those who have fallen asleep in death. For since death is through a man, resurrection of the dead is also through a man. For just as in Adam all are dying, so also in the Christ all will be made alive.'"

Jodie stood stony silent, tears running down her cheeks. On one side of her was Jameson, on the other

240

Latham. Across the grave, a small sob broke from Mrs. Purcell's lips. Leah, standing between her mother and father, was rigid and pale, with absolutely no expression on her drawn face.

"'For if we have become united with Him in the likeness of His death, we shall certainly also be united with Him in the likeness of His resurrection. Sleep lightly, Will Jameson, for the Father has approved of giving you the Kingdom.'"

It was a generous eulogy. Most ministers would have shied away from suggesting that Will had a secure place with the Lord. At the end of it, Leah began sagging at the knees and Tom Purcell had to support her weight. At the end of the service he hurried her off to a waiting car. Jodie tried to speak to her as she went past, but Leah just stared into her face for a brief moment, and went on.

The small gathering broke up quickly, because of the rising heat. Latham walked to the car with Jodie and Jameson. Jameson got into the car with a brief parting remark to Latham, and waited inside for Jodie. Jodie and Latham stood there together for a moment, Jodie staring toward the Purcell car, which was just pulling away.

"Do you think Leah will be all right?" Latham said.

"I don't know," Jodie said numbly. "I'm worried about her, Mark."

"She didn't cry," he said. "She didn't cry at all."

"I'm going to stop past later and see how she is," Jodie said.

"Would you mind if I drove you?"

She looked at him. "No, I'd like it, Mark."

Inside the Purcell car, as it left the cemetery, Leah sat in the back seat with her mother and stared blankly ahead. Her entire world had seemed to fall apart, in the past week. She could not bring herself to believe that Will was gone, on a conscious level. Yet, deep inside her somewhere, a voice kept crying out to her. That she was alone. That everybody was alone. That the world was an ugly, dangerous place.

That there was little purpose in all of it.

When she arrived back home, Purcell took her up to her room, and turned two fans on there. He asked her if she wanted something to eat, and she declined. He asked if there was anything he could get her, and she said no. She wanted to be alone now.

When Purcell had left, Leah sat on a chair with a fan directly on her and stared across the room. In a corner near her bed, a clock ticked loudly, audible above the fans. She sat that way for nearly an hour, without moving. Purcell came back and asked if she wanted to go out to the store with him and her mother, and Leah declined. A few minutes later, she heard the car pull away, outside. She was alone in the house.

She felt cool inside her, despite the heat. She went and turned the fans off, then sat back down in the chair. She felt amazingly comfortable, and tranquil, suddenly. None of it was affecting her anymore, nothing was bothering her. She felt smug about it, a little superior. She gave a small laugh, aloud, and it echoed dully in the room.

It was becoming clear to her now. She could be like this always, if she wanted to. She could fix it so she was never touched again by any of it, she could place herself out of reach of all the ugliness and trauma. It was easy, really. And somehow beautiful. The beauty was in its completeness, and its finality. Will must have understood that, lying in his father's arms. She was sure he had.

Leah rose from the chair, and moved numbly into an adjacent bathroom. It was all so cool now, so comfortable, now that she understood. Nothing could touch her, nothing would ever be able to hurt her again. She reached into the medicine chest and found the bottle. Her mother had brought it up there just yesterday, and given Leah a pill to help her sleep. Leah opened the bottle, poured a handful of pills into her hand and stared at them. Absolute protection lay in those white, innocuous discs. Eternal comfort.

She ran a glass of water, and began swallowing the pills. There were a lot of them, and it took several minutes. She felt wonderful. Almost exhilarated. She wondered why it had not occurred to her before. It was all so very easy.

She was finished. She looked down at the water in the glass, and it was brown. It had taken a couple of minutes to draw, just dribbling out of the tap. None of that mattered now, either. None of it mattered. She set the glass down, and walked back into the bedroom. She lay down on her bed, and stared at the ceiling. She felt as if she were floating, it was like she was not touching the bed. It was strange. But peaceful.

She heard a knocking on the outside door, downstairs. There was a voice somewhere. But then it all faded from her, the sights and sounds, like a film going out of focus. Fade to black. She smiled at the comparison.

Downstairs, Jodie and Latham came inside the house. Jodie often had before, the Purcells expected her to. She had seen that the car was gone, outside, but was sure that Leah must be there somewhere.

"Leah?" Jodie was calling out, looking up toward Leah's room.

"We'd better take a look," Latham said.

They went up the stairs together, and Jodie's heart

began pounding in her chest. She threw Leah's door open up there, and saw Leah on the bed, with all her clothes on.

"Oh. She's resting," Latham said quietly.

But Jodie went into the room, and stood over Leah for a moment. There was something about her. Jodie could hardly see her breathing. She turned quickly and went into the bathroom. She saw the pill bottle. *"Mark!"* she called out.

He came and glowered darkly at the bottle. "Goddam, Jodie!" He turned and hurried back to the bed. "The extension phone! Get an ambulance here!"

Jodie hurried to the phone while Latham bent over Leah on the bed. Jodie was dialing.

"She's still breathing," he announced.

He picked Leah up off the bed, and held her upright, her feet touching the floor. He slapped her face lightly a couple of times. "Leah! Wake up! Speak to me, Leah!" He started dragging her around the room, trying to get her feet to move. Her eyes fluttered open, and then closed again.

Jodie was giving the address to the ambulance service. She hung up and came and helped Latham hold Leah up. Leah opened her eyes again, and Jodie spoke to her.

"Leah, dear Leah!" Jodie said to her. "We love you, honey! You don't want this! We all need you and love you!"

They dragged her around the room. In just moments a siren wailed in the distance, and then it came to a noisy stop outside. Latham went downstairs to meet them, and a few minutes later Leah was being carried out of the house on a stretcher.

"We'll get the pump on her," the driver said. "She'll

be okay."

Latham nodded.

"I'm going with her," Jodie told him. "Try to get in touch with the Purcells."

"All right," Latham said. "I'll drive over to Wesley Hospital as soon as I can get there."

"It's all full, they're taking her to St. Joseph," Jodie said.

"I'll be there as soon as I can," he told her.

A moment later, the ambulance drove off with both Leah and Jodie inside.

Latham went back into the house, and used the downstairs phone in a potted-palm-grown foyer, trying to locate Tom Purcell. But the Purcells had gone off shopping and were unreachable. Latham had just decided to lock up the house and follow Jodie to the hospital, when the phone rang. He returned to it, hoping it was Tom Purcell. But it was Hollis Sprague on the other end.

"*Mark, what are you doing there at Tom's place? I've been trying to get in touch with you ever since I got back here to the lab. Is everything all right over there?*"

"Not really, Hollis," Latham said. "It's Leah. She took some pills, but she's going to be all right."

"*Oh, hell,*" Sprague said heavily.

"Jodie is with her. I've been trying to get in touch with Tom, but can't locate him."

"*I wish I could help you,*" Sprague said pensively. He sounded very fatigued. "*I know you don't need this on a day like this one, Mark. But I thought you'd want to know, I just heard it on television.*"

"Heard what?" Latham asked.

"*About the Russians,*" Sprague said darkly. "*Yuri*

245

Mazurov just made a public statement. He's admitted their experiment failed."

"Oh, Jesus," Latham said.

"*He says his latest observations prove that the upper stream currents refused to be bullied back into their old path. He says there was some movement, but not enough. Blames our equipment and support technology. He says we're just going to have to wait, that eventually it will swing back into its usual route.*"

"Eventually?" Latham said acidly. "Good God. This is just what I expected from them."

"*He and Potamkin and the rest of them will be flying out of here tomorrow, Mark,*" Sprague said. "*I guess the President tried to keep them here, but they say there's no point. There's going to be a big psychological letdown in this city when they're gone.*"

A long pause. "Well. I'm going over to St. Joseph Hospital, Hollis. That's where they took Leah."

"*Are you sure she's going to be all right?*"

"Yes, I'm sure of it. They're going to use a stomach pump. It's her mental condition I'm concerned about. Listen, I'll be back to the lab just as soon as I can break away."

Sprague's voice sounded lead-filled. "*No hurry, Mark. There's nothing going on here that you can't miss.*"

Latham sighed audibly. "I know, Hollis," he said in a low, subdued voice. "I know."

FOURTEEN

Mazurov and Potamkin and their entourage did not lose any time in leaving. They were gone before noon the next day.

In late afternoon gangs and mobs began emerging into the streets. Going wild. Shouting, cursing, screaming obscenities. Destroying property, attacking each other. By nightfall it was so bad that Jameson ordered his troops to keep out of their way, to adopt defensive postures only. Police headquarters and the armory became armed camps, sandbagged on the outside, bristling with guns within. Municipal offices were closed for the duration of the emergency, and martial law was declared across the city and state. Similar situations existed in Iowa City, Topeka, Colorado Springs, Houston and other communities.

Anarchy reigned.

In the hot, sunny morning following the departure of the Russians, less than twenty-four hours after they had left, the exodus began.

Anybody who still had the strength and will to leave the area started packing up and going. Vehicles of all kinds streamed onto the highways and streets: cars, trucks, vans. Furniture was piled high on open trucks, tied down with makeshift bindings, and was stacked on car roofs. Station wagons were jammed from floor to ceiling, vans had paraphernalia sticking out of windows and rear doors.

Many locals got all packed and loaded, only to find that either their gas tank or radiator had been siphoned dry by thieves, or that their tires had been slashed by vandals. Some of these unfortunates picked up as much as they could carry and started out along the hot streets, out of town. Others just gave it up and went back into their homes and sat down in front of a fan, if they owned one. The ones that started out walking usually dropped all baggage and paraphernalia by the time they hit the city limits, and then kept on without any belongings whatever. Some of these turned around within a few miles of the city, when the sun got hot, and stumbled desperately back to shelter.

A few of those on foot stopped cars at gunpoint, and stole the vehicle from its owners, contents and all. Others fought with each other over a canteen of water, or a can of soup. Drivers in cars had engine trouble, in the heat, and many vehicles stalled useless just a short distance from the city. Some refugees banded together with guns and attacked farm houses, taking them by force. A few farmers were killed.

This lasted for a couple of days, and then most of those who were leaving—usually for the north or east—were gone. But most of the local residents were still there, frying alive in heat that consistently reached a hundred twenty-five degrees in the shade.

Nobody in his right mind went out on the streets of the city now. It was too bake-oven hot in the daytime, and too

248

dangerous at night. A mood of resignation had set in.

There was no greenery in Wichita now. Leaves had burned off most trees, and shrubbery had become brown stalks. There was no grass. Only dust and more dust. The crews at the power company had given up on trying to keep the machinery going at full capacity. Brown-outs were usual and increasing in frequency.

The President came on television and declared a dire national emergency, promising food and medicine to the worst-stricken areas. The implication was made that scientists were still working on a solution to the drought, but everybody knew that if the Russians could not undo their own wrong, it was unlikely that American technology could. Water finally arrived from several foreign sources, and one load came to Wichita. It was like a drop of rain in a desert. Almost all of it went to the sick and disabled, and some was rationed out to the most needful ambulatory of the public through clinic water stations. That lasted for a couple of days, and the need was as great as before.

Latham and Sprague did not give up. They still made their observations and calculations, still bombarded each other with theories and ideas. But their energy, too, was giving out. Sprague was feeling sick most of the time, and was really just going through the motions.

Leah Purcell was not the same person when she came around from the pills. She had withdrawn almost completely into herself. The only persons she would speak to were Jodie and her father. She was placed in a psychiatric ward at the hospital, where she sat in a white room in front of a floor fan and stared out of a bright window, unseeing. The attending psychiatrist assured

249

the Purcells and Jodie that she was still reachable, though, and that she ought to come back, given sufficient time.

Paula Betancourt was quite sick, and could not seem to recover. She had been under the impression that Wichita was getting a lot more water from overseas than just one planeload, and when she learned the truth, that set her back psychologically and physically. One hot morning at the end of August she came into Jodie's office and heaved herself onto a chair across from Jodie at Jodie's desk.

She looked very different from the robust woman who had come to Wichita. She was thin now, and pale and drawn-looking. Her eyes had lost their luster, and also her thick hair. She looked very tired, and she was.

"Jodie, I wanted you to be the first to know," she said wearily after she had slouched on the chair. "I'm leaving Wichita. I've been given permission to return to Washington."

Jodie sat leaning onto her desk. Her auburn hair did not have the neat look it had had a few weeks ago, and there were dark places under her eyes. Her skin was pale and dry. Nobody was sweating now. They did not have enough body water for sweat. It was all beyond that.

"Nobody will blame you, Paula," Jodie said. "You should have gone long ago. You're in no shape to continue on here."

"I feel like a rat deserting a ship," Betancourt said. "You know I'm a fighter, Jodie. You know what I've gone through to get the little water we've had from outside sources, and medicine. But I don't have any more ideas, even if I felt well enough to act on them. I'm frankly played out. This damned drought has beaten me."

"It's beaten all of us," Jodie told her.

"The Secretary says I'll be replaced by somebody. But I wouldn't hold my breath, if I were you. The people of Kansas are going to have to take care of themselves any way they can, Jodie. I know that sounds hard, but I don't have any other suggestions. I spoke to the President personally yesterday. I told him I felt people should be forcibly evacuated from this area, whether they want to go or not. He told me that the logistics problems alone would be staggering. Unless people can move out on their own, they're going to have to find a way to survive here on their own. That's what it boils down to."

"Even camels couldn't survive in this indefinitely," Jodie said. "Have you gone out into the streets recently? There are wild animals out there, Paula, looking for water. I've seen them at night. Gangs of armed kids go hunting in our streets at night. If they don't find a coyote to shoot, they end up shooting at each other."

Betancourt met Jodie's gaze with a sober one. "Jodie, come out of this with me. You'll get sick, too. It's just a matter of time. Come back to Washington with me, where there's at least a little water for drinking. You're not going to be of any use here if you come down with hepatitis or worse."

Jodie hesitated. She wanted to accept the offer more than anything she had ever wanted in her life. She wanted to be out of it, if just for a little while. She wanted to breathe cool air again, have a glass of refrigerated water. Get really clean. Sleep deeply and restfully.

"I can't, Paula," she finally said. "I can't."

Betancourt nodded. "I figured as much."

"New patients are coming in every day, and there aren't enough people to tend them."

"I understand."

251

"Paula, you've been invaluable to us here through this, and we'll always remember you for your help. I want to wish you well, in Washington, and I hope you feel better soon."

"I'll be all right. You just take care of yourself, do you hear me?"

"I will, Paula. I promise."

With Betancourt gone, it seemed as if even Washington were deserting them, to most residents. Stanley Kravitz was still out at McConnell, monitoring the weather along with Ed Keefer, but nobody had ever looked upon Kravitz as any kind of savior. He just did not have that kind of stature, in the eyes of the locals.

The same day that Betancourt left, Jodie decided to go pay Leah a visit at the hospital. When Latham heard that she was going, he offered to drive her, and she acquiesced. He did not like to see her driving across town by herself now. It was dangerous for a lot of reasons.

It was early evening when they started out for the hospital. The temperature was suffocatingly high, even though the sun was almost down. Latham drove a university car, a recent model Olds with a cracked windshield where a rioter had hit it with a brick. It seemed that nothing was undamaged nowadays, or worked properly. That was the way it was, and they were all beginning to accept it as a fact of life.

They drove slowly, carefully across town along Central Avenue, past tall buildings steaming under the incredible thermal blanket that covered the city. Everything was dust-covered. Buildings were locked up and boarded up. There was almost no vehicular traffic. Latham found himself wondering if it would look as bad after a nuclear war. He wondered if archaeologists would dig Wichita out from under a mountain of sand one day and deduce what had happened to end a thriving city's life so abruptly. That was a possible future happening for this area, he knew. It would not be the first time that nature had ended a dream of man, with a vengeance.

"Have you heard how Leah is doing?" he asked Jodie as they drove. "I think Tom was hoping she'd be back home by now."

Jodie looked over at him. She had not been intimate with him since Christine's visit to him, and she did not expect to be. She still felt deep affection for him, and it gave her comfort to have him around, near her. But she was afraid now, apprehensive about giving of herself emotionally. To Latham or anyone. There was no permanence in anything, it seemed. You could not depend on things to stay the same. You could, in fact, expect the worst, and usually be right in your expectation. Fathers changed, brothers died, best friends withdrew into dark corners of themselves. The world was a hot, dusty, dry place that was not fit to live in.

"The doctor says it will be a while," she finally said. "The Purcells and I are the only things she has to hang onto the real world with, Mark. So I figure I should be there as often as I can. To help her remember that somebody cares."

"I hope to God she'll be all right," Latham said. The air-conditioner was on in the car, but the temperature was almost unbearable.

There was a sound in the sky above them, and Latham looked up and saw a big jet landing at Midcontinental Airport. Airline flights across the Midwest had diminished, too, in past weeks. Nobody was traveling there, if they could help it. Latham stared at the vapor trail behind the plane, as he had done in California, and realized how odd that thin cloud appeared in the hot sky, now. He sighed heavily, and then stared back out through the windshield, pensive.

"Here, don't miss the turn," Jodie told him.

Latham turned right off the wide street, onto Hillside Avenue. Only one moving car was visible on the entire length of the street. Jodie looked ahead and saw a knot of animals along the curb, and squinted down, then put a hand to her mouth.

"What is it?" Latham asked.

But then he saw, as they approached. Four rabid coyotes had joined into a pack and had been emboldened by lack of human traffic on the streets to come out to hunt in broad daylight. The four of them had cornered a weakened, scruffy dog, had it down on the ground, and were ravaging it.

"Don't look!" Latham told her.

They drove past quickly. There was the sound of deep snarling, and some weak yelps from the dog. Latham glanced toward the bloody scene, and saw the coyotes tearing and ripping, their eyes wild, looking like small wolves.

"Jesus Christ," Jodie murmured, when they were past.

They did not speak the rest of the way to the hospital. When they got there it was almost dark, and lights were going on around the city. Latham parked on the parking lot and they went in together, Jodie going to the administration offices first, where she checked on new cases of hepatitis and dehydration. Then they walked down to the psychiatric ward through corridors crammed with beds, cots, people standing and sitting. There was no room for all of them, and the hospitals were beginning to turn some away.

They spoke to a doctor first, a short man in a white frock and horn-rimmed glasses who looked completely worn out. They stood in a corridor not far from Leah's room and discussed her quietly.

"She's in better touch with reality, I think," the doctor said to them. "She speaks quite freely with her father, less so with her mother. She asked about you today."

"Oh, I'm so glad I came," Jodie said.

"There are still areas of disorientation. She's mentioned Will Jameson only on two occasions to my knowledge, and when she did, she spoke of him in the present tense, as if he's still alive. I said nothing to disabuse her of that notion. It's too soon."

"Do you think it would be all right if I saw her with Jodie?" Latham asked.

"I think so. She knows you well, and there's no reason for her to associate you with any of her traumas."

"We won't stay long," Jodie said.

"You can walk her out in the garden, if you want to," the doctor told her. "She hasn't been outside today."

"Can she take the heat out there?" Jodie said.

"Oh, yes. She told Tom Purcell that it's too cool inside here."

Leah was sitting in an overstuffed chair when they went into her room, staring at a magazine on her lap. She did not have it open so she could read it, but was merely looking blankly at its cover. It featured a brunette model wearing a wide, pleasant smile.

"Hi, Leah," Jodie greeted her.

Leah looked up quizzically, studying Jodie's face. "Oh.

It's Jodie." She looked over at Latham. "And you're—Mark."

Jodie swallowed hard. "Yes, Mark wanted to say hello to you too this evening. It's all right, isn't it?"

Leah thought about that for a moment. "Yes. Mark is all right." She wore a plain hospital garment and sandals, and she had no make-up on. She looked washed-out and tired, yet her eyes were glittery.

"Have you been feeling well, honey?' Jodie asked her.

"Oh, yes. I feel all right, Jodie. How's everything at— the clinic?"

"Oh, everything is fairly well under control," Jodie told her.

Leah stared at her. "Under control."

Latham and Jodie exchanged dark glances. "Yes, we're doing quite well keeping up with the traffic," Jodie said. "Paula Bentacourt asked me to say hello to you. She left for Washington earlier today."

"Betancourt," Leah said to herself.

Jodie sighed inaudibly. "The doctor said you could take a short walk outside if you want to. Shall we got out together, the three of us?"

Leah thought for a moment. "All right, Jodie. That would be nice. A walk ought to be nice."

They led her outside, into the darkness beside the building. What had been a garden area there was now just a series of walkways through brown stalks and sand and dust. It was still quite hot outside, but Leah did not mind it. She walked between Jodie and Latham, rather like she was drugged, without turning her head to right or left. They walked to a bench, and sat down on it.

"It gives you a change of scenery," Latham said to Leah.

She looked at him. "Yes."

"It's not too hot out here for you, Leah?" he said.

"I like it here," she told him. She regarded him closely. "You haven't made it rain yet. Have you, Mark?"

He shook his head slowly. "I'm afraid not, Leah."

"The Russians went home, didn't they?"

"Yes. The Russians went home," he said.

"Will doesn't like the Russians much," Leah said. "I think you and he have that in common, Mark." She smiled a shy, pitiful smile.

Latham regarded her with a sober look that grew into a pseudo-grin. "I suppose that's true."

Leah clasped her hands in her lap in a tight-fisted, final way, as if she intended for them to grow together there. "Will never liked the Russians, not from the beginning."

Jodie looked away for a moment, fighting back tears. When she turned back to Leah, her face was tight-lined. "Tom says you'll be going home soon, honey. After you've had a little more rest here. We all kind of envy you, with the air-conditioning and the bottled water." She gave a strained, little laugh.

"I'd rather be at home without it," Leah said seriously.

"Yes, of course," Jodie said.

"I don't think Mother wants me home, though, Jodie."

Jodie regarded her curiously. "What makes you think that, Leah?"

"I make her nervous, I think. I remind her how bad things are."

"Oh, that's not true, Leah," Jodie protested. "I heard her say just yesterday how glad she'd be when you got home."

"Did she say that?" Leah asked, her eyes watery.

"Yes, of course," Jodie said. "She and Tom are both hoping you'll be back soon. It's the doctor who thinks you should stay here for a little while, but that's for your own good. You need complete rest, and quiet."

"I'm glad she said that," Leah said. "I know Ed Keefer wants me back, I'm valuable to him. But I can't handle that yet, Jodie. All those phone calls, all those angry voices."

"Of course not," Jodie said.

Leah caught Jodie's gaze. "I'm sorry, Jodie. I'm sorry about the pills. I don't know what got into me. I was just feeling so badly, when I got back from—I can't seem to remember where I'd been that morning. It seems like I was with Daddy and Mother. Did they mention it to you, Jodie?"

Jodie bit her lip. "I—don't think so, Leah," she said.

"Maybe it isn't important," Leah said. "Where I'd been, I mean. I would like to know, though."

"I'm sure you'll remember," Jodie said. "Just don't force it, honey. It will come."

"Well," Leah said, after a long silence. "I seem to be getting tired. I hope you two won't mind if I go back inside."

"No, of course we won't," Latham told her. "We didn't think you should stay out here very long."

They all rose and began walking back to the side entrance to the building. Jodie had been looking forward to this visit, but now she was very low. The night seemed particularly black, and the heat especially oppressive. She glanced toward Latham, and wondered why she should fear intimacy with him, when there was so much else to cause real fear around her. She was still mulling that thought, when they turned a corner around a dead shrub, and there it was confronting them.

A diamondback rattler, coiled directly on the walk.

Ready to strike.

Leah let out a small scream, and Jodie grabbed her.

"Stand still!" Latham said quietly.

The snake was a five-foot one, and shaking its rattles loudly. Latham had heard about snakes making intrusions into the city, but this was the first he had seen.

"Back up. Slowly," he said.

Jodie followed orders, pulling Leah with her. Leah had frozen, and was difficult to budge. All her muscles were stiffened, her eyes very wide. Jodie moved her backwards one step, then two.

The snake struck out at Latham.

Latham jumped sidewise, and the fangs sank into his trousers leg. There was another outcry from Leah, a stifled, moaning one. Latham jammed his foot down hard onto the rattler's head, and caught it squarely. There was a cracking of bone, and some writhing, and at last the snake lay lifeless on the dusty walk.

Leah was shaking so violently that Jodie could hardly hold her. Jodie was scared and angry and frustrated. "Easy, honey. Easy. It's all right. It can't hurt you now, really."

"Get her back inside," Latham said in a low voice.

Jodie led Leah in a wide circle around the snake, and into the building. Latham went over to the snake and kicked at it. It was dead. He picked it up and threw it into the nearest dead bush.

When he got back inside, Leah and Jodie were in Leah's room, with the doctor. The doctor was giving Leah a sedative, and Jodie was angrily criticizing the hospital, unreasonably, for allowing wild animals to come onto the grounds. In a few minutes she came out into the corridor, where Latham awaited her.

"She's resting now," she said tiredly. "But that didn't do her any good, Mark. Damn, this is frustrating, seeing her this way."

"You're just going to have to be patient, Jodie," he told her. "She'll heal, with time."

The doctor came out into the corridor, looking somber. He pushed his horn-rimmed glasses further up onto his nose. "I'm sorry this had to happen," he said, "especially during your visit."

"I shouldn't have blamed you or the hospital," Jodie admitted. "I'm just very uptight at the moment, doctor."

He smiled. "I understand perfectly. I don't know what can be done about these wild creatures coming into town. The police certainly have their hands full already, as does the Guard. There are quite a few roving coyotes now, and wild dogs. Some of the animals are rabid, I'm sure. It's another reason to stay off the streets at night, that's for certain."

"They're only trying to survive," Latham said. "Like us."

The doctor eyed him narrowly. "Do we have to give up on this thing now, Dr. Latham? I mean, since the Russians have left?"

Latham met his gaze pensively. "We'll never give up on it," he said. "But at the moment we have no miracles up our sleeves, doctor."

"Then I guess it's up to us to bear down and last through it," the doctor smiled uncertainly.

"That's about it," Latham told him.

"I'll keep you advised about Leah," the doctor said to Jodie.

"I appreciate that, doctor," Jodie said.

When Latham took Jodie home later, she made no invitation to him to come up and stay a while. She was still too upset about Leah to want to do anything but rest. Latham was disappointed. He felt a great need for Jodie that night, a need he had never felt for Christine. But he knew he could not force it between them. Jodie had to want it as much as he did, and it had to come naturally. She had to be convinced somehow that her affection would be returned, and not just momentarily. Words would not convince her, she had to be reached in more subtle ways. It might take time.

Latham wondered how much they had.

He did not go to bed that night. In his quarters at the university he sat up in an armchair, his feet on a stool, and pondered the very real life-or-death situation the Midwest was in. In another week or two there would be absolutely no water in Wichita, for example. Tom Purcell did not like to think of what would happen beyond that, nobody did. But people could not live without water. By the end of September, homes, buildings, the streets would be littered with corpses, with nobody to bury them. They would rot, stinking, in the open. Vultures would come in off the plains—Latham had already seen some, in the high, hot sky—and feed on the carrion. Then they, too, would die.

Even most insects would succumb to the drought. Maybe the scorpions would survive, across the plains and Southwest. They had survived everything else over a period of four hundred million years. Sitting there alone in his darkened room, Latham saw a great irony in that. The scorpion that man habitually crushed underfoot, that was beneath man's notice or concern, had managed to survive hundreds of times longer on the planet than *homo sapiens*, and some day when man was gone, it would probably still be here, crawling under rocks, getting along on next to nothing, lasting. It was a kind of joke on this godlike biped, if you could see the humor.

Latham sat there all night. He dozed off just once, for over an hour, then he seemed to be refreshed for renewed concentration. There had to be a solution. There almost always was, somewhere. Latham stared across the room into the darkness, hunched into himself, straining every nerve fiber in him. Thinking. Calculating. Ruminating.

When dawn illuminated the eastern sky outside his window, Latham was still at it. There seemed to be something tugging at the edge of his consciousness that was important, but which he could not quite catch hold of. He dressed, ate a light breakfast of dry cereal and raisins, with just a taste of precious water. He walked slowly to the lab, and when he got there he isolated himself in his small office, shunning Sprague and the others, withdrawn completely into himself.

The jet stream was unable to make clouds for them, he thought, for the thousandth time. Because of its out-of-kilter position. If there were clouds, they could be seeded. If. Man did not know how to make clouds. Only the jet stream did.

An idea blossomed in Latham's head.

He leaned forward on his chair, not wanting to lose it. Turning it over and over, examining it closely. No, it was absurdly impractical, just like all his other notions. *Isn't it?* he thought.

There was a knock on his door, and he figured it was an assistant. *"Not now!"* he called out. *"Come back later!"*

But then he heard Jodie's voice out there. *"It's Jodie, Mark. I'll just be a minute."*

He rose, went and opened the door. "I'm sorry, Jodie. I thought it was one of my people. I'd asked them not to disturb me. Come on in."

"I don't have to," she said, noticing his red-rimmed eyes and tired look. "I just wanted to tell you about the reservoir."

"No, please," he said, stepping aside for her. "I need a break. Come in and sit down."

She did, and Latham resumed his seat behind the small desk that was paper-littered.

"You look terrible," she said with concern.

"Thanks, I needed that," he grinned, joking.

Jodie felt herself blush slightly. She would not have made that remark to just anyone, she realized. Only to a person she accepted as very close to her. Maybe she was not as afraid of Mark Latham as she had thought.

"I'm sorry, but you know what I mean. Didn't you sleep last night?"

He shook his head. "Not much, Jodie. I've been wrestling with some crazy ideas. What is it about the reservoir?"

Jodie sighed. "Tom Purcell just called me, less than an hour ago. We're down to a two-day supply, Mark. Tom couldn't believe it, we both thought there was more than that. We'll be out by the end of the week. Then there will only be hoarded water. I'd rather not even think about how awful it will get at that point. I was coming over to the clinic here, so thought I'd stop past and let you know."

"All the news is bad nowadays, it seems," he told her.

Jodie turned toward a table fan to let it cool her flushed

face. Her hair was caught up behind her head, but ringlets of it had fallen loose, and she looked very pale. "I wish I knew how to keep them alive," she said to herself more than to Latham. "Just keep them alive."

Latham nodded understanding.

"You said you were doing some deep thinking," she said, turning to him. "Would you mind sharing some of your thoughts with an outsider?"

Latham grinned. "You're not an outsider, Jodie. There's nobody closer than you."

She averted her eyes, staring at her hands.

"Just before you came," he went on, "I was thinking of those vapor trails we see all the time across the city, from the landing jets. And I remembered."

"Remembered what?" she wondered.

"It's only happened a few times where competent meteorologists could observe the phenomenon," Latham said, leaning back on his chair and staring blankly past Jodie, now. "But there are cases. Where several vapor trails close together caused clouds to form. Clouds with high moisture content."

Jodie was listening casually. Now her interest quickened. "You mean, real clouds formed just from those narrow, white streaks we see all the time trailing out behind the jets?"

"That's right. But small clouds, and no rain has been reported coming from them. Also, the clouds would occur over a very small, limited area, of course. We need cloud cover over thousands of square miles, to make any difference, even if seeding were possible."

"Well, do you see any possibility of doing something with that idea?" Jodie asked with mild excitement. "Could you seed such clouds, if you could make them?"

"Ordinary methods might not work," he admitted. "Silver iodide particles wouldn't form sufficient ice crystals up there to do the job, in my opinion. But I've been working with a new seeding agent that involves electrified 'chaff,' or minutely cut metal foil, and a catalyst gas that helps crystals to form. This type of seeding would be done from far above the clouds themselves. Say, from Skyhook balloons."

Jodie leaned forward on her chair. "Well?" she said. "Isn't it worth a chance? Why can't we try it?"

Latham was shaking his head. "Jodie, everything I've said is the wildest theory. For instance, it would take literally hundreds of jets—no, thousands—to concentrate enough vapor up there over a big enough area. Then, if we got lucky and clouds formed, we'd have to collect tons of particulates here and in other sites strategically located around Kansas. I say Kansas because it's the center of the drought, and the place where we should concentrate our effort. If we could get it turned around here, it might spread out into other plains states. Anyway, after collecting a mountain of seeding agent—and making much of it ourselves, incidentally—then we'd have to get hold of hundreds of Skyhook balloons from all over the country, and at least one volunteer pilot for each balloon. There are only a few men who have been up on Skyhooks, Jodie, all over the country." He paused, watching her face. "Am I beginning to get through to you? The whole idea is logistically unfeasible. It's too bad, too, because if it could work, the conditions we set up could act as a force to nudge the big streams back where they belong. At least it would have as good a chance as the Russian radio-bombardment method."

"My God, you're absolutely brilliant," she said in a low voice.

Latham smiled at her. "Thanks, Jodie. But what good is an idea that won't work? By the time we could do all I've outlined—if we could do it—everybody in Kansas would be—well, it would be too late."

Jodie sat there, thinking. "I wonder," she said.

Latham studied her with a thinning smile. "What is it, Jodie? Do you have a magic wand in that medical bag? Are you really the Good Witch of the West?"

"Maybe we do have a wand," she said slowly. "A wand of power that is ordinarily not available to us. We have the raw power of both the governor and the President available to us, in this national emergency. Also, there are two other factors. Most airlines are almost down completely at the moment, their jets sitting empty. And the President personally knows three different airlines presidents, I heard Tom Purcell say so."

Latham pursed his lips, thinking.

"If Tom can convince the governor you have a good idea," Jodie said, "and the governor can convince the White House, I think we could bring the fleets of a dozen airlines to bear on this problem. And I mean immediately, within twenty-four or forty-eight hours."

"That might be several hundred planes," Latham admitted.

"And you can add the bombers of SAC to that," Jodie said, warming to her subject. "The squadrons from all over the Midwest. The President need only give the order."

Latham nodded. "That still wouldn't be enough, of course. But maybe we could run them across the same air space say, three or four times. We could accomplish such

266

a criss-crossing in a matter of a few hours, with the big jets."

Jodie's face had brightened. "Oh, God, Mark! But what about this 'chaff' you spoke of? Where will we get it?"

"There are several places that manufacture that kind of thing. We could get them all putting out at once. In just a couple of days we could have a lot of it here, I suppose. By plane, again. But there's still the Skyhooks and men to man them, Jodie."

"Doesn't the Weather Service have constant-altitude balloons?" Jodie wondered. "Keefer and Kravitz could get us a lot of them."

"If they would," Latham said sourly. "You can be sure Kravitz will do everything in his power to obstruct a project that originates here on campus."

Jodie shook her pretty head. "Not if he gets orders from the White House."

Latham smiled. She had latched onto his idea with a fervor that surprised him and won his respect. She had forced him to open up his thinking, and broaden it, in the area of application of theory.

"You know, you're right," he grinned at her. "And I think I know where I can get me some pilots."

"Where?" she asked.

"I belong to two national sport balloonists' organizations. There must be thousands of enthusiasts across the country who would be competent to man a Skyhook, and with a little instruction, do some seeding for us. I could call the presidents of these outfits, both of whom I know well, and have them make the personal calls to the members for us. I'll bet the response would be terrific."

"Another wonderful idea," Jodie said, smiling warmly for the first time in weeks.

"I didn't believe in any of this until you stopped by," he told her. "But now I think I do. I really think it's possible."

"Then let's give it a try," Jodie said. "What do we have to lose, Mark?"

He rose and came around to her, and pulled her to her feet. "Exactly," he said quietly to her. He touched his mouth to hers, and she felt the old excitement tingling her flesh. "What do we have to lose?"

FIFTEEN

The five of them sat around Tom Purcell's office tautly.

Floor fans hummed at them, making the stifling air barely breatheable. The temperature in the room was one hundred ten. Jodie, Sherwood Jameson, Tom Purcell and Hollis Sprague were all staring toward Mark Latham; Jameson and Purcell rather incredulously. Latham had just summarized his proposed project to them, and even Sprague was getting more detail than he had previously.

Sprague turned to Purcell. "What do you think, Tom? It's a damned bold idea, of course. That's characteristic of Mark's thinking. But scientifically speaking, I think it has a reasonable chance of success."

"It's a staggering notion, logistically," Purcell said.

"That's where we'll need your help, Tom," Sprague said. "And yours, Colonel."

Jameson shook his head slightly. "I don't know, Mark. You're going to have to get the cooperation of a lot of people." He had seemed to accept Latham, Jodie thought, now that Will was gone. "If you fail to get the support of the White House, the plan will be in immediate trouble, I'd think."

"Well," Mark said, "it shouldn't take long to find out.

The big thing will be to impress on the people involved that there's no time for committee meetings and arm-waving. This has to happen within the next few days, or we can forget it. That's how long we'll have water."

"Ninety percent of the preparations," Jodie said, "will have to be made on the long distance telephone. I'd think we can know by late today whether we can go ahead or not."

Purcell leaned onto his long desk. He looked washed-out, his skin flaccid-looking. Sprague looked even worse, and was getting stomach symptoms now. Jameson sat ramrod-stiff in his fatigues, his square chin jutted out. But he was not the same man since Will's death. He doubted himself, his mission, the possibility of survival. He tried not to let it show, but Jodie could see through the tough exterior to the wounded soldier beneath.

"I'll get on the wire to the governor as soon as we break up," Purcell said, and they could all hear the small excitement building in his voice as he spoke. "I'll try to get him to call the President directly. I'll impress on him that we have to know something before the day is over. Of course, the White House and we would have to get in touch with the heads of several airlines, and get definite commitments. I suppose if we got too many negative replies, the White House could commandeer those fleets, send troops to fly the jets."

"Even now, through all of this, the President would be reluctant to do anything like that," Jameson said. "But maybe we'll get enough affirmative answers so a showdown isn't necessary, particularly if the government promises reimbursement from federal funds. I know a couple of Air Force generals personally, and might be able to implement the use of SAC aircraft, so these people are not just going through motions for the President."

"I'll go ahead and place orders for metal chaff for the seeding, in case we need it," Latham said. "We can have enough in a couple of days, I'd guess, if we have it flown here and to other balloon-ascension sites that Dr. Sprague and I will agree on."

"I don't think you'll have any trouble getting Skyhooks," Jameson said to Latham, "if Tom mentions the need to the President. For God's sake don't go through Kravitz."

"We wouldn't even consider it," Sprague said with a weak grin.

"I can help you start making calls to sport balloon people," Jodie told Mark. "Also, just in case. These people will all have to get to Kansas, and quickly."

"I'll dip into municipal funds to get them here," Purcell told her. "The least we can do is pay their transportation, if they volunteer to help out. The job would be rather dangerous, wouldn't it, Mark?"

Latham nodded. "To some extent, yes."

"Where will you be placing these various kinds of aircraft?" Jameson asked. "To begin the operation?"

Latham blew out a long breath. "The idea will be to saturate the air space over Kansas with jet vapor trails. We'll want some here, and in Topeka, Kansas City, Omaha, Pueblo, Tulsa, maybe Oklahoma City and Amarillo. They'll work a criss-cross pattern through one long morning of flying, and they'll all be at about the same altitude, so we'll have to coordinate the flight patterns exactly so nobody is colliding up there."

"What about the balloons?" Purcell asked.

"They'll be spread over the same area, only at more

sites. I'd say a couple hundred sites, at least, and some sites may utilize more than one balloon. It will be a massive job to get all these craft ready to seed in a brief time, but there will probably be personnel at each air field who will be willing to help out."

Jameson was studying Latham's handsome face closely. "Do you really think that these vapor trails can make clouds that will rain on us?" he said doubtfully, when Latham was finished.

Latham held Jameson's sober gaze. "I just don't know, Colonel. I think the potential is there. And, of course, if this were not a disaster situation, the idea would be completely unrealistic, to spend millions and millions of dollars and man-hours like this, just to make it rain. To mount a federally funded program of this proportion, twist the arms of private industry, call on volunteers from all walks of life. But we are in a disaster, Colonel, of unprecedented proportions, one that makes this great risk of time and money, this one-time gamble, seem worthwhile. We're down to saving lives, now. That's all we expect out of this, if we expect anything. Of course, a by-product benefit might just be to save this great bread basket of the world from permanent destruction."

Jameson nodded. "Well, at least you've given us something valuable already, Mark. Something that all of us need very much right now, just to get through another day. You've given us hope back."

"Exactly," Tom Purcell said.

"I'd never have pushed this," Latham said, "if it hadn't been for Jodie. It was she who had hope first, even before me."

Jodie shrugged. "It was faith that I had, Mark. Faith in a great idea. And in a man."

Jodie and Latham's eyes locked in a sure embrace, and Jodie was suddenly embarrassed. Purcell smiled, and Jameson studied the two of them seriously.

"I hope your faith is justified, Jodie," Latham said. "Now that I have the backing of all of you here, I have this sudden attack of cold feet. It's awesome to think of the machinery we're going to try to put into motion in the next couple of days. Awesome and humbling."

Sprague laughed in his throat. "A little humility is refreshing," he said. "After the Russians."

The rest of that day was a busy, tense one. All of the five who had met at Purcell's office, and many assistants, were placing calls all across the country. Latham realized, in those hours, what a miracle of the modern age the telephone was. In the 1800's there would have been no hope at this juncture for the residents of Wichita or Kansas, because of lack of communications and transportation. Before the twentieth century, time was a much more deadly enemy. Now it could be beaten occasionally, with luck.

Latham hoped they all had some, in the next few days.

By dinner time, nothing had been settled. The governor of Kansas was still trying to get in touch with the White House, and he was not going to commit himself unless the President did. Latham had started things going on production and shipment of seeding agent, and had made some calls, with Jodie, to balloonists. They had some big commitments to the project already, but it all hinged, still, on goverment backing, and on the cooperation of the big airlines.

Jodie, Latham and Jameson all had dinner together at Jodie's place that evening. It was not much of a meal, despite Jodie's cooking ability. There was no meat now, no eggs, no canned goods. They had a wilted salad, some fresh fruit for moisture, some toast. Jodie turned on her water faucet in the kitchen and just a few brown drops came out. Then it quit completely. She brought out a small ration of tepid water, and they all had a drink of it at the end of the meal. But it did not slake their growing and insistent thirst.

There had been increasing lawlessness through that day, and Jameson's troops were becoming fatigued with overwork, and short-tempered. There were some subordinate officers who openly espoused the notion of lining offenders up against a wall and shooting them. Jameson had to fight that sentiment among his people, but it was becoming increasingly difficult to do so with each day that passed.

Because of the extra trouble through the day, Jameson was obliged to leave Jodie and Latham earlier than he would have liked, in early evening, to attend to his duties. He was picked up by a tough-looking captain and two sergeants in a military jeep, and they drove him around the night city, checking on the deployment of troops.

It was at their third stop that they ran into trouble that evening. Jameson had posted a four-man squad at the intersection of Oliver and Twenty-first Street, near Aurora Park. When the jeep approached that area, Jameson heard shooting up ahead, and he knew immediately that his people there were in trouble.

When the vehicle pulled up to the intersection, the occupants saw three of the guardsmen crouched in the cover of their own jeep and a parked car. They had been attacked by a roving band of hoodlums who had been run off at a looting across town by a larger Jameson force, and were now here to wreak some kind of twisted vengeance on the Guard by killing these other soldiers.

One soldier lay in the street near the jeep, shot but not dead. Two of his comrades were crouched against their jeep, and a last one huddled beside a bullet-dented Buick sedan at a curb. The firing at them was coming from two store fronts across the intersection, and a building closer to them. The guardsmen were returning fire, but appeared to be outnumbered by about two.

"There, in that doorway!" Jameson yelled, as the jeep squealed to a halt almost in the line of fire. *"Go after them first!"*

The besieged soldiers saw the colonel's jeep pull up, and looked very relieved. Now the captain and sergeants were piling out of the vehicle and heading for the building where three of the five assailants were firing from cover. They all carried submachine guns, and began raking the doorway with heavy fire. The surprised assailants now turned their fire on the newcomers, and one of the sergeants went down. Jameson and the other two kept on toward the building, firing off clattering rounds. The besieged guardsmen were now able to turn and concentrate their fire on the nearer building, where two more assailants were still firing at them. Someone yelled from that direction, and then at the store front that Jameson was assaulting, a crazy-looking young man stepped out of the shadows and cover shouting obscenities and firing a big pistol toward them. The captain rattled off a burst from his submachine gun, and the youth threw his arms into the air and went running backwards under the hail of hot lead, his eyes open very wide. He hit the pavement hard on his back, and his right leg drummed at the concrete for a moment.

A second fellow came out with his hands high, and then the third. Across the way, the unwounded assailant in the nearby building also came out into the open, hands raised.

"*Okay, okay!*" this last one yelled. "*You've got us, for Christ's sake!*"

"*Yeah,*" the first one out on Jameson's side called out. "*We surrender, pigs!*"

Jameson walked up to him, grim-faced. "Now you surrender, you bastards. After you've shot two of my men."

The surviving sergeant came up to the second man out, and grabbed him by the shirt. "Over to the jeep, you sonofabitch!"

"*We're secure over here, Colonel!*" one of the besieged men called out.

"*All right,*" Jameson replied. "*See to those wounded men.*"

It was a moment of relaxation. Jameson had turned away from the assailant he confronted, the first one out, and suddenly the fellow went into his shirt as Jameson turned back. He had a small handgun in his right fist and a twisted grin on his narrow face.

"Surprise, Colonel!"

Then he fired the gun pointblank at Jameson.

The shot took everybody by complete surprise. Except that Jameson, in a reflex movement, raised the submachine at his side and fell into a half-crouch at the same moment in time. The shot from the handgun, instead of hitting Jameson in the heart, where it was aimed, caught him in the shoulder.

Jameson stumbled backward a step, and then pressed his finger on the automatic weapon. It banged out its message again into the night, making yellow explosions in the darkness, and the assailant was hit across the low chest by three hot slugs. He pirouetted off his feet, spinning in a tight circle, and plunged to the pavement on his face.

Jameson dropped to his right knee, his left hand going to his shoulder, his face white and drawn. Blood seeped through his fatigue jacket and onto his fingers.

"*Colonel!*" the captain yelled, from ten feet away. "*For Christ's sake!*"

Jameson knelt there trying to get some strength back. Raw pain ricocheted through his shoulder, his chest, his arm and head. The burly captain's face had gone an odd color, and he now strode over to the downed assailant whom Jameson had just shot, but who was still alive. "*You creep!*" he yelled. "*You yellow bastard!*"

Then he aimed his automatic gun at the fallen figure and blasted off several rounds into its head.

Jameson was trying desperately to focus on what was going on. The figure on the pavement jerked and jumped for a moment, then was still. Something had hit Jameson's trousers leg, and he squinted and saw that it was a bloody bone fragment from the shot man's skull.

The sergeant with the disarmed prisoner had seen what the captain did. "Yeah," he muttered hoarsely. He turned and aimed his gun at his prisoner and squeezed the trigger. Another three shots erupted into the night, and the surprised prisoner was knocked violently off his feet, slamming against the parked car that the besieged soldiers had used for cover, then sliding slowly to the ground. He had crimson holes in his side, his middle chest, his neck. Blood was on the car and on the pavement.

Jameson finally understood what was happening. *"No, damn it!"* he gritted out. Across the street, another soldier had taken his cue from his superiors and was leveling his gun on his prisoner. Jameson shouted toward him, angrily. *"Hold it, by God!"*

The soldier glanced at the downed Jameson, hesitated, and slowly got himself under control. He took another look at the man before him, then lowered his gun.

"Jesus Christ," the surrendered man gasped out.

One of the soldiers who had been besieged came and bent over Jameson and pulled him carefully to his feet. He had not done any of the wanton shooting, but he could not look Jameson in the eye. Jameson staggered with his help to the jeep he had come in, and stared toward the two executed prisoners. Finally, he looked up at his captain, only a few feet away.

The captain was standing there breathing shallowly, with a stoic, defensive look on his face.

"Those bastards deserved it, Colonel!" the hysterical sergeant said from where he had shot down the second prisoner. His eyes were wild, opaque-looking. *"They wanted to kill all of us, couldn't you see that?"*

Jameson ignored him, still staring stonily at his burly captain. It was the same man who had come into his office that time when Jodie had been there, and whom Jameson had described to Jodie as a good officer.

"I—lost control for a moment," the captain said in a low, quiet voice. "I just—lost control." There was no apology in his voice, no remorse. Just fatigue.

Jameson sighed heavily. It was hard to place blame, in a situation like this, difficult to judge a man too harshly. But there had to be rules. Otherwise none of it made any sense. "You're relieved of command, Captain," Jameson said in a hollow, unreal voice.

"Yes, sir," the captain replied without emotion.

"Place yourself and the sergeant under close arrest," Jameson went on mechanically, "and then get an ambulance over here. We're going to need one."

"Very well, Colonel."

"Colonel," the soldier who had helped him to his feet said now, "what you want done with them bodies?"

Jameson looked at the soldier darkly. "Just leave them where they are, Private. They're not going to bother anyone anymore. Not in this life, anyway."

It was only just over an hour later that Jodie and Latham arrived at the hospital anxiously, to see Jameson. Latham had heard about the shoot-out first, through Hollis Sprague, and he had driven back over to Jodie's place immediately. It was ten p.m. when he picked her up, and it took them only ten minutes to reach the hospital.

Jameson was just coming out of a local-anesthesia surgery when they arrived, and the bullet had been removed from his shoulder and the wound was draining well. He was sitting up in bed when they first saw him, using the telephone, issuing directives despite his condition. When he hung up the phone, he gave them a weak smile.

"I asked them to tell you not to come," he said to Jodie. "I'm perfectly all right, Jodie. I'll be out of here tomorrow, it's just a scratch, really."

They stood beside his bed. Jodie looked at the thick bandage on her father's shoulder, and the dark spot showing through it, and knew that it was more than a scratch. But she was so grateful that he was alive, she felt strangely elated. "Oh, God, Dad!" she mumbled, bending and embracing him.

Jameson patted her back. "It's okay, honey."

Jodie straightened, still holding his hand. "Thank God," she said quietly.

Latham came around beside Jodie, looking very weary. "I hear you had quite a battle scene out there for a while, Colonel."

Jameson's face clouded over. "Something ugly happened out there tonight, Mark. I've seen it coming, but there was nothing I could do about it when it happened. My people executed a couple of disarmed men."

"Oh, no," Jodie said.

Jameson stared past them. His shoulder hardly hurt, with the drugs in him. "I'm responsible, of course. I should have headed it off. I should have done something."

Latham studied Jameson's grim face. "We can't control the actions of everybody we answer for," he said.

Jameson shook his head slowly. "First Will, and now this," he said. "It shakes a man. Makes you wonder what you've accomplished, what you've stood for, through it all. Whether the people around you might not have been better off with someone else calling the shots."

Jodie gripped his hand tightly. "You've been a good father and a fine soldier. Don't let this ruin it for you."

Jameson clapped his other hand onto hers. "Hey. I'm sorry to unload this onto you two. I guess it's just that I don't know what to do with my two people involved. I guess it's that I know how close I was to the same thing myself. That's what's bothering me." He sighed heavily, then looked at Latham. "Has Tom Purcell heard anything?"

"Not yet," Latham said. "The President has called in

some members of the Cabinet for an all-night meeting. We're supposed to hear something tomorrow morning. But we're going ahead with the rest of it."

"If we get a go-ahead from the White House, I'll start making some calls to some old friends in the Air Force," Jameson said.

"I got a call from Stanley Kravitz tonight," Latham told him. "He's already heard about our proposed project. He was incensed that we'd make plans for something this big without going through his headquarters at McConnell. He doesn't know we're in contact with the White House. He insists we hold in abeyance all plans involving weather control until he and his staff have had a chance to study them in detail. He wants detailed prospectuses sent over to him, and meetings between us and his people. I told him there was no time for all of that, that we'd clue him in personally if he'd just stop past. He hung up on me with a couple of threats."

"Typical of him," Jameson said. "He can't cause us trouble, can he, Mark?"

"I don't see how," Latham said. "I'll keep you advised about the President, Colonel. Just get well. Don't make any decisions about your two men until this is over, you may feel differently then."

Jameson smiled weakly. "That sounds like good advice, professor."

"And please don't get out of this bed until the doctor tells you it's okay," Jodie said. "Will you promise me?"

"Okay, Jodie," Jameson said. "I promise."

It was a hot drive back across town to Jodie's place, and Jodie was quiet all the way there. When they got there and Latham was parked on the lot beside the building,

Jodie turned to him sober-faced.

"Thanks for the ride, Mark. I think Dad liked it that you came."

"He's going to be all right," Latham said. "The wound isn't a bad one."

"Well. I guess I'll go on in. We both have a big day ahead of us tomorrow."

Latham was staring through the windshield. "I have this ugly feeling, Jodie. That even if we get the co-operation of the government, and the airlines, and all the people we need, that it won't work. That my idea was a bad one from the beginning, and that it will all be a stupendous failure, an even bigger one than that of the Russians."

Jodie looked over at him. "Don't think about it, Mark. It's probably best not to second-guess yourself at this stage."

"I keep seeing Wichita as a windblown dust pile, with rotting corpses in the streets and buzzards floating high in the hot air, looking for carrion."

Jodie watched his somber face, not knowing what to say.

"We'll be taking up our last time available, with this," he went on. "If this crazy plan of mine doesn't work, we'll have wasted any time we had left for something else."

Jodie touched his face softly. "There isn't anything else," she reminded him. "Nothing, Mark."

Latham turned to her, his gaze intense. "Don't send me away tonight, Jodie. Not tonight."

Jodie looked quickly away, uncertain.

"I need you, Jodie," he added urgently.

She looked back at him. "All right," she said.

They went up to her apartment in silence. Upstairs, it was very hot and stuffy. Jodie turned on all the fans she owned, and threw open all her windows and the French doors. She made no attempt to make small talk with him. She went into the bedroom and pulled the covers off and piled them on a chair. There was only a sheet and two pillows remaining on the bed. She aimed a floor fan toward it, pulled curtains away from two windows there. It was at that point, then, that she noticed the tension building inside her, the anxiety—the heat. Now she hurried slightly in her movements as she went into the small bathroom and undressed. Latham had come into the bedroom now, and was disrobing also. When she came out into the bedroom, nude, he was standing in a corner, facing away from her, unfastening his trousers. She climbed onto the wide bed and lay down on it on her back, legs separated, arms at her sides, waiting.

When Latham turned and saw her, he just stood there for a very long moment, a moment that seemed like an eternity to Jodie. Then he came over and got onto the bed beside her.

"You don't know how much I've wanted this," he said huskily.

"Yes," she said. "I do."

Latham rolled onto his side, and suddenly he was touching her all along their lengths. She gasped slightly. His hand moved onto her full breasts, and her breathing became shallow and irregular. "Oh, God," she murmured. "Oh, God."

"You're what I've waited for all my life," he breathed, "without knowing I was."

283

A little moan from her throat.

"There'll never be anyone else, baby, I know that now."

She turned to him. She had never felt such a heat inside her, it was almost unbearable. If he did not take her immediately, she felt, she would go crazy with the fever for him. He reached and pulled her to him closely, hugging all her rich curves against him, and kissed her hotly on the mouth. Jodie responded with an urgency that slightly surprised him. There was a long moment of fiery probing and touching and caressing, and then she was gasping for breath, eyes wide in wonder at her unquenchable heat.

"Jesus!" he whispered hoarsely. "I—can't wait, honey. I can't—wait."

"I don't—want you to," she gasped out. "Go ahead. Please. Now!"

Suddenly she was smothered by his weight, his muscular arms enveloping her, his kisses on her face, her throat, her breasts. She took him in hand feverishly and joined them with a hard thrust of her hips, crying out into the darkness of the room with quick, heart-jolting pleasure.

There was no casual approach to climax this time. It was as if both of them had been building emotionally for this moment all through their lives, and could not wait for its release. There was a desperate reaching and grasping, an entwining and merging of such seeming permanence that there was no past and no future, only that torrid moment in eternity. At the climax of passion Jodie's unrestrained outcries resounded off the room walls exuberantly, and Latham mauled her with hard savagery, and she clutched him tightly to her damp flesh with a fierceness that bruised and cut his back and arms.

They lay together afterwards for a long time. Jodie did not want him to ever leave her body, she wanted that sweet fire inside her to burn forever. This was the only island of beauty and truth in a madhouse of a universe around her, and she wanted to pretend that this was all there was.

When they finally separated, a long while later, Latham lay there weak and exhausted and staring into the darkness above him. "I love you, Jodie."

She looked over at him.

"I never want to lose you," he added.

The fire inside her had been quenched. She was slowly cooling down, and with the lessening of heat came reason and caution.

"Let's not talk about permanence tonight," she whispered.

Latham stared at her lovely body for a moment, then turned and cast a sober look toward the ceiling without making a reply to her. There was no need to comment on her suggestion, they both knew what she meant.

In a couple of weeks, it might be over for all of them.

But that was something nobody said aloud.

SIXTEEN

"That's right, operator, this is Tom Purcell. Who? The President of the United States? Yes, I'll hold." The mayor cupped his hand over the phone, and turned to Latham and Sherwood Jameson, who were sitting before his desk. Jameson had left the hospital at noon, with his doctor's okay, and it was now three p.m. Purcell had been expecting a call from the governor, and had gathered Latham and Jameson to him to discuss the plan they now referred to as Operation Big Seed, while he awaited the call. He was very surprised, at this moment, that the call was directly from the White House. "It's the President himself!" he whispered to them.

Latham and Jameson exchanged glances. "I'll be damned!" Jameson said.

Purcell was listening into the phone, his face flushed, his shirt open at the collar and soiled-looking. Everybody looked a little soiled and wilted these days. "Yes?" he said suddenly. "Yes, Mr. President, this is Tom Purcell."

"*Tom*," the deep voice came to him, "*I've just gotten out of a second cabinet meeting with my top advisors here. There was some small opposition to your Big Seed project, but the bottom line is, we've decided to go ahead with it.*"

"That's wonderful news, Mr. President," Purcell

grinned. He cupped the phone again. "We've got a go-ahead," he said to Latham and Jameson.

"By God," Jameson said.

Latham just sat there, silent, feeling the responsibility more heavily than he ever had felt it before.

"Now, this is going to be a massive effort, as I understand your plan," the President went on. *"How many planes do you think you'll need for this fly-over?"*

Purcell grunted into the phone. "Just as many as we can get, Mr. President. Literally. We can't have too many, according to our expert here. Yes, that's Dr. Mark Latham, University of California at Berkeley. He's the physicist who's been mentioned to you previously."

"You're talking big money here, Tom," the President said solemnly. *"These jets don't fly on peanuts, you know. I'm going to have to promise some federal funds reimbursement. I've already talked with some congressional leaders, and they say they'll appropriate money for the reimbursement."*

"What about the airlines, Mr. President?" Purcell asked. "Have any of them been approached yet?"

"I've made a couple of calls myself. To TWA, National, Pan Am. I've got my aides checking out the others. I think we can guarantee you close to a thousand jets, if you really need them."

"Latham says we do," Purcell said.

"All right. I'll have an aide call you back later, to give you a list of firm commitments, with a breakdown of numbers of planes. I understand you want this to happen in the next twenty-four hours."

"We'd like to have the jets in place and fueled by then, Mr. President."

"All right, you work through my aide regarding where

287

you want them—Wichita, Omaha, et cetera. The airlines will work out flight schedules in accord with this Dr. Latham's orders. We'll have to get on this immediately, because of the complexity. I'm also issuing orders to several SAC bases this afternoon. My aide ought to be in touch with you by dinnertime."

"I can't tell you how much we appreciate this," Purcell said soberly. "For us here, it's a matter of life-or-death."

"I'm aware of that, Tom," the President said.

"Oh, one other thing," Purcell added. "Are we going to have some National Weather Service balloons at our disposal?"

"That's no problem. I've already spoken with the Director, and he's getting some ready to ship out by air later today. Latham said you needed three or four hundred. I'm trying to get five."

"I'll advise your aide where we want them," Purcell said.

"Fine. Anything else I can do?"

"Nothing I can think of, Mr. President. Thanks again, and we'll be in touch."

"We'll be watching this with the gravest interest," the voice came from the other end.

When Purcell hung up, he turned to Latham and Jameson with a grin decorating his sallow features. "By God, we're on a green light!"

"Damned good," Jameson said. He had taken Latham's advice and delayed any decision on his captain and sergeant, merely giving them limited, essentially clerical duties until Big Seed was over one way or the other. "Damned fine, Tom." He grimaced, touching his shoulder.

Latham made a face. "I'm scared to death," he admitted.

"We know there's no guarantees," Purcell said to him. "The President knows it, too. We made that very clear to him. We're just glad to have something to try, Mark."

Latham rose from his chair. "Well. I have a lot of calculations to complete, and about a thousand calls to make. I might as well get at it."

"Good luck, Mark," Purcell told him. "And for God's sake, tell us what you need. I'll call you when I've heard again from the White House."

"I'll be there," Latham said.

For the rest of that day, Latham and Jodie isolated themselves together in Latham's office, making calls to sport balloon organizations and to individuals. Jameson visited the commander at McConnell Air Force Base, and got a commitment from him to implement the President's directive as expeditiously as possible, which meant making bombers available within the next twenty-four hours. He also called several other generals around the Midwest, expressing the urgency they felt in Kansas for immediate help. At just after seven p.m., the White House aide called Tom Purcell and advised him that the President had commitments from almost every major airline in the country, including a couple of foreign-based ones. Purcell, in accord with Latham's instructions, suggested to the aide where the planes should be situated, and in what numbers, for the big upcoming fly-over. Maximum and minimum flight altitudes were discussed, with the suggestion that the airlines themselves coordinate flight patterns within those boundaries.

When Purcell called and told Latham, Latham and

Jodie had just finished with their calls for the evening. Latham listened quietly to the news, and then thanked Purcell for letting him know.

"We got them?" Jodie said when Latham had put the phone down. "We really got the planes?"

"There will be between nine hundred and a thousand," Latham said. "And that excludes military jets. If my theory holds any validity, we have the equipment to get the job done now. Tomorrow we're getting three plane-loads of Skyhooks, distributed over Kansas and parts of Iowa and Oklahoma. We'll have the military there in those places to receive them, and they'll distribute them even further, to airfields large and small over this whole area. Our balloonists are on their way to all those sites right now. The area military will advise them about time coordination, and I've already mimeographed instructions about installation of seeding equipment and seeding operations. Those are being delivered specially by the Post Office to the take-off sites. God, I hope I haven't overlooked anything important."

"I'm impressed," Jodie said. "Maybe Christine is right. Maybe you should be an administrator rather than a scientist."

Latham recognized the remark as a joke even before he saw the smile spread onto Jodie's lovely face. He returned it, glad she could see any humor in Christine's past influence over him. "Maybe," he said. "But I don't think so."

"I have to admit that all of this problem-solving is good for me, at least," she said. They were sitting across his desk from each other, with fans on them. "You tend to forget that so much hinges on the outcome."

He nodded. "I know what you mean. But there are

little reminders for us. Hollis Sprague went home sick this afternoon earlier. I didn't tell you because I didn't want you to worry through the work day."

"Is it his stomach again?" Jodie said, sudden concern in her face.

"I'm afraid so. He can't seem to keep anything down now, not even water. He's lost to us, I think, Jodie. For the duration of this God-awful trouble."

"He tried so hard not to succumb," Jodie said. "I'll, have to look in on him. Has he had a doctor in?"

"Yes, I made sure of that. Jesus, if this doesn't work, Jodie—"

She watched his straight-lined face and felt the almost unbearable weight of his responsibility. "It will, Mark," she said softly. "It will."

Latham glanced over at her. "How is Leah, by the way? You called the hospital, didn't you?"

"Yes," Jodie said. "I meant to tell you, but you were on the phone. She mentioned Will's funeral."

"Really? That's good, isn't it?"

"The doctor says it's very good. She seems to be slowly allowing herself to recognize the truth of Will's death. She could go home in a couple of weeks—if that's otherwise possible."

"Yes," Latham said. "If it's otherwise possible."

There was a knock on the office door, and Latham called out permission for entry. A young man came in, one of Sprague's lab assistants.

"There's a couple of pieces of mail for you, Dr. Latham," the fellow told him.

"Okay, thanks," Latham said. He took the mail, and the fellow left with a nod to Jodie.

Latham glanced through the small pile of mail, and

stopped and stared hard at one thick envelope. "Well, well," he said.

Jodie frowned slightly. "Something important?" she wondered.

"It's from the court in San Francisco," he said.

Jodie wished she had not asked. He opened the envelope, took out a thick sheaf of papers stapled together with a blue cover.

"It's divorce papers," he said heavily. "A summons and bill of complaint."

Jodie watched his face. He skimmed the pages quickly, turning sheets of paper. "Mental cruelty," he said. "Lack of love and affection." He put the papers down onto the desk. "I should be elated, Jodie. But I don't feel anything." He stared at the dropped papers.

"Maybe you'd like to be alone," she suggested.

"God, no," he told her. "I'm all right. Really."

"Will you have to go to San Francisco?"

"I don't think so. There's nothing to haggle over in this one. We had no real estate, no kids. There was damned little we did have together, come to think of it."

Jodie was silent, listening, assessing his words.

"We didn't read the same books, or even the same magazines and newspapers. We liked different kinds of furniture. She had her car, I had mine. She always liked to use separate hand towels. If we had ever had children, we'd have had to have one for her, one for me. That's the way it was with us. I suppose that in a few years, we'd have had separate beds."

"Some people are that way, Mark," Jodie finally said.

He nodded. "Oh, I know. But it was more than that. Separate was not enough for Christine. She had to try to control my side of the dichotomy. She wanted to dress me

292

for an outing, for God's sake. If I had my own idea about which shirt to wear, there would be a big argument about it. She even bought my clothes, in the last year. She arranged for parties without my consent or knowledge. If I invited a colleague to our home that she did not find 'exciting' and 'fun,' she would veto the invitation.

"Of course, it was partially my fault. Because I was so wrapped up with my work, I didn't take much notice, didn't care, for a long time. Then it was too late. There was no going back."

"I had some of that with Lou Falco," Jodie said quietly. "With a little male chauvinism thrown in."

Latham looked at her, focused on her for the first time in several minutes. "My God, the things we find to kill something that starts out good," he said.

"Yes," Jodie agreed.

"I suppose the most basic difference between Christine and me was our priorities," he now concluded. "I had never had money, and put little importance on it and the things it could buy. Christine, on the other hand, had always had it, was accustomed to all the creature comforts. She couldn't understand why the work I was doing was more important to me than earning more money, moving up in the world. I suppose she never will understand."

"The mis-matching of people is very sad," Jodie said. "It can spoil lives, when it isn't caught early. But maybe some skill can come with experience."

Latham held her gaze. "I'm hoping so," he said deliberately.

Jodie averted her eyes noncommitally. She was still afraid to think in terms of lasting affection, apprehensive of thinking past this week, or even tonight. Not just

293

because of Christine and what she and Latham had meant to each other, at one time, but because there might not be a future for them in Wichita. Any of them.

There was a second knocking on the door behind Jodie, and Latham glanced over there with irritation. "Damn," he said. "Yes, what is it?"

The same young fellow poked his head into the office. "Sorry to bother you again, professor. But there's somebody here to see you."

"Oh?" Latham said. "Who?"

"It's Kravitz, over from McConnell."

Latham and Jodie exchanged dark looks. "Oh, hell," Latham said.

"You'd better see him," Jodie suggested.

Latham nodded. "All right, send him in."

The lab technician glanced over his shoulder. "Oh. Here he is. You can go on in, Mr. Kravitz."

Latham and Jodie rose as Kravitz blustered into the room past the lab man, flushed in his meaty face and scowling. The technician closed the door behind him, and was gone. Kravitz came and glared hard at Latham, without speaking, and then glanced toward Jodie. He looked bad. His eyes were red-rimmed, and he had developed a small twitching at the corner of his right eye.

"Well," he said in a low growl. "I'm glad I caught you here."

"I'll be running along," Jodie said. "So you two can have some privacy."

"That's not necessary," Kravitz said in a hard voice. "You might as well hear this, too."

Jodie and Latham looked at each other. "Will you have a seat, Kravitz?" Latham said.

"No, I will not!" Kravitz told him. "What I have to say

is better said on my feet!"

Latham shrugged. "Anything you say."

The three of them stood around the small office, stonily. Kravitz turned hostilely to Latham.

"You've been trouble to me from the moment you arrived here," he grated out. "You made the Russians feel unwelcome, you threatened obstructive and competitive projects. And now this!"

"Now what?" Latham said.

Kravitz's face flushed even a deeper color. "Now you embark on this complex, expensive, foolish project without clearing it through the Weather Service! I know what's been going on in the past twenty-four hours, don't bother to deny it! You've gone ahead despite my warnings to you, and contacted airlines, the Weather Service headquarters in Washington, even the White House!"

"Why should I deny it?" Latham said. "We've done all that and more to implement Operation Big Seed. We couldn't stop to clear everything with you personally, Kravitz. There just wasn't time. Anyway, you wouldn't have gone along. Would you?"

"*You're damned right I wouldn't!*" Kravitz fairly yelled at Latham. "I think this is an absurd attempt to show Washington that we don't need foreign supervision of this problem, that American science has answers of its own! I think you're trying to mount a monstrous project that will be catastrophic in its failure! Jet vapor for cloud-producing! That's university theory, Latham! I'm telling you once and for all, abort this silliness and let the Weather Service and NASA handle this problem!"

"We tried that," Latham said sourly. "Now we're going to have our turn, Kravitz. We already have White

House approval for it."

Kravitz' face sagged into long lines of dismay. "You what?"

"The President himself has okayed the project," Latham said with a certain amount of satisfaction.

Kravitz fumed. "I don't believe that!"

"You might as well," Jodie put in. "Tom Purcell just called us. Not only the White House is behind us, but much of the Congress. We've obtained the cooperation of airlines, private manufacturers—even your National Weather Service."

Kravitz looked wild-eyed. It was obvious that the heat had taken its toll on him. He had never been a pleasant individual, but now he had become quite neurotic about it all.

"You went over my head to Washington!" he said to Jodie. He turned back to Latham. "Behind my back! Turning my superiors against me! I knew you had!"

"We didn't even mention your name," Latham said flatly.

"Damn you!" Kravitz said, shaking slightly. "You're out to ruin me, aren't you? Make me look bad, so that my career will be finished! You and your Ivy Tower people!"

"I told you," Latham said. "We weren't thinking of you. We have a disaster on our hands here, Kravitz, remember? Time is of the essence in a situation like this. We did what we had to do to get this thing off the ground. Now, if you don't mind, we both have work to do here."

"You think this is the end of this?" Kravitz said loudly. "Do you really think you can write me off like this?"

"Kravitz—" Latham said.

"I'll put the skids to this, you wait and see," Kravitz

said, his heavy face shaking with rage. "I'll call the White House, too. I have friends there, you know. They'll speak to the President, make him realize he's made a mistake in dealing directly with you and that Sprague. I know people in Congress, too. I'll get this whole crazy plot stopped right where it is! You hear me?"

"We hear you, Kravitz," Latham told him. "Now get to hell out of here. You're wasting our valuable time."

"You'll hear from me, you bastard!" Kravitz yelled as he opened the door to leave. *"Don't forget it! I'm not taking this lying down, by God!"*

A moment later he was gone from the room, and they could hear him shouting at someone in the corridor. Latham went and closed the door quietly, and then stood there pensive for a long moment. "That man is going to pieces fast," he said after a while.

"It affects all of us differently," Jodie said. "His job is done here, and he failed in what he thought was a great project. He can't admit it's all over for him, that he wasn't the savior of the Midwest."

"I just wish he'd move out of the way," Latham said, "and let us try our way now. Without all of these threatening gestures."

"Can he hurt us now?" she wondered. "At this late moment in time? Can he change the President's mind?"

"Would he change yours?" Latham said.

Jodie shook her head. "I see what you mean."

"I think all he can do if he really makes those calls is hurt himself in Washington," Latham said. "Anyway, I suspect it's too late for him to undo what's been done. Airlines are massing jets to fly to Kansas. The Skyhooks are already on their way. One voice—a crazy-sounding one—isn't going to turn all that around. The White

House is committed now, as are a lot of other organizations and individuals."

Latham returned to his desk, and slumped heavily onto the chair there. Jodie knew that he had had little extra strength for the verbal assault of Kravitz. He looked very tired, now.

"Well," he said. "There are no more calls we can make tonight. I suppose I should double-check some calculations I made earlier. About seeding techniques. The timing has to be exact, and the amount of seeding material used."

"You know," Jodie said, "there's a point beyond which it doesn't do much good to go on. You need a rest, Mark. You've had a terrible day."

"I'll rest when it's all over."

"You'll do a better job tomorrow morning, on those calculations. You'll approach them with more energy, and a clearer head."

Latham glanced over at her. "There's nothing else for me to do, anyway, until bedtime," he said. "Did you have something in mind?"

Jodie smiled a very pretty smile. "Yes," she said. "Relaxation."

"Oh?" he said.

"I want you to come home with me," she said. "Now."

"That's the nicest invitation I've had all day," he grinned wearily.

Stanley Kravitz stopped past the mayor's office too, after leaving Latham and Jodie, but he did not find Purcell there. He vented more anger on a clerk and a secretary, making a big racket in the corridors at City Hall. Then he drove out to Rawdon Field and found Ed

Keefer just about ready to leave the weather station there. He met Keefer in a corridor outside Keefer's office, and began raging to him about Mark Latham.

"That sonofabitch has gone too far!" he told Keefer loudly. "I'm going to bring him down, Ed! And you're going to help me!"

Keefer had visited Leah Purcell that afternoon, and had spoken with the mayor about how she looked better, and he had begun to feel closer to Purcell and Sprague and Latham than to Kravitz, who was an outsider.

"In what way, Stan?" Keefer asked, looking thin and pale in the dim light from an overhead ceiling fixture.

Kravitz' face was very intense. He gave the impression that he wanted to strike out physically and hit something or someone. "I want some ammunition against this bastard," he said hoarsely. "He's in the middle of a divorce, isn't he?"

"Why, I believe so," Keefer said curiously.

"I want you to get on the wire to California, and find out about that. See what dirt you can get on him. Talk to his wife, maybe a couple of people at Berkeley. I want to really paste this guy when I call the White House tomorrow morning."

Keefer stared at Kravitz as if he had never met the man before, as if he were a complete stranger. "I—don't think I could do that, Stan," he said slowly.

Kravitz' face changed again. Emotions crossed it that were very frightening to Keefer. "You—what did you say?"

"I couldn't do that," Keefer said more firmly. "Latham seems an all right guy to me. And his effort to stop all this is probably the last chance we have around here. I just couldn't get involved in anything to bring discredit on him."

"An all right—" Kravitz seemed incapable of speech for a moment. "You couldn't get involved? You don't want to discredit him? Goddam it, Keefer, I'm not asking you this! I'm telling you for Christ's sake! I can't get all this done, myself!"

Keefer took a deep breath in, raised himself up a little taller. "I won't do it, Stan."

Keefer was sure that Kravitz was going to hit him. There were some gutteral sounds in Kravitz' throat, then he pointed a finger into Keefer's face. "You refuse me, and you've had it, boy! Do you understand that?"

"I'm beginning to," Keefer said. "But my answer is still the same."

Kravitz spat the words out at him. *"You're fired, Keefer! Don't show up tomorrow morning here, because you're through!"*

"All right," Keefer said quietly.

"You won't ever work for the Weather Station or any other federal agency again! You can count on that!"

"Good evening, Stan," Keefer said coldly. He turned and walked away then, leaving Kravitz standing there red-faced.

It was almost ten minutes later when Kravitz got himself together enough to go down to his car and drive back to his quarters at McConnell. On the way, a roving pack of dogs came out in front of his car, and he swerved and side-swiped a parked vehicle, and kept on going. He was not thinking about driving. He could not get Mark Latham out of his head. He did not know it himself, but if he had had a gun in his hand at Latham's office, he probably would have shot him. He had lost almost all control over his emotions.

300

The gate guard at McConnell passed Kravitz through routinely, and Kravitz drove to a barracks building where he and other project people were quartered. The building was out on the edge of the base, away from traffic and noise, and Kravitz' small two-room apartment was at the rear of the place, on the first floor. He always drove around to a parking area at the back of the place, and entered through a door back there. Tonight he did the same, parking his car without even consciously knowing what he was doing. On the way from the car to the building, he heard a rattling noise under a nearby dry shrub, but it did not register with him.

He walked on past the noise, up to the doorway, and noticed that someone had left the screen door wide open. Ordinarily that would have angered him, because he hated to let flying insects inside. But tonight he took no interest. He went into the hot hallway and down to the first door on his right. It was ajar. He thought back, and recalled leaving in a hurry, Latham on his mind. He had forgotten to close and lock it. Well, that was the advantage of living on the base. You did not have to worry about burglary much there. There would have been no vandals or thieves about, in all probability. He went in and turned the lights on.

Everything looked normal. In this larger room there was a bed, three chairs, a short sofa, a desk. In an adjacent kitchenette were stove and refrigerator, and a table for eating. He stepped in there, and in a tiny bathroom, to make sure he was alone. Then he went and closed and locked the outside door behind him.

"Damned ungrateful subordinates," he muttered to himself.

He looked over toward the bed. Yes, he had turned it

301

down before he left, so it would be all ready for him when he returned. He turned away, and headed for the bathroom, and heard the sound again. The rattling sound. Less distinct this time. He turned back, listening. It must have been from outside, he figured.

He went into the bathroom, passed some water, closed the toilet lid on the waste that he could not flush because of lack of water. He felt let down by the Russians. If they had succeeded, Stanley Kravitz would have been a big man. He had headed the project. He would have been a kind of hero. Now, it was all different. The President ignored him, his own bureau chief ignored him now, and dealt with outsiders.

"We'll see. We'll see, by God."

He came out into the larger room, turned off the overhead light, leaving only a dim night light on beside the bed. He had intended to make a couple of calls before he turned in, but he was too fatigued now. He blamed Keefer for that. He went to the bed, and did not see the lumps under the turned-down sheet. He got into bed, shoving his legs and hips between the sheets. He always slept with a light cover, no matter how hot it was.

There was movement against his thigh. And another one against his foot. Slithery movements, sliding, angry ones, and the rattling noise very loud.

Kravitz felt the fangs sink into him, just below the hip. And more, at the ankle.

"*Aahh!*" he cried out. "*Aaagh!*"

He jerked the sheet up and off the bed in a quick, spastic motion, and saw them. A big rattler poised at his hip level, and a smaller one just showing at his feet. The smaller one turned and glided off the edge of the bed, and the larger one struck at him again, at close range, hitting him in the low abdomen. This time it bit through his undershorts and into his torso just above the groin, and then it, too, slithered off the bed.

Kravitz had jumped again at the third bite, then he just sat there half-propped on the bed, staring toward the fang marks on his belly. He knew there were also bite marks on his leg and ankle.

"Oh, my God!" he grated out.

He felt very faint. He jumped out of bed, and found the overhead light and switched it on. There were both snakes, across the room, coiled defensively in a corner. They had only wanted to rest for the night, like him, and had been as surprised as he at the confrontation. He stood there shaking, looking past his bulging stomach at the bites. Yes, there were three, all right. They began to hurt. They hurt very much.

Kravitz went to the bed, sat down on the edge of it. He picked up the phone. Already he was feeling queasy, dizzy. He felt himself break out into a cold sweat in the heat, and wondered how much was fear, and how much from the venom. He dialed a number, and waited. He was getting very weak, very dizzy. He had heard that a man can absorb one rattler bite quite well, two not so easily. He was certain that three could kill.

"Yes?" the voice on the other end came to him. It was a duty officer on the base.

"I need—help," Kravitz grated into the phone. "Call me an ambulance."

"*Hello? You'll have to speak up, sir, I can hardly hear you.*"

"Listen to me. I've been—snake-bitten. They came in

from—outside the building. Get me a—doctor."

"Snakes, did you say? What barracks is that, sir?"

Kravitz was feeling hot and chilled at the same time. He was beginning to shake all over. "I'm in—F Quarters. Stanley Kravitz. Please. Help me."

"Quarters F. Did you say you need a doctor there?"

"Yes." A deep shiver. "A doctor."

"You'll have to call the infirmary, Mr. Kraggiss. Or go on over there, that might be better."

"I can't—go there—you idiot!" His leg and ankle were burning now, and his abdomen was beginning to distend. He felt knife-like pains shooting through his body and into his head. The room was spinning around him.

"Just a minute, Mr. Kraggiss. Maybe I can transfer this call. Just hold on a minute."

"No, wait—" Kravitz said with a thick tongue.

The phone went dead. Kravitz held it for a long moment, sweat popping out on his face, cold shivers running through him. But then he felt himself hit the floor hard on his side, without knowing how he had gotten there. He grunted in more pain. He did not have the phone in his hand now. He squinted down, looking for it. He saw it lying only a couple of feet from him. He reached out for it, and found it difficult to move his arm. It was as if he were straining, against bonds of some kind. He got the receiver in hand again, and it was now slippery in his grasp. Across the room, the bigger snake made a soft rattling sound, like a last reproach. Kravitz remembered Latham and Jodie at Latham's office.

He could not be proud. Not at a time like this. The room swam in his vision. He reached out again and pulled the phone off the night table. It fell beside him, making a crashing noise. With great difficulty he pulled it to him.

He had to think of the number. Seven digits, ending with four-four. Darkness edged in on him. He looked down, and he had lost his grip on the phone, and the crotch of his undershorts was wet.

A violent knife thrust ripped through him, and his lips formed his last words, silently. *It wasn't—my fault.*

Then Stanley Kravitz was dead.

SEVENTEEN

The same night that Stanley Kravitz died, five other persons were killed in Wichita by wild animals, or animals gone wild.

Rioters and looters were not much in evidence on the night streets now, because of that and because of sickness. A few hardy youths were still roaming the night streets, as predatory as the dogs and coyotes, looking for victims to mug and rob.

And rape.

And murder.

Sherwood Jameson's troops, and the police department, were finally able to respond to trouble as they would like to. But they usually got to the scene of a crime too late.

Jameson had detailed a kind of death squad for animals. The squad roamed the streets at night looking for any animal loose on the streets, for extermination on the spot. Some residents' pets were killed unnecessarily, but most of them found were dying, anyway. Dogs that had gone wild were not so difficult to find and destroy, but coyotes, it turned out, were very clever. They learned very quickly to distinguish a military jeep from other vehicles, and to fear the green fatigue uniform. If a rifle was pointed at them, they disappeared like ghosts into alleyways and building crevices.

Jameson was even bolder in his personal participation than he had been before being shot. His stiff, erect figure had become a familiar sight on the night streets, riding high on a jeep, arm in sling, jaw thrust forward, as if daring someone to shoot him again. Jodie was not aware of this foolhardy bravery, so was not able to make an issue of it.

The curfew in Wichita was moved up to dusk, and anyone seen out after that hour was deemed suspect, and there was a good chance of being shot. There were people with passes, of course, including Latham and Jodie Jameson, and they were required to drive in vehicles clearly marked on their sides with a big "CP" for Curfew Pass.

Latham did not like the idea, but he had obtained a revolver to carry with him when out on the streets. It was a Sturm Ruger .357 Magnum that Tom Purcell lent him, and he carried it in a belt holster at waist level. He did not like guns, had never owned one. But things were different, now. Danger was literally everywhere.

Latham and Jodie slept together that night that Kravitz was killed, and Latham was surprised by a sudden and dramatic impotency, particularly after the frenzied outburst of the previous evening. But the tension had gotten to him now. It was even greater for him, now that he had the backing of the government and the others. He sometimes felt that he had pulled an enormous practical joke on the world, in making it believe he could save it. It was bothering him more than he realized, and now it had gotten between him and Jodie, on a physical level.

The morning after Kravitz' fatal encounter with displaced denizens of the plains, things began happening fast in Operation Big Seed. Airports around the Midwest began reporting in that the big jets were massing at those sites, and pilots were awaiting final instructions concerning their fly-over patterns. Also, balloonists were slowly arriving at those sites and others, ahead of the Skyhook shipments. It appeared that everything would be in place by that evening, and that the massive operation could take place the following day, if all of the seeding material arrived at the various bases of operation. However, at noontime Latham received a call from the biggest of the manufacturers of the metal chaff, saying that the entire order would not be filled and in place until noon or so of the next day. So it appeared that Operation Big Seed would take place in two days. The date would be September 12.

All city water would be gone September 11.

Just minutes after Latham's call from the chaff manufacturer, an assistant called him from Midcontinental Airport to advise that the Wichita shipment of Skyhooks had arrived. Latham decided to go out there and personally oversee the unloading and placement of the balloons, and Jodie decided to go, too, when Latham called her. They drove out there just after lunch, and the temperature was one hundred twenty-seven degrees in the sun.

The crates containing Skyhooks were being unloaded when they arrived on the airstrip. Latham and Jodie got out of their car and went and stood under a temporary canopy raised to keep them out of the sun. There were several airport personnel there, and a couple of balloonists who had arrived earlier. Latham had a hot but pleasant talk with the balloonists as the crates came off the big transport plane, and Jodie enjoyed meeting them. They were both athletic-looking, rugged young men who also engaged in other physical sports, such as sky-diving and hang-gliding.

Several of these balloons were going to be launched from that airport, a couple from Rawdon Field, one from McConnell, and a few from sites around Wichita close. Trucks were standing by to take those others to their destinations, and on a section of the airport removed from the traffic of planes and vehicles, supports were being erected for launchings. Skyhooks were not inflated at launching, as sport balloons were. They had only a capsule of gas at their crowns, which held the thin bag upright but almost empty. When the balloon was released, the bag slowly filled as the balloons rose in height and the helium gas expanded to press on its polyethylene sides.

After watching the unloading, and helping supervise it, Latham drove over to where the launching platforms and supports were being erected under his direction. Balloon crates were already stacked at that site, and several platforms were partially constructed. They went over to the shade of a construction hut and were met there by a burly man in a yellow hard hat.

"Oh, so you're Latham," the middle-aged fellow said when Latham had introduced himself.

"That's right," Latham said to him. "And this is my associate, Miss Jameson."

The fellow nodded. "Kovak here. We're getting your guillotines built for you. They ought to be finished by this evening." He referred to the appearance of the platforms, with their high parallel supports that held the balloons upright until they had been injected with a gas bubble.

"That's good, Kovak," Latham told him. "We'll have them in plenty of time."

The fellow narrowed his sun-squinted eyes on Latham. "You think this is really going to work, Latham?"

Latham met his gaze. The foreman spoke for all of Wichita, all of the Midwest, in his concern and his doubt. "I hope so," Latham replied.

"Did you see the TV this morning?" the foreman asked him. "About the Russians?"

"No," Latham said. "You mean Mazurov and Potamkin?"

"Yeah, they're doing some mouthing off over there in Moscow. They heard of your project here, and they said you don't know what you're doing."

Jodie felt anger well into her chest. "I guess that would be a natural reaction," she said coolly, "for the directors of a failed project like theirs here."

Kovak grunted. "I'm just saying what I saw on the tube, lady. The Russians say this will all go on until the winter, and then the weather will settle back to normal."

"Let's hope they're wrong," Latham said soberly. "Because in a couple of weeks, all life will have ceased to exist here, if we can't make it rain."

The foreman's face changed slightly. "Well. Of course, we're all pulling for you, Latham."

The foreman went off to supervise some work activity then, and Latham and Jodie stood and watched a couple of men nearby who were attaching an unrolled

310

balloon envelope to a completed platform, with the use of a small crane. Jodie watched the operation wide-eyed, never having seen a Skyhook before.

"It's big," she said. "And so thin-looking."

"The skin is thinner than cellophane," Latham told her. "But incredibly strong. These will weigh two or three thousand pounds when we get the gondolas attached to them, and they'll lift a couple of tons off the ground."

"That's incredible," Jodie said.

"Each one will carry a ton of chaff, several containers of gas, the apparatus to expel it, and one or two pilots. The balloons won't look much different from now when they lift off. They'll look almost deflated, even with all the equipment and personnel they have to raise. As they go up and the atmosphere thins, the gas in the envelope will make the balloon spherical, or almost. The balloon will rise to a pre-determined height, according to the amount of gas we inject here on the ground, and it will stay there while the seeding is done."

"Why wouldn't the balloon keep rising," Jodie asked, "since the atmosphere keeps getting thinner all the way out to black space?"

Latham grinned. He liked it that she thought things through so well. "It would," he said, "except that the size of the balloon limits the ascension. More lifting beyond a pre-established altitude will merely force helium out of the open neck at the bottom, which stabilizes the volume of gas inside and the altitude of the craft."

"How big is the balloon when it's fully inflated?" Jodie asked him.

"These will be about a hundred fifty feet across, when they get up where they're headed," Latham told her. "At about forty thousand feet. That will put them above the vapor they're seeding."

"This all sounds just a little dangerous," Jodie said. "You say you've done this several times before?"

"Oh, yes," Latham said. "If you get a good launch, and you know how to operate the few controls we put on them, it should be a safe flight. Of course, you have to wear oxygen masks in this work, and you have to dress properly. As you found out from our low-altitude flight, it can get cool up there. Where these balloons are going, it will be downright frigid."

"Oxygen masks," Jodie mused. "It sounds a little like diving in the ocean."

Again, Latham was impressed. "Exactly." He looked out into the blinding sun, where the balloon was being attached to its support masts. "When these crafts are unmanned, they sometimes stay aloft for weeks. Some have circled the Earth several times before coming down. But we'll bring them down immediately after our seeding is done, of course."

Jodie's face was straight-lined. "Why are you going up, Mark?"

He looked over at her. "Why, because I'm one of those best qualified to man a balloon."

"You have plenty of people here to man balloons," she said.

He grinned slightly. "Hey. You're not scared by all this, are you?"

"I'm not sure. Should I be?"

"Of course not. You've been up. You know that it's safe up there if you know what you're doing."

312

"I didn't go up forty thousand feet," she said. "It seems to me that you're needed more on the ground than in the air, Mark. You're the one in charge of all this. It wouldn't be so great if something happened to you."

Latham touched her flushed face. It was beautiful, even though it looked fatigued and washed-out. "The ballooning will come at the very end of the experiment. It will be too late for further supervision then, Jodie. But the important thing is, I can't ask all these other balloonists to go up there, and stay on the ground myself. I'm just not built that way. They'll want to know I'm up there too, freezing to death, sucking oxygen through a mask, dropping chaff just like them. And I want to be."

Jodie sighed. "I guess you've got it all figured out."

"Jodie, it makes me feel damned good to think you worry about me. But this will just be an ordinary flight, except for the height." Actually, Skyhooks were very difficult to land, in comparison with a sport balloon. But he saw no point in telling her that. She had enough to think about, as it was. "Now. I'm going to stop past the Weather Service at Rawdon. Ed Keefer stayed on there despite an apparent firing by Kravitz. I'll offer my condolences for Kravitz' death. Would you like to come, or do you want to get right back to the department?"

Jodie had almost forgotten the bad news about Kravitz, in the excitement of Big Seed. She felt unreasonably guilty for a moment, and wondered if all this were making her insensitive to the suffering and death around her. If this second Great Experiment did not work, she supposed, the drought would suck all of what was human out of them before it killed them. It was not a thing to look forward to.

"No, I'll go with you," she said. "It's the least we can do, I think. After all, he did try very hard in his own way to save us all. We can't forget that."

"No," Latham said seriously. "We can't."

Jodie worked hard the rest of that day at the department clinic, trying to keep her mind off what was happening all around the state. It did not help to think about it, to sit before a TV and listen to last-minute updates. There would be no real knowledge now until it was over.

In early evening, before meeting Latham for a quick dinner at the university, Jodie made the rounds of the hospitals before darkness set in. At St. Joseph she looked in on Leah for a few minutes, and was pleased to see Leah eating and watching television. Leah talked freely about the drought, and about the news on TV, and seemed in very good spirits. As Jodie was about to leave, Leah mentioned Will.

"I know now, Jodie," she said quietly.

Jodie frowned slightly.

"About Will. I know he's gone."

"Oh," Jodie said. "That's good, Leah."

"I think I can handle it now. I—think it helps that we're trying again to make it rain."

"I'm glad there's some hope for us," Jodie said. "We'll know in a couple of days."

"He's really gone, isn't he, Jodie?"

Jodie felt a thickness in her throat. "I'm afraid so, Leah. Will was a victim of the drought. Just as much as if he'd died of thirst or disease. That's the way we have to look at it." She wondered if her father were also a kind of victim already.

"He wasn't my brother," Leah said. "But I loved him, Jodie."

"I know, honey," Jodie said. She averted her gaze. "Are you getting enough to eat?"

"I think so," Leah said. "We need water, though, Jodie. Do you think you could send us some water?"

"I'll see," Jodie said.

When Jodie left Leah, she realized that if Latham's Operation Big Seed did not work, Leah would possibly lapse back into a traumatized state. But then if Big Seed failed, it would not make any difference, she guessed.

Out in a corridor, she found the administrator. He was a hefty middle-aged doctor who was wearing thin in the heat and whose patience with shortages was about gone.

"We lost eleven patients today," he told her in what she thought was a rather harsh tone. "They can't fight back with dehydration, damn it! It's the same all over town. There must have been thirty or forty deaths today in all hospitals and clinics, and God knows how many more there were in private homes, unattended. This has to stop, Jameson. It has to stop now!"

Jodie eyed him quizzically. "Dr. Latham is doing his best to see that we turn this around," she said. "In a couple of days we'll know whether this seeding project will—"

"Seeding project! Are you people still talking about making it rain, for God's sake? Don't you think it's time we concentrated our efforts on keeping people alive? These projects to change the weather aren't going to

315

work, that's apparent! We're wasting time on things like that, when we should be figuring how to get water here from outside sources!"

Jodie's face crimsoned slightly. "We have been concentrating our efforts on keeping people alive, doctor, or haven't you noticed? We've eliminated sources for outside water, and even if we hadn't, Operation Big Seed doesn't compete with those efforts."

The doctor leaned toward her, neurosis in his beefy face. "We're almost out of water, Jameson. You're in charge over there at the Health Department, you're doling the stuff out. Why isn't St. Joseph getting its fair share anymore?"

Jodie could not believe his naivete. "None of us are getting water now!" she said incredulously. "I've had to cut down on all the hospitals in the past few days! Maybe you didn't know it, but our reservoir is dry! We're doing the best we can, doctor, with what we have. You're going to have to do the same."

"I'll bet the patients at your clinic are getting water," he said a little breathlessly. "And proper medication. So the department will look good!"

"Look good!" Jodie said, wide-eyed. "My God, next you'll be accusing our staff of hoarding the water and medicine for ourselves!"

He grinned a hard grin. "Well?" he said.

Jodie's face had hardened. "The department is carefully rationing water and medication to all health facilities in this area, on a day by day, worst-need basis," she said slowly and deliberately. "We're doing our damnedest to be equitable. But we're almost out of everything, including water. If you can't accept that hard fact, I'm very sorry. But don't blame the Health Department."

He waggled a thick finger in her face. "I'm calling Topeka about this. We never had trouble like this when Ben Webster was running the show over there! I think you're into a job that's beyond your capabilities, Jameson, and I'm going to tell them so in the capital, and at City Hall!"

"Do what you think is necessary," she replied in a throaty voice. She spun on her heel and strode quickly down the corridor to the outside.

Out on the parking lot, she leaned against her car and tried to calm herself. She might have known, she thought, that Stanley Kravitz would not be the only one affected mentally by the heat. In another few days of this they would all be at each other's throats, tearing and slashing like wild animals.

It was almost dark. Latham would be waiting for her at the university, and he did not like her out after sunset. She drove across town in fading light to College Hill, and went directly to the cafeteria when she arrived there. The hot anger had subsided inside her, but she was down again. It hurt to think that anyone could accuse her of malfeasance after what she had been through, working day and night, worrying and fretting about it all. Even if the someone was obviously not himself because of the heat and extreme fatigue. Was even Mark Latham really himself? she wondered. Maybe if they all survived this somehow, he would be a different man. Maybe if everything returned to normal one day, he would see their affair as just that. A temporary thing he needed to get through the emergency, but nothing to base a life on. Divorce proceedings could be aborted. Lawyers could be dismissed. Nothing was irrevocable.

Except death by dehydration.

Walking along the corridor to the cafeteria, Jodie wondered for a brief moment if, from a selfish point of view, she should not have accepted Lou Falco's invitation to go to Kansas City, where things were slightly better. She had heard a rumor that he had flown to Maine to get out of the drought. He would have taken her with him, and they would have sat it out in some relatively cool place, clucking their tongues at the poor unfortunates at Wichita. There would never have been anything permanent with Falco, but that did not seem so important, now. Maybe what he had offered was all she wanted, or needed. She would not have the complexity of the Mark Latham relationship, nor would she be berated by a medical man for staying and fighting.

Latham saw her mood as soon as she walked into the cafeteria. He was alone, and they ate a quick sandwich well away from the few other people eating there. There was no water offered at the cafeteria now, no liquids of any kind, no fresh fruit or vegetables. There was no cook, only a clerk and a cashier. Jodie ate her dry sandwich quietly, not looking at Latham, and he wondered what was wrong with her.

"So some of the chaff will be here tonight, and the rest tomorrow morning," he was telling her. "It will be delivered simultaneously at several other cities, and distributed according to my instructions from there." He saw that she was staring at her sandwich. "Is everything all right, Jodie?"

318

She put the sandwich down. She was no longer hungry at mealtimes, and that was not good. "Oh, it's nothing, really. I just got some ear-blasting by the administrator at St. Joseph. He has the idea that he's not getting his fair share of water and medicine."

"Oh, for God's sake," Latham said.

"It's a bad position to be in," she admitted. "In charge of doling out what people need for life. I hate it, Mark."

"Somebody has to do it," he told her. "And there's nobody around who could do it any better."

She gave him a look. "I wish I could believe that."

"Paula Bentacourt told the President personally that you're doing a great job," he said. "Remember?"

Jodie tried a smile. "I'm sorry, Mark. It must be the heat. I don't react to things the same as I used to. None of us does, I guess."

"I know what you mean," he said.

She eyed him closely. "Will it be different with you, if we get through it, Mark?" she said in a half-whisper. "With us?"

He reached out and put his hand on hers. "I can only speak for myself, Jodie. I know my true feelings, even now. I want you with me always. I want to tie the legal knot and everything, go the whole distance. Do you?"

She looked away. "I—don't know," she said quietly. "I'm sorry, Mark, but I can't think straight, it seems." She had thought about it, though, and it all seemed so complex. She had her career there, he had an even bigger one in California. It seemed to her that their lives were irredeemably headed off in different directions for a number of reasons.

"It's all right,' he said. But he was disappointed.

"We'll talk about it later."

More than anything, Jodie figured, the last-minute tension was getting her now. For her, and probably for Latham, this was a facing up to death that they were involved in now. Her own death had not seemed like a possibility to her, all through the drought, until the Russians left. Now, she could not escape the conclusion that both she and the man she so deeply loved—yes, it was Mark Latham, she knew—were marked for death if his great experiment became a second failure in the fight against the drought. They could both leave, but neither would. She would stay to make dying easier for those who could not get out, or would not. He would remain hoping there was something he could do, but knowing there was not.

It was a grim thought.

When they finished eating, they went down and got into Jodie's car. The temperature had dropped about twenty degrees, and the air seemed breatheable outside. It was dark now, past the curfew hour. Latham got behind the driver's seat. He was going to drive them to Jodie's place, and he was going to stay overnight again with her. Not for any physical love, but for mutual comfort. They both felt more relaxed, less lonely and afraid, with each other.

Latham drove out of the parking lot and onto a campus street. There was nobody out, on campus. Even the People's Brigade, some of which had found their way back to the univeristy grounds, was quiet now. Latham drove out onto a main boulevard, and headed for Jodie's place. There was a big moon overhead, in a cloudless sky. Dust was banked at curbs, piles of it had drifted up in places on the sidewalk and parkways.

"Look," Latham said as they passed a row of store fronts.

Jodie had already seen the two shadowy figures coming out of the broken-glass store front, carrying office chairs. The food in the store had long ago been looted. These two were a couple of the few crazies still going out at night to steal, vandalize, and terrorize.

Latham felt for the Ruger revolver at his waist, and was reassured by its heavy presence there. Night before last, three youths had stopped a curfew car at a light and dragged its two occupants out and beaten them so badly that one had died at a hospital emergency room.

At the next block they passed a standing jeep with four of Sherwood Jameson's men in it, sitting with heavy guns across their legs, waiting. Waiting for trouble. Latham waved to them, and they saw the big yellow letters on the side of Jodie's department Ford, and waved back.

It was almost a mile further along that they saw their first animal on the streets. It was a single dog, a big German shepherd, and it was slinking along building walls, foaming at the mouth. It was headed in the direction of Jameson's troops, so Latham figured they would see it.

Then, about a half-mile further along, they saw the woman.

She was standing in a park area, not far from the street, and she was surrounded by what looked like dogs.

"Hey. What the hell is that?" Latham said, pointing through the windshield. He slowed the car as it approached the scene.

"A woman," Jodie said breathlessly. "My God, they have her surrounded, Mark!"

Latham pulled the car to the curb not far from the scene. Now they could hear the animals snarling and making gutteral noises, and the woman yelling.

"They're not dogs," Latham said, squinting toward them. "They're starving coyotes!"

Just as he uttered that observation, one of the animals dived in at the woman, snarling and biting. She yelled, hitting at it with a heavy-looking purse. It grabbed at the purse and almost tore it from her grasp. Her dress was torn in two places, and there was blood running down her right leg.

"Oh, God!" Jodie gasped out.

Latham turned the engine off and drew the Ruger. "Stay in the car!" he said to Jodie. He swung the door beside him open then, and jumped from the car, running around to the curb side.

Jodie reached for the medical bag that sat beside her on the seat, and ignoring Latham's command, climbed out of the car on the curb side. She could not let him go out there alone.

Latham came up behind the animals, yelling now. There were six of them, and they all looked ferocious. Ordinarily, coyotes were rather friendly to humans, but these were psychotic and desperate. They looked like timber wolves, with their fangs bared at him. Three of the six turned toward him, snarling, as he aimed the gun at them. The woman saw him, and began screaming at him.

"*Jesus, help me!*" she yelled. "*They'll kill me!*"

Latham uttered a snarling yell at the animals, to

scare them off. But they were not afraid of the gun this time. They were too hungry. They just looked upon Latham and Jodie as two more potential meals. One lunged at Latham savagely.

Latham saw the animal coming, and fired while it was in mid-air. The bullet caught it in the head, and jerked the coyote sidewise as it came. It hit at Latham's feet, jerking spasmodically on the pavement.

Another one lunged at the woman, and grabbed her in the lower leg. She screamed and went down. Latham moved closer, but two animals barred his way. The coyote at the woman was back at her now, going for her thigh. Latham swallowed hard, aimed and fired the Ruger a second time. The coyote jumped two feet in the air, as if from a coiled spring, and landed just beside the woman, howling and biting at itself.

Now one threw itself at Latham, while he was distracted by the woman. He felt the teeth in his leg, and the weight of it knocked him off his feet. He hit the ground about fifteen feet from the woman, and a second coyote came in on him immediately. Then he got a glimpse of Jodie, swinging the medical bag wildly at the animal.

"*Jodie!*" he yelled. "*Get back!*"

The coyote that Jodie had distracted was now turned on her, baring its yellowed fangs. In a moment it would be on her. Latham aimed and fired again, and the animal was hit in the spine. It was knocked sidewise to the ground, and then jumped and flailed there.

Now there were only three of them left, and they sensed that the odds were going against them. One of them started in on the fallen woman, and she swung out at it with the purse she still had clutched in her hand. It backed off, growling.

The coyotes were more subdued now. Latham aimed at the one nearest him, and it slunk back a couple of steps, showing its teeth. He fired a fourth time, and it yelled gutterally and fell awkwardly to the ground, tried to get on its feet, fell again lifeless.

The last two were finally cowed by the gun. They gave Latham a last look and reluctantly turned and ran into shadows, disappearing across the park area.

Jodie was already over to the fallen woman, kneeling beside her, quieting her. "It's all right. They're gone now."

"They were trying to—"

"I know," Jodie told her. She opened the bag as Latham came up to them, holstering the revolver.

"I thought I told you to stay in the car," he said breathlessly.

"I couldn't," she said. "Not with you out here."

There was a long look between them, then Jodie was cleaning the woman's shallow wounds and putting temporary bandages on them. In just a few minutes, they had her on her feet and were helping her into the car. The shot coyotes were all dead now, and peace reigned over the boulevard.

"I didn't see them—until they were right on me," the woman was saying, less hysterically. "I'd never broken curfew before. I just went out to find my boy. He's sixteen, and you can't talk to him. I just know he's going to get into trouble."

Jodie found herself wondering if the woman's son was one of those skulking figures they had seen earlier. "We'll drive you to the hospital now. They'll take care of you there, you need some stitches but you'll be all right."

But as they drove off again, the woman seated between them in the front of the car, Latham found himself wondering if any of them would ever be all right again. He wondered if it was not probable that a couple of weeks from now, Wichita would be richly infested with rabid animals, circling vultures, diseased people, and death.

It was a future that was more likely than not.

EIGHTEEN

It was the morning of September 11.

Across the Midwest, they sat poised in position. Boeing 707s, 727s, even the jumbos. DC-10s, 8s and Stretch-8s. Big cargo jets, military craft including SAC bombers still fully loaded with nuclear weapons.

Glistening in the sun.

Ready.

In even more diverse locations, hundreds of enormous Skyhooks hung like giant cocoons from their platform supports, gondolas attached, equipment installed. Pilots milling about, squinting in the heat.

Throughout that morning, the last shipments of seeding material arrived at the balloon launch sites. By telephone, Latham gave detailed last-minute instructions to those few who did not understand the written ones. Unlike the airplane pilots, these men might not go up at all. The balloons would be used only if the first stage of the operation produced moisture-laden clouds, clouds that would hopefully gather much more moisture to themselves, from the upper reaches of the atmosphere. Clouds with the potential of rain.

Sherwood Jameson and Tom Purcell asked for permission to go up on two SAC bombers from

326

McConnell, and got it. They wanted to watch the operation from close-up. Jameson and Jodie had another talk that morning, when Jameson stopped past the Health Department to tell her about his intended bomber flight, and Jodie thought he was getting past Will's death and the implications of it. His entire attention was focused on Big Seed now, and that was good for him. Hollis Sprague dragged himself out of a sick bed to be at the lab on this important day, and insisted on checking some calculations for Latham.

Throughout the afternoon the seeding material was loaded aboard the balloon gondolas and into dispersal apparatuses, and by dusk that day, all was in readiness. Latham considered the idea of making it a nocturnal operation—the absence of the sun was a small factor in their favor—but there was more danger to the pilots, and to the operation, if the entire project was carried out in darkness. He compromised in the last hours by deciding to start sending the big jets up three hours before dawn, the following morning.

Latham and Jodie ate almost nothing that evening together. They had no appetites. It was getting too close now, and it was too important. Latham returned to Jodie's apartment with her, and they sat around her living room nervously, Latham scribbling last-minute calculations on a yellow pad, checking and re-checking, his work punctuated by phone calls between him and his command headquarters at the university lab.

It was about mid-evening when Jodie came and sat with him on a sofa near her French doors, and asked him when the Skyhooks would be going up, if they

327

went up.

"Well, it shouldn't take long for this to work, if it works," Latham told her from beside her. He was sitting slumped heavily on the sofa, his head back on its cushions, a thin shirt unbuttoned down the front to partially expose his tanned, muscular chest. "The jets will all be down by nine or ten, and we should know already at that juncture whether there's any point in sending the balloons up."

"The majority of balloons will have a two-man team, you said," Jodie went on.

"Yes, that's right. Where we can afford the manpower."

"But you're going up alone."

He looked over at her. She was wearing a sheer, low-cut dress that showed a bit of her to him. At any other time, he would have had an overpowering hunger for her. He touched a ringlet of her thick hair, looked into her deep blue eyes. "We've been through all that," he said gently. "I can handle it alone."

Jodie eyed him defiantely. "I want to go up with you, Mark."

He regarded her soberly, with a small frown. "Jodie."

"I mean it. I was up with you before, and you said I have a knack for it. I can help you with the controls. Together, we can be assured of a better job."

"You're a health officer, not a balloonist. You're needed right here on the ground," he said.

"Not for those few hours. I want to be up there with you."

He looked away from her. "Jodie, this isn't like sport ballooning. You're up there in unbreatheable air at the top of the flight. Small mistakes can be deadly. And landing one of these big fellows can be tricky. Accidents happen."

"With two of us, an accident is less likely," she argued.

"Jodie, you just don't know enough. There are things you do on landing—on impact—that prevent injury. You learn these things over a period of time, by going through it over and over again. I couldn't risk it with you, I'd never forgive myself if you were injured."

"You can help me, you'll be there right beside me," Jodie said. "I learn fast, you told me so. I can take care of myself, Mark."

"No," he said. "I won't take you."

Jodie thrust her jaw out. "Damn it, I'm going, Mark! You'll have to station two men at the balloon to keep me off it!"

He eyed her narrowly.

"I mean it. I'm not letting you go up alone. I want to be with you, helping you do the job that has to be done. It's my right!"

His sober look melted into a slow grin. "You're pretty serious about this, aren't you?"

"I've never been more serious about anything, ever," she said.

"Does that mean you love me?" he said, watching her face. "That you've decided you can't live out your life without me?"

"You know I love you," she said.

"That's an incomplete answer."

"I know."

"Commit yourself, honey," he said quietly. "Now, tonight. It would mean a lot to both of us."

She hesitated, shook her head. "I can't."

She supposed it was because, deep down inside her, she had not been convinced by Latham that he was committed to her. Whether or not that was his fault. She did not even know what she wanted, what it would take. That was the frustrating part of it.

Latham nodded. "Okay."

"Okay, what?" she said.

"Okay, I understand."

"What about the balloon ride?" she said. "Are you going to beat me off the gondola with a club?"

He grinned again. "No, I guess not. If you want to go that badly, I'll take you."

Her eyes moistened. "Thanks, Mark."

"None of us may have to go up, anyway," he said.

"I think we will," she said.

"You know that we'll have to spend the next couple of hours teaching you about the seeding controls, and about the balloon?" he said to her.

"We weren't going to get much sleep, anyway," she said.

"All right. You're on."

It was only three a.m. when Latham and Jodie arrived at Midcontinental Airport, and it was a madhouse there. Vehicular traffic was heavy around the terminal, and Jameson's troops were everywhere, trying to keep early sightseers away from trouble. There were more jets than the airport had ever had there on the ground at one time—it was almost a hundred—and they were taxiing for take-off already, in assigned order. Some had passengers, a few carried cargo. But most were empty except for their crews. In a far corner of the field, the Skyhooks rose against the night sky, ghostlike, and pilots milled around them, restless. Latham knew that the same scene prevailed at McConnell and Rawdon Field to a smaller extent, and at several other cities around Kansas and the Midwest.

When Latham and Jodie got out onto the concrete apron behind the terminal, they saw an enormous crush of big planes and crews, with traffic controllers moving about among them, waving flags and speaking into headphone mikes. A few were already out on the field in position to take off one after the other, and tower controllers were giving them last-minute instructions. Vehicles with flashing lights were moving about like fireflies around the heavy, sleek jets, and cars with official markings were everywhere.

Latham got on a microphone hook-up for traffic control, and addressed the crews already in the planes, giving them last-minute orders about re-fueling at their destinations and getting into the air again. Jodie went on over to the Skyhook platforms and climbed aboard the gondola of the balloon she and Latham would be going up with, to familiarize herself with the balloon and the controls.

Over at McConnell, Purcell and Jameson were climbing aboard two separate bombers, and getting ready to take off. Purcell was flying with a couple of city commissioners, and Jameson would be with the base commander. They all felt as if they were more in the center of things, aboard one of the many flights.

At about three-thirty a.m., the planes began taking off, two at a time, and at two-minute intervals. They would not all be gone until about five a.m. Then, at about five-thirty or six, the first planes would be

331

arriving from other take-off points, having left their vapor trails across the morning skies all the way to Wichita. They would re-fuel, those needing to, and then turn around and head back to their original point or some new one, according to a complex schedule.

Latham stood alone watching the first jets get airborne. They rose raucously into the night sky, thundering overhead one after another, making the ground vibrate and the building shake. Latham, with Jodie halfway across the field, felt very alone and uncertain at that crucial moment, and more sure of failure than at any other time. As he stood there on the concrete watching the big jets go up, a car drove up and Sprague and Ed Keefer got out of it and walked over to him. They looked a lot happier about the big event than Latham.

"Well, there they go, Mark!" Sprague said when he came up to Latham. He looked pale, sickly. "God, it's all pretty impressive!"

Latham turned and acknowledged them, and Keefer offered his hand and Latham shook it, "I couldn't stay away," Keefer admitted. "I can't think about anything else."

Latham smiled weakly. "I know."

A big jet roared overhead, and another right with it. They all watched the lights on the sweptback wings fade into the blackness.

"Absolutely nobody is working today," Sprague said, a moment later. "I mean, outside the project. Nothing seems to have any importance now, except for this."

"Nothing does," Keefer said. He turned to Latham again. "I want to take this opportunity to thank you,

332

Latham, whether or not this works."

Latham nodded. "I appreciate that, Ed."

"And I want to apologize for Kravitz," Keefer added. "At his best, Stan wasn't the easiest guy to get along with. But in the past couple of weeks, the heat had gotten him. It fried his brain, Mark. He wasn't responsible."

"Hell, Ed," Latham said. "You know I don't blame you for Kravitz. I don't even blame Kravitz."

"I wish I could be as generous," Keefer said. "If he had cooperated with you and Hollis here all through this, you might have had this parallel project going a lot sooner."

"I doubt it, Ed," Latham said honestly. He waited for the roar of more jets to disperse. "I don't think the idea would have occurred to me earlier, no matter what Kravitz did or didn't do. Anyway, Kravitz may yet turn out to be right. This all may come to nothing."

They both regarded him darkly. "Let's hope not, Mark," Sprague offered in a weak voice. "Let's hope to hell not."

At about four-thirty, a big SAC bomber rose into the air at McConnell with Tom Purcell aboard. He sat up with the navigator, headgear on, and the two commissioners sat back with a couple of technicians. These planes had been pulled off their rotation duty in air defense for a few hours only, and would be back on duty in the latter part of the day. The crews were still combat-ready and had the capability to respond to an emergency at a moment's notice. Nuclear bombs were stored in their undercarriages, and guns were mounted and loaded.

When they were in the air for a half-hour, Purcell began seeing the white vapor trails of other jets that had preceded them in their take-off. They were like white snakes in the dark sky, burgeoning and thinning with every moment that passed, expanding and widening. When there were enough of them, it was hoped, they would merge in places, draw more moisture to themselves, form stable clouds. The navigator that Purcell sat with was disgruntled about it all.

"I'm sorry to say it, Mr. Mayor. But it's crazy duty. I've never heard of anything like this before, in twenty years of flying."

The engines droned in Purcell's ears. He was dressed just like the crew, in blue fatigues and cap. His square face was lined with exhaustion. "This is an unprecedented problem we're facing, Lieutenant. It requires unprecedented procedures to solve it. That's what Mark Latham has come up with."

"As soon as that sun comes up," the navigator said, "it'll burn this sparse stuff off like fog on the desert."

Purcell looked out the black windshield for more white snakes in the sky, and could not find any. And in that moment, he believed the navigator was right. "Latham says it won't," he said without enthusiasm. "Not if we get enough vapor distributed up here."

The navigator was nevertheless shaking his head. "Crazy duty," he grumbled under his breath.

When dawn came, gold-flecking the eastern sky with its unwanted heat, the operation was well under way. Ed Keefer had returned to Rawdon Field, and now reported to Latham over the phone that his scattered instruments around the state showed that there were hundreds of jet trails up there at around thirty thousand feet, and they were holding fairly well. More were being created with every half-hour that passed, as the jets criss-crossed the state, unloading their exhaust into the skies. The university and McConnell labs reported the same thing.

Down on the ground, the vapor-trail clouds could be seen with the naked eye now. They were long, cumulus-type clouds barely visible and very thin, and some seemed to be evaporating away. They did not look like they were growing in strength yet.

Up in the airport tower, Latham paced the floor like a caged animal, not speaking to anyone, hardly looking up from his dark concentration. This was it for him. The next hour or two would tell the tale. At mid-morning, he would have to make a decision based on observation of the sky. To send the Skyhooks up or not to send them up. Jodie was up there in the tower with him, but she stayed out of his way. She knew what he was going through. This first phase had to work, or there would be no second phase. And even then seeding might not work. Two unprecedented happenings had to occur for him now, or it was all over. For all of them.

At just past nine-thirty the last of the big jets touched back down at Midcontinental Airport, and at just past ten they were down all over the Midwest, including McConnell. Jameson and Purcell had viewed the whole operation up close, from the air, and Latham was beginning to wish he had done the same thing. There were a lot of vapor streaks across the morning sky at Wichita, but nothing much seemed to have happened to them yet. At 10:21 Latham received a call from the university, and it was Hollis Sprague on the other end. Jodie got the call.

"Yes, Dr. Sprague," Jodie said into the phone in the tower. She cupped a hand over her other ear. There were several traffic controllers guiding jets in taxiing maneuvers near her, and Latham was speaking with Ed Keefer on another phone, but not learning much. "Did you want to talk to Mark?"

"*I have some good news for him, Jodie,*" Sprague said with excitement in his voice. "*Put him on, will you?*"

Latham had just hung up on the other phone, and was turning to Jodie. "It's Dr. Sprague for you," Jodie told him. "He says it's good news."

Latham looked worn out. His face brightened some, though, and he took the phone from Jodie quickly. "Yes, Hollis? What is it?"

"*It's happening, Mark!*" Sprague's voice came. "*Kansas City reports cloud cover forming over eastern Kansas! They say that the clouds are filling in from the vapor streams, just like you predicted! They say it's happening right before their eyes! They're very incredulous!*"

Latham's voice was hoarse with sudden emotion. "That's terrific, Hollis!"

"*Also, Hutchinson and Topeka are reporting the same phenomenon,*" Sprague added. "*I'm telling you, it's working, Mark! Wait a minute, here's a report from one of our observers.*" There was a long silence on the other end, while Latham waited impatiently, then Sprague returned. "*Yes, it's happening here, too. To the west of town, a big build-up of cloud cover. Damn, it looks like the balloons will be going up, Mark!*"

"Thanks, Hollis," Latham said. "I'll be back in touch

with you. I'm going out to take a look."

When he hung up, Latham turned to Jodie. "Come with me," he told her. He grabbed her by the arm, and pulled her through a doorway into a corridor and then out onto an open deck through an outside door. The wave of heat from the morning sun struck them hard, but neither of them noticed much.

Latham squinted into the sky, through sunglasses. "By God!" he whispered softly. "Look at that!"

Jodie had already seen it. To the west of town, and slightly to the north, clouds were clearly visible. They were high, and they were dark-looking, and they appeared to be growing.

"Oh, Mark!" Jodie said, her eyes damp now. "It's working! It's really working!"

"I have to call Hollis back to put the order out," Latham said. "The second phase is on. The Skyhooks can go up immediately."

"Those are the first clouds I've seen since May," Jodie said in wonderment. "Real clouds. My God, I never realized how beautiful they are."

"Let's hope they're moisture-laden," Latham said. "And that I know how to properly seed them. They're high, and they're very delicately formed. Also, time is very important now. If we don't seed quickly, or not well enough, the clouds will pass over and dump whatever load they have in the Gulf of Mexico."

"Well, what are we waiting for?" Jodie said with a flushed grin.

Latham nodded. This was the climax of his work, and his life. Nothing would ever come close to this in importance, ever again. Not for him. "Let's get it over with," he said.

NINETEEN

A hush had fallen over Wichita.

Local citizens stared up at the sky and could not believe what they were seeing.

A heavy cloud cover was quickly forming over the city and the state, a sky locals had not viewed in months.

They knew it was the result of Latham's big experiment, and hope soared. If he could do this, maybe he could make it rain.

Pulses raced, and stomachs tightened. Sick persons stumbled out of bed, to go and stare at the heavens and murmur exclamations in quiet tones.

At the airports, another melee was starting. Helium gas was being injected into Skyhook balloons, in just the amount that would raise the lighter-than-air crafts to the desired altitude above the cloud cover. Pilots were receiving last-minute instructions, and were getting fluttery in their insides. Almost none of them had ever flown a big weather balloon, and they all knew there were risks.

At 10:53, the balloons started their ascension at Midcontinental Airport. Latham supervised their launching, to make sure everything went well, saving his own launch until last. Each balloon would receive a shot of helium from a gas tanker truck standing beside its platform, and suddenly the balloon would no longer be sagging on its supports. It would have a bulbous crown, with most of the envelope still hanging loose below that. The crown and gondola would then be released from their moorings, once the two-man crew was aboard, and the craft would start floating upward. This was a tricky time, because the gondola was less stable than later, when the envelope was properly inflated.

The gondolas were sizeable, because they were carrying a rather heavy load, with the seeding machines, the seeding material, and the crew. But, surprisingly to some observers, the big balloons lifted all that off the ground with an ease that was beautiful to watch. One after one the big balloons rose into the now-gray sky, like giant moths toward an occluded lamp.

As it came Latham and Jodie's turn, they noticed an unusual phenomenon. Jodie felt her face with her hand, and turned to Latham as a ground crew put steps up to the gondola of their craft for them.

"Have you noticed the temperature?" she said to Latham.

He turned to her, and took in a deep breath of morning air. "You're right," he said. "It must be down fifteen degrees from nine o'clock."

"Maybe twenty degrees," Jodie said. "My God, I can actually breathe, out here in the open!"

They were both wearing jump suits, bright orange, and light-weight crash helmets. Everything was aboard their balloon, and now the bag was shot with an injection of helium at its crown, so that it strained at its moorings, swaying slightly in a warm breeze from

339

the west.

One of the ground crew came over to Latham and Jodie, who were now on the platform, standing beside the gondola. "Dr. Latham, you wanted a couple of pieces of measuring equipment aboard, I understand, from your lab. But it hasn't arrived yet."

Latham nodded. "Okay, we won't delay. It isn't important to the operation. Let's get this thing off the ground." He looked upward, and saw three other balloons up there, one reaching the cloud cover already, and disappearing into it.

"We're ready to send you off," the ground crewman told Latham.

Jodie preceded Latham up the ladder and into the eight-foot gondola. Latham watched her rounded backside go over the gunwale, and wished he had been able to talk her out of this flight. But it was becoming increasingly clear that she had a mind of her own. He had to admit he liked that about her.

Latham climbed into the gondola, too. Beside them in the gondola were the hopper of chaff attached to a seeding machine that dropped chaff from the bottom of the gondola, the machine itself, a tank of special-mixture gas that would be released in a jet from the side of the gondola. The controls for the balloon were attached to a metal ring at the base of the envelope, above their heads. Strong metal supports attached the gondola to that ring. With Latham and Jodie in the gondola were jackets for the cold, and gloves, and oxygen masks with oxygen tanks.

"Did you get the upper-level weather readings from Ed Keefer?" Latham asked the crewman as he removed the ladder from the side of the gondola.

340

"We have a pretty good picture, Dr. Latham. This first phase of yours has caused some turbulence up there, but it ought to be fairly smooth sailing for most of you."

"That's what we want," Jodie said brightly, in a good mood. "Smooth sailing."

Latham looked over at her. "Are you scared, honey?"

"A little."

"You still have time to change your mind," he said. "If you insist on me having someone with me, maybe one of these crewmen would volunteer."

"I don't want one of them with you," she said. "I want to be there. It's settled, Mark."

He grinned at her. "All right. It's settled."

Jodie took a deep breath in, and let it all out slowly, and she felt a little shaky inside. She was more than a little scared. She was very scared. But she did not want Latham to know that.

"*All right, cut her loose!*" Latham called out to the three-man crew below them.

There was a nod of acknowledgment, and then a release of mooring for the gondola, and finally a couple of levers pulled on the mooring masts. Far above their heads, the crown of the envelope tugged hard at them, and there was a jerking motion upward, and they started lifting off the ground.

"Here we go," Latham announced.

As they watched, the crew grew smaller and then the control tower across the airport, and finally the airfield itself shrank in size. Unlike on the sport balloon flight, which had been a nocturnal one, a real panorama opened up to them on this one. Downtown Wichita, brown and barren-looking, and around it a countryside that was already beginning to look desert-like. They rose and rose upward, and the gondola swayed widely for a while, and Latham could see the whiteness creep into Jodie's lovely face. He grabbed onto her and held her, and she smiled up at him from under the rim of her white helmet.

It was not long before they were in the cloud cover that Big Seed had created, and Latham wished he had the measuring instruments with him, so he could test the fabric of his home-made clouds. The ground disappeared from view, and the sky around them, and they were suddenly immersed in a damp, foggy whiteness that cut their visibility to zero. It seemed a long while that they floated like that, with little sense of movement, seemingly suspended in an infinite nothingness that chilled and sobered them. But then, after their jackets had gone on and Latham was getting their masks ready, they felt rather than saw a brightening of the white mass around them, and suddenly they broke into the open again, above the clouds.

The sun was bright on them once more, and the sky a cobalt blue. Below them now lay the heavy blanket of fluff that was so important to the future of the Midwest. Their masks went on, and they breathed more easily. Latham got some controls ready, and found he needed his gloves. They were both shivering now from the sudden cold. Their bodies could not adjust so quickly from the overpowering heat to this. Jodie helped Latham with some adjustments on the seeding apparatus, and then turned to look out over the sunny vista around them.

"Look!" she said to Latham through her mask.

Latham turned and saw what she was pointing at. It

was another Big Seed balloon, hovering above the cloud mass only a half-mile away, looking beautiful in the sun.

Latham grinned. "Nice, huh?"

Their balloon and the one they were looking at had expanded now to almost full inflation, and were spectacular silver spheres hanging like Christmas decorations above the clouds. Latham turned, and touched Jodie's shoulder. "There. Another one."

Jodie turned and saw the black speck further off, in another direction. It was a third balloon. They were all getting in position, reaching their appropriate level, maneuvering in the breeze.

"I've never seen a more lovely sight," Jodie's muffled voice came from behind her mask.

Latham was glad she was there with him, sharing this moment, regardless of how it turned out for them. He came and hugged her to him, and Jodie felt a warm affection for him unlike anything she had previously felt.

"You're some woman, Jodie Jameson," he told her.

She held his gaze. "The feeling is mutual, Mark," she replied.

"Come on," he said. "Let's see if this is going to work."

In the next twenty minutes, Jodie helped Latham seed his man-made clouds. They dropped the metal chaff after releasing some gas, and the stuff twinkled in the sun dazzlingly, as if they had seeded with cut diamonds. It was everywhere, below the balloon. Looking off to the nearest other Skyhook, they could see the glittery chaff descending from it, too. It was all slowly disappearing into the clouds below. Across the state, Latham knew, the operation was being repeated hundreds of times.

Finally the chaff was all gone, the operation finished. Latham closed off the valve on the machine beside him, and turned to Jodie, still behind his mask. "Well. That's it. Now we wait and see."

"No matter what happens here today, Mark," Jodie told him, "I'm proud of you. Really proud."

Latham wanted very much to kiss her, but it was not possible. She resembled a space man just landed from Mars. "That's nice, honey," he finally said. "Let's get this thing down now. We're finished up here."

"I'm ready to be Earth-bound again," she admitted. Her breath came loudly to her through the oxygen hose from the tank and then out through the exhaust port, like the sound in an operating room. She would be glad to breathe fresh air again, no matter what its temperature.

"Grab that lever and release some helium from the envelope," Latham said to her. "While I close off this gas tank. Just open the valve for about fifteen seconds, and we'll see how that drops us."

"All right, Mark," she said.

She went to the lever on the control panel just above her head, and unclasped a lock on it, and pulled. Nothing happened. She pulled harder, and with no result.

"Mark, I'm sorry, but I can't budge it," she said. There was no real concern in her voice. She figured she was doing something wrong. She watched as he turned and came over to her.

"It must be me," she said apologetically.

"Let's see," he said. "Sometimes these things stick."

He made sure it was unlocked, and then pulled hard on the lever. It would not budge. He pulled again, with all his strength. Again, nothing.

Now Jodie felt fear, creeping into her chest from some dark, hidden place. "What is it, Mark?"

Latham's face had gone suddenly grim. He checked the working parts of the lever, then looked upward, into the bright interior of the balloon. "It's not the lever," he said. "It's the valve at the crown of the envelope. It's stuck in position—closed."

Jodie swallowed back her fear. "What can we do?"

Latham was still looking upward. "I guess I'm going to have to go up there. Over the exterior of the balloon. On the shrouds."

Jodie felt a raw tingling of panic race through her. "On the outside? My God, you can't, Mark! We'll try to do something from down here! Let the balloon float, if we have to!"

Latham turned to her. "We can't do that, Jodie. These things go for weeks sometimes, unattended. The envelope could burst, eventually. No, I have to go take a look."

"Oh, my God," Jodie moaned.

He reached to the floor of the gondola, and found a pliers there, and a small can of grease. He stuck them into his pockets and turned and grinned at Jodie through his mask. "I wish there had been enough parachutes to go around down there. But don't worry, I've done this sort of thing before. There's a rope ladder on the shrouds, and I'll be very careful."

"Can't you go up inside the envelope?" Jodie asked hoarsely.

"There's nothing to climb on inside," Latham told

her. "I'll be okay, Jodie. Really."

"Oh, my God," Jodie said, looking up at the glistening, bulging side of the balloon. It would be almost like mountain-climbing. He would be on the underside of the curve at first, until he got up around the bulge of the balloon. "Please don't!"

"I have no choice," he said quietly.

There were no preliminaries, no long looks. Suddenly he was grabbing at the rope ladder and inching himself upward and outward. For a couple of minutes he was over the gondola, when it was most difficult, and then he was hanging out over blank space. Jodie could not look. She made a small sound in her throat, and turned away. When she looked back, he was climbing vertically, and his going was easier. *"Be careful!"* she called up to him, through her mask.

Then he went out of sight over the curve of the envelope.

Up on the top of the balloon, Latham paused and tried to catch his breath. He would not have told Jodie, but he was terrified of that first part of the climb, when he was trying to grab on upside-down, like a beetle. That had taken almost all his strength, and he had to get some back now. He lay there on the soft plastic, breathing hard, his fists knotted on the rope ladder. Finally he moved on up toward the crown, now lying on his stomach as he approached the closed opening at the crown. It was a circular place about a foot across, set in metal with a metal closure door that was supposed to swing on pivots, when the lever below was pulled. He was up beside it now, examining it, ignoring the feeling that he was pole-sitting on top of a forty-thousand foot pole. The bag of the balloon dropped off all around him gradually, in a gentle curve, so that it was like lying on top of a rounded, snowy mountain top. Except that beyond the curve of white was a bottomless abyss of sky.

Latham tried to move the closure by hand, and it did move, but very stiffly. He let go of the shrouds with one hand again, and got the grease and pliers out. He unscrewed a couple of pivot screws so they were loosened, and applied some grease to the joints. He had to be careful, though. He could not leave the closure so loosely affixed that he lost it. They could plummet to earth very suddenly if he lost all the helium in the bag. In fifteen minutes he was finished. He worked the closure, and it moved easily. He opened it manually, all the way, and allowed gas to escape into the air for fifteen seconds. Then he allowed it to close on its return spring.

He could feel the balloon begin to descend gradually. He pocketed the tool and grease, and took a deep breath in, and started back down, backwards.

The first part was not bad. But then he was suddenly out over sky-space again, with just his hands and feet holding him to security. Below him was the blanket of white clouds, and far, far below that, hard ground. He climbed down vertically again, and then he came into view of the gondola. He was getting tired, but the difficult part still lay ahead.

Jodie could see him again now, and she was holding her breath as he came around the big bulge of envelope. She could see his feet dig into the small spaces between the rope ladder and the fabric, and his hands grab desperately at the rope.

"Go slowly, Mark!" she called up to him.

347

Latham was now heading into the lying-supine position again, the part he disliked most. It was difficult to get his feet secured, so they did not allow his body to hang straight down away from the balloon, with only his hands holding him. He came a rung at a time, breathing hard, straining for purchase. He was not yet over the gondola. He came another couple of feet.

His left foot lost its grip on the ladder.

In just a split-second, that weight pulled his second foot free, and he was swinging from his hand-holds, over open air.

"Oh! God!" Jodie gasped out.

Latham released his hold with one hand, and took hold of a rung closer in toward the gondola. Then he did the same with the other hand, his legs still swinging free. His grip was very weak now. He tried to make the move in again, and when he released with his left hand, his right could not hold. He gasped as he felt his grip releasing, and swung his legs inward.

He fell.

Jodie screamed as he came. She thought he was going on past the gondola. But because he had swung his legs inward, they now hit the gunwale of the gondola and broke his fall. His hips and legs were on the gunwale or side-wall of the gondola, but most of his weight was outside it, and he now began slipping on over the edge. He reached upward to catch himself, but could not reach the edge.

He was going.

Jodie, frozen with terror, shook herself into action and reached desperately for his closest leg. She grabbed it with both hands, and held onto it psychotically. He stopped slipping over. He hung there outside the gondola for a moment, gathered strength. Then he reached up and found the edge of the gunwale.

He gripped it as he had never gripped anything in his life. Jodie pulled harder on his leg, and with his help, got him up so he could grab the edge with both hands. Slowly he got his hip back up onto it, and then his chest, and then he was pulling himself up and over.

He tumbled into the gondola, head first.

They both collapsed onto the gondola floor, gasping in their oxygen masks. Jodie glanced back toward the gunwale of the gondola, and could not believe for a moment that Latham had not fallen to his death. She finally came and fell into his arms, sobbing.

"It's—all right," he grated out. "It's all right now."

The balloon was descending. Suddenly they were wrapped in dense clouds again. They got up from the floor heavily, still clinging to each other. Latham looked into her blue eyes. "Thanks," he said.

"Oh, Jesus, Mark!"

Latham went over to the controls. He was bruised and hurting, but he was alive. He pulled on the release lever, and it worked. He let some more helium out of the balloon. The balloon continued on down through the clouds, and then broke out into the open again. Fields appeared below, and tiny farm houses.

"Can you tell where we are?" Latham asked Jodie.

"It looks like we've drifted about ten miles east of Wichita," Jodie told him, still trembling inside.

"I want to descend pretty close to here," Latham told her. "Where there are open fields. I'll let some more helium out, so we descend more rapidly. Then I'll throw some ballast over later, to slow us up near the ground."

He opened the valve at the crown again, and more helium escaped. The balloon began descending more rapidly, heading in an easterly direction. Latham turned back to Jodie. "Okay, we can take these things off," he said, pointing to his mask. "We're going to need as much mobility as we can get in the landing."

By the time they removed their masks, and then their jackets and gloves, the balloon had descended to only a couple of thousand feet. They could see the desert-like terrain plainly below, not looking quite as harsh because there was no sun. Latham pulled on a shroud to stabilize the balloon, and then looked ahead of them.

"Damn, that's a woods up there that we're drifting toward. I hope we can miss it."

"Shall we drop some ballast?" Jodie said, breathing in the fresh air around her. The temperature was even lower down below now than it had been when they ascended. It was not much over a hundred degrees.

"Yes, we have to slow this thing up," Latham told her.

They picked up the gas tanks used in seeding, and dumped them over the side, and then detached the chaff container and it went over, too. The balloon slowed its descent, but was still headed for the wooded area ahead of them.

"I think we're going into the trees at the far side of the woods," Latham said. He pulled on two control shrouds, but was not able to alter the course of the balloon much. He turned to Jodie. "Remember what I told you, honey. Hold onto these handles on the gunwale until you're on the ground. Don't let go no matter what. After we've hit, separate yourself from

350

the balloon as quickly as possible. That's where it can really hurt you, if you can't get clear of it after it's down. Do you understand that?"

"Yes, Mark. I'm all set."

"Don't worry about me. Take care of yourself. If we get hung up in trees, get into the tree as quickly as possible, and climb to the ground from there. You may be a long way off the ground."

"I'll be careful, Mark."

They were only three hundred feet off the ground. They could see the bare, withered trees rushing up at them fast. An air current had caught them and was pulling them right into the trees, the gondola trailing the big bag of the balloon by a short distance.

"Here we go!" Latham told her. They were both hanging onto the gondola tightly, and Latham had an arm on Jodie's shoulder.

Latham braced himself as the gondola began scraping the tree limbs, moving swiftly across the tops of them. There was a cracking and crunching of wood beneath them, and the gondola jerked about fitfully for a moment, and then it caught on a limb and tipped completely onto its side, the big envelope of the balloon pulling it sidewise. Jodie yelled loudly, and then she felt herself being jerked free of her hold on the gondola and thrown through the air. She screamed again, and then she hit a limb hard, saw a flash of sky and balloon above her, then dropped through some branches again. In the fall, she caught sight of Latham below her, crashing through some thick, dead foliage just beneath her. She saw him hit the ground hard, and then she was hung up on a low branch, tangled in twigs and dead leaves, on her back.

The balloon tore on through the trees, and there was a snapping sound as the gondola tore off its supports. It plummeted to the ground, too, at the edge of the trees, and the torn, deflated balloon blew on out into an open field, where it settled down into high weeds, an enormous ground cover out there, all twisted and lumpy.

Jodie managed to turn onto her side. With great difficulty, she grabbed onto a sizeable branch beside her and turned to face it. She could see Latham on the ground, crumpled there, and he was not moving. Her heart jumped into her throat, and she began making little sounds there, muffled and urgent, as she kicked and fought her way through the dead debris on the limb, down to a cleaner part of it, toward the trunk of the tree. It seemed an eternity to her, but finally she reached the trunk, bruised and cut on her face and arms. She was only ten feet off the ground. After another couple of acrobatic maneuvers, she hung by her hands from the limb where it met the trunk of the tree, and dropped heavily to the ground.

Pain rocketed up into her legs when she hit, but she did not break anything. She turned and saw she was only a few yards from Latham. He was either unconscious or dead. She whimpered in her throat and crawled over to him.

Latham was lying in high, brown weeds. His left leg was bent awkwardly at the knee, and his clothing was torn, and his square face was rather pale-looking. Jodie bent over him, looking for some sign of life, and could not see any.

"Oh, no!" she murmured. "Oh, God in heaven, no!"

She bent his head back, forced his mouth open in

preparation for artificial respiration. She could not allow herself to even contemplate the possibility of losing him. She put it out of her head, and bent down to touch her mouth to his.

He moved.

His head turned, and his eyes fluttered open. He focused slowly on her. "Jodie?" he said in a thick voice.

"Yes, Mark," she replied, tears running down her cheeks suddenly.

"I must have—hit my head. I was out, wasn't I?"

"Yes, just shortly," she told him.

"Are you—all right?" he asked her.

She nodded vehemently. "Oh, yes. I'm very all right."

He raised up, looked at the balloon where it lay crumpled out in the field, billowing lightly in the breeze. He tried to straighten the bent leg, and yelled in pain.

"What is it?" she asked him.

"It's my left knee. I've torn something, I'm afraid, Jodie. And maybe I have a cracked rib on the right side."

"I'll go try to find the flare," she said. "Then I'll be right back. Don't move."

She got up and ran to the busted-up gondola, which lay near the huge envelope of the balloon. After searching through the weeds for a few minutes, she found the flare that was put in each gondola, to guide mobile rescue and recovery units to downed balloonists. With the flare was a big-barreled pistol that fired the flare into the air. Jodie got it all put together, and then closed her eyes and fired the gun. The gun kicked in her hand, and the flare went sailing high, exploding up there.

Next she located a first aid kit that had stayed with the gondola, and found two lengths of metal tubing that could be used as splints. Returning to Latham, she splinted the left leg so he could support his weight on it, and taped his ribs on the right side. Latham got up and leaned on her, and felt pain in his throbbing knee. But he was ambulatory.

"You're not bad to have around," he grinned at her.

She smiled at him, broadly. "I was hoping to hear you say that."

"How do we get out of here?" he asked her.

"I got a glimpse of a road over there about two hundred yards. We'll go over there and wait for help."

It was a long walk for Latham, but Jodie helped him along. Soon they reached the road, and Jodie got Latham between the strands of a barbed wire fence. They were just climbing up onto the road surface, when they heard the vehicle engine coming down the road.

"Now that's what I call service," Jodie said.

The car with the red light on its roof pulled up just beside them, and two young men climbed out. "Well, I'll be damned! It's Dr. Latham! We win the pool!"

Latham and Jodie exchanged glances, smiling tiredly. Jodie was amazed that Big Seed had given these men so much hope that they had been wagering on who would recover Latham. They were moving about Latham and Jodie now with solicitous remarks, and helping Latham into the back seat of the car.

"How did it go?" one of them asked Jodie as she went around to get in beside Latham. "Did it work?"

"We're still waiting to see," Jodie told them. "If it rains, it worked. If it doesn't, it didn't."

The fellow glanced up at the dark, overcast sky. "Right," he said.

Jodie was just about to get in beside Latham, when she heard the sound in the distance. A slow rumbling, from the gray sky. It was thunder. She leaned down to look in at Latham. "Did you hear that?" she said.

He nodded, smiling. "It's a good sign, no doubt about it."

"God, let's keep our fingers crossed!" the driver of the car said in a hushed tone, as he climbed into the front with the other fellow. "Wouldn't it be something? Wouldn't it be great to see rain again?"

Jodie got in last, and as the car turned around and drove away from the landing site, both she and Latham looked over toward the white-billowing Skyhook that had carried them so high and then dumped them so hard. It seemed enough to Jodie, at that moment, that they had both survived their high-atmosphere ride.

"Do you want to go to the hospital with that leg?" the driver asked Latham as the car kicked up dust, heading back toward town.

Jodie looked over at Latham. "You'd better get that knee looked at," she told him.

But he shook his head at her, then turned to the driver. "No, take us directly to City Hall," he said.

"You've got it," the fellow responded.

Latham turned to Jodie. "Everybody will be there. Hollis Sprague and Tom Purcell were going to meet there. Your dad will be there, too. I don't want to miss the Big Moment, no matter how it turns out."

Jodie smiled up at him, pushing a wisp of hair from her scratched and dirt-smeared face. "Okay, Mark. It's City Hall."

*   *   *

It was twenty minutes later when they drove into Wichita, coming in along Central Avenue, and a strange sight awaited them in the city. Everybody was out in the streets. Everybody. The sick, the getting-sick, the disillusioned, the hopeful. The sidewalks and roadways were jammed with crowds of people, masses of them. Most of them were craning their necks backward, staring up into the gray, heavy sky. The car moved slowly through them, and when a few people saw Latham in the car, they ran alongside and called out to him, asking him if it was going to rain.

"I've never seen anything like it," Jodie said in awe. "The whole city is out. There's never been anything like it!"

"It was almost this bad when we left on patrol," the fellow beside the driver said. "They all are beginning to think it might rain."

Jodie glanced at Latham, and saw his tense face. He looked skyward through the open window of the car as it moved along. A clap of thunder exploded almost overhead. "Come on," he muttered under his breath, tautly. *"Come on!"*

When they arrived at City Hall, the area directly before the building was a throng of milling, excited citizens. The streets were packed solid from building to building, everybody staring skyward. The car moved slowly through the crowd, with the help of Jameson's troops, who had been trying to keep a lane open up to City Hall. When they got to within a hundred yards of the front entrance, they could not drive further. Latham and Jodie disembarked, and people turned to them and watched them pass between the thick rows of them, Latham limping badly. Up by the front entrance of the building were Sprague, Jameson, Purcell, and several city commissioners. Jameson was holding a walkie-talkie, and was in touch with a command post inside the building, where news was coming in from the university lab, and from the Weather Service. When Purcell saw Latham and Jodie, he hurried to meet them.

"Jodie! Mark! You're all right! Thank God, we've all been worried over you! There have been some accidents reported, with the Skyhooks!"

Latham and Jodie came up to them, and Latham shook Purcell's hand. "Good to be back, Tom." Now Sprague and Jameson came up, too. "If it hadn't been for Jodie here, I'd never have made it."

"Mark brought me down at the risk of his life," Jodie told them. "We might be drifting across the Mississippi by now."

Jameson came up and hugged his daughter to him. "It's good to see you again, honey."

Sprague looked very fatigued, but happy. "It's going to happen, Mark. I can feel it in my old bones. Smell the moisture in the air? It's going to happen, I tell you!"

Not far away, a minister of God had raised his eyes to heaven and was mumbling a prayer skyward. Latham saw him, and hoped that act of faith was being repeated all over the country. He needed all the help he could get.

"There was some lightning in the western sky just a few minutes ago," Purcell told Latham and Jodie. "And Hollis here says those are heavy rain clouds overhead. What do you think, Mark?"

Jameson, Sprague and Jodie all turned to Latham.

Latham looked out over the milling crowd, and listened to its soft murmuring. He raised his eyes skyward, studied the cloud formations directly over them.

"I—think it's going to rain," he said.

The three of them broke into grins. Jodie came and embraced him warmly. "I think you should get off your leg, Mark," she said quietly. "Why don't you come inside? It could be a long time before we know—"

At that moment, though, Jameson received a message on his portable transceiver. He held up his hand for quiet among them, and replied to his command post inside. "Yes, this is Charlie One, Command Center. Do you have news for us?"

They could all hear the response. "*We just got word, Colonel. It's raining in Kansas City.*"

"Oh, Mark!" Jodie exclaimed.

Sprague let out a little yell of joy, and Purcell began laughing and slapping Sprague on the back. Jameson was grinning very broadly at Latham. People around them had heard, too, and word was spreading through the crowd like wildfire. The transceiver sputtered, and the voice came on again.

"*Here's more, Colonel. It's now confirmed that it's raining in Omaha, Topeka, Pueblo, and Oklahoma City. It's started to rain in other places, too, across the Midwest.*"

Sprague yelled out again, and Purcell grabbed at him. "Damn!" he said, over and over again.

Just a split-second after his exclamation, a heavy clap of thunder boomed out over the city, and all eyes turned skyward. Then, in the next moments, the drops began coming down.

One hit Jameson on the hand, another splashed

358

onto Sprague's shoulder, wetting his shirt. Then one brushed Jodie's cheek, and one touched Latham's neck.

"*It's raining!*" someone from the massive crowd shouted hysterically. "*It's goddam raining!*"

In just moments more it began coming down hard. More thunder roared, and a deluge began. It quickly wet down everybody and everything in the open area before the City Hall. It came down hard, pummeling and splattering, bouncing high off the pavement underfoot. Jodie and Latham grabbed each other in pure ecstasy, and stood there enjoying the soaking like everybody else in the city. Jameson's walkie-talkie became water-jammed and he did not care. Sprague held his face heavenward and let the rain pound into his mouth, his closed eyes, his nose. Purcell did a little dance around them, acting like a kid. Then the chanting arose through the drenched crowd, and in just moments, it had risen in volume so that it carried above the noise of the storm.

"*Latham!*" the shout rose through the wetness. "*Latham, Latham, Latham!*"

The clamor built and spread until it was a pounding that rumbled through the city, and it went on and on.

And it rained.

TWENTY

For the rest of that day, there was dancing and singing in the rain-clogged streets. People just would not go indoors. The dust that had choked the city turned into mud, and the mud was washed away in rivulets of fresh, clean water from the sky. Trees and shrubbery took on a slightly fresher look, where any leaves were left on them. Grass was revived and began sending up new shoots. Out in the countryside, fields were wetted down and loam became loam once more.

That evening the rain ceased for a while, and then it started coming down again. It rained off and on all through that night. Rivers and streams began to flow again, and lakes started to fill back up. After the first deluge, the rain came down steadily but not in a heavy downpour, so most of it soaked into the soil, and there was little run-off. The water table began rising, and reservoirs began filling slowly.

Latham spent that night at St. Joseph Hospital, while a cast set on his left leg and his ribs were taped more heavily, and Jodie slept alone, waking regularly to listen to the rain.

The next day, it rained off and on all day. Latham insisted on discharging himself from the hospital as soon as breakfast had been served there. The nurses and everybody else were treating him like some kind of hero, and he had to get away from that. Also, he wanted to get back to the lab, to confer with Hollis Sprague about the new weather. He called Jodie, and she came and drove him to the university. It was raining all the way there. They sat and smiled at each other and did not talk much. When they got to the lab, Jodie went inside with Latham. Purcell was in Sprague's office, and he could not seem to get the grin off his face.

"Well, if that doesn't look great!" Purcell said when Latham and Jodie came into Sprague's office wearing slickers. "Raincoats and galoshes! Damn!"

"Hello, Tom," Latham grinned. "What are you doing over here? I thought you'd be out planting your garden today." He was walking on a cane now, stiff-legged.

Purcell went and got an armchair for Latham, and helped him onto it, as Latham greeted Sprague. Latham got into the chair with his leg stuck out in front of him. "Damn knee," he said, "Torn cartilage, they tell me. I'll be limping around for a while, I guess."

"Tom came over to ask about the national weather outlook," Sprague said from behind his desk. He was looking a little better. Faucets were starting to flow again, and there was drinking water for everyone. "Can I get you a footstool for that leg, Mark?"

"No, it's all right," Latham said. "What is the weather doing?"

"We just got supplemental reports from Ed Keefer," Sprague said. "It's raining all the way from California to New York and Florida. Several inches are expected over the Great Plains."

361

"Why, that's just wonderful!" Jodie said happily, sitting now on the arm of Latham's chair.

Latham had not spoken of her and him since the balloon ascent, and Jodie thought she knew the reason why. Latham would be returning to California soon, and she still had her work to complete here in Wichita. That meant that they would be separated for a while, whether they wanted it or not.

Jodie knew now that she wanted to be with Latham always—take care of him, have their babies, make them a home, eventually—and she hoped very much that he might ask her to come to California when the emergency was over here, and when his divorce was final. She had lost her fear of commitment when she had helped Latham drag himself back up into that balloon gondola at forty thousand feet, and later when she had thought he might be dead, on the ground. But violent trauma had been known to make a man more cautious. He had not called her from the hospital until it was time to check out, and had not mentioned their future on the way to the university together, when he had every opportunity. Now Jodie feared that Latham had decided to return to California without making any commitment to their future, and see how he felt after he had been alone there for a while, and his life had gotten back to normal.

Sprague was telling Latham some more good news. ". . . and now we're getting some good readings back from up above. There's definite evidence that the jet stream is edging back toward its old path, encouraged by our man-made low system that extends from coast to coast."

"That's what I was hoping for," Latham said. "I'm

very gratified, Hollis."

Purcell was standing beside Sprague's long metallic desk. "I'm also advised that our city power system will be able to withstand our lesser demand soon now, and we will be able to hook up our air-conditioners, refrigeration units, and so forth," he said. "That will make life more comfortable for all of us again. It ought to allow me to bring Leah home from the hospital sometime in the next week."

"She'll be so pleased," Jodie said.

"Incidentally," Purcell added, his tall, square frame looking more vigorous today, "your father the colonel will be leaving us within the next few days, Jodie. I got a call from the governor, expressing his pleasure with developments. He says all troops will be removed from Wichita by the end of the week."

"I figured as much," Jodie said. "It's been nice having him around, frankly. I guess I'll stop past there later, at the armory, and see if he knows exactly when he's going."

"There's going to be an influx of people back into Wichita and the farm country hereabouts," Purcell said, "and it will probably start almost immediately. We may wish we had Sherwood here to direct traffic. But our police chief assures us he can handle it." He caught Jodie's gaze with a serious one. "I had a long talk with the colonel, Jodie. We talked about Will some. I think your father is going to be all right."

"I think so, too, Tom," Jodie said with a smile.

Sprague leaned forward on his chair. "Congratulations are pouring in from all directions to you, Mark," he said brightly. "From all over the country, and from abroad. We're collecting the messages for you on your desk, I think you'll be pleased."

"Thanks, Hollis," Latham said. "But we all know this was anything but a one-man show."

Sprague caught Purcell's eye, and Latham saw him wink at Purcell. Then he looked back toward Latham. "There's a very special pat on the back coming up, too," he said. "We were going to have the call put through to the hospital, but now you can take it right here."

Latham furrowed his dark brow. "What call?" he said.

"Don't tell him," Purcell grinned. "Let him guess. Who do you think might be calling you, Mark? That would be especially appreciative?"

Latham was not in the mood for guessing, though. "As long as it's not Yuri Mazurov," he said sourly.

Sprague laughed. "No, I suspect you'll have to presume that he's properly grateful," he said. "I suppose we'll have to tell him, Tom. It could be some time before—"

The phone on Sprague's desk rang, and Sprague looked up at Purcell. "I'd guess that's it," he said.

Purcell answered the call. "Yes?" he said into the receiver. "Oh, yes, operator, we've been waiting." He handed the phone to Latham, in the armchair. "It's for you," he said with a smile.

Latham glanced at Jodie, then took the phone. "Latham here," he said soberly.

"*Just a moment for the President, Dr. Latham,*" the female voice came to him. Sprague had pushed a button so that all of them present could hear the conversation at both ends. Jodie and Latham exchanged surprised looks, and a slow smile spread onto

Jodie's pretty face.

"*Good morning, Dr. Latham,*" the deep voice suddenly came to them. "*I hope you slept to the patter of rain on your roof last night!*"

"Good morning, Mr. President," Latham replied. "Yes, it's still raining off and on here in Wichita. We're all very pleased here."

"*It's even raining here in Washington,*" the President said jovially. "*I don't know what kind of magic you performed out there, but it worked to perfection, professor. Some of my cabinet members are talking about starting an ark here!*"

Latham smiled broadly, and Purcell laughed aloud. "I don't think there's any immediate danger of flood, Mr. President," Latham said.

"*Well, seriously speaking, Dr. Latham, we all owe you a great debt of gratitude. Not just in this country, but all around the world. And I think you know how especially pleased we are, and how proud, that a Californian succeeded where the Russians so miserably failed.*"

"Our team is happy about that, too," Latham said. "I just hope due credit will be given to all the people who worked so hard to make this happen here, and to the citizens of Kansas and the Midwest who endured this terrible time."

"*You may be assured of that, Dr. Latham,*" the President told him soberly. "*Congratulations again to you, and to your fine research team out there.*"

A moment later the phone was dead, and Purcell was taking it from Latham and returning it to its cradle. Everybody was smiling except Latham. He sat there very sober, remembering all that had gone before, and thinking what it would be like at that moment if the experiment had failed. Jodie watched his face and knew what he was thinking.

"The President has already demanded a treaty with the Soviets," Purcell was saying. "To prevent this kind of thing from happening again. Let's all pray it works out."

"Amen," Sprague said. He turned to Latham, studying Latham's sober face. "Did you mention to Jodie what I talked with you about last night?"

Latham glanced at Jodie, beside him. He had been waiting for a private moment to talk with her. It had not seemed right, in the car coming over. "No," he said. "I wanted to have some time to think about it first."

"Well. Maybe you'd like to discuss it," Sprague said. "We can give you some privacy right now."

"I think that's an excellent idea," Purcell agreed. Sprague rose from his desk. "If you need us," Purcell added, "we'll be in your office, Mark."

"All right, Tom," Latham said.

Jodie was wondering what Sprague had been referring to. Sprague and Purcell filed from the room, and closed the door. Jodie rose from the arm of Latham's chair, and went and leaned on Sprague's desk, facing Latham. "All right, what were you two talking about?" she said.

Latham wondered if she were in the right mood. He could not delay it further, now. "Hollis Sprague stopped by the hospital just after you left last evening," he said slowly. "He's retiring, Jodie, he won't be heading into the fall semester. He says he's put in his time."

"I suppose that doesn't surprise me," Jodie said.

Latham watched her face. "He spoke with the university president, Jodie. About me. They want me to succeed Hollis as head of his department."

"Oh, my gosh!"

"There will be more money than I've been making at Berkeley. But more importantly, I'll call the shots in research. No interference. I called my dean last night, and he encouraged me to take the step up."

"Well, that's just great, Mark," she said noncommitally.

"I haven't given Hollis an answer yet," Latham said. "You see, it all depends on you."

Jodie looked into his deep eyes.

"If you want me, Jodie, I'll stay. Otherwise, it would be rather awkward. For both of us." He averted his gaze for a moment. "I'm talking permanency, now. I'm talking a winter wedding, if I get my papers by then. Nothing less would be acceptable to me. If you still have reservations, I want—"

Jodie rose, and came and put a slender finger to his lips. She bent down and kissed him lightly, her vision blurry. "Yes," she said simply.

He regarded her searchingly. "Yes?"

"Yes," she repeated.

Latham rose, and they embraced silently there, not speaking, only feeling their strong emotions. Finally Jodie separated them. "No more work for you this morning. You're coming back to my place, and we're going to have a nice lunch there, and talk about us."

"I was hoping you'd suggest that," he grinned.

A few minutes later they emerged from the building, and out into a drizzling rain. They had not even stopped to tell Sprague and Purcell they were leaving.

There would be time for conferences and talking, later. Jodie glanced up at the threatening clouds over their heads, and she and Latham looked at each other and smiled.

It was a perfectly awful morning. It was wet and muggy, dark and dreary. You could not go outside without getting soaked to the skin. It was just right for catching colds, feeling your arthritis, getting your feet soggy through your shoes.

It was the most beautiful day of the world.